Stitch by Stitch

Marie-Therese Hernon

Published by Marie-Therese Hernon, 2021.

NANOWRIMO

For Mom and Dad,
Until we meet again.

ONE

O nce again, Russell failed her. An anxious bead of perspiration rolled off Elizabeth's forehead and plopped onto the keyboard of her geriatric laptop. She checked the bank that cradled her meager funds and found an available balance of $144.56, which had to last until he sent the support check, if and when that ever happened. Now the phone company would stick her with a late fee during back-to-school season. She mentally reviewed Trevor's supply list. Since when did a nine-year-old need a graphing calculator? So far, she hadn't found a decent model for less than a hundred dollars.

She studied the spreadsheet. August. Bailey would soon start preschool at an additional expense of eight-fifty a month. Elizabeth had no choice but to stick the first payment on her mounting credit card bill. She owed her divorce attorney too, but she should sue the lazy wench for malpractice. It became clear the woman had botched discovery when Russell, who cried poverty all through the divorce, rolled up to fetch Trevor in a new Lexus. Trevor returned from that weekend to reveal his father had put a down payment on a newly constructed house downtown with a three-car garage and five bed-rooms. Right now, however, he still resided in the firetrap with the sagging porch he'd rented for the poverty show. Elizabeth feared let-ting Trevor spend the night there, but the court left her no choice. She consoled herself that if some ancient wire fizzled and torched the thing, a firehouse was three blocks away.

After seven solid days, the rain let up. The weather service reported the wettest Connecticut summer on record. Between rain and heat, ants might invade any minute, and Elizabeth could not afford the expense of an exterminator. She examined the kitchen counter for offending insects. Finding none, she nibbled on a cookie. It teemed with a sharp, poisonous artificial sweetness, the days of paying extra for non-GMO confections made with pure cane sugar behind her. Today she would allow herself a single fake sweet to ease paying the bills, if you could call looking at bills paying them.

She heard the swollen front door scrape open along the wood floor in the front of the house, announcing Trevor, back from racing worms in bottle caps on a puddle on the driveway. Every now and then, she'd watched him from the window on his haunches blowing worms towards the finish line.

He tossed the mail on the table. "MP is picking me up for dinner."

"Wash your hands." Typical of Mary Pat to assume she could take Trevor without permission. "When did you see her?"

"She drove by ten minutes ago."

"Right, well, do your pleasure reading first."

"I'm halfway through one of the books we took from the library this morning."

Elizabeth ruffled his hair. "Good going." Her own parents had to beg her to read. Music had come easily, though, and until she'd figured a way around her dyslexia, she hated reading. Thank God Trevor had the music gene but not the learning disability.

"We're getting pizza and ice cream. MP said me and Hughey can watch *Transformers*."

"Hughey and *I*, and I don't like you watching that violence."

Trevor slid the empty cardboard roll from the paper towel rack and waved it like a saber. "*Shwoo, shwoo*! I am here to bend you to my will, Minion."

"Case in point."

"This isn't *Transformers*, Minion. This is a product of my imagination."

"Racing worms was a product of your imagination."

Trevor deepened his voice ominously. "Silence, Minion."

"Call me minion again, and you can forget Hughey and spend the night in your room."

Trevor slumped into a chair. "Daddy's taking me to Disney for Christmas. Aunt Mary Pat and Hughey are going too."

"Is that so?" Russell had steadfastly avoided any discussion of Disney during his marriage to Elizabeth. He said if he was going to spend that kind of money on a vacation, they'd go to Europe, although they never got farther than Rhode Island. He never minced words about his sister, whom he claimed to despise. Now it seemed he and Mary Pat were gay old friends, planning trips to Disney together. Elizabeth had been so busy hunting for back-to-school bargains she'd forgotten she would spend Christmas without Trevor. From now on, she'd get him every other year until he turned eighteen, just nine years away. That gave her four measly Christmases before he left for college, and then maybe for good. The thought caught in her throat. How could this be happening? But she had no one to blame. She'd done it to herself.

Tires crunched to a stop on the driveway. "That aunt of yours doesn't waste time."

The kitchen door opened. Without invitation, Mary Pat appeared in the kitchen. "Remember your cleats," she told Trevor.

"I thought they were getting pizza and watching TV." Elizabeth glanced at the calendar. "Practice doesn't start until – ."

"Informal practice starts today at *my* house. I'm not messing around. Colleges want scholar athletes, Elizabeth. These boys need to get a head start." Mary Pat smoothed her skirt. Even on a sticky late summer day, she looked pressed and put together. No halo of frizz crowned that raven-haired head of hers. Elizabeth's thin dirty blonde hair clotted messily around her shoulders. She hadn't found a product on the market that could fix that mess.

"They're nine, Mary Pat. It's a lot of pressure."

"These kids have to start like *yesterday*." Mary Pat nodded toward Trevor, who rooted around the hall closet for his cleats. "It's not enough to be some Straight-A Poindexter anymore. You gotta be able to catch a ball."

"David Beckham can breathe easily around Trevor." And Hughey, too, she might add. The kid spent enough time on the bench last season to put a dent in it. "He's better off concentrating on his music."

That reminded Elizabeth; she still owed Christian for last month's lessons. If she could bring herself to touch the piano again, she could teach Trevor herself and save a hundred and twenty dollars a month. But, no, she'd made herself a promise. She would never play again.

Mary Pat leaned a slim hip against the counter. Forty-two years old, and she still had the body of a high school cheerleader. "Pianists are a dime a dozen. You, of all people, should know that. If a kid wants a scholarship, he'd better play the tuba. Tuba players are not a dime a dozen. Do you know why? Because no kid in his right mind wants to be the loser playing the tuba in the high school band. No kid in his right mind wants to be in the band because band kids are the ones who get picked on. You know what they call band kids, Elizabeth? Band Geeks. Do you want your kid to be a band geek?"

"He loves music. Who cares what anyone else thinks?"

The washing machine shifted into spin cycle and commenced its noisy rumba from behind the door off the kitchen. Elizabeth had learned to ignore it. The dryer had stopped working altogether. She'd managed by hanging clothes on the line all summer, but with fall closing in, she'd have to corral funds for a new one.

Mary Pat clapped her hands to her ears. "Oh, for Pete's sake. Put a grass skirt on that thing and sell tickets."

The machine had started acting up months before Russell left. He told Elizabeth to cancel the appointment with the repairman; it only needed "a little part," which he'd pick up at the hardware store. And didn't. Elizabeth wouldn't get into it now with his sister.

Trevor came jostling down the stairs in a soccer jersey with a hem inches above his waistband.

"You can't wear that," Mary Pat said.

Elizabeth ran her hand through the hair she hadn't bothered to comb. He'd outgrown his uniform, which meant she'd incur yet another expense. "He doesn't need a uniform to practice in your backyard."

"The hell he doesn't. You ever hear of mindset? It helps to look the part." She flung her forefinger at her nephew. "Take that thing off, Trev. Hughey has a shirt you can borrow."

Elizabeth felt punched in the stomach.

Mary Pat eyed the tub of substandard cookies. "Formal practice starts next week. Trevor will need a uniform."

How does it feel to be perfect? Elizabeth wanted to ask. How does it feel to be the successful real estate agent everyone recognizes from the billboard on Route 16? How does it feel to drive a Range Rover with four good tires? Or laze by an inground pool watching your kid bobble in water you paid somebody else to clean? Elizabeth would wring Mary Pat's neck, if she weren't grossed out by that Frankenstein bolt of a mole popping from the side of it. It was Mary Pat's only physically unappealing attribute. Elizabeth thought for sure she'd have had it removed years ago, but Mary Pat hadn't. For Elizabeth, the ugly blob of skin served as a metaphor for her sister-in-law's character. She never concluded a conversation with her former sister-in-law without giving that mole a good three-second glare.

"No offense," Mary Pat said. "But what are your plans? You can't sit home forever."

"I'm raising two children."

"Exactly. You need an income."

"My children need someone to take care of them. Decent day-care is twelve hundred dollars a month, and when you factor in dry cleaning, transit, and the fact that a job would leave me zero time with the kids, I'm lucky if I'd break even. I don't see the point."

"Yeah, another excuse."

Elizabeth resisted telling her former sister-in-law the truth: If Bailey turned out to have a learning disability, she'd need a full-time advocate. Elizabeth would probably still be in first grade if her own mother hadn't stayed home to give her the extra help she needed.

"Get What's-Her-Name to watch the kids," Mary Pat demanded.

"Who?"

"The one across the street who helped out when you went to court."

"Nancy. I don't want to take advantage of her."

Mary Pat shrugged. "It doesn't sound like she has much going on. Sometimes you need to take advantage of an opportunity."

"I don't feel comfortable doing that."

Mary Pat threw a derogatory glance at the heap of unread mail on the table beside the blob of grape jelly. "It seems to me you're entirely too comfortable. How do you live like this?"

Elizabeth turned to her son, who, in the tight jersey, resembled a pound of sausage in a half pound casing. "Trevor, would you get the mail?"

"I already got the mail."

"Oh, that's right. You did." She pulled a half-full garbage liner from the can and tied it. "Bring this out then."

"Do I have to?"

"Yes."

Elizabeth focused her eyes on the bit of hair that obscured the offending mole, her vow to not mention Russell's shortcomings to his sister frayed to a thread. "If your brother sent the support check on time, we'd be okay. He's been playing games all summer."

Mary Pat pulled a face. "You brought this on yourself."

Everybody in town knew what Elizabeth's father had done to her mother. Everybody. So, when Russell made his "misstep," as he called it, Elizabeth overreacted. Which was normal and understandable, her therapist said, when she could still afford the copay.

She held up bitten nails. "Please go. Take good care of my son, but please go."

"My pleasure." Mary Pat turned to go. She spun back around and looked Elizabeth in the face. "One of these days I'll tell you exactly what I think. I'm tired of being polite. I've had to take down my wedding pictures because you're in them." From behind Mary Pat's perfect orthodontia, Elizabeth perceived a glint of froth.

"I'm sorry you feel that way." The self-help book Elizabeth had taken from the library recommended the use of *I'm sorry you feel that way* when confronted by toxic individuals like Mary Pat. Even so, it felt passive-aggressive.

"Sorry I feel that way? Sorry that you're a whore?"

"I'm sorry you feel that way," Elizabeth said again, with more enthusiasm.

"You should be sorry that you committed adultery and gave birth to a bastard."

"Keep your voice down. The bastard is taking her nap."

The sunny blue eyes that made Mary Pat famous in high school went dark. "Do you even know whose baby that is? It's not my brother's baby. That baby is nothing to me."

Elizabeth worried Trevor would burst back in any second. "Please keep your voice down."

"What, you don't want your son finding out? Because one of these days he will find out. You are going to hell for what you did to him and my brother. How can you even look yourself in the mirror?"

"Please leave." The book advised readers to speak slowly and confidently when addressing the toxic individual, and to maintain eye contact. Elizabeth squinted and located the mole. She didn't have the courage to meet Mary Pat's hateful stare. She felt safer talking to the mole.

"I feel sorry for you, Elizabeth, because everybody knows what you are," Mary Pat said, jutting her delicate chin. "You're garbage. I should tell your son to throw you in the trash, where you belong, but I won't because I'm not that kind of person. But one day, somebody will. When that day comes, this whole fantasy world of yours is going to fall apart."

The Mother's Day card Trevor handmade for Elizabeth last May hung on the refrigerator, its edges curling in the humidity. Mary Pat plucked it from under the magnet. "Treasure this little piece of crap," she said. "Don't count on getting too many more of them."

Mary Pat slammed the door behind her. Elizabeth gripped the edge of the table, certain she would faint.

TWO

Bailey woke up from her nap with another ear infection, her third in three months. This required a trip to the pharmacy for a refill on drops. The child must've inherited the weak ears from her father, a one-night stand Elizabeth probably wouldn't recognize. She'd picked him up in a rage after she'd borrowed Russell's laptop and discovered it cluttered with porn. If it had been garden variety *Playboy* stuff, she'd have felt creeped out and betrayed, but therapy might smooth out those emotions. What she found instead turned her stomach, a photo of a naked woman with a bag on her head in action, captioned "Uses for an ugly girl," the *piece de resistance*. Elizabeth's respect for Russell drained out of her in an instant. She wanted revenge.

She strapped Bailey into her car seat and hit 'play' on one of the nine hundred Grateful Dead shows she'd burned onto CDs over the years. She started to sing along to "Deal."

"Mommy," Bailey shouted. "I want Elsa. No more Dead! I want Elsa."

"Ah, come on."

Should Elizabeth give in? The kid had an earache. She ejected the Dead and slipped in the soundtrack to *Frozen*, her face hardening into a scowl.

Mary Pat's comment about the uniform infuriated her, more than the bit about her being a whore. Why couldn't she and Mary

Pat get along? In the early years of Elizabeth's marriage, the question kept her awake. Why wasn't she good enough? She hadn't been good enough for Mary Pat and her clique in high school, either. Elizabeth wished she had the cash to resume sessions with her therapist. The self-help books from the library could only do so much to ease her mounting anxiety.

She steered the van past the rock walls on her street, her windshield wipers thumping out of time to songs she never wanted to hear again.

While waiting for the prescription to be filled, she perused the hair color aisle. No gray yet, but the idea of looking new and different tempted her. Also, Elizabeth had fallen for the line that coloring your hair could leave it healthier than if you didn't bother, and she could use a bit of renewed smoothness. She'd been a pretty girl in that wholesome fair freckled kind of way, but if you weren't careful in the sun with that kind of skin you could end up looking like a deflated balloon. She caught sight of herself in a mirror and saw a MOM staring back at her, someone who'd relegated taking care of herself to the last thing on the list. The specter of the coming school year made her listless: Checking homework, coordinating SNACK MOM schedules with other MOMS for Trevor's soccer team, and running to the pediatrician did not excite her. Elizabeth couldn't imagine not being a mother, but she did not like the business of being a MOM.

She looked up from the mirror and straight into the eyes of one Sean "Red" Garcia, Stonesbury Class of 1998 and Prom King to Mary Pat's Prom Queen. He had an Irish-born mother, a father from Spain, and skin that turned gold when he went out for the mail. Elizabeth had been in love with him. He said he was in love with her, until Mary Pat entered the picture. For all Elizabeth knew, he still carried a torch for her former sister-in-law.

"Hey, I know you," he said.

She swept an errant lock of hair out of her eyes. She'd heard he'd served in Iraq but lost track after that. Since her separation, out of what she swore to herself amounted to curiosity, she'd combed social media platforms searching for him but came up with nothing. Not that it mattered. He'd had his chance in high school and didn't take it. Elizabeth's recent emancipation from Russell would change nothing.

"How's it going, Red?" She willfully slowed her breathing to prevent him from hearing her thundering heartbeat. "I haven't seen you in a million years."

"Lizzie Candew! It really is you!"

Despite a chaste hug that involved shoulders but not much else, a bolt of electricity shot through Elizabeth—even though she should head for the exit after what he did. But that was years ago, and Red still had the goods. The green eyes shimmered with flecks of blue and gold. He'd maintained his high school physique, the trim torso and gently muscled shoulders that Elizabeth once rested her head upon. It unsettled her how his overwhelming attractiveness seemed not to affect him. Why couldn't he be a conceited ass? That way, she could enjoy some laughs at his expense over drinks with Cathy, her best friend who knew the whole deal. They never understood what he'd been doing with Mary Pat, who wielded her good looks like a tire iron.

Meanwhile, Bailey smiled at him and fluttered her eyelashes. Then she sneezed, loudly, and sprayed everything within a three-foot radius.

Red didn't flinch. If she'd sprayed him, Elizabeth couldn't tell.

She rummaged through keys, three lipsticks, ninety-seven wrinkled receipts, a leaky pen, and pulled a crumpled tissue from her purse. She blew the kid's nose with all the glamour she could muster.

"I heard you served in the marines. Thank you for your service." Elizabeth balled up the wet tissue in her fist, resisting a compulsion to curtsey. Imagine if she'd curtseyed! What a dork move! She had yet to master the art of thanking military personnel for their service without making a fool of herself.

"You're very welcome." Red gestured to the box in her hand. "Lucky Caramel, huh?"

The hottest guy from high school had busted her in the hair color aisle. "I guess caramels get lucky," she blurted. And winced.

"You look good, Lizza." *Lizza.* He was the only one who ever called her that. "What's this little person's name?"

"Bailey."

"Hello, Bailey." Red bent over to meet the child's eyes and shook her little hand. Bailey tucked her head and giggled. Why couldn't she hate the guy and throw a tantrum?

He stood up to his full height and smiled at Elizabeth. *Kryptonite.* "I've been back for a long time."

"I'm surprised we haven't run into each other."

"Me too." He rolled back on his heels a bit. Was he as nervous as she was? *No way. He couldn't be.*

"Well," Elizabeth said. "I guess I should go." She attempted an insouciant wave and returned the hair color box to the shelf. Fretting the wave came off like a swat, she headed to the pharmacy counter and broke into a humiliated sweat. She gave the clerk the baby's name.

The clerk reached into a drawer. "Here we are, Mom," she said. "There's a twenty-dollar copay."

Elizabeth handed over her credit card. On her way out of the store, she decided she needed the hair color, after all.

She headed back down the aisle and nipped it off the shelf. She spotted Nancy, the neighbor who'd provided complimentary babysitting service while she spent the month of June in divorce court, at the checkout. Elizabeth could use a night out, badly, but to ask Nancy to watch the kids again would be taking advantage. She couldn't afford dinner or drinks anyway. Hell, she couldn't afford hair color.

Nancy knicked Bailey's chin with her knuckle. "How's my little angel?"

Bailey narrowed her eyes warily.

"Your pretty mommy is just the person I want to see!" Today Nancy had on jeans that drooped from her flat backside like a diaper. Elizabeth could never quite figure her age; between the wire glasses and tight black curls that made her head resemble a burnt muffin, she could be a young sixty-two or an ancient thirty-five. The lineless complexion threw everything off.

Bailey pulled at the seat belt on the cart, angling for escape. "I want to get out!"

"One second, Bail."

"I want to go now!"

Nancy ruffled the child's hair. "Sit pretty for Mommy, Baby Girl. Sit pretty for Mommy."

Sit pretty? Why did people speak to little girls like that? Elizabeth resisted rolling her eyes. "What's up, Nancy?"

"I fixed that jerk who took Fido for a crap on my lawn," Nancy announced, loud enough for everyone else in line to hear.

"Another spell?" she whispered. In addition to being a self-proclaimed ardent Christian, Nancy dabbled in witchcraft.

"I had a spell, but it called for sage. I only had marjoram."

Elizabeth pulled at her eyebrows nervously. "If someone's walking his dog on your lawn, wouldn't you be better off calling the police?"

"I called them months ago, after Fido made the first drop. Do you know what that officer said to me? He said, 'You can't prove that excrement belongs to that dog.' You know what I said to him? 'What? You want a DNA sample?' The police are useless."

"Hence the spells. But Nancy –," Elizabeth looked around to make sure nobody could overhear her. "Isn't witchcraft inconsistent with Christianity?"

Nancy put up a hand, exasperated. "I am a witch who loves Jesus. We witches revere the earth our Lord gave us. Some yo-yos confuse us with Satanists, which we are not. I can be a witch and a Christian at the same time. The intelligent mind can contain more than one idea."

Elizabeth thought the speech sounded rehearsed. "You really are full of surprises."

Nancy bowed, displaying silver roots. Elizabeth tried to imagine her as a Lucky Caramel. "So, how'd you end the problem with the dog?"

"YouTube. Did you know that dogs hate cayenne pepper? I just happened to have a jumbo size jar in my cupboard and carpeted my lawn with it. Then I sat back and watched that sucker steer his schnauzer onto my property, but Fido wasn't having it. Wouldn't go near it. The joker's standing there, scratching his head, wondering why Fido's gone off his favorite crapping spot."

"Clever, Nancy, as long as it didn't hurt the dog."

Nancy looked as if she'd been shot. "I'd never hurt a dog."

"Of course not. I just wish you wouldn't get so worked up. Call the police again. Maybe you'll get a more responsible officer."

"All the police are good for in this town is supervising construction sites. You can bet somebody's getting a payoff." Nancy raised a badly penciled eyebrow. "You have to take matters into your own hands."

"Well, you sure did."

"Yep, and good luck finding a new crapping spot, Mister. If he tries it again, I'm going to upload my own video advising other victims of jackass pet owners. Anyway, I'm glad I ran into you. I was going to stop over to invite you to a party."

Elizabeth dreaded going to any party of Nancy's. "What can I bring?"

"I've got it covered," Nancy winked at Bailey, who stuck her thumb in her mouth. "It's a fashion party. Lady Lily Wear. Have you heard of it?"

Had she heard of it? Elizabeth had fended off multiple invitations to attend Lady Lily Wear parties. Suddenly, every woman in a five-mile radius either sold the stuff or agreed to host a party where her friends and acquaintances would be expected to buy it.

"I have heard of it," Elizabeth said. "When's the big night?"

"Not this Monday but next." Nancy bent out her elbows like a chicken. She shuffled her feet. "A little vino to start the week off right."

"I'd love to, Nancy, but Trev's tied up with sports." Now that Mary Pat had commenced the personal backyard practices, it wasn't a lie.

"I'm sure he is. They all are." Nancy pulled at her turtleneck, which had strawberries on it. "I don't know how you moms do it, all that driving back and forth to ball fields. We kids used to throw our books on the table and run wild until dinner time. Our mothers didn't know where the hell we were, and they didn't care, but then they didn't spend their lives behind a wheel of a van, that's for sure. They wouldn't have recognized a child car seat if it bit them on the leg."

"Hard to believe."

"Eh, look at me. I turned out all right. In high school, I babysat for a pregnant lady who hung out on her driveway blowing smoke rings with her girlfriends. Anyway, don't let Trev's practice stop you. You come after." Nancy leaned in conspiratorially. "I'll save you plenty of vino."

Nancy leaned in closer. Elizabeth smelled her perfume, a fussy scent that brought to mind her first-grade teacher and the shame of not being able to keep up with the star readers, "I know you're getting back on your feet," Nancy said. "Don't worry about buying anything. I just like to get the girls together. I ran into Cathy Allret at the library. She's coming too. You like her, don't you?"

"Yes, I like her." Elizabeth bristled at the mention of her best friend, whom she hadn't seen in weeks. How had Nancy been able to get hold of Cathy when she hadn't?

"So, come." Nancy slapped Elizabeth on the shoulder. "Have a glass of wine. After what you've been through, God knows you deserve it."

"Maybe you're right." Right now, Elizabeth merely wanted a quiet afternoon and an iced tea. "But that perfume you're wearing. What is it?"

"Daydreamer by Benchley. It's been my signature scent since eighth grade." Nancy sniffed the inside of her wrist and giggled. "Isn't it glorious?"

"Yes," Elizabeth fibbed, not wanting to offend the person who'd treated the children so kindly during the divorce. She agreed to go to the party and wheeled Bailey through the exit. The sky went black and opened up halfway to the minivan.

THREE

As soon as they had three days of dry weather, Mary Pat leaned on Coach Mike to call in the team for an unprecedented preseason practice schedule. He resisted, fearing he'd alienate parents who'd planned last-hurrah-of-the summer family vacations, but Mary Pat convinced him that even if just a few kids attended the drills the team would be better poised to trounce the competition come fall. Her offer to pay for team jackets sealed the deal. Mary Pat knew how to get what she wanted, and now Elizabeth spent scorching August afternoons on an unshaded ball field with a sniffly toddler. She prayed for rain, but the sun shone as though Russell had put it on his payroll. She handed out small bottles of water and snack packs of popcorn, paid for with the credit card, desperate to fend off any gossip that might elicit from her divorce. She needed Trevor to be accepted. *She* needed to be accepted, expenses be damned.

How boring she found soccer, though. From the sidelines with the baby on her hip, she watched Trevor run listlessly in the ball's general direction. Elizabeth shielded her eyes from the sun and spotted her former sister-in-law in the distance, gesturing wildly while speaking to another parent. Elizabeth froze, praying the mole would distract the parent from absorbing anything Mary Pat might say about her, which might include the fact that the child in her arms resulted from a one-night stand. Bailey wriggled, seeming to read her thoughts. More likely, she wanted to run around like a normal

17

child. Elizabeth put her down on the grass. The heat was brutal, but she took comfort in the fact that the weekend and all the running around it entailed would be over soon enough. But then she remembered yet another soccer practice and Nancy's party on Monday.

It turned out Elizabeth's best friend would be away on business until Friday and unable to make it to the party. It hurt Elizabeth's feelings that she had to come by this intelligence from Nancy, a mere acquaintance, when she and Cathy had been friends since the year her mother put her foot down and divorced her father. Cathy had been a savior. She came from a stable family, the kind seen on TV, where the parents and siblings sat around the kitchen table together and enjoyed it. There was one constant at Cathy's house that was missing from Elizabeth's: laughter.

After college, Cathy married a guy seemingly rare as a unicorn: one who made his wife's happiness a priority. She achieved the most glamorous job in the world, VP of International Marketing for an organic skin care line that held its annual sales conference in Los Angeles, an event that featured a parade of A-list celebrities out of the pages of *People*. Cathy herself appeared frequently in *Forbes* and on the business pages of *The New York Times*. She lived in a rock-solid four-bedroom Colonial that had sustained every major New England storm since 1850, unlike Mary Pat's hastily slapped-up McMansion, which had a basement that turned into a second swimming pool every time a nor'easter swept through.

AFTER PRACTICE ON MONDAY, Elizabeth pulled into her driveway. She unstrapped the baby from her car seat.

"Let's go, Trev."

"I'm tired. I don't want to go to a party," he protested. "And Nancy gives me the creeps."

"Then stay in her basement and watch TV."

"I'm old enough to stay home alone. We live across the street, for Pete's sake."

"You're nine years old. I could be arrested for leaving you by yourself." Elizabeth shifted the baby on her hip. She unsnapped the diaper bag to ensure she had one bottle left. *Check.* "That's the last thing I need."

Trevor's legs stiffened. "I don't want to go."

"We're going."

"I do not want to go."

Elizabeth bent over, met her son eye-to-eye. "Look, Kid, I don't want to go, either, but I don't have a choice. Put a smile on your face and come on, or you can kiss soccer goodbye."

Elizabeth said a silent prayer Trevor wouldn't call her bluff. She walked towards Nancy's house, willing him to follow. Another day, she would have looked up and observed the arch of maple trees connecting the cookie-cutter houses, leaves quivering noiselessly, and been thankful for it. The long summer had left the branches heavy and tired. Elizabeth, too.

Trevor relented. "Aunt Mary Pat says you can't get into college without soccer."

"Tell that to Stephen Hawking."

FOUR

Nancy held a tray of pigs in blankets. Elizabeth had never seen her look so splendid. She'd set a flattering poppy lipstick against a crimson jumpsuit that magically lent shape to her flat rear end. *If she'd only grow her hair long enough to keep it from shrinking up around her ears.*

"Here's our Elizabeth!" The hostess turned to face the little group assembled around her small coffee table, each of them poking chips into a bowl in its center, heads bobbing to unfamiliar music. "The lady I've been telling you about!"

A woman in a Yankees cap clapped tortilla chip crumbs from her hands. "We've heard all about you. I feel like I know you for years! I'm Susan, I'm divorcing my husband, and I need to pick your brain."

Elizabeth shivered in the aggressive air conditioning. She should have remembered her jacket. "I'll try to help if I can."

"A juice box for Princess Bailey?" Nancy asked.

"I brought water, but thank you anyway," Elizabeth said.

"Juice," the little girl protested, holding her Elsa doll by the hair. "Juice!"

"The princess has spoken."

Nancy returned from the kitchen with a box of red-colored liquid. Elizabeth feared for Nancy's light-colored rug. She gave in and let Bailey take it, though, not possessing the energy to fend off a meltdown after a hot buggy session on the soccer field.

20

"I picked up a case of that electrolyte stuff for the star athlete. How about it?"

Trevor stiffened. "Sure, thanks."

"I put out some snacks in front of the TV downstairs. Why don't you and the princess head down there and put your feet up?"

"Excellent." Trevor rolled his eyes.

Where had he picked that up? "Be polite, Trevor." Elizabeth said.

"Oh, leave him alone. He's tired from all that school and sports. Why can't a kid just be a kid anymore is what I want to know."

A tall sleek woman, a stark contrast to the varying degrees of unfashionable women around the coffee table, swooshed into Nancy's living room.

"Louisa Davenport. Lady Lily Wear Designs." She shook Elizabeth's hand, pinching her cold flesh with a large diamond ring.

Elizabeth shifted the diaper bag on her shoulder to cover the extra weight around her middle. "Elizabeth Candew, Neighbor."

"Well, Neighbor," Louisa gave Elizabeth the once-over in what appeared to be the most loving and concerned fashion, which Elizabeth took to mean, *I can fix you.* "Tonight is your lucky night."

Elizabeth laughed. "I'll bet you say that to all the girls."

"She didn't say it to me," said a woman sitting in front of the onion dip in a pair of flip flops. "I'm Marlene, by the way."

"Didn't say it to me, either," said another.

"Well, then I guess I'm excited," Elizabeth said.

"Have a piggie," Nancy held out the tray and a napkin. "In fact, have several."

All Elizabeth had eaten for dinner was mini-pretzels and water on the soccer field. She took a seat at the table, eager to put warm substances into her body.

Nancy tilted the tray towards the Lady Lily Wear rep.

Louisa shook her head. "No, thank you."

"That's why she looks like that, and we look like this," said a woman with the name of a high school swim team running down the arm of her hoodie.

Elizabeth looked at the hoodie longingly, gooseflesh appearing on the backs of her arms. She sank into the couch, the waistband of her jeans strangling her waist. When would she stop wearing jeans? They didn't flatter her, and they didn't feel good. Nancy sailed over and plunked a wine glass filled to the rim in front of her on the coffee table. Elizabeth popped a cocktail frank in her mouth and washed it down with an immodest gulp of wine. *Why not? I'm not driving!*

She set down her glass, sensing eyes upon her. They belonged to Louisa, who said, "I used to be in the same boat as some of you, but I wanted something better, and that's why I wear Lady Lily Wear. It's also why I *sell* Lady Lily Wear."

"I seen the car you drove up in," said a woman perspiring visibly along the armholes of her sleeveless top. "I can see why you sell it, too."

The woman fanned her face with a church bulletin with one hand and dunked a stack of chips in the onion dip with the other. Elizabeth hoped to God Nancy didn't take the fanning as a signal to jack up the air conditioning. She had yet to be introduced to this guest or the others except Marlene, and she didn't care. She had no energy to make small talk.

"Well, yes, the car is one of the many perks." Louisa folded her manicured fingers into a prayerful position. "And it's definitely the reason a lot of ladies sell Lady Lily Wear, but for me, my reason is a bit different." She extended her arm, summoning Nancy. "I need my model, please."

Nancy set the pigs on the coffee table. She squealed and clapped her hands. "I get to be a fashion model."

"You can turn up that music you had on earlier, if you like," Louisa told her. She winked at the guests on the couch. "Put her in the runway walking mood."

"I'll get it," Elizabeth said, hopping up. She pushed play on a CD player, sending an unfamiliar song into the suitcase-sized speakers wedged into opposite corners of Nancy's living room.

"Ba-ba-ba-ba-buh-ba-buh-ba-ba!" sang along the one fanning the church bulletin, joined mid-ba by the fashion model herself.

"What are we listening to?" Elizabeth asked.

"Um," Nancy said. "The Partridge Family."

"The *who*?" Elizabeth asked.

"No, honey, definitely not The Who." The woman in the hoodie laughed, winding her arms around her thigh and pulling herself into a straighter sitting position. "David Cassidy? You ever hear of David Cassidy?"

Elizabeth shook her head.

Except for Louisa, the women exploded into riotous laughter.

"The Partridge Family were only the biggest thing in the world in 1970. Where the hell were you? Timbuktu?" said the perspiring one stationed over the onion dip. "The things I dreamed about doing to that boy when I went to bed at night."

A bead of sweat dangled from a hair along the woman's upper lip. Elizabeth's stomach turned. "I wasn't born yet."

"Well, that explains it," said the one in the hoodie.

"Elizabeth is quite a bit younger than the rest of us," Nancy said. "Louisa too."

"Have you ever heard of The Partridge Family?" Elizabeth asked Louisa.

"Oh, yes. I'm the youngest of seven."

"Nancy's the only one I know who actually plays, let alone owns, a Partridge Family collection," said the one with the bulletin. She hopped up and pulled a metal box with a multi-colored school bus on it from the mantlepiece.

Nancy rushed over. "Hey, be careful with that!"

"Oh, nobody's going to break your Partridge Family lunchbox."

The woman dangled the box by its handle. "Google the Seventies, and you'll come up with the contents of Nancy's closet. We're shocked she even owns a CD player. Thirty-three-and-a-third is more her speed."

"I don't even know what that means," Elizabeth said.

"How old are you?" Marlene demanded.

"I'll be forty-two."

"You're a child," Marlene said. "That explains it."

Nancy shrugged. "Make fun if you want, but the Seventies were a far superior decade to this one – or any of them."

"Tell that to Nixon," Marlene said.

"Or Patti Hearst," said The Perspirer. "Does anyone remember the Iran hostage crisis? Or that freaking gas shortage where you had to wait in a damn line that snaked around for a quarter mile?"

Louisa looked eager to put Nancy back at ease. She changed the subject. "Oh, the Partridge Family was the biggest thing ever. My sisters had posters of Keith all over their bedroom until David Bowie swept them off their feet."

"I know who he is," Elizabeth said.

"Thanks be to God," said the one in the hoodie.

Nancy returned the lunchbox to its perch. She turned up the music and shout-sang I THINK I LOVE YOU while flashing her shoulders in an awkward attempt at model-like movements. Had Elizabeth been in her place, she wouldn't have bounced back from the ribbing so quickly. And it bothered her the others hadn't thought her too young to have heard of the Partridge Family. How old did she look?

"Now, come here. Stand still," Louisa directed. She ran her manicured nails along the seams of Nancy's jumpsuit.

"Now, the first thing you'll notice is the quality," she said, meeting the eyes of each of the guests. "Quality is in the fabric, but it's also in the stitching. When I show you our gorgeous new line today, please pay special attention to the quality. The other thing. Everything in this line is wash-and-wear. Bonus, it holds up in the dryer. I want to underline that. We have tested every item in our line to ensure that it stands up to no less than one hundred go-rounds in the hottest, most abusive dryer. That means the fabric *and* the colors."

The women averted eye contact and fixated on their refreshments. Elizabeth felt bad for Louisa. These people didn't care about clothes. The one in the hoodie hopped up and popped open a beer.

The woman with the fan fanned harder. "You don't say!"

Nancy slit her eyes, but Louisa carried on unflustered. "Let's talk fit. Notice the darts."

Louisa took Nancy by the shoulders and turned her sideways. She ran her fingers along Nancy's breast. "Every Lady Lily Wear item is designed to flatter a woman's shape. Not a girl's shape. Or, heaven forbid, a boy's shape. Maybe you've given up on buying clothing. A lot of women have. Do you know why? Because a lot of the clothing you try on in stores doesn't fit you. It makes you look lumpy and misshapen and wrong. Maybe you've left the fitting room feeling horrible about yourself."

A couple of the women stared into their laps and nodded.

"It's just easier to wear yoga pants," said a woman wearing yoga pants.

"Yes," Louisa whispered, oozing empathy. "Of course it is."

"Those clothes aren't going to make any of us look like you," the one in the hoodie protested.

Louisa removed a photograph from her jacket pocket. "I didn't look like me so long ago, either."

She passed it around. It showed a heavily overweight woman in a man's shirt with a baby lying on thighs the size of canned hams.

"That isn't you," said the woman with the fan, staring ruefully into the empty onion dip bowl.

"Look at the face. What do you see?"

"This lady has a mole on her cheek."

"I had a mole on my cheek." Louisa bent over the coffee table for the women's inspection. "See the scar? I had it removed."

"My sister-in-law has a mole like that," Elizabeth said to nobody in particular. Would it be rude to ask Nancy to turn off the air conditioning? She slid her eyes toward the woman still fanning herself and whose eyes remained on the bowl. "She should have hers removed, too. I suspect she hates herself, and the mole serves as a means of self-flagellation."

"Well, I guess I'm glad I'm not your sister-in-law then." Susan twisted the bill of her Yankees cap and rolled her eyes.

Elizabeth burned from the inside out. Had she said that out loud about Mary Pat? Time to cut down on the wine.

The blonde in the yoga pants took the photo of Louisa. She squinted. "That really is you. What the hell happened?"

"Let's rewind nine years when Lady Lily Wear was in its infancy." Louisa folded her hands again, like a humble preacher. "I was coming out of church one Sunday in hubby's sweat pants, and some angel of a parishioner invited me to a party. I was in the throes of post-partum depression, and if I had to deal with one more dirty diaper or up-chuck in my hair, I thought I'd jump out a window. I self-medicated every night with wine and a box of Ho-Hos. Woke up feeling worse and worse every single day, but I said yes to the Lady Lily Wear invitation." She lowered her voice to a whisper. "Between you and me, the only reason I said yes was for the free wine and to get a break, God forgive me, from that beautiful baby."

"I'm so glad I don't have kids," said the woman with the fan. "You're telling me you lost all that weight because you went to a party?"

"That's what I'm telling you." Louisa folded her plump pinkened lips. "Ladies, I have been there. I've left fitting rooms despising myself. I figured what exactly is the use of exercising and depriving myself only to look like hell. I thought it was me. I thought there was something wrong with my body, but it wasn't my body. It was the clothes. They are designed by men to an impossible beauty standard. Why do we read the stories about supermodels being strung out on drugs and subjecting themselves to disfiguring surgeries? Because, Ladies, they need to fit in the clothes. They need to fit in clothes God never designed their beautiful bodies to fit into."

"Men are a problem," Susan said.

"They sure are," agreed Marlene.

"Let's forget about the men for a minute." Louisa clapped, lightly. "Look at the way this jumpsuit fits Nancy. Isn't she just a glamour queen?"

"She looks good," Marlene agreed. "It fits her nice."

The cold air made it hard for Elizabeth to concentrate. She had a vague idea the thermostat might be on the wall near the bathroom. Maybe she could excuse herself and give it a nudge. "What else did you do to lose all that weight?" she asked Louisa.

"Nothing extreme. Once you start wearing clothes that honor your body, you honor yourself. You find yourself eating better. Exercise almost feels good, and *having* exercised feels even better."

"I don't believe that," Marlene objected. "Let's not get carried away here."

"When you decide to do it for yourself, you'll make it happen. Don't waste your time doing it for a man." Louisa lowered her voice dramatically. "That is the truth."

"I've had just enough of patriarchy," said the one in yoga pants.

Susan rubbed the tops of her thighs. "Who the hell hasn't?"

Everybody laughed. Nancy disappeared into the kitchen. She came back and spooned more dip into the bowl.

"If I looked like you," said the Perspirer, brightening at the sight of the refill. "I'd find myself a fella who can pick up his own socks." She turned to Elizabeth. "After I kicked my current husband out on his ass."

"Oh, I'm keeping my husband," said another woman, who spoke for the first time. "But if I looked like Louisa I'd have a ton more sex!"

The other women hooted.

"I'd be screwing like a rabbit," said somebody else. "Who wouldn't?"

Elizabeth shook her head. Sex led to nothing but trouble.

"What about you, Joanie?" Louisa asked a brunette. "What would you do if you felt better about your weight and appearance?"

"I guess I might feel more confident at work."

"Fit people make more money," Louisa said, holding in her fingers an invisible piece of chalk. "It's not fair. It's not legal. But it's absolutely true."

She rested a hand on Nancy's shoulder. "Now, I know you're all very, very eager to see the new line, but before I bring it out, I want to tell you what else makes Lady Lily Wear extremely special. Exceptionally special. These clothes are designed by women for women, and they are manufactured by women in developing countries. These women are paid a fair wage for their beautiful work, so that they can feed their families, build schools, and dig wells. It would not be an overstatement to say that Lady Lily Wear is in the process of changing the very world we live in, Ladies. We are changing the world stitch by stitch."

Every woman in the room had stopped eating and drinking. They were listening to Louisa, open-mouthed.

"And here's the best part. You can not only buy, wear, and enjoy Lady Lily Wear Designs, but you can do what I do and build a profitable business that you can hand down to your children. Nobody can take it away from you." Louisa gestured towards the window. "You can drive a car like the one you see parked on Nancy's driveway. I did it, and you can too."

"Sign me up," Joanie said.

"See me after the trunk show, and let's talk." Louisa smiled so that her eyes crinkled. "I'd like to share another part of my story first, though. My husband and I were in crippling debt before I started this business. We were up to our eyes in medical bills due to his cancer." She lifted her eyes to heaven. "From which he has been cured, thank God. Not only did we have credit card debt, we also made the very grave mistake of letting ourselves be talked into taking an adjustable mortgage. I'm sure I don't have to tell you what happened there."

"The interest rate hit the ceiling," Susan shouted.

"That it did, and we could not afford it." Louisa hung her head. "We fought about money constantly, which led to an unhealthy environment for our children. Hubby threatened me with divorce and went so far as to see an attorney we couldn't afford either."

Elizabeth listened, transfixed.

"Since starting my Lady Lily Wear Designs business, we are free and clear of all debt. We paid off our mortgage. We sold that house and moved into our dream house. Our children go to private schools. Best of all, I retired my husband. Let that sink in, Ladies."

"You retired your husband," Elizabeth said. "What does that mean?"

"It means I make so much money that he got to quit his soul-crushing J-O-B," Louisa said. "And do you know what happens when you retire your husband?"

"More sex!" squealed the brunette.

"Yes, that, definitely, but we spend time together. We have money for vacations. We have fun. Do you know what it's like to fall back in love with someone you thought you hated? Who thought he hated you? That is my Lady Lily Wear Designs story, Ladies. It would be my honor and privilege to help you write yours."

Elizabeth needed an income. Elizabeth needed new clothes. She didn't have cash, but she did have credit. A voice inside said, *Do not do it*, but for all she knew it was the same voice that told her to marry Russell. She didn't trust it. Another voice said, *Do not walk away from this opportunity. You believe in these clothes, you believe in this message, and you can sell it.*

AFTER THE SHOW, SHE sat down with Louisa.

"I'm just nervous because I'm afraid I can't afford it," Elizabeth told her.

Louisa took her hand and squeezed it. "Honey, I know. You know my story, and you know I've been in your shoes. Give yourself the love you deserve. Have faith and make this investment in yourself. Fast forward ten years from now. What do you want your life to be like? Think about that little boy and girl downstairs. What do you want their lives to be like? I have a kid in college. No loans. No scholarship. We were able to pay for it out of pocket. Let me tell you, that's a good feeling."

Elizabeth did the math. She'd paid the minimum on the Citibank bill, which had a balance that hovered around $2500. At the rate she was going, she'd never pay it. This opportunity looked more and more like something she should not pass up.

"How much is the investment?"

"Well, luckily for you, Lady Lily Wear Designs offers three tiers to entry. The first gets you fifteen pieces of your choosing for seven-fifty, but with the higher tiers you get more for less. This could be an even better option for you. Fifteen hundred gets you forty pieces. Three gets you ninety."

"Three thousand?"

"It's a phenomenal deal." Louisa laughed gently. "And remember whatever entry tier you choose, you get me as your personal mentor. I'll teach you everything I know."

Elizabeth bit her lip, her stomach filling with anxiety. "Do you think fifteen pieces to start would be enough?"

Louisa nodded sympathetically. "I don't, actually." She rested her finger on the sales sheet, on the middle figure. "I usually advise team members to start here at the very least."

Fifteen hundred, plus the twenty-five hundred I already owe the credit card company equals? Four thousand. Elizabeth took a deep breath.

"No pressure, but every single woman bought at least one item at tonight's trunk show and three of them are in line after you to make an investment to start their own Lady Lily Wear Designs businesses. Next month at this time, they'll be well on their way to building their own downlines because, let's face it, these clothes sell themselves."

"I completely agree," Elizabeth said. "And I'm going to take Nancy's jumpsuit in Royal, in a Medium. Would it be all right with you if I took home the consultant agreement and slept on it?"

"Absolutely," Louisa handed her a folder lettered with the words *Your Dream Life Starts Today.* "But I have a feeling about you. I think you're going to be one of us."

Elizabeth relived the sensation of jumping off a high dive for the first time. She thought she'd drown, but she didn't.

"I have a feeling I'm going to be one of you, too."

FIVE

Deep, gutteral sounds came from Bailey's room. Elizabeth snapped open her eyes and checked the phone on the night table: 3:42 AM. She'd drunk four and a half glasses of wine at Nancy's, more than a bottle, and now she would suffer. She dragged herself out of bed to find her daughter bent over the crib, upchucking on the rug decorated with the cow that jumped over the moon.

"Come to Mommy, Baby." Elizabeth lifted Bailey out of the crib and pressed her cheek to the hot little face. "Does your tummy hurt?"

The child nodded.

Elizabeth slid the tip of the digital thermometer into the child's ear, praying for no fever. The day would go easier if she had eaten something that didn't agree with her.

"103.4. I guess we're going to the pediatrician." The office wouldn't be open for hours, so Elizabeth gave Bailey the quickest and gentlest sponge bath, paying special attention to the sour-smelling head. She changed the child's diaper and slipped her into a onesie. The temperature hovered around ninety. It was too hot for anything else.

She went downstairs and settled Bailey, who fell asleep immediately, on her lap. Elizabeth couldn't sleep, not with the headache, not with the heat. The humidity made it impossible to breathe. She put on *Friends* and started to relax. Familiar faces, and everything worked out in the end. She needed everything to work out in the end.

AT NINE O'CLOCK THE phone rang, waking the baby and startling Elizabeth. Had she fallen asleep? She had. She'd hoped to have beaten the rush by making an appointment by now. Now she'd be lucky if she could get a doctor to see Bailey by two o'clock. She hated afternoon appointments. By that time, doctors were tired. Even worse, they ran late at that hour, and Elizabeth had to get Trevor to soccer practice by 3:30.

She picked up the phone. It was Louisa, who obviously believed the proverb about the early bird and the worm.

"Good morning," she said. "I'm not getting you too early, am I?"

Elizabeth did her best to hide her annoyance. "My little one is sick. We're getting ready to go to the pediatrician."

"Awww. What's the matter?"

"I think she has a stomach bug. I'm not sure, but she's miserable."

"Oh, that is the worst. It's so hard to watch our babies suffer, isn't it? It's the absolute worst part of being a mom."

Louisa sounded less charismatic on the phone. Less magical. Elizabeth found her precise annunciation annoying.

"Well, I won't keep you. Maybe I'll call you later to see if you have any questions related to our discussion last night. One of the best things about repping for Lady Lily Wear Designs is the built-in business mentoring program. It's kind of like having a Harvard MBA in your pocket, except some of our reps have considerably larger incomes than Harvard MBAs."

"Right, yes, well, I'm not sure what time we'll be back. I'm expected on the soccer field today."

"Are you very involved with your son's team?"

Elizabeth looked at the clock. This one didn't know when to hang up. "Yes, parents are required to be or our kids can't play."

"So you probably know a lot of parents."

"Can we discuss this later? I really have to go."

"Oh, honey, yes. You go. *Go!* But during your day today, ask yourself who you know that a) loves wearing wonderful clothing, and b) is ready to start their own business."

"I will do that, Louisa. I'll talk to you later."

"Yes, Elizabeth, we will most definitely talk later. I am so excited for you and for this big change you are about to make in your life and in your children's lives."

Elizabeth gave the clock another glance. "All right, thanks. Bye now."

"Oh, one more thing. Another advantage of your Lady Lily Wear Designs business is that you'll be free to take your children to the pediatrician whenever you need. Not so when you have a J-O-B."

"That's a great point, but I'm going now. Goodbye, Louisa."

"One more thing. When you're in the doctor's office, why not jot down a list of those people you know. We advise new stylists to come up with one hundred names."

"I'll do my best."

Elizabeth hung up.

The pediatrician's office crawled with coughing kids, crying kids, kids fighting over a dump truck on the WELL side of the wall. Elizabeth steered Bailey and Trevor onto the SICK side but away from the toy box and the microbes it hosted. She observed runny-nosed toddlers and sullen adolescents flicking at devices from under hoodies. She inhaled shallowly. In the few minutes since they'd arrived, her face had stiffened against the aggressive air conditioning. Why had she forgotten to pack warm jackets?

She took a magazine from the coffee table. Inside it offered weight loss hacks, recipes for confections to make your family love you, and tips on giving the perfect blowjob. Elizabeth would like to find a men's magazine crammed with best practices for pleasing a woman sexually or otherwise, but men's magazines generally focused on how to get a woman into bed for his pleasure, not hers.

Elizabeth flung it back on the table, ignoring the parenting magazines altogether. She had subscribed to one shortly before she gave birth to Trevor, and her mother had given her a gift subscription to another for Christmas that year. Reading them gave Elizabeth a claustrophobic feeling, and she noticed they gave conflicting advice on everything from nursing to teething to time-outs. She hated them.

She'd already decided to ignore Louisa's advice to write a list of one hundred people she knew. Louisa had struck her as an entirely different person this morning, pushy and self-serving. Clearly, she didn't care that Elizabeth had a sick baby on her hands. She was single-minded in her goal to recruit new reps. If succeeding at Lady Lily Wear required that kind of ambition, Elizabeth had bad news for Louisa. She didn't have it, and she didn't want it.

They drove to the pharmacy to pick up Bailey's prescription, an expense Elizabeth could do without. She wanted to go home and take a nap, but soccer practice left them time for nothing more than a quick late lunch. She stopped the minivan at the mailbox at the bottom of her pitted driveway and removed the mail. It did not contain a check from Russell.

That man is going to hell! Elizabeth furiously liberated Bailey from her seat, the buckle clipping the baby's hand. She wailed wildly, her nose running all over her Minnie Mouse tee. Elizabeth recited, "Mommy's sorry, Baby," over and over. *Damn you, Russell!*

It turned out Bailey had no appetite. Maybe they could both squeeze in a fifteen-minute nap, after all. Elizabeth sang the *Barney* theme song until Bailey fell asleep. Elizabeth had fought valiantly to shield her from Barney, who gave her the creeps, but Nancy had shown the movie while Elizabeth went to court. From then on, the child had refused to sleep until she heard "I Love You, You Love Me" at least three times. Elizabeth put the blame for Bailey's Barney fixation squarely on Russell. If not for his porn addiction, Nancy and *Barney* never would have entered the equation.

She made a grilled cheese sandwich for Trevor. "I'm going out for a minute," she said.

Trevor shrugged and bit into his sandwich. Elizabeth brought the phone onto the driveway to give Russell a piece of her mind without the children overhearing. For once in his life, he answered on the first ring.

"The check is fifteen days late," she said.

"Or maybe it's going to be fifteen days early," he said.

"What are you talking about?"

"When are you supposed to get the check, Elizabeth?"

"The first of the month. I shouldn't have to tell you."

"Have I ever sent it on the first of the month?"

"No, you haven't. I should take you back to court."

"See how that works out for you."

"Where's the check, Russell?"

"You agreed not to take alimony, Elizabeth."

"It's not alimony, you jackass. It's child support."

"Do you have a job?"

"You know I don't."

"And you're supporting yourself how? How are you supporting the child you had with another man?"

"Frugally."

"Wrong. The correct answer, Elizabeth, is that you are supporting yourself and your bastard with the money I send for the support of my son."

"I'm raising your son five days a week. Where the hell are you during the school year when he needs help with his homework? Or when somebody says something mean to him? It's me who takes care of him. You pop in for the fun stuff while I'm here in the trenches all day. I have to take him to soccer practice, Russell, and I'm just back from the pediatrician with a sick baby."

"Somebody has to work for a living, and that person is clearly not you. Get Mary Pat to take him to practice. Trevor knows *she* cares about him. Meanwhile, you are in contempt of our agreement. You're living off your kid's money, you and that runt of yours. It's time for you to get a job."

"Did you ever think to yourself that the court might not see it that way, Russell?"

"Nope. But even if they didn't, I have the money to go back to court. It's no skin off my nose, but you don't have any money. If you want your attorney to bill you up the wazoo to shake me down, be my guest."

"Russell, I'm done apologizing. I made a mistake."

"That was some mistake, Babe. You picked a bad time to go off the pill."

"*We* picked a bad time to go off the pill. You're the one who wanted another baby."

"Yeah, *my* baby. Not the spawn of some slimeball you picked up in the local tavern."

"Look who's talking about slimeballs. You're a porn freak, which is gross on so many levels, but you knew damn well about my parents—"

"Oh, boo hoo. Your parents! Get over it already. Get help. I hate to break it to you, but you're not the first person whose family broke up due to infidelity. Just because your father did it to your mother didn't mean I would do it to you."

"You promised you wouldn't go there. You wouldn't go to those sites. My father read those magazines, and then he cheated on my mother. Porn is a gateway drug, Russell."

"I should tape these conversations so you can hear yourself. You sound crazy, Elizabeth. Every man reads those magazines. Grow up. Men look at the pictures and go into the bathroom and jerk off. End of story. Looking at those magazines doesn't mean you're going to cheat on your wife."

"Some people would say jerking off *is* cheating."

"Some people are morons. Even Christie Brinkley's husband liked porn."

"And she divorced him."

"Yeah, well, you're no Christie Brinkley, and I didn't cheat. Your father may be a dirtbag, but I'm just a normal red-blooded American male."

The comment about Christie Brinkley threw Elizabeth off her axis. She'd absorbed the message that if you wanted love and admiration, you had to be beautiful. She wanted to be beautiful. And now the man she'd married told her she didn't make the grade. Furthermore, if Christie Brinkley couldn't keep a man faithful, could anybody? Elizabeth vowed to never fall in love again. She found the very idea exhausting.

"You're not necessarily normal, Russell, just ordinary. I wonder how you'd have liked it if I locked myself in a room with a vibrator."

"That would have been the wiser course, Sweetheart. But you had to run out and bang another dude."

"What's done is done. If you really care about your son, *you* can get your sister to take him to practice. I am limiting my exposure to that woman."

SIX

Trevor returned from soccer practice to become one with the iPad Russell gave him after the divorce became final. The sun disappeared beyond the kitchen window. The night air wrapped around them like a filmy blanket. Bailey whined incessantly.

She clung to her mother's hip and refused to be put down. Elizabeth turned on the oscillating fan, but the sound of it whirring back and forth made her tired. She squinted. The couch she and Russell purchased after their honeymoon had faded along its top and arms. It wouldn't be long before she would be ashamed even to invite Cathy over. Russell was right; Elizabeth needed an income, and the Lady Lily Wear deal still scared her.

Last week a cashier slipped a *Now Hiring!* flyer into her groceries advertising a competitive wage but no benefits. Elizabeth had excellent medical and dental insurance and a 401K as Marketing VP at Bullseye Entertainment, but she'd talked herself into quitting to raise Trevor. What if he turned out to suffer the learning difficulties she once did? With a job in Manhattan, she'd be too busy to advocate for him. She wouldn't have the energy to read *The Cat in the Hat* after a two-hour commute, and she knew damn well Russell wouldn't do it.

Since the divorce, Russell's insurance covered Trevor, but Elizabeth paid dearly to provide for herself and Bailey. She needed money. With two children, she needed to make her own hours. She needed more than a "competitive" cashier's wage; any babysitter she paid while she worked would take every cent.

Elizabeth seated Bailey in her lap at the kitchen table. She picked up the form Louisa gave her: *One Hundred People*. She wrote down a name:

Cathy

She couldn't think of anyone else. Her mother was dead. She didn't speak to her father and had ceased communication with his sisters. She had no siblings. She had a couple of cousins in New Jersey she kept in touch with over Facebook. She wrote down their names. She thought about people she ran into in her everyday life: Mary, the clerk at the library. They'd become more than passing acquaintances in the fourteen years Elizabeth had lived in Stonesbury. They both had tastes that ran from Neil Gaiman to Philippa Gregory. Maybe Mary would be interested in hosting a trunk show. Maybe she'd be eager to start a profitable business. How much money could the town be paying her to work at the library?

Elizabeth went to bed. Maybe during the night other names would come to her. In the morning, she wrote down a list of people that included the notary at the UPS office. She'd become friendly with Rhona —Rhonda? — during the dispensation of her mother's tiny will. She added Mabel from the dry cleaner's, and also Sheila from the coffee shop. Her hand shook, but the anxiety lessened when she reminded herself she didn't have to twist arms to get people into the business. Getting them in would bring in the most money, but Elizabeth only had to invite them to her party, and then gently ask if they'd be interested in joining during the presentation. If not, maybe they'd agree to host a trunk show. The free items they'd earn would certainly be an inducement. Elizabeth brightened; she might actually be able to succeed at this business, and if she did, she could do more than replace the cracked window in Trevor's room. She could wriggle out from beneath Russell's thumb and send Trevor to college with her own money, without the help of a tuba scholarship.

She added some women who had boys on Trevor's soccer team, even Lisa Nasta, who'd rolled her eyes when Elizabeth turned up as Snack Mom with donut holes from the supermarket instead of the swanky new bakery on Turner Avenue. Maybe Elizabeth did provide substandard snacks, but she'd honed her skills in sales and negotiation in Corporate America. If she were to succeed at Lady Lily Wear, she must keep reminding herself of that fact. If she set her mind to it, she could out-Louisa Louisa.

Elizabeth picked up the phone to report the good news.

"You're coming on board," Louisa trilled. "I knew it!"

The woman was infuriatingly presumptuous. "Uh, I think so. Your instructions say I need one hundred people. I have fifty-nine. Is that okay?"

"Oh, it's better than okay. One hundred is a guideline, although – you watch – you'll wake up in the middle of the night and find that forty-one more come rushing at you."

"I'd like to get started as soon as possible, but I don't have childcare. Is it all right if I do shows with my children? Trevor's generally pretty well behaved. Bailey's a work in progress."

"That would be up to each individual hostess, but while you're getting your feet wet, you might want to host a few shows at your own home. That way, your children could be around without sacrificing your professional image."

Elizabeth glanced at the couch. How much would it cost to have it reupholstered? Too much, probably, but she might be able to spring for a microfiber slipcover.

"If I do everything to the letter, how soon do you think I can see a full-time income?"

"I've had girls who've taken in profits in the low five figures after the first five weeks."

Elizabeth bristled at the use of the word girls to describe women over the age of thirty-five. "We're talking, what? Ten thousand dollars over the course of a month? A quarter?"

"A month," Louisa said. "A four-week period. Work your buns off, and it's totally doable. Women love to buy and wear Lady Lily Wear Designs."

Which meant Elizabeth could work off her Second-Tier investment of fifteen hundred dollars in no time. What's more, she could pay off her credit card balance in full. The reservations she'd felt earlier that morning evaporated.

"And you will be my mentor?" Elizabeth asked.

"Exactly. The best part of coming in is that you get me. I don't mean to brag, but well, listen, talk is cheap. Why don't you bring Bailey over to my house this afternoon? We can go over everything."

"Sure, if you don't mind being around a sick toddler."

"Not at all. I've been there, and being around other working moms who understand your situation is just one of the benefits of getting in with this fine company."

"I'm just going to change, and I'll be right over."

"Excellent. Coffee or tea?"

"Tea, please."

"I'll put the kettle on," Louisa said. Then came a pause. "Elizabeth?"

"Yes."

"Remember your credit card."

MARY PAT CALLED, SUMMONING Trevor for a playdate. Elizabeth dropped him off and eyed the gas gauge. *Good to the last drop.* It had been Russell's idea to buy a minivan. She'd been dead set against it, said it would swallow up her youth, but now she had to hand it to him. The thing got 36 miles to the gallon. Also, from the outside, where you couldn't see the juice stains, it didn't look horrible.

After the meeting, she'd invest in a full interior/exterior car wash to ensure the elimination of all yogurt smears and pretzel crumbs. The minivan would roll up to trunk shows gleaming like an emerald, with an immaculate interior to keep her clothing line in top flight condition. Elizabeth's clothing line! She was doing this! She'd wait to replace the balding tires until after she banked her first commission check.

She headed towards Louisa's house, eager to see if it lived up to expectations. She turned onto Maple Leaf Drive, and then onto Sterling. She'd seen pictures of this community in realtor magazines she'd picked up in the waiting area of the Sunnyview Diner, but she'd never been beyond its gates. She stopped the car at a security kiosk designed to look like a small medieval tower.

The guard glanced at the minivan. By his expression, he didn't see a lot of them.

"You're here to see who?"

"Louisa Davenport at –."

He cut her off. "Fourteen Dudley."

"She must get a lot of visitors." Elizabeth looked beyond the courtyard fountain to see a riot of impatiens and marigolds. She'd heard there were over a hundred houses tucked away in this sub-community, which contained a small supermarket, a package store, a dry cleaner, and a clubhouse with an Olympic size swimming pool.

"Oh, everybody knows Louisa Davenport," said the guard, a square-jawed young man, whom Elizabeth guessed to be a college student working to pay tuition. "I'll need to see your license."

"These people don't mess around." Elizabeth reached into her bag. Behind her, the baby slept soundly.

"I need to make a copy," he said.

"Really?"

"Them's the rules."

She fished her license from her wallet. The young man copied it and handed it back. He smiled. She smiled back. Did he find her attractive? Despite the trouble sex had gotten her into, it still mattered to her that men, even younger men, considered her pretty. She wanted to please them. And why? What had any of them ever done to please her?

"All right, ma'am," he said. "Make a right at the first lane beyond the fountain. Pass the clubhouse and follow the signs."

Elizabeth followed his directions, rolling along Belgian Block curbs that gleamed in the sunlight. She sang along to "Deal" by the Dead, taking in the fleet of gardeners buzzing across lawns on shiny equipment. Purple hydrangeas and Black-eyed Susans burst in every direction. Only five years ago, Elizabeth had stormed City Hall to decry the destruction of a farm that predated the Revolution to build this development. Now she looked beyond her smeared windshield and figured it might have been worth it.

She took a right at Gable Lane. The mailboxes, etched with the occupants' house number in gold plate, probably cost more than new tires. On Longfellow Elizabeth made the left onto Dudley. Along Louisa's lengthy driveway, a line of beech trees waved in the breeze above a koi pond.

She unbundled the sleeping baby and climbed the steps to a double front door. The bell sounded like the smash of a mighty gong. Elizabeth felt tiny, like Dorothy demanding to meet the Wizard of Oz. She tried to make out her reflection in the glass. Did she still look presentable? Bailey's damp bangs clung to her forehead. Elizabeth blew her own out of her eyes.

The heavy door opened, slowly.

She tilted her head in anticipation, heart racing. She'd read about a poor guy named Reverend Ike who used to walk past exclusive shops in Manhattan telling himself, "This is for me." His subconscious had taken him at his word, and he became rich. Elizabeth took in the huge cast iron lanterns at either side of Louisa's massive door. *This is for me!*

The door opened fully to reveal a small middle-aged woman in a white uniform. "I will tell Louisa you are here," she said. "Please come in."

Elizabeth held out her hand. "I'm Elizabeth Candew. Nice to meet you."

The woman didn't accept the hand. "I will tell her you are here."

Elizabeth stepped gratefully into the air conditioning, onto black-and-white tile that reminded her of floors she'd seen in the foyers of better wedding receptions. The wrought iron chandelier imparted an industrial vibe, a chic contrast to a Queen Anne table on which a splash of purple hydrangeas exploded from a rectangular vase.

Elizabeth fully expected Louisa to descend the grand staircase like Scarlet O'Hara. She didn't. Instead, she emerged from the back of the house rubbing a dish towel.

"Welcome, welcome, welcome!" She extended her hand. "Excuse the damp. I've just been out in the garden."

"You have a business and children, and you have time to garden?"

"I live to put my hands in the earth, Elizabeth. There's nothing quite so therapeutic. Trust me, I've had therapy. We're all the same in the end, you know. Broken, and in need of fixing."

I could use some fixing. Elizabeth followed her hostess into a massive kitchen with industrial sized appliances, every one of them gleaming and free of finger marks. Louisa opened her refrigerator, which approximated the size of a Manhattan apartment.

She held up a bottle of prosecco. "I got us a treat."

What happened to the kettle she said she'd put on? Elizabeth surveilled the stovetop. No kettle.

"Would you have any iced tea, maybe?"

"You sure you wouldn't prefer prosecco."

Of course Elizabeth would prefer prosecco. She shifted Bailey, thumb in mouth and eyes closed, onto her other hip. "I can't drink and drive."

"Oh, relax. We'll spend some time." Louisa took a tea towel from a drawer, unwound the safety netting from the bottle, and popped it open with nearly silent precision. "Bailey looks ready for a nap. Why don't you lie her down in the family room? Don't worry. We'll hear her if she wakes up."

Elizabeth did as instructed and laid Bailey on a couch across from the stone fireplace.

Louise followed, lightly swinging the bottle. "There are clean blankets in the closet over there."

Clean blankets? As opposed to just blankets? Elizabeth changed sheets every Wednesday, but she rarely got around to washing blankets. This woman had her act together, but she also had help. Which she could afford. Because of Lady Lily Wear.

Louisa handed Elizabeth a glass. "So refreshing, especially after a morning in the hot garden.

"Or any time in late August," Elizabeth said.

"I'm done with summer. Bring on the fall, please. Now let's go back to the kitchen," Louisa whispered conspiratorially. "For some girl talk."

She settled onto a kitchen stool and lifted her prosecco glass to indicate Elizabeth should do the same. "Can I see your list of names?"

"Oh, I'm sorry. I didn't know you needed me to bring it."

The sunlight coming from the kitchen window illuminated the deepening furrow between Louisa's brow. "You must always be prepared in this business. You must always be ready to go."

"I thought my having a list was enough. I didn't know you'd need to see the names on it." Elizabeth watched the bubbles rise in her glass.

"How are we supposed to strategize if I don't understand the nuances of your relationships with these names?"

"Of course. You're right. I'm sorry."

"Don't ever be sorry, Sweetie." Louisa took a delicate sip. "Be better."

Elizabeth didn't know whether to be inspired or insulted.

"Now can you remember the names? The categories?" Louisa said over the rim of her glass.

"Categories."

"Meaning where you know these people from. I'm guessing some of them are family, others are friends, and then you have the people you bump into every day running errands and at your children's activities."

"Most of them fall into the last category."

"That's most common. I advise my new stylists not to lean too heavily on friends and family. This is a business, not a guilt rally."

"Oh, good. I really didn't want to hit up the New Jersey cousins."

Louisa brought a notepad out of a drawer. "Give me the names you remember."

"I told you I had fifty-nine, right?" Elizabeth closed her eyes and tried to remember. She came up with fifty-five.

Louisa ran a manicured finger that defied the rigors of gardening down the list. "Your first step is to invite your soccer and preschool moms to a show at your house."

Elizabeth remembered her faded couch. A new slipcover wouldn't hide the cracked window and crumbling driveway. "I think I'd be more comfortable doing shows at other people's houses. You know, the way you did with Nancy."

"Relax." Louisa rested a startlingly cold hand on Elizabeth's. "One of the benefits of being a stylist in my group is that you have the option of presenting your first trunk show in *my* home. I don't call my gals Davenport's Divas for nothing."

Certain words bothered Elizabeth, *gals* being a chart topper. "Here?"

Louisa waved from the wrist, like a queen. "Here."

"Oh, that's genius. If I do my party here, it might induce people to see the possibilities and sign up to become hosts themselves?"

"Might induce? *Will* induce. Better yet, it'll have them killing each other to sign up for the stylist opportunity."

Elizabeth didn't necessarily want people killing each other. "But you didn't do Nancy's show here? Why?"

"Because this perk is exclusively for new stylists. Nancy was merely a hostess."

Merely. Elizabeth felt a twinge of anxiety, but from beyond the kitchen the rail of the circular staircase gleamed reassuringly.

"Can you see yourself living in a home like this?" Louisa asked.

"Not yet, but I'm definitely open to the possibility."

"I won't sugar coat it. It takes hard work and dedication. You can't be shy. Let me ask you something. Your son plays lacrosse, yes?"

"Just soccer."

"You know what I'm getting at. Every single coach wants something from you, right? And wait'll school starts. Every scout leader, the PTA moms. They suck your blood. They've got you buying snacks, bugging your friends and family to buy giftwrap and cookie dough. Somebody's always got a hand in your wallet."

"Oh, yeah." Elizabeth hated it. "Might as well hook a vacuum to my bank account."

Louisa sighed expansively. She poured more prosecco.

"Now, the beauty of owning your Lady Lily Wear business is that you get to make that nonsense work for you. You're putting yourself in the driver's seat. *You* get to run a fundraiser through your own business, which will benefit *your* child's team or school. It will also benefit *you*." She chuckled darkly. "And you will be doing society a favor by getting half the American population out of yoga gear and into presentable clothing. We do a lot of good with this business, and I have a feeling that you'll be one of my brightest stars. Something tells me you'll really go for it."

"Thank you." Elizabeth took a long sip of prosecco. Why didn't she drink prosecco every day? She promised herself to locate the gated community's package store on the ride home and treat herself to a bottle. She'd pretend she lived here. Fake it 'til you make it.

Louisa disappeared into another room and returned with a folder festooned with the Lady Lily Wear logo. Elizabeth realized with horror she'd forgotten the one Louisa gave her at Nancy's. Strike two.

"I'm sorry. In the rush to get Bailey to the doctor, I forgot mine." Louisa picked up her pen. "Don't be sorry."

"Be better," Elizabeth replied.

"We talked about you going in at Top Tier, is that right?"

"Second Tier," Elizabeth said. She fished around in her pocket for her credit card. She did the math again: Fifteen hundred plus twenty-five hundred is four thousand. The money Louisa predicted she'd make her first month would not only lift her out of debt but also remove Russell's golf shoe from her neck.

Louisa rubbed her palms together. "Good news, though. Lady Lily Wear is doing its once-a-year special for new stylists. You can get in at Top Tier at three thousand, with the ninety pieces we talked about *plus* an additional ten, and also a mix-and-match collection of accessories."

"A fifteen-hundred-dollar investment is more comfortable for me."

"Sure, I can see why you'd say that. I felt that way, too, getting started, but I'd have gotten further up the ladder so much faster if

I'd had that extra product to show. You see, for just fifteen more you don't just get bigger quantities of the same items. You get a wider selection of items in the usual quantities. In other words, you'll have items that other stylists won't because they didn't qualify for that level of inventory. It gives you a big edge. No pressure, though. Just a thought."

Louisa opened another bottle of prosecco. Elizabeth hopped up and found Bailey still sound asleep. Why not accept another glass? She enjoyed the early afternoon buzz. The sight of a hummingbird alighting on the window sill over the sink delighted her. The graceful line of the faucet qualified it as a piece of modern art.

That's for me.

"What are you thinking?" Louisa asked, pouring.

"I'm thinking I love this kitchen. I'm thinking I love this house."

Louisa took a look around. "If you told me I'd be living in a house like this one day, I'd have said you were nuts. It just goes to show anything is possible."

"I could get used to living like this. I have to tell you, though. I fought this development. My ex and I used to take our son to the farm that stood on this land for ice cream."

"The farm may be gone, but nobody can take your memories. Now what do you say we build something solid for yourself and your children?" Louisa set her pen on the Top-Tier description on the contract.

A wave of anxiety surged through Elizabeth's buzz. She'd never sleep tonight. She could handle a four-thousand-dollar credit card bill. Fifty-five hundred would put her over the edge.

"I don't know," she said.

"Let me be frank, Elizabeth. My stylists who go all in are always more successful than those who go halfway. Always. They make an average of one hundred and fifty percent more in sales than my other ladies. Again, no pressure. Just something to think about."

"Really? One hundred and fifty percent more in sales." Elizabeth stared at the contract so intently the numbers blurred.

"I have good instincts about people, and from the minute I met you, you struck me as a go-getter. Someone who gets things done."

"I have an ex who would strongly disagree with you."

"Why? Because you're the one who stayed home with the kids? Because you have a full-time job for which you receive no money and even less gratitude?"

How many times had Russell told Elizabeth to get off her fat ass and get a job? She imagined the look on his face when she drove over to his house to pick up Trevor in a car like Louisa's. She imagined it when he dropped Trevor off at her new house in Louisa's development.

"Think about it." Louisa said, reading her mind. "How it will feel to show your ex how wrong he was about you."

"I would really enjoy that," Elizabeth said. The prosecco started digging a small hole in her stomach. "What if I go in at Middle Tier now, and in a week or two move up to Top?"

"Right, but this special deal with the free add-ons is only offered at signing, I'm afraid. You snooze, you lose." Louisa smiled to reveal movie star orthodontia. "Listen, Sweetie, I know this is a tough call, so I'm going to get my mentor on the phone to help you make a sound decision. Would that be all right?"

Elizabeth nodded. She needed to make a sound decision. Besides, it couldn't hurt to talk to Louisa's mentor to get an idea of the success she'd achieved in this business. Due diligence demanded she hear another story before she pulled the trigger. She drained her glass.

Louisa pressed a single button on her phone. "Toni, it's me. You're on speaker."

"Great," the voice said. "I've been expecting your call, Weezy."

"Listen, I have Elizabeth Candew with me, the one I told you about." Louisa winked at Elizabeth. "As I said, she's got everything we look for in a star stylist. Personality, spunk, and drive."

Elizabeth shifted on her stool, flattered. Should she reach for another glass? Or wait to be offered?

"Hello and welcome to the Lady Lily Wear Family, Elizabeth!" the voice said. "You are going to love, love, love this business. That is a promise. Louisa tells me you're a mom of two, is that right?"

"A single mom," Louisa chirped, preventing Elizabeth from answering for herself.

"Ah, the great unsung single mom," Toni said. "The American superhero. I don't know if Louisa mentioned it, but I was a single mom myself in a former life, struggling from paycheck to paycheck. I don't know if you can relate. Maybe your situation is different."

"I can definitely relate," Elizabeth said.

"I thank my lucky stars for the gal who introduced me to this wonderful company."

Elizabeth didn't allow the use of the word *gal* to stop her from listening eagerly.

"I got in, hit the ground running, and never looked back. I made a lot of money in this business. And bonus, I met the man of my dreams and married him, too."

"This is a good story," Louisa said. "Tell her, Toni."

"Oh, it's better than good. I met my loving husband, Todd, through one of my show hostesses. She happened to be Todd's sister. He showed up to rescue her son and take him to a ball game, because what young man in his right mind wants to hang around with a bunch of women. Am I right, Ladies?"

Elizabeth felt her stomach clamp up. Sure, most kids would prefer a game to a fashion show – she would too when she was a kid! – but she disliked women who disparaged their own sex.

"When Todd showed up," Toni continued, "I happened to be showing a scarf from our elegant Britannia collection. He announced he needed a gift for his mom's birthday. The next thing you know he was asking for my number."

"A Lady Lily Wear romance," Louisa trilled. "You should write a book."

"I should, and the funny thing is, Todd's mom was dead. It was just a line."

"So romantic," Louisa said.

"Yup, and no meddling mother-in-law trouble for me." The sound of Toni's husky laugh filled the room. "As a single mom, Elizabeth, you may be glad to know lots of stylists meet husbands. You meet lots of wonderful people in this business altogether. You start getting to know folks you previously just said hello to. Now, Elizabeth do you belong to a church?"

"Not really."

"You might want to join one. Churches make excellent soil for cultivating hostesses, in addition to bringing women into your business. That's how you build a solid downline. You also might want to explore volunteering at a soup kitchen or homeless shelter. The other people who help out in those places tend to have a deep need to be of service, and you can induce – no, induce isn't the right word. Help me out here, Louisa."

"Coax, maybe?" Louisa offered.

"Yes, much better." The husky laugh again. "Elizabeth, you can gently *coax* those people into joining your business. Teaching Sunday school is another option. You'll meet tons of moms."

Toni's ideas struck Elizabeth as slimy, but Louisa said, "So not only would Elizabeth be doing a public service, she'd be helping the people she brings into her business achieve their own dreams. Everybody wins."

"Everybody wins indeed," Toni said. "Now let me tell you about the house my recruit Shari Colter just closed on. Shari seized the Lady Lily Wear opportunity, oh, just about 18 months ago. Since then, she has retired her husband and bought her family a five-bedroom, four-bath center hall colonial on six acres, which gives them all the room they need for their three kids and two cocker spaniels. Pretty great for a family that once squashed a Christmas tree into a milk crate apartment over a pizzeria."

"Tell Elizabeth about your place, Toni."

"Sure thing. You know I never pass up a brag opp, Louisa. Thanks to LLW, Elizabeth, my husband Todd finally broke free of his J-O-B, and we built our dream house."

Louisa held up four fingers. "It's four acres overlooking a lake. You could literally slip two of my houses into Toni and Todd's. It's that big."

"I won't pretend I didn't work my tush off for it."

Elizabeth despised the word *tush,* but the prospect of owning lakeside property prompted her to let it slide.

"To succeed in this business, Elizabeth, you'll work your tush off too, but from what Louisa tells me, you have what it takes. There's no doubt in my mind you can achieve your dream of financial freedom."

Elizabeth did have what it took. It had been a long time anybody had encouraged her to reach for anything beyond finding a good deal on a 3-ring binder, unless you counted Cathy, and she didn't. Cathy was biased. "Thanks for putting your faith in me, Toni. Right now, my children's education is my first priority."

"Oh, honey, that's cake."

Louisa snapped her fingers. "Easy McPeasy."

"Are you excited?" Toni asked. "Because, I for one, am very excited for you, Lady Elizabeth."

Louisa clapped her hands. "I'm excited, too."

"It would be a dream come true not to worry about paying bills," Elizabeth said.

"Has Louisa had a chance to tell you about our Lady Lily Wear Global Sales Conference yet?"

"I was just about to get there," Louisa said.

"Oh, do yourself a favor and book your flight now. This year, we're going to be in Austin, Texas for four days and three nights celebrating everything Lady Lily Wear."

"It's a blast," Louisa said. "The company launches its new line each year at Conference, and there are tons of very profitable trainings."

"Not to mention extremely inspiring testimonials."

"And vats of prosecco."

"Prosecco's pretty much the official beverage of Lady Lily Wear," Toni declared.

"It's true" Louisa held up her glass. "Best of all, Toni's the keynote this year."

"Oh, and I'm delighted. It'll be an honor to tell my Lady Lily Wear success story to thousands of stylists from all over the globe. I can't wait to count you among us, Elizabeth."

Behind Toni's voice, Elizabeth heard a door slam and a male voice. She thought she heard the voice say, "How long are you going to be on that freaking phone?" but she wouldn't swear to it.

"Oops, the man is here to fix the boiler," Toni chirped, "I'll let you ladies go."

"Thank you so much for your time," Louisa said. "We both really appreciate it."

"Oh, it's my pleasure. You're a blessing to me, Louisa. And welcome aboard, Elizabeth."

The line went dead. Louisa poised her pen above Top Tier. "Well, shall we?"

Elizabeth had just enough prosecco to thoroughly quell the fear in her stomach. "If three thousand dollars means I get to sleep again, sign me up."

"I'm proud of you for making this investment in yourself." Louisa handed Elizabeth the pen.

Elizabeth took a deep breath. She copied down her credit card number. As she signed the document and returned it to Louisa, she heard the rumble of the garage door.

"That will be our Stephanie. Speaking of education, she goes back to Brown on September 9th."

"Wow. Good school," Elizabeth said. "You definitely know about tuition then."

"I sure do." Louisa tore off the pink copy of the contract and handed it to Elizabeth. "My daughter's dreamed about going to Brown since third grade."

"Really?" Elizabeth thought about Trevor and his bottle-cap worms. "My son's a good student, but he hasn't made any decisions about college yet."

"Oh, well, Stephanie has always been a big achiever. She knows what she wants, and she gets it. Not only did she decide on Brown, she decided she'd marry a Brown boy in the campus chapel. She's very determined."

"She decided all that in third grade?"

"She's a force of nature." Louisa fingered a thorn on the roses she'd set in a vase between the sink and stove. "I admire her determination, although sometimes I wonder if it might backfire. She did manage to find the boy. I hope he's the right one."

"I hope so, too," Elizabeth said.

Stephanie came rushing into the kitchen and slammed the door leading to the garage. She threw her keys on the counter and stuck her head in the refrigerator without acknowledging her mother.

The kid may be a big achiever, but she's got rotten manners.

"I'm fine, Steph, thanks for asking. How are you, Dear?" Louisa said.

"Hi." The girl kept her face in the refrigerator. When she emerged, Elizabeth saw she had her mother's height and cheekbones. "There's no food in this house."

"There's plenty of food."

"Yeah, if you count radishes, peas, and assorted heads of lettuce."

"Open your eyes. There's chicken."

"Which I have to cook. No, thanks." She turned back towards the garage. "Don't worry. I'll hit the food court at the mall. I need clothes."

"I thought nobody went to the mall anymore. Anyway, I just got a shipment."

"Mom, you know damn well I wouldn't be caught dead in that crap."

Louisa folded her arms across her chest. "Kids," she told Elizabeth. "I'm sure you know the feeling."

Stephanie turned back. She grabbed a green apple from a bowl on the counter and gave Elizabeth the once-over. "Are you a mom from Quincy's group?"

"Quincy's group?"

"My sister has special needs. I guess you're not part of it." The girl forced a smile. "Well, good luck."

Stephanie pulled out of the garage, and Elizabeth felt her buzz subside. She woke Bailey. Louisa waved goodbye to them, dangling her garden gloves.

SEVEN

Elizabeth woke up the next morning with a major case of buyer's remorse. What had she gotten herself into? She brushed her teeth, looked herself in the eye, and told herself out loud everything would be okay. She had the work ethic to pull this off. She had the desire. And she didn't have a choice.

But what if she couldn't? What if she didn't have what it took?

She texted the one person who could peel her off the ceiling.

Good morning, Cathy. I've done something crazy. I need you to talk me down.

She deleted the text before she could hit *send*. She'd already burdened Cathy with the responsibility of carrying her through her divorce. After countless late-night phone calls seeking advice and anxiety relief, the relationship had become one sided.

It was time to balance the scales. She could invite Cathy to lunch. No, she couldn't; she was already fifty-five hundred in the hole. Then again, what difference would another sixty dollars make?

Can I take you to lunch? Saturday? I miss my best friend.

Lately, Cathy had taken her time texting back, providing Elizabeth another source of anxiety. Was Cathy genuinely busy, or did she want distance? Elizabeth added a GIF of Will Ferrell dressed as Little Debbie to induce a quick response. Cathy and Elizabeth were steadfast in their love and admiration for Will Ferrell.

Cathy responded immediately.

Forget lunch. His new movie opens Friday. Wanna go?

Elizabeth mentally compared the cost of a movie versus lunch. It would work out cheaper, even with snacks. She did a celebratory jig. But wait. She figured in the cost of a babysitter. This Girls' Night Out would be expensive. She couldn't impose on Nancy again. Could she? No, she couldn't. Something told her to keep her distance.

As long as I can find a babysitter.

Cathy didn't respond. Elizabeth stared at her phone, willing the moving dots that indicated typing to appear on the screen. None came. Had she said something wrong? She read back the texts. God, she was getting paranoid. She could jump out of her skin. After five minutes, she got into the shower.

When she came out, she found the blessed response.

Patrick said to drop the kids at our house.

Cathy really had married the greatest man in the world!

God bless Patrick! Thank him for me!

Emboldened, Elizabeth thought about launching into a rant about Russell's late check and his wacko sister calling her a whore, but those subjects might be better received in person than in a text.

Dinner before the movie? Cathy texted.

Elizabeth had planned to fling a frozen burrito into the microwave before hitting the theater. She hadn't factored in a restaurant expense. Dinner on top of a movie would cost her an arm and a leg, but she hadn't seen her best friend in ages. What could she do?

Sure!

And drinks, Cathy texted back. *Patrick will pick up Trevor and Bailey and drop us at movie. The kids can sleep over. Uber to and from restaurant.*

Uber signified a leisurely night of tequila consumption, with margaritas costing ten dollars a pop. Elizabeth would have to sell a lot of Lady Lily Wear to catch up.

Yay, Uber!!!!!

Elizabeth signed off with a happy-face emoji. With a trembling hand, she put down her phone.

TWO HOURS TOGETHER watching their hero, Will Ferrell, put an end to Elizabeth's fear that Cathy had gone cold on her. They waited for their Uber driver to arrive on the landing outside the theater, both in white jeans under a fat late summer moon, just like old times.

"He's mastered using blubber around his middle to maximum comic effect," Cathy remarked.

"The way he purses his mouth into that little *O* gets me every time." Elizabeth pursed her mouth in the little *O*.

Cathy bent over laughing. "Stop it! I'm going to wet my pants."

Elizabeth did it again.

"I am going to kill you!" Cathy spun to face the honeysuckle bush billowing its fragrance into the hot breeze. She squeezed her eyes together. "Please, *please* stop."

"And that look in his eye," Elizabeth continued.

A gleaming black Toyota Tacoma rolled up. "Saved by the Uber!" Cathy straightened her shoulders, composing herself.

Elizabeth stepped up into the vehicle behind Cathy. The interior had exquisitely cared for leather seats. Cathy strapped on her seat belt. "But he is hot, I'll give you that."

"Hell, yeah, he's hot," Elizabeth said. "It's about time *People* magazine got with the program and made him Sexiest Man Alive."

"George Clooney, my ass," Cathy said.

Rosary beads hung from the rearview. Strictly speaking, rosary beads weren't meant to be used as good luck charms, but they gave Elizabeth confidence that the driver would be divinely guided from making dicey left turns and slamming the Tacoma into a pole.

"Enjoy your movie, Ladies?" he asked.

"Oh, yeah. Somebody deserves an Oscar," Cathy said.

"I take it we're talking about the Redmayne and Meryl Streep thing."

"The Will Ferrell thing," Elizabeth corrected.

"Will Ferrell?" The driver made eye contact in the rearview. "He's disgusting. He's always taking his shirt off."

"He's our hero." Cathy sighed.

The driver took his eyes off the road to glare at them. "Have you ladies been drinking?"

Cathy looked at Elizabeth. Elizabeth looked at Cathy. Elizabeth's shoulders trembled. She was about to lose it.

"Not yet," Cathy said.

CATHY HAD CHOSEN COMIENDO Feliz, a lively Mexican place with blue, yellow, red, and orange tile walls. She and Elizabeth chose a high table near the bar and ordered margaritas. A bus boy dropped off chips and salsa.

Cathy opened her menu. "Guacamole is a necessity."

"Definitely. How's work going? I hardly see you."

"The job is great. It's all-consuming, but the self-esteem initiative we're pushing for girls and young women makes it worthwhile. If you asked me ten years ago if I saw myself making a career in a cosmetics company, I'd have asked what you were smoking."

"Yeah, me too. Your mother had me hold you down so she could put lipstick on you for the prom."

Despite her position at Beauté Rayonnante, Cathy still limited her makeup routine to a coat of mascara and lip color that disappeared into the day's first coffee.

"But Beauté Rayonnante isn't just a cosmetics company, Cathy. Between the Fair-Trade ingredients and biodegradable packaging, you can say you're making a difference."

"Let's not get carried away." Cathy held up a tortilla chip in protest. "The constant air travel is unnecessary, and it's not exactly lightening our carbon footprint."

Under the pendant light above their table, Elizabeth noticed circles under Cathy's eyes. Was Cathy, who seemed to enjoy a charmed life, losing sleep? Or had age caught up with her? And if age had caught up with Cathy, how bad did Elizabeth look in this light? They'd looked mighty fine in the selfie they took at the movie theater.

Cathy scooped salsa onto the chip. "On the other hand, we are a woman-owned company with an all-female board of directors. The big news is, we're expanding into Asia. I've been asked to relocate to Beijing."

Elizabeth swallowed hard. "Meaning?"

"Meaning I think I'm moving to China."

Elizabeth swallowed hard. "And Patrick's good with it?"

"Patrick doesn't know." Cathy signaled the waiter to bring another round.

It flattered Elizabeth that Cathy revealed this information to her before telling her husband. "How will you break it to him?"

Cathy rolled her eyes. "Break it to him? It's the opportunity of a lifetime."

"Yeah, but what if he doesn't want to go?"

"I want to go. Why is it when a man is offered a relocation opportunity and a pay raise, his wife falls into line and starts packing? When a woman has an opportunity, people imply she's self-centered."

"I didn't imply anything."

"Maybe I am being self-centered."

"I don't think so. But you'll have to uproot the kids."

"Yeah. It'll be an adjustment for them, for sure, but it could be the gift of a lifetime. They'll go to school in China."

"Your children rise to every challenge."

Cathy shifted uncomfortably. "It's not as if I have a choice. Either I go, or I'm out."

"They can't do that."

"Oh, they wouldn't fire me. That's not how it works. They'd stick me in an office without a window, make it uncomfortable for me to stick around. On the other hand, the package they're offering includes rent, tuition, and a membership to a club for American expats. When the boys come back to this country, they'll be speaking Chinese. That'll open doors."

Doors to what? Elizabeth wondered. So-called "desirable careers" that would entitle them to unrelenting stress? Where did it end? In Elizabeth's experience, corporations operated under the assumption they owned their employees. Whatever happened to boundaries? What happened to the idea that a person should be paid for thirty-five hours' work per week, free to bobble their weekends away in the family swimming pool? Why did they have to fly to Cincinnati twice a month to attend some time-wasting meeting that could have been held over the phone? Or forced to relocate from beloved hometowns to flimsy new construction on the outskirts of Sioux Falls? Elizabeth glugged her second drink. She had come out for advice and a few laughs. She hadn't expected getting slammed with the bad news her best friend was moving to China.

"It will be an adjustment," she said finally. "For everybody."

"If I don't take this deal, I might regret it later. Anyway, I'll have to find another job at a company that might not be as good to me. Then again, I don't know if I want to leave Connecticut. I don't want to leave you, that's for sure."

Now that Cathy uttered the words Elizabeth hoped to hear, she felt guilty about holding her back. Real friends didn't do that. "If you want to go, you should go. You're right. It really would be a great opportunity for the kids."

"Thank you. I needed your blessing." Cathy dug into the chip bowl with renewed gusto. "Now I have to get Patrick on board."

"But he's your— ." Elizabeth started to say *best friend*, but she reserved that position for herself. "He's your champion. You know that."

"I think I'm in for a hard time."

"You won't know until you ask him."

"What if he doesn't want to do it? I'll end up resenting him for the rest of our lives. I'll end up divorcing him, I know I will, in which case I'd be better off just divorcing him now."

"You're overthinking this."

"Maybe." Cathy drained her drink.

Cathy had stopped talking about her salary years ago, but at one point she was taking in 250K plus an annual bonus. "I'm guessing the compensation will be decent."

"It will be," Cathy agreed. "But Patrick's mother's cancer is back."

"Oh, no."

"She starts chemo Monday. They're optimistic, but it's a bad time to split for Asia."

"Would Patrick stay back until she's out of the woods? You guys could FaceTime."

"He might end up staying here until we sell the house, anyway, if the market isn't with us."

"Wait. You're selling the house?"

"We'd been talking about selling it for a while."

Ten years ago, Cathy and Patrick bought a dilapidated 1735 Colonial and restored it to its original beauty, while equipping it with state-of-the art appliances that complemented the existing architecture. *New England Historic Homes* magazine named it Number One Historic Renovation of the Year.

"Do you know how much I want to live in that house? You can't sell it. I won't let you."

"Do *you* know how much work it is to maintain that house? Especially with the boys' schedules? I can't even get the mail without taking my life in my hands. The traffic never stops. It's not 1776 with a horse and carriage plopping past." Cathy put her hands over her ears. "It's so noisy I can't hear myself think."

Elizabeth thought about it. "It has taken me ten minutes to get out of your driveway."

"It's taken us twenty. It's time to move." Cathy held her head in her hands. "Lying awake trying to figure out my life has devastated my intellect."

"You're sharp as ever. You'd still make captain of the debate team." Elizabeth laughed. Maybe the rings under Cathy's eyes had nothing to do with being slightly north of forty, after all. "Talk to Patrick. He won't disappoint you. Butter him up with *Blades of Glory.*"

"Patrick hates Will Ferrell."

"What is wrong with people?"

The waiter circled the table. Seeing Cathy and Elizabeth's menus still open, he sighed and walked away.

Elizabeth took the hint and closed her menu decisively. Cathy smiled at their waiter. They settled on nachos for an appetizer and chimichangas for the main course.

"Now, guess who I ran into at the pharmacy," Elizabeth said to Cathy.

"Will Ferrell."

"If only. I'll give you a hint. High school."

"Male or female?"

"Definitely male."

"Hot or not?"

"So hot I got burned."

"Red Garcia?"

"Ding ding ding. Red Garcia."

"How is old Red Garcia?"

"Not old at all and still hot, unfortunately. I fantasized about him being fat and bald."

"Damn," Cathy said. "What's he up to?"

"I scared him off before I could find out."

"Do we know if he's married?"

"I was too preoccupied to check for a ring."

"Too preoccupied, or too flustered?"

"I wasn't flustered in the least." Sometimes Cathy made annoying presumptions, like she had the power to see into Elizabeth's soul. "He's back in the area, so maybe I'll see him again. Not that I want to see him again." She looked into her half-empty glass, debating whether she'd order another drink. After getting the news about Cathy's probable relocation, she deserved another. "Maybe I'll leave town."

"Let *him* leave town, the jerk. Did he ask for Mary Pat?"

"He did not. I wonder if flying up I-95 and spotting her scary face on a billboard is hard for him. I mean, if he still carries a torch."

"That relationship came to an abrupt ending, as I remember," Cathy said. "And that billboard is hilarious."

"Now that Russell and Mary Pat are chums, how much you wanna bet I'll be driving along Route 8 and spot him on his very own billboard leaning against a giant tooth?"

"Yeah, because nothing inspires trust like a dentist pictured with a tooth."

"True story. It's interesting how Mary Pat never mentions Red. Not to me anyway." Elizabeth sighed. "Listen, enough about Red

Garcia. I'm not letting that guy live in my head rent-free again. In other news, you've heard of Lady Lily Wear, right?"

"Refresh my memory."

"It's this clothing line that everyone wears. People our age, anyway."

"Oh, yes." Cathy popped a chip in her mouth. "One of Jackson's den mothers sells it. It's an MLM."

"They don't call it an MLM."

"What do they call it?"

"Direct sales."

Cathy rolled her eyes.

"You don't approve?"

"No, it's not that. I mean, the stuff seems nice enough, but I don't know that anybody makes any real money at those things. Are you telling me you're selling clothes?"

"Actually, I was going to tell you I'm starting a business."

"A Lady Lily Whatever Business?"

"Cathy, you're making me feel really foolish."

"Yeah, but you have a track record in corporate America. You could go back, you know."

"I'm a single mother who's been out of the workforce for a decade. What kind of salary am I going to pull? And corporate America doesn't provide childcare. I need something flexible, and this opportunity fits the bill."

"Look, I get the attraction. I just don't want to see you get burned. The den mother keeps hitting me up to join her downline. I've heard the pitches." Cathy rolled her eyes. "She's relentless."

"I don't know about other people, but I have no intention of doing business that way. I was skeptical, too, but the woman who recruited me is going to train me to do business the way she does, and she does very well. She's even letting me do my first show at her house. You have to see where she lives, Cathy."

"Your first show?"

"They call it a trunk show." Elizabeth shrugged. It did sound pretentious.

"Okay."

"Will you come?"

"If I'm in town, I will definitely come, but please tell me you didn't invest your life savings in this."

"Not my life savings, no." Elizabeth felt a sliver of resentment. Did Cathy think she was some kind of idiot? No need to mention the crippling unsecured debt she'd racked up to finance the deal then.

"I take it you signed some kind of agreement."

"Yes."

"It should contain a clause letting you change your mind within a certain number of days and get back any money you invested."

Elizabeth also wouldn't mention she'd been too deep into a prosecco glass to read the contract. "Good to know," she said.

"Promise you'll give it a little more thought."

Elizabeth promised.

EIGHT

The clock on the night table said 3:36 in the morning. Elizabeth bolted upright, fizzing with anxiety. She blamed it on the alcohol, which messed with the nervous system. She'd drunk enough to fell a manatee.

She searched her murky memory. Had she said anything to Cathy that could have been perceived as hurtful or inappropriate? She rejected the idea of Cathy moving to Asia. Had she said so? Out loud? She strained to piece their conversation back together. Her brain throbbed, hangover setting in. No. No. Elizabeth had been supportive. She hoped so, anyway.

Okay, on top of Cathy's announcement she was about to move across the planet, she discouraged Elizabeth's participation in the Lady Lily Wear opportunity. Elizabeth got the feeling she considered it an opportunity to be ripped off. And Cathy had excellent instincts.

She downed two cups of strong coffee and made good on her promise to re-read the contract. She located the clause Cathy mentioned:

Enrollee has three (3) business days from the date of signing this contract to render it null and void.

"Yes," she said out loud. The caffeine quickened her heart rate. Elizabeth gulped four ibuprofen and breathed. She could get out of this deal if she wanted. *Good.* But that would entail a confrontation with Louisa. *Not so good.* Louisa would talk Elizabeth out of backing out.

If she did get out, though, she'd sleep better.

Elizabeth flopped onto the couch, her mind racing with competing thoughts. A dagger-like sensation pulsed behind her left eyelid. She'd paid for top shelf tequila, but she suspected the bartender served her a cheaper deadly brand.

People did that kind of thing. People cheated. People lied.

ELIZABETH TAPPED OUT Louisa's number, her anxiety mounting. She would gladly cut her own head off to take away the stubborn pain in her head. Above it, she heard the sound of Bailey's feet. She'd make this quick. *Louisa,* she'd say, *I'm going to need to give this more thought.*

The swollen front door grinded open, and Trevor burst in swinging his overnight bag.

"I'm quitting the team!" He flopped into a chair at the kitchen table and covered his face with his arms.

Elizabeth put down her phone. She took a look at the clock: 8:38. She still had a few hours to get out of the contract. The call could wait.

"Where's your sister?"

"At Cathy and Patrick's."

"I wasn't supposed to pick you up at Cathy and Patrick's until ten. It's not even nine."

"MP dropped me off."

"Mary Pat dropped you off? What are you talking about? You slept at Cathy's. Where's your sister?"

"MP showed up at Cathy and Patrick's and told them you said I could have a sleepover with Hughey."

"I said no such thing. How did she even know you were over there?"

"I texted Hughey."

"And, what? Told him to get his mother to get you out of there?"

"No, Mom. MP just came over."

"That is crazy." Elizabeth pulled at her own hair. "What did she say to Patrick?"

"That you changed your mind and wanted me to stay at her house."

"She said that? He must think I'm nuts. What did he say?"

"He believed her. I mean, he looked confused. But she is my aunt, so I guess he thought it was okay."

Elizabeth didn't know whether to be embarrassed or furious. Embarrassment won out. *What must Patrick think?* Now she had three uncomfortable phone calls to make, not just to Louisa, but to Patrick and Mary Pat. *I'll punch her in the nose!*

"If you slept at your aunt's, why are you home so early? She usually takes you guys for breakfast."

"I asked her to take me home. Her kid is a loser. I'm never talking to that kid again." Trevor slumped into his usual chair at the table.

"Are we talking about Hughey?"

"She has one kid, Mom."

"I'm trying to help here, Trev." Elizabeth massaged her temple. How long had it been since she'd taken the ibuprofen? How much could she safely take? Strictly speaking, she'd already overdosed.

"Last night, I'm minding my own business and Hughey tells me Noah and Joseph say I'm the worst kid on the team."

"You're not the worst kid on the team." *Hughey is the worst kid on the team.*

"Noah and Joseph took a vote, and I got voted worst kid. It was unanimous."

Elizabeth pictured Joseph's rat-like face, with its undiscernible chin and twitchy, pointy nose. Noah, on the other hand, possessed the charisma of a young Justin Timberlake. If either of them had done anything to hurt her son, she'd pray they'd wake up on their thirtieth birthdays bald as beans.

'Unanimous, meaning every single person on the team voted you worst?"

Trevor webbed the fingers in front of one eye. Elizabeth could see he'd been crying. "That's what unanimous means."

"And Hughey didn't stick up for you?"

"What don't you understand about unanimous, Mom?"

"You're his cousin, for Pete's sake. You're a better player than at least several of those kids."

"Tell them that."

"I don't understand any of this. I mean, after you stood up for Hughey in front of all those bigger kids."

"I won't stand up for him next time. I'm not the worst kid on the team. He is."

"I'll speak to your aunt about this."

"No, Mom. Please. She's not that nice to me as it is."

"What do you mean she's not nice to you? Why is she always inviting you for sleepovers and driving you to practice if she's not nice to you?"

"I have no idea." Trevor rubbed his eyes in his fists. "I don't even want to go to Disney. I mean, I want to go, but I don't want to go with her and that fat loser Hughey."

Elizabeth resisted the urge to chime in and call Hughey a fat loser. She had to set an example. "But Daddy is going with you."

"Yeah, and all he does is fight with MP. They fight about everything."

"I'm sorry, Trevor. I didn't know. That must be stressful."

"MP and Dad are even worse than you and Dad." Trevor pulled at an eyebrow and gave it a good twist. "It stinks."

Elizabeth called Patrick, but he'd run out for bagels. She asked Cathy to pass along her apology for Mary Pat's kidnapping Trevor.

"If anyone needs to apologize, it's us," she said. "Patrick should have texted before he let Trevor go with that mad woman."

"Why would he, though?" Elizabeth didn't remember mentioning the problems with her sister-in-law around Patrick. "He couldn't have known."

"Did you tell her off?"

"Mary Pat? Not yet. I don't know if it'll do any good, or if I'll end up being subjected to another tirade about my substandard washing machine. Trevor's said he doesn't want to be around Hughey anymore, so the problem may have solved itself."

"Let's keep our fingers crossed," Cathy said.

ELIZABETH MADE TACOS for dinner, Trevor's favorite. She questioned the wisdom of eating beef two nights in a row, but she didn't have the energy to make a separate meal for herself. Also, she'd read that mothers who ate special meals facilitated eating disorders in their children.

Trevor cleared the table and put the dishes in the washer. Elizabeth re-read the contract, determined to cancel. Before she could pick it up, her phone buzzed.

Louisa.

"ESP. I was just about to call you."

"Great minds think alike," Louisa said. "Let's put a date in the calendar for your premiere trunk show."

"That's why I was calling," Elizabeth said.

"Listen, we're still doing it at my house, but I was thinking – and if this doesn't work for you, be honest and let me know – that we'd postpone it until the first week of next month so that we can get the biggest crowd possible to attend. Now I know you said you were struggling to get to 100 people, so I was thinking I could invite some of my peeps."

Peeps?

"But you must've gone through all your peeps by now."

"One of my keys to success is AMNP. Translation: Always meet new peeps. It is my goal to meet new people every single day and expose them to this business. I talk to people on airplanes. At the gym. Crops of fresh moms are always cycling into my younger daughter's activities. But don't worry. Some of my stylists are shy gals like you. I'm happy to give you a head start with my resources. The beauty of this business is that when I help my downline, they help my bottom line. You can see why it's a gorgeous business model."

"That's really nice of you, Louisa. I mean it, thank you, but listen – "

"Ordinarily, I like a new gal to hit the ground running and do her first show within the week. Acting fast helps eliminate that fear factor, but I'm going to be holding your hand all the way, so it's not so urgent that we schedule your first show so soon. We have time."

"And we'll do it at your house?"

"Absolutely, we will do it at my house. All I ask is that you contribute a couple of bottles of prosecco."

"The official drink," Elizabeth said, the specter of cancellation evaporating from her mind. "I can do that."

"So, we'll do your show the first week of September. Sound good? The kids will be back in school, and the ladies are ready to treat themselves."

"I like that idea. What else do you need me to do?"

"We need to get you started with your first training. How's Thursday, mid-afternoon? We'll go over some fun stuff, like the color wheel and which shades flatter which skin tones. I'll show you best practices for taking orders and scheduling deliveries. It may sound like a lot, but you'll love it."

Best practices. "As long as you don't mind Bailey coming along."

"Mind? That baby is an absolute cherub. In the meantime, I'll put together a list of people I can invite to the show. See if you can add a name or two to yours. Otherwise, we're set."

"We're set," Elizabeth repeated happily. "Thank you again, Louisa. Thank you. Thank you."

NINE

The delivery man tapped his foot impatiently.

"It's a big shipment," he told Elizabeth, thumbing at his truck parked along Elizabeth's pitted driveway. "You want it in the house or the garage?"

Elizabeth, still in her pilly bathrobe and needing a shower, couldn't vouch for the integrity of the garage roof, which could spring a leak the next time it rained.

"The house."

The man breathed hard, running the back of his hand along damp clumps of hair clinging to his scalp.

"You sure? It's a ton of boxes."

"I'm sure."

"Two more years of this crap, and I'm going to Vegas." He hopped down her steps and slammed open the sliding door of his truck.

"Thank you," she said after he crowded Elizabeth's tiny dining room with the boxes.

"Good luck with that," he said.

"Thanks." Elizabeth closed the door and rested her cheek upon it. Did he know something she didn't?

She brought a razor blade from the bathroom, cut open the boxes, and went through them. She fingered a wrinkle-resistant dress Cathy could pack for Beijing. The color would brighten Cathy's blue eyes; the A-line shape would flatter any figure, despite assaults by airplane food drowned in sodium. Elizabeth reassured herself she'd made the right decision to seize this opportunity. She would succeed. Necessity plus quality plus a fair price could add up only to profit.

ELIZABETH ROLLED DOWN her window to give her name to the guard, but, except for a sweating cup of iced coffee, the kiosk was unoccupied. *Security breach!* Well, how much could you rely on a kid expected to trap himself in a broiling booth for slave wages?

She bumped the front of the minivan gently under the gate to prompt the arm to go up. She'd learned this trick in college, from a fellow student paid to monitor the faculty parking lot. The gate did as she intended, and Elizabeth glided into the development toward the buzzing lawns. Hydrangeas and Black-Eyed Susans burst from all directions.

She made a left on Gable Lane, admiring those iron mailboxes. *That's for me.* She turned onto Dudley Drive, singing along to The Grateful Dead's "Deal." Coincidentally, the same song came on the last time she approached Louisa's house.

She spotted the pulse of flashing lights. On Louisa's driveway.

A policeman approached from behind yellow tape and signaled Elizabeth to roll down her window.

He was so young she could have once been his babysitter. He ran his tired eyes along the length of the minivan. "Where are you headed?"

"Here. I have an appointment with a homeowner." She turned the volume down on The Dead. Had there been a robbery attempt? She thought about the unmanned security booth. *Well, I guess somebody's getting fired.*

The kid ducked his head in Elizabeth's window to check the contents, which contained a sleeping toddler and an assortment of flattened juice boxes. He ducked back out and muttered into his radio. The radio muttered back.

"Ma'am, I'm going to have to ask you to pull in. I'll need to ask you a few questions."

It didn't take a detective to tell she didn't live in the development. The minivan made that clear. *Am I going down for a robbery?* Elizabeth obeyed the officer. Hansen, his badge said.

"What kind of questions?" she asked. "Officer Hansen."

"Who were you meeting?"

Whom.

"The homeowner, as I said. Louisa Davenport."

"I'm going to need to see your license."

Elizabeth reached for her purse, hoping he wouldn't notice the jumble of tissues and candy wrappers.

"Your name is Elizabeth Candew. You are here to see Louisa Davenport."

"That's right." What didn't he get? She watched a contingent of older officers amble along the driveway, coolly flicking on sunglasses.

"And what is the nature of your relationship to Ms. Davenport?"

Elizabeth, who hadn't thought to define it, thought for a second. "It's business."

"What kind of business?"

"She recruited me into her multi-level marketing business." It sounded pie-in-the sky, even to her. Pathetic. What nonsense had she gotten herself into?

"Have you heard of Lady Lily Wear Designs?"

"No, ma'am. Can you tell me how well you knew Ms. Davenport?"

Knew? Elizabeth broke out into a cold sweat.

"I met her last week. What happened? Did something happen to her?"

"I'm sorry to tell you this." The officer scribbled on a pad and handed Elizabeth back her license. "Mrs. Davenport is dead. We may be in touch to ask additional questions."

"She can't be dead." Later, Elizabeth would pray for Louisa's soul. She would also hate herself for the next words that flew out of her mouth. "If she's dead, I'm out three thousand dollars."

TEN

Elizabeth had missed the cancellation deadline. Now her mentor was dead. She called the 800 number on the contract and sat through a lengthy welcome recording: "Hey, Lady, welcome to the washable-y chic world of Lady Lily Wear Designs. Please listen to the options as our menu has changed. To speak to Customer Service, press one."

She pressed one. A voice that sounded annoyed answered. Elizabeth began her story.

"Wait." The rep changed her tone. "Your mentor died?"

"Stabbed, apparently."

"Oh my God. That's awful." The woman lowered her voice to a whisper. "Did she live in a high crime community?"

"Not in the least."

"And her name was?"

"Louisa Davenport of Stonesbury, Connecticut."

"Zip code?"

"06885."

"Okay, I see her." The rep let out a low whistle. "She had some numbers. Solid producer."

"Executive National Vice President."

"On track to become Ultra Executive Vice President, top of the heap."

Enough about Louisa. Elizabeth felt uneasy asking for her money back under the circumstances, but hey. "Due to the unfortunate circumstances, I'd like to cancel my agreement and get a refund for my investment."

A dog barked in the background. Elizabeth got the feeling she was talking to one of those work-from-home customer service reps companies hired to avoid paying benefits. At this point, she might take a job like that herself.

"If I'm reading this right," the rep continued. "In the event of your upline's death, your new mentor is *her* upline."

"Toni Badden. I've spoken to her, but she's out of state."

"Uh, let me see if there's any provision for that."

Elizabeth tapped her fingers on the kitchen table. If worse came to worst, Toni could mentor her via Skype, but she wouldn't have the advantage of hosting her first show on Louisa's enviable property. That had been the selling point.

"I'm not an expert in legalese, so let me speak to my supervisor. Can you hold?"

Elizabeth watched the numbers on the oven change from :13 to :21 before the rep returned.

"Sorry for the wait," she said.

"What did your supervisor say?"

"She says all you have to do is to report to your next-up, which would be Toni Badden, who you can train with via Skype. According to Google, she's only about three hours from your house, so you might even make a weekend trip for training. Good excuse to take the hubby and reconnect!"

"I'm a single mother," Elizabeth said flatly.

"Oh, well, did your previous mentor steer you towards the website?" The rep's voice pitched higher. "Our state-of-the-art website provides access to the Lady Lily Wear library of training materials.

If you haven't taken a look at it, you should. I think you'll be impressed."

"Let me ask you something. Are you a Lady Lily Wear Rep?"

"No, I'm just inside support."

"Have you ever considered becoming a stylist?"

"I'm pretty happy doing what I'm doing now."

"For what? Ten, twelve bucks an hour? And I'll bet they're not giving you medical insurance."

"Uh, that's kind of personal."

"I'm just wondering why you, a person who works for this company, and sees firsthand all it has to offer, hasn't seized the Lady Lily Wear Stylist Opportunity."

"It's not for everybody."

"That's not what they're telling people like me, is it? So, I have to wonder what you might know that I don't know."

"Look, Ma'am, I understand that you're upset because your upline is no longer available, but your new upline is equally successful in this business. More so, in fact. You've signed up for an opportunity to change your life. Why don't you give yourself a few days to process the loss of – " Elizabeth heard the click of a keyboard. "Louisa Davenport?"

"What don't you get? I want to cancel my contract."

"Ma'am, you're not listening." The rep's voice went dark. "You missed the deadline. You can't get your money back. Your best bet is to contact your upline. Take the steps to success."

"My next step is consult an attorney." Elizabeth didn't have money for an attorney, a fact this company probably counted on.

"If that's what you feel you have to do, Ma'am. Is there anything else I can help you with?"

ELIZABETH FRIED A CHICKEN cutlet. She put it on a ciabatta with jalapeno mayonnaise and roasted red peppers. Her mind swirled with too much activity for the flavor to penetrate her taste buds.

The doorbell rang. She wiped her fingers and tiptoed towards the window to see if she should answer it, lest she be talked into changing her religion. She'd already been talked into quite enough.

Red Garcia stood on her doorstep.

She scraped open the door slowly, her heart speeding up. "Hi, Red. What can I do for you?"

"Hey, Elizabeth."

Hey. He said it casually, as if he hadn't fallen off the map for decades.

"I'm here to speak to you about Louisa Davenport."

Did she have a smear of mayo in the corner of her mouth? With her luck, probably. She couldn't remember if she'd brushed her hair.

"I take it this isn't a social call."

"No," he said. "Unfortunately."

Elizabeth took a good look at the badge on his crisp turquoise button-down shirt. He flicked up his sunglasses, revealing the sparkling eyes. Despite the wilting humidity, the man looked infuriatingly cool. With the back of her hand, she daintily pressed at the perspiration pooling on her forehead.

Her face burned at the thought of the mountain of laundry she'd left in front of the TV, which she'd forgotten to shut off before making lunch. She had no choice but to admit him into the graceless house.

"Come on in."

"Thank you." The officer stepped into the living room, which crackled with negative vibes emanating from *Dr. Phil*. Elizabeth cast a glance at his left hand. No ring, but that didn't mean anything. Not that it mattered to her. At all.

"So," she said. "Louisa Davenport."

"Can you tell me the nature of your relationship?"

"I signed up for her MLM business. She was going to help me get started." Elizabeth felt stupid. "Do you know what an MLM business is?"

"I'm familiar."

"Yes, so I was on my way to her house for my first training."

"How well did you know Mrs. Davenport?"

"Not well. I'd only really just met her."

"And you signed up for her business."

"Yes. Why? That's how it's done in the MLM business."

"And did you make a large investment in this MLM business?"

"I gave three thousand dollars to a stranger, if that's what you're asking."

"No judgment here, Elizabeth."

"It's always seemed to me that when people say 'no judgement,' they've already judged you."

"I'm not judging."

"Maybe you should. It's a ton of money," she said.

"If it makes you feel any better, other people invested more."

"It does, and it doesn't. I saw on Facebook Louisa was stabbed nine times. Somebody must've had it in for her."

"Facebook." Red shifted his weight.

"Yes, on the Stonesbury Parents Keeping it Klassy page."

"I've seen it. It's a lot of gossip. There are more credible news sources."

"You're saying she wasn't stabbed?"

"She was."

"So, it really was personal." Elizabeth snapped off the TV and led Red into the kitchen. "Coffee?"

"Sure, thanks."

"I keep planning to un-like that page, but it's like a traffic accident. I can't not watch."

He smiled, almost. "The department is aware of the bullying that goes on among parents on Facebook."

Elizabeth scoured her memory. She never bullied anyone, but she'd defended those who had been. She'd gotten salty. Had Red seen any of her comments? Had he checked out her profile? How long, exactly, had she been on his radar?

"I'll bet you solve a lot of cases on Facebook." She stopped digging her fingernails into her palms. *Sends the wrong signal.*

"Yeah. You wouldn't believe the things people post."

"Oh, yes I would." Russell had recently shared a photo of himself wrapped around his new girlfriend, Tammi. He captioned it with a winky-face emoji and the announcement they were "enjoying each other."

"Do you know anyone who had a beef with Mrs. Davenport?"

"As I said, I didn't know her well, but everyone at the party where we met admired her. She had a lot of charisma."

"She signed two other people up for her business at that party, is that right?"

"She said so, but that's the last I heard of it. I did think it was unusual that she wanted to train me without them. I figured she'd want to save time and train us together."

"Maybe she didn't want you getting too chummy. People are easier to control if they can't compare notes."

"I hadn't thought of that." At the time, Elizabeth wanted to believe Louisa truly considered her the gem of the people she'd recruited at Nancy's party.

"What we're getting on Louisa Davenport is a habit of signing people into her business and reneging on her responsibility to train them."

"She didn't train me, but it wasn't her fault."

"I'm letting you know a pattern is emerging."

"You think the person who killed her was someone in her down-line?"

"That's one thread we're following, but if you have any other ideas, call me. I'll give you my card. "

"You're telling me Louisa signed people up and left them holding the bag?"

"That's what I'm telling you. I'm sorry."

She watched him get into his car. She ran the raised type that bore his name under her fingers.

ELEVEN

Trevor dragged a French fry through a puddle of ketchup.

"It's good manners to use a fork, Trevor," Elizabeth said. She forgave herself for letting him microwave fast food leftovers for breakfast, reasoning that it encouraged independence.

"Nobody eats fries with a fork, Mom. I tried that at school last year. People treat you like you're from another planet."

"What in the world is happening to civilization?"

Trevor shrugged. She sat across from him at the table. He seemed bigger this morning, broader. Soon he'd be ten, then twenty. She squinted, trying to picture it. Would he be his father's son? Or hers? Would the divorce sour him on getting married himself one day? Would he grow up to distrust women?

"How are things going with the team?"

"They're still low-key bullying me."

Low key? Elizabeth had heard that expression from teenagers but not from a fourth grader. "Bullying is bullying. What are we talking about?"

"They're not punching me out or anything. They just say stuff and let me know they don't want me around. Hughey's such a big shot, joining in. Meanwhile, they don't even like him."

"Yeah, well, what goes around comes around. Life has a way of catching up with people." Elizabeth couldn't wait.

"I don't know why you have to go to this thing," he said, changing the subject. He meant Louisa's wake. "It's not like you even knew the lady. I just want to stay home tonight."

Elizabeth hoped to avoid a fight. The clock had barely struck eight, and already the hot sun screeched through the window.

"It's respectful, honey. I'm sorry I have to drag you along."

"I don't even know this lady."

Neither did Elizabeth, really. She examined her conscience. Did she want to go to the wake out of respect – or nosiness? She blotted her damp forehead with the back of her hand.

"Freaking Hughey. I coulda went to his house if he hadn't turned on me, but I'm never speaking to that weasel as long as I live.

"Could *have gone*. Listen, we'll stay twenty minutes. Tops."

"Can I stay in the car?"

"It'll get too hot in the car. You know that."

"I don't even know these people. What am I supposed to say?"

"Look them in the eye, put out your hand, and say you're sorry for their loss."

Trevor popped a bleeding fry into his mouth. "Maybe it's not a loss. Maybe they're glad somebody stabbed her."

"What a thing to say! I'm surprised at you, Trevor."

"Somebody must have really hated her guts." He lifted his glass of milk. "That's all I'm saying."

TWELVE

Elizabeth hoisted Bailey on her hip. She handed Trevor the diaper bag, in which – fingers crossed! – she no longer had to carry diapers but juice boxes and pretzels. Bailey's ear had improved to the point where she could bring her to the wake, but it still harbored just enough fluid to facilitate excuses for a quick exit. It turned out Trevor had outgrown his button-downs and slacks, so Elizabeth steered him into a pullover and the darkest jeans in his dresser.

Traffic slowed to a stop a full block away from the funeral home. It took fifteen minutes before she got close enough to the parking lot for a policeman to direct her into the last free spot behind the massive mock Victorian.

"Louisa must have had a lot of friends," Elizabeth remarked, pulling in.

"Or a lot of enemies," Trevor observed.

"When did you get so cynical?" Maybe the break from Hughey and Mary Pat was for the best. Those people were pure poison.

Elizabeth observed the crowd milling on the funeral home's wraparound porch; she hadn't expected this kind of turnout for a woman with a reputation for cheating people.

She mounted the stairs nervously, Bailey digging the heels of her sandals into her hips. Despite what she'd told Trevor, "I'm sorry for your loss" didn't seem adequate when someone had been stabbed to death. She wanted to say something meaningful, but no words came to mind. What was to prevent her from going back to the car and peeling out of the parking lot?

Elizabeth pulled open the heavy door, thick with shiny white paint layered over many decades. She nearly lost her balance. Why had she worn high heels again? Oh, right; Red Garcia might show up, although she didn't want to attract him one bit. She mentally cursed the three grave-looking men in suits chatting along a foyer wall. Not one of them so much as flinched to help her.

She thought it might be fun to see if she could pick Toni Badden out of the crowd. She aimed to hit her up for sales training via Skype to make some back some money. Elizabeth expected Nancy to be around; she could be counted on to put her at ease by jumping on her like a lonely Labrador. Without her, this evening would be awkward.

"The place is packed, Mom." Trevor sighed loudly.

According to the death notice online, Louisa Davenport turned 43 shortly before the murder, which explained the three-deep line of mourners snaking from the entrance to the room that contained her body. It had been Elizabeth's observation that anybody under sixty, however good or evil, could count on an excellent turn-out for their wake.

"Juice, Mommy."

Bailey's eyes looked clearer, a good sign. "What do you say?"

"Please."

"Will you get her juice, Trevor?"

Trevor rolled his eyes and unzipped the bag. "We're never going to get out of here. Daddy says you shouldn't be dragging me to this. It's morbid, and I shouldn't have to have to know about these things."

"Why? Because you're a child, and you need to be protected from the facts of life?" Russell's family thrived on telling lies. His nut-so sister told Hughey their Siberian husky went to a camp with carnival rides after she got sick of vacuuming his hair and had him put down. "I hate to break it to you, Trevor, but we're all going to die. Seize the day and get used to it."

"It smells in here," Trevor said.

"That is not polite," Elizabeth said, despite a heavy oily smell of orchids invading her nostrils. She didn't like it either. They reminded her of something. A wedding. Hers.

The line of mourners crept closer to Louisa's casket, past drawings and Mother's Day poems her children had written over the years. There were photographs, too, of Louisa as a young girl sitting in a row boat; looking sassily into her husband's eyes as he lifted her wedding veil; with siblings on church steps, her knobby knees poking from under the hem of a First Communion dress. The last photograph came as a surprise. Louisa had been adamant in telling Elizabeth she considered herself "a Christian but definitely not a Catholic."

"This stinks," said a women in line behind Elizabeth. She wore a skirt that fell to the tops of bright white sneakers. Elizabeth had first taken her for fifty, but closer inspection put her under thirty-five. The outfit, combined with glasses and a high-on-top haircut, threw her off.

"I can't believe she's dead," said her companion, similarly dressed and a few years older. Elizabeth took them for sisters.

She offered a sympathetic smile. "Did you know her well?"

"Oh, we knew her all right," the older one said. "From church. Quite the dynamo."

"What church, again? I know she wasn't a Catholic."

"Catholics." The woman said the word as though she had a hair caught in the back of her throat. "Catholics play a lot of Bingo."

Elizabeth wouldn't challenge her. She wanted information. "We can take comfort that Louisa is with our Lord now."

"We can't assume that," the woman said. She had pretty blue eyes once you looked past the turquoise eye pencil.

"But Louisa was a good person," Elizabeth suggested. "And we can pray for her."

"We can't pray for her. That drawbridge went up. Once you're dead, Jesus judges. And was she a good person? That depends who you ask."

"Are you a Catholic?" the younger one asked gently. "I only ask because Catholics pray for the dead."

Elizabeth hadn't been inside a church since Bailey's baptism. She told herself it was on account of the abuse scandal, but really it was a matter of not wanting to twist Trevor's arm to go to Mass. Or have to keep Bailey on her best behavior for an hour. Besides, Trevor had to be on a soccer field on Sunday mornings. He'd need a scholarship to get into college. Surely God took these things into consideration.

"Yes," she said. "I am definitely a Catholic."

The older woman twisted her mouth disapprovingly. "You should come to our church. We get a lot of recovering Catholics."

"You'd love the pastor," the younger one said. "Everyone does."

"I think Louisa might have mentioned him," Elizabeth lied. "She really liked your church."

"Why wouldn't she?" said the older sister. "She used it as a quarry for that business of hers. And don't get us started on her relationship with Pastor."

The younger sister shook her head. "That's gossip, Jackie. Pastor is friendly to everyone."

"I'm not blaming *him*. But some of these women." Jackie lowered her voice. "They're hard up. Louisa wasn't hard up, but –."

"But what?"

Jackie pinched her lips together, giving them the look of a testy worm. "I'm just going to say it. She liked attention from the other sex. People say she crossed lines."

"I got the impression Louisa had a happy marriage," Elizabeth said.

"Louisa was very big on image," Jackie said. "And as far as her business went," she made air quotes around the word *business*. "When she wasn't hawking her wares, she was sweet-talking other families into making investments they couldn't afford."

The younger one studied the floor.

Jackie jerked her thumb in her sister's direction. "This one nearly got taken for fifteen hundred bucks. Tell her, Sam."

"I got out before the cancellation deadline."

"*I* got her out before the cancellation deadline."

"Good for you," Elizabeth said sincerely. She'd withhold the nugget that Louisa took her for three thousand.

"Nobody that bought into that business ever made enough to buy a hill of beans," Jackie said.

"Except Louisa," Sam said.

"Correct. Louisa lived in one of those big houses off Ashford. Poor Julie Ombianelli got hosed out of five thousand bucks. She said it's some kind of magic palace that induces suckers to sign on the dotted line. Regular people didn't get to see it. Except Pastor, of course."

"How did you know Louisa?" Sam asked Elizabeth, changing the subject. "Are you one of the moms from the special needs group?"

"My neighbor introduced us. I believe she goes to your church? Nancy Spinner? She had Louisa over for a trunk show. She invited me."

"She knew better than to invite us." Jackie widened her nostrils.

"There are so many people here," Elizabeth counted ten people waiting for the water cooler. "Somebody must've liked Louisa."

"Oh, a lot of people liked her. The superintendent of schools is here, for Pete's sake. In addition to ripping people off with her MLM business, she made a name for herself as an advocate for children with autism and learning disabilities."

"So, maybe she wasn't all bad," Elizabeth said.

Bailey took her thumb out of her mouth and wriggled to get down.

"How old is that little girl?" Jackie inquired.

"Nearly three. Just about to start school, right, Bailey?"

"Isn't she big for you to be carrying her around like that?"

Elizabeth felt cut through the heart. It was bad enough that Russell and Mary Pat assailed her parenting skills, but it doubly hurt when it came from a stranger. Even Cathy had gently suggested she stop referring to Bailey as "the baby." Elizabeth would consider this more fully later, over a glass of wine.

She let Bailey out of her arms. "Can I count on you to keep an eye on her, Trevor?"

Trevor twisted on one foot. "You said we'd be here twenty minutes. Do I have to?"

"You have to, and I didn't realize we'd be here so long. I'm sorry."

Jackie nodded at Trevor. "There's a good boy," she said, turning the subject back to Louisa. "The only reason she got involved with disabled children is because her kid has dyslexia or ADD or ADHD, or whatever they're calling it these days."

"And a peanut allergy," Sam offered.

"I didn't know anyone who had a peanut allergy when I went to school. Kids today are so weak."

"I knew some," Sam said. "They put them at a separate table in the cafeteria."

Jackie waved a hand. "Anything for special treatment."

"What was the name of your church? You never did tell me." Elizabeth had a sneaking suspicion it wasn't Episcopalian, Lutheran, or any other respected denomination.

"The Stonesbury Army of God." Jackie puffed out her chest. "You really should come. You'll love Pastor."

Elizabeth threw in some lingo. "He must be quite a shepherd."

"He is, and so dedicated. Services at ten and one. You won't be disappointed."

"If you're in a hurry, I would attend the ten," Sam said brightly. "Because sometimes the one o'clock doesn't let out until dinner because nobody wants to leave."

"The Stonesbury Army of God," Elizabeth repeated. She had no intention of going. "Maybe I'll make it some time. I haven't seen Nancy tonight. Have you?"

"Nope," Jackie said. "She has to be around here somewhere though."

Elizabeth bounced anxiously on her toes. "Maybe she had something else to do."

Jackie snorted. "If busy means watching *The Partridge Family* with her cat."

Weary of the conversation, Elizabeth inched forward in line, behind a family waiting at the door to the room containing Louisa's casket. Ten minutes passed. A group of mourners moved out, making space for a group that included her. Over her shoulder, she saw Trevor diluting his sister's sippy cup at the water cooler. She waved him over.

"We are going to die in this place," he said.

She bent over to meet his face. "Remember: eye contact, hand shake, I'm sorry for your loss."

"I heard you the first time." He eyed Bailey, who sucked at her cup like a beached fish. "Why don't you tell *her*?"

Elizabeth drew a sharp breath. Last weekend Bailey threw herself kicking and screaming on a supermarket floor. How fast could they get to the casket before she had a meltdown? Elizabeth stood on her toes and spotted a hunched man in a tight suit standing in front of it, his face bleached of expression. *The husband.* An elegant young woman in a black A-line dress took his arm. *Stephanie.* Elizabeth felt sorry for the girl. Her own mother died at just fifty-two.

Despite the pretty dress, Stephanie looked tired. She seemed much older than the day Elizabeth met her in her mother's kitchen, no longer a spoiled, ungrateful daughter but a woman who'd been handed an unfair share of sorrow. Overhead florescent lighting cast deep hollows under her large dark eyes. Why did funeral homes insist on lighting that made people look even worse than they felt?

Rows of flowers surrounded Louisa's casket. From Elizabeth's vantage point, it looked to be an expensive one, nothing like the economy number Russell and Mary Pat tossed their mother into, reasoning Anita would want the savings funneled into their bank accounts.

Elizabeth's gaze fell upon a massive heart bouquet festooned with a blue sash that read BELOVED MOTHER. She had the uneasy sensation of eyes boring into her back. She turned around. Red Garcia watched her from against a wall, next to a comically large Grecian statue.

She gave a small wave. *Wave, smile, keep walking, as Mother used to say.*

"Here we go, Trevor," she whispered, approaching the casket. She cleared her throat. Nudging Bailey forward, she held out her hand to the widower. "Mr. Davenport, I'm Elizabeth Candew, one of Louisa's new recruits. I'm so sorry."

"Thank you for coming." He held out his hand. "Please call me Dave."

Stephanie squinted, as if trying to place Elizabeth.

"We met in your mom's kitchen," Elizabeth said.

"Right." Two red splotches burst on both sides of Stephanie's face. "I wasn't very nice to Mom that day. Or to you. I'm sorry."

Elizabeth had been young once. There had been scenes in her own mother's kitchen.

"Don't be." She tapped Trevor on the shoulder. "Your mother was an inspiration to a lot of people."

"I don't know what I'm going to do." Tears came down the girl's face in sheets. "Excuse me."

Dave Davenport sighed wetly and watched his daughter walk away. Elizabeth had expected him to be fit and attractive, like his wife, but he had rounded shoulders, and a stomach that protruded over his belt. His face swelled beneath a crew cut, giving him the look of a hypertensive pug. The wrinkles in his pants suggested he'd pulled them from the back of a closet after so many years he didn't know he'd gotten too fat for them.

"We're still in shock," he said. "It was nice of you to come."

"Of course you're in shock. I'm so sorry," she said again. What else was there to say? Except *sorry* yet again and *goodbye*. The air closed in like the walls of an oven. Elizabeth couldn't breathe.

She saw Red Garcia still standing there, the heat of his stare dampening her blouse. *Focus.* She averted her gaze and looked into the widower's eyes.

The spouse was always the first suspect in a murder case. Could this guy have stabbed his wife to death? He seemed legitimately grief-stricken, but for all Elizabeth knew, he'd once been the guy who got the lead in every high school play.

"Have you met my other daughter?" he asked. "Quincy, come here next to Daddy. I'm sorry. What did you say your name was again?"

"Elizabeth Candew. This is my son, Trevor, and my daughter, Bailey."

Trevor extended his hand to Louisa's husband. He looked him in the eye. "I'm sorry for your loss, Mr. Davenport."

"That's a fine young man you have there," Louisa's husband said.

"Thank you. My daughter's less predictable," Elizabeth said, observing Bailey chewing busily on the lip of her empty cup.

"Quincy," Dave Davenport said again. "Come."

A small girl with brown hair tucked under a pink barrette hopped up, leaving an iPad on the chair. "I found a tyrannosaurus rex," she told Trevor.

"Quincy is fascinated by dinosaurs," her father said.

The little girl bounced on her toes. "Terradactyls are the best."

"Terradactyls are cool, but I really like the dracorex," Trevor said.

The girl beamed. "They're cool, too."

"We're going to the Museum of Natural History in New York this weekend," Dave said. "When this is all over."

"You'll like it," Trevor said. "We went with the Cub Scouts a couple of years ago."

Quincy didn't seem to hear him. She looked up at Elizabeth. "Your lipstick is dark," she said. "Do you like wearing that dark lipstick?"

"She wouldn't wear it if she didn't like it," Dave Davenport said. "Quincy says things sometimes. She needs to learn to keep a lid on it."

"Oh, I don't know." Elizabeth winked. "I find it refreshing to know what people really think."

Bailey started whining, signaling it was time to bolt. Elizabeth slipped gently through the crowd, but a wall of people obstructed her path to the exit. A fight or flight response seized her; Bailey picked up on it and started shrieking.

A man in his early sixties seemed to deliberately block her exit. Since when did men wear madras shorts to wakes?

"Somebody needs a nap," he said, petting Bailey's head.

The child shrieked louder, causing people to cover their ears.

"She's had a long day," Elizabeth shouted over the crowd. Mourners swirled around her.

The man remained stock still. He seemed determined not to let her pass. "She's a pretty baby. Just like her mama."

So creepy. Was Elizabeth jumping to conclusions about him? She was an anxious single mother trapped in a hot funeral home with an after-work crowd sorely in need of breath mints. It would be easy to misread things.

"Thank you," she said. "I'd better get home."

"You do that," he said, taking in the full length of her as she walked away.

Elizabeth focused her sight on the door to avoid greeting Red Garcia, whose eyes she instinctively knew followed her movements. Even if she were still attracted to him – which she was not – she would not say hello to him. This whole claustrophobic scene made her jittery; she'd exceeded her quota for small talk with Dave Davenport. If ever talked to Red again, she'd cut to the chase: *I thought you liked me. Why did you dump me for Mary Pat? Do you still carry a torch for her, or have you regained your mental health?*

The only other thing that bore discussion with He-Who-Dumped-Her would be Louisa's murder. Did Red suspect Elizabeth? She sneaked a quick glance and met his eyes, causing her to swell with anxiety. She had a motive, after all, a good one. Louisa had cleaned her out of three thousand dollars!

The detective made his way towards her. She became aware of the wet fabric under her arms. The persistent orchid odor rose into her throat, suffocating her. She blew damp bangs out of her eyes, her hip tingling numbly under Bailey's weight.

"Hello, Red," she said casually. "Big crowd."

"Massive," he said, leaning back on his heels. The left hand remained free of a wedding band, not that it was any of her business.

"Nice to see you again, Elizabeth. How are you?"

How much did he already know? That she'd cheated on her husband and given birth to another man's child? While investigating the case, he might have interviewed relatives and acquaintances; for instance, Russell and Mary Pat.

A tall man in a suit and tie, better dressed than most of the mourners, approached.

"This is Elizabeth Candew," Red told him. "Mrs. Candew, this is Detective Michaels."

Detective Michaels had a thick neck under a pristine starched collar and seemed impervious to the heat. Elizabeth got a feeling he'd already been filled in about her. She shifted the baby's weight and offered her hand.

He didn't take it. "Whoa, Ma'am. You don't want to drop that little girl."

"I won't drop her," Elizabeth said. "I've never dropped either of my children."

Michaels ignored her. "You must be the man of the house," he told Trevor.

The boy's face shone with admiration. His hand disappeared into the detective's meaty one. "I sure am."

So, Red and his partner *had* discussed Elizabeth. "The man of the house starts school tomorrow. We'd better go," she said.

"Not so fast," Michaels said.

Elizabeth's heart stopped "Excuse me?"

"You're about to miss the best part," Red said, his eyes following the man in the madras shorts who'd blocked her exit.

"Here comes the man of the hour," Michaels looked at his watch. "How long you give him, Red?"

"Twenty minutes, easy."

"I'm going for, oh, twenty-eight."

"You want to put a beer on it?" Red asked.

"I'll put a six-pack on it."

"Big stakes," Elizabeth said. "I really have to put my children to bed, though."

"And miss out on the good pastor's remarks?" Michaels slid out of his jacket, folded neatly it over his arm, and loosened his tie.

"That joker is the pastor?" Elizabeth was dying to know what words of comfort he would impart from his madras shorts. She shifted Bailey gently onto her other hip. "I guess we could stick around for a minute."

"What does the man of the house have to say about that?" Michaels asked.

"Sounds good to me," Trevor said, basking in the attention of this powerful, older male.

Elizabeth gritted her teeth. She already disliked Detective Michaels.

The pastor silenced the crowd with a clap of his hands. He fiddled with a cordless mic and introduced himself.

"What can we say about our beloved sister, Louisa?" His authoritative voice boomed over the sound system. He slid one large hand over the shiny surface of the casket, pausing for effect, and the other in the pocket of his brightly-colored legwear. He sighed deeply.

"This is a difficult time for Dave. For Stephanie. For Quincy. For us, her family at the Stonesbury Army of God. For the Special Needs community. But we persevere. I exhort you to remember at this time of difficulty the words of Romans 12:12: 'Be joyful in hope, patient in affliction, faithful in prayer.' We must be all of these, joyful in the hope that our sister, Louisa, is in the arms of our Lord Jesus Christ, patient in the pain of her death, and faithful in our fervent prayers for our brother, Dave, and his daughters. As you know, Louisa was a force of nature, to a fault." He paused here, gave the casket a good rub, and chuckled. "We Christians know the ladies' primary role is to be helpmeets to their husbands, who are the spiritual head of the household, and Louisa – bless her—sometimes missed the memo on that, isn't that right, Dave?"

Elizabeth stood on her toes to see Dave's reaction. He didn't seem to be listening.

"The guy's a piece of work," Red muttered.

"You're telling me," Elizabeth said. "He's making me itch."

Michaels examined the backs of his thick fingers, one of which strangled in a wedding band. "This is a police matter, Ma'am."

"You're the one who told me to stick around, Detective." She shot Red a look: *What's the deal with this guy?*

"I'm going for water," Red said. "Can I get you some water, Elizabeth?"

"And miss the show?"

"Are you kidding? This guy is so loud they can hear him in Chile." He pointed his fore- and middle fingers at his own eyes, then at hers. "And I don't miss a thing."

Was he flirting with her? Or warning her? "I'll take some water."

She watched him thread his way through the room, casually surveilling the vicinity.

He returned, pinching four conical paper cups between his fingers. He handed one to Trevor, who suddenly seemed to be enjoying himself.

"We're ten minutes in," Michaels said, accepting a cup from his partner. "When's this windbag going to wind it up?"

Red looked at his watch. "You'd better hope he keeps it up for eighteen more, or you're down a six pack."

"No real loss when the winner drinks watered down domestic, Lightweight. You'd better hope he wraps up fast, or I'll put you on the hook for a pricey microbrew."

Elizabeth took a swallow of the blessedly cold water. Michaels squashed his cup and hooked it into a nearby wastepaper basket.

"Nice shot," Red said.

A woman wearing a long skirt and slab-heeled sandals swiveled her neck to shush them. Elizabeth and Red smirked at each other. The pastor quoted Ephesians 5, with special emphasis on the verses about wives submitting to their husbands.

Elizabeth rolled her eyes. "The wife's in a casket. She's not submitting to anybody."

"He's reading it for the benefit of the living," Red said.

"Why doesn't he read something else? Something Jesus said, for example?"

"Jesus didn't say wives should submit to their husbands?"

"No. Paul did," Elizabeth said. "Paul isn't Jesus."

"I don't read the Bible, so I wouldn't know."

"I do," Elizabeth said. "That way I can call these co-called Christians out when they quote Jesus to oppress people or promote their own psycho agendas."

Michaels checked his watch. "Fifteen minutes and no sign of slowing down. Blow the dust off your wallet, Garcia."

"Red bet twenty minutes," Elizabeth reminded him. "You bet twenty-eight. The closer man wins."

"Thank you for saving me from this bully." Garcia puffed up a little, making Elizabeth wonder again if he was flirting with her.

"Light beer is the beer to have when Garcia's having more than one," Michaels chortled. "Because he's a total lightweight."

"That's Schaefer," Elizabeth corrected. "Remember the commercial?"

"How old *are* you?" Michaels asked. "Schaefer went out of business when *I* was a kid."

"I'm forty-one. My father drank it."

"I'd have put you at thirty-six, tops."

"The preschooler threw you off. Without her, I look 50."

"You're funny," Garcia said. "I'd forgotten."

"Women aren't funny," Michaels said.

The pastor gestured to a bouquet of daisies. "And everything in life has a life cycle. These flowers will wilt and die, as will we all. Think about that, Ladies and Gentlemen. Think about your immortal soul. Where will it go when you're lying in a box like Louisa? Because, my friends, that day is going to come. Louisa is beyond us now. She has met her Creator, but Stephanie and Quincy and Dave remain with us, and they need our prayers. Let us bow our heads and ask for God's blessing upon them."

"When I get home, I'm going to pour myself a big glass of wine," Elizabeth said.

"In Jesus' name," the pastor said.

"In Jesus' name," the crowd responded.

Michaels poked his watch. "Twenty-five and a half minutes, Garcia. You owe me a six pack of not light beer."

The pastor accidentally dropped the mic, sending a screeching reverb throughout the funeral home. People held their ears. Startled, Bailey snapped open her eyes.

"That'll keep you awake." The pastor chuckled sadistically. "Now we will hear from Mrs. Patti Parisser, whose child benefited from the good works of our spirited sister, Louisa Davenport."

Mrs. Patti Parisser, either a young forty or a sun-damaged twenty-nine, stood at the casket holding a tissue. She had a blonde pony tail and a sleek pair of side-zip pants that didn't come from Lady Lily Wear.

"Thank you, Pastor," she said. "And please call me Patti because I'm not Mrs. Parisser. There's no Mr. Parisser, but you can say hello to my wife, Jenny, who's standing along the wall over there."

She blew Jenny a kiss. A mix of horrified and gleeful murmurs followed. Patti Parisser pulled a piece of loose leaf from her pocket and cleared her throat.

"All of us in the special needs community have a pain in our hearts this evening. We are at such a loss. How can we fully express the transformations Louisa effected in our lives through her tireless advocacy for our children? Pastor, you called Louisa spirited, as if it were a failing, but unless you have a child who's told she'll never measure up, she'll never be like other children or fit in with them, you don't understand what a treasure Louisa Davenport was in this world. She banged on the doors of our Board of Ed members. She packed a bus full of mothers and fathers and children to fight our state representatives for services we needed and deserved."

A group of parents near the water cooler hooted their approval.

"Pastor, I am not a believer in your God, so I am beyond your jurisdiction. But if there ever was a person on this earth who defined a Christian, a person who loved her neighbor as herself, it was Louisa Davenport." Patti Parisser began openly sobbing into her tissue. "And, I for one, was honored to know her."

A father from the contingent blew his nose into a handkerchief. Several congregants from the church shouted Patti Parisser down and made a show of heading for the door.

The pastor clapped his hands for attention.

"Now, Brothers and Sisters, get back here. Come back inside."

They obeyed. The pastor resumed his position on center stage.

"We don't have to agree with every word this lady said or approve of her lifestyle, but let's not turn our backs on her," he said. "She doesn't have the advantages we have in the love and mercy of our Lord Jesus Christ, but we can agree with some of the points she made. Sister Louisa was an asset to the special needs folks, and to the community at large. Some of you took your children off the artificial flavors because of Sister Louisa. Some of your kids aren't bouncing off the wall anymore and can even sit still long enough to learn to read. Look at her little girl, Quincy, over here. You've made tons of progress haven't you. little girl? Last year at this time, we wondered what would become of you. We couldn't even get you to talk." He turned back to his audience. "This child's mother's determination had spillover benefits for a lot of you. Don't make me ashamed, Brothers and Sisters. Make me good and proud."

"Holy Mac," Michaels remarked. "This guy could sell ice cream in hell."

"He's good," Red agreed.

Elizabeth readied herself to leave. Still no sign of Nancy. Elizabeth said goodnight, gathered up her children, and flipped through the guest book on her way out. Still no sign of Toni Badden, either.

THIRTEEN

Cathy had a habit of checking the local papers online whenever she was away on business, hence the call to Elizabeth early Monday morning from London about the Louisa Davenport case.

"I don't think there's ever been a murder in Stonesbury," she said. "People must be in shock."

"You'd be surprised. Some of the people I spoke to from her church thought she had it coming. And then others regard her as some kind of saint."

"Stabbed nine times? That's gruesome."

Elizabeth shuddered. "I don't like to think about the actual murder. I'd like to solve it, though."

"Stabbed," Cathy said again. "That's personal."

"Yeah, that's what I was thinking. Her detractors said she made herself unpopular with the clothing line. Put people in debt and reneged on her promise to teach them the business."

"Sounds like the real business was taking their money and running. I read a piece in the *New Yorker* that confirmed my suspicion that only the people at the very top make any money in those multi-level marketing things."

"I hope that's not true. I invested more than I could afford."

"Do you need a loan?"

"Let me explore a couple of other options first." Elizabeth couldn't take money from Cathy. She already felt like a loser. "Thanks, though. Really."

"Did you look into canceling your contract?"

"I missed the deadline."

"Yeah, but your upline is dead. That should count as a special circumstance."

"I asked. They pretty much told me to get lost."

"Threaten legal action if you have to."

"I did. It didn't make much of an impression. What's all that noise in the background?"

"Work party on the Thames. We're about to board our boat."

Elizabeth whistled. "I hope the weather's good for it."

"It's about eighty degrees. Sunset in a half hour."

"Sweet deal." Screw Disney. One day Elizabeth would take Trevor and Bailey to London. If she ever had the money. "Whatever you do, don't work too hard."

"Oh, don't worry." Cathy's voice became muffled, as if she'd run her hand over her phone. "I'll be right there, Clive."

"Clive? Who is Clive? Should I tell Patrick?"

"You know me better than that. Clive's a colleague."

Elizabeth did know Cathy better than that, although she almost wished Cathy would do the wrong thing once in a while. It would make her feel so much better about herself.

LOUISA HADN'T PROVIDED Toni's number, so she tried Lady Lily Wear headquarters again. Maybe a different rep would issue a refund.

This rep identified herself as Sheila. She sounded younger and friendlier than the last one.

"Oh, I'm very sorry about your loss," Sheila said cheerily. "Unfortunately, you didn't cancel in time to qualify for a refund."

"I'm a single mother trying to feed two kids under the age of ten."

"I wouldn't worry about that. You can work your business through your upline. It's in their best interests to help you."

"Yes, but my upline is out of state. I can't be running up to New Hampshire every time I have a question."

Sheila didn't say anything for a minute. "You do have a computer, don't you?"

"Yes."

"Are you familiar with Skype?"

"Yes."

"Yay, then you are all set to meet your upline face-to-face at your convenience. Beats paying tolls, right?"

Elizabeth rolled her eyes.

"And with our online library of trainings, you should be all set. It's very comprehensive. One of the beauties of this business is that it's not at all complicated."

"By any chance, are you a stylist, Sheila?"

Sheila waited a beat before answering. "No, Ma'am, I am not."

"And why is that, Sheila?"

"Because, um, I don't like working on commission."

"So, what you're saying is, you prefer the stability of a paycheck. You can't count on a steady income from a Lady Lily Wear business."

"I didn't say that."

"It sounded like you said that."

"If you want, I can provide you with the phone number for your upline. Would that be helpful?"

Elizabeth sighed. "To tell you the truth, I'm not sure it will. But give it to me, please."

Sheila read off the number with a wounded tone in her voice. "I wish you the best of luck," she said. "I really do."

Elizabeth would not take no for an answer. Maybe Toni Badden, from her perch on the top tier of the company, could get her money back. She tapped in Toni's number and got a chipper recording:

"Hello, Lovely. If you're calling Toni Badden to discuss the endless possibilities Lady Lily Wear Designs offers for work, evening, and play, leave a message. I'll get right back to you. And if you're calling to explore the Lady Lily Wear stylist opportunity that has helped many a mom retire her husband and put her kids through the finest universities, definitely leave a message. I can't wait to catch up."

What did Elizabeth's mother used to say? *What a load of mullarkey.* She left a short message and recited her phone number, slowly and twice. *Call me the second you hear this!* she wanted to say, but she knew it would sound desperate. Nobody wanted to deal with desperate people.

TREVOR'S FIRST WEEK of school had come and almost gone. Still no word from Toni Badden. Elizabeth's phone rang. She leapt for it, hoping for Toni. She got Mary Pat.

"Yes?"

"Russell asked me to pick Trevor up from school and take him for the weekend, but there's an issue."

Elizabeth looked at the clock on the microwave. School let out twenty minutes ago.

"Wait, is he okay? What kind of issue?"

"Your son won't come with me, and the secretary can't make him."

"It's Russell's weekend. Shouldn't you be calling him to pick him up? Why are you calling me?"

Mary Pat launched into her most indignant tone. "I'd have thought you'd care more about your child than to blame Russell for not picking him up."

"I'm counting on Russell to take care of our child when it's his turn to take care of him. He's his father, not a babysitter. He's not doing anybody any favors."

"Well, he can't make it, so he's left it to me."

"And did he inform the school you'd be picking Trevor up?"

"He's not a moron, Elizabeth." Mary Pat huffed. "The problem is, Trevor is being a Class-A Brat and refuses to come with me."

"Let me talk to him."

After some muttering on Mary Pat's part, Elizabeth heard her son's voice.

"Hey, Trev. What's going on?"

He whispered into the phone. "I don't want to go to MP's."

"I know you don't. Have you explained the situation to your father?"

"He told me to suck it up."

"Why couldn't he take you this weekend, did he say?"

"He's got this girlfriend. Tammi. She's okay, but when I'm with Dad, I just want it to be me and Dad. He invited me to go to Vermont with them, but you could kind of tell they were hoping I'd say no."

So much for Elizabeth watching *Ray Donovan* and *Fleabag* with a couple of glasses of wine. "I'll pick you up. Put your aunt back on."

"What?" Mary Pat huffed.

"I'll get him," Elizabeth said.

"Hughey will be highly disappointed," Mary Pat said, "and it's also bad parenting. Give into him now, and it'll bite back later. Mark my words."

"You know what else is not good parenting? Ignoring the fact that Trevor doesn't want to be around Hughey, and there's a reason for it you need to address."

"There's nothing going on between the boys, Elizabeth."

She couldn't resist. "Maybe they aren't comfortable talking to you, Mary Pat."

Her sister-in-law's voice dropped an octave. Elizabeth pictured her gritting her teeth. "I'm in the principal's office. I don't have time for your drama."

"Surely there's another kid you can invite over to play with Hughey," Elizabeth said, knowing full well there wasn't. "Go home. I'll be at school to get Trevor in ten minutes."

FOURTEEN

Things were different when Trevor started preschool. Russell took the day off, and the three of them sat around the breakfast table as a family. Russell cooked scrambled eggs and bacon to ensure Trevor consumed adequate protein, instead of sugary cereal that would leave him jittery and susceptible to behaviors which would make him unlikely to make friends. He and Elizabeth let Trevor dress himself in the outfit they'd agreed upon the night before, while Elizabeth packed a snack bag with mozzarella sticks and prayed her son wouldn't turn out to be *that kid*, the one his teachers actively disliked. She couldn't wait for the first day to be over so that she could hear all about it.

Today Elizabeth would take Bailey to preschool for the first time, alone, a single parent. From this day forward, Bailey would go to school every year until she finished college. She would go to college. Would she? Would Elizabeth even have the money?

Bailey would be younger than the other children in the program; she wouldn't turn three until mid-November. Elizabeth debated keeping her back a year to make sure she could keep up with her classmates, but her financial situation forbade it. She needed to stop messing around and earn an income.

Elizabeth carried Bailey out to the car.

"School," she said.

"You'll make friends," Elizabeth said.

She hoped to God it was true. There had been a mean girl named Simone in Trevor's class, who had a habit of getting in with two established friends, and then inviting one but not the other to her house for playdates until one of the original friends was vanquished from the group. At the time, Elizabeth marveled that a child so young could already be so destructive.

A packet had gone out two weeks before first day explaining the drop-off protocol for Threes: Parents must hand their child to the teacher at the door and "not linger." If the child started crying, they should wave and keep walking. In nearly every case, they promised, the child would calm down as soon as the parent was out of sight. Somebody from the school would call the parent afterwards to assure them this happened. While waiting for the call, the parent should "have a cup of tea."

Elizabeth braced herself. She parked on the street in front of the little school attached to the Eastern Orthodox church, and walked around to the back, where a scarily high slide loomed above a play yard full of ride-on jeeps and turtles. The air carried the metallic scent of rain.

She set Bailey down gently on the concrete. The kid still had her thumb in her mouth. Would her child be the only kid in class who still sucked her thumb? No doubt some boy in class would still be at it. They developed slower than girls.

"Hold hand, Mommy?"

"Of course. Are you excited, Bailey?"

"I'm going to school, Mommy."

"I'm excited, Bailey. We're going to meet your teacher."

"Trevor has a teacher, and I have a teacher."

"That's right."

They took their place among the other children and parents. They waited for their turn to get to the top of the line. A father at the front held things up taking pictures. Everybody else had taken pictures, hoping to capture the first encounter between child and teacher, but this man switched between an SL-35 and an iPhone and micromanaged his daughter's poses and also the young teacher, whom Elizabeth suspected was too new to know better.

"Lift your chin, Miss. A little lower." He backed up and snapped. "There you go."

Elizabeth rolled her eyes. She planned to take pictures, too, but like a normal person.

At last, she and Bailey got to the door where the fresh-faced teacher crouched to make eye contact with her youngest new student.

"I see you've brought your Elsa doll," she said.

"Is that all right?" Elizabeth breathed through a wave of anxiety. "Bailey is obsessed with all things *Frozen*."

"Of course it's all right." The young woman held out her hand. Bailey took it and walked into the classroom without looking back.

When Trevor started school, he made sure Elizabeth and Russell suffered. They heard him yowling all the way back to the car. This woman won Bailey's trust without earning it.

It scared Elizabeth witless.

ELIZABETH POURED A cup of tea, as if following the school's directions to the letter would magically avert any potential problems for her small child. She decided against peeling open a snack pack of peanut butter crackers. It wouldn't kill her to lose five pounds.

It had been days since her Lady Lily Wear shipment arrived, yet she hadn't the heart to go through it again after Louisa died. Its presence in her house taunted her, as though she'd fallen for a bad joke.

Toni Badden. Maybe she hadn't returned yet from the end-of-summer vacation Elizabeth imagined for her and her husband and children. Give people the benefit of the doubt, her mother always said, but look where it had gotten *her*.

Elizabeth went into her recent calls list and pressed the one with the New Hampshire area code. She cleared her throat and waited. She listened again to the recording of Toni's fruity voice. It struck her differently this time, although it hadn't changed. Toni seemed overly friendly and enthusiastic. There was a word for it: Phony.

Don't jump to conclusions, Elizabeth. There's nothing uglier than a cynical woman.

Elizabeth's mother's words again. Not hers. Sometimes she had trouble telling them apart.

She left a voice message. "Hello, Toni," she said. "This is Elizabeth Candew, Louisa Davenport's new stylist. The one you spoke to on the phone recently?"

At Elizabeth's first job after finishing college, Tom Stoddard said that if she wanted someone to call back, "You gotta consider the WI-IFM factor. What's in it for them? Make it about them, not you."

Elizabeth heeded that advice. "I know you want me to hit the ground running, Toni, and I've received my inventory. I want to be one of your top producers, so that I can make a major contribution to your bottom line, not just mine. If you call me as soon as it's convenient, I can get started. I'm eager to jump in and do my first show. Any advice or pointers you could give me would be really, really appreciated."

She glanced at the clock, which gave her sixty-five minutes before she had to pick up Bailey. *Please let her be having fun. Please let the teachers be kind and encouraging.* She'd read enough self-help books to know that the words a person heard as a child could influence their success and happiness for the rest of their lives.

Elizabeth poured another cup of tea. *I'm releasing extra fat as I drink.* Now, there was an affirmation. While waiting for a call back from Toni, she might as well take Sheila's advice and watch the training available to her online. She logged onto the Lady Lily Wear website and launched the introductory video.

An attractive blonde woman in her mid-thirties appeared on screen.

"Hello, I'm Holly Ann Holliwell," she trilled, bracelets glimmering from the cuffs of a pink angora sweater. "Congratulations on your new Lady Lily Wear business. You are about to embark on a journey that will change your life, your partner's life, and your children's lives. Not only do you have the opportunity to reap considerable financial benefits from your new business, but as I'm sure you know by now, that legions of Lady Lily Wear stylists have already a) retired their husbands from their dreaded J-O-B-S, and b) earned fun and extravagant vacations for their families where they built magical memories that will last a lifetime."

A collage of vacation photos, ostensibly of successful Lady Lily Wear stylists and their families, replaced Holly.

"Just meet Rhonda Beckley of Brooklyn, New York. In April 2015, Rhonda's husband suffered a massive heart attack, which caused him to tragically leave behind not just Rhonda but also their two kiddos, Frances and Owen. Rhonda signed onto Lady Lily Wear and guess what happened next?"

A snapshot of Rhonda on a stage with a man clasping a medal around her neck replaced the portrait.

"Today, Rhonda Beckley is a Regional Vice President, steadily earning money to put food on her table and provide solid educations for her kiddos."

If she says kiddos one more time, I'm going to scream. Why did Holly feel the need to launch into the sales pitch yet again? Oh, right. Probably because reasonable people had second thoughts after signing away a fortune. They needed reassurance. Elizabeth stopped Holly in mid-sentence and clicked on the next video in the series,

GETTING STARTED IN YOUR LADY LILY WEAR BUSI-
NESS.

Bingo.

Holly Ann Holliwell appeared again in her pink sweater, holding
a white mug.

"Okay," she said, after an introduction Elizabeth fast-forwarded
through. "Let's get comfortable because now we're going to get down
to the nuts and bolts of running a Lady Lily Wear business. Maybe
nuts and bolts isn't the right word. We like to do things stitch by
stitch, so let's start by threading our needles here, shall we?"

Get on with it. Please!

"The first thing to remember is that you're representing not only
a company that is at number twenty-five of the fastest growing companies in the United States in *Incredible Income Forever* magazine,
but you're representing yourself and your business."

Incredible Income Forever magazine? Elizabeth made a note to
Google it.

"Every item you present to your customers should be in excellent
condition with no stains or signs of wear whatsoever. That's why we
include the complimentary single-item cases with your order."

Does she mean those flimsy cellophane baggies?

"We recommend that you store your items in the cases at all
times, except of course, at your Trunk Shows. Now you know how
people are. I don't have to tell you that some of the ladies who come
to your shows are less respectful than others. Some of them will
spill coffee and wine on your beautiful samples, so there is another training on the topic of stain removal where you can get lots of
tips on keeping your samples fresh. However, I will tell you that your
best weapon against stains is a product we've developed called Lily
Fresh, which is like a magic wand for cleaning even those dastard-
ly wine and coffee stains from your inventory. Really, it's unbeliev-
able. Ladies, let me tell you right now, that Lady Lily Wear employs

not only the most talented designers to develop our enviable clothing line, but also engineers who make sure your product arrives at your home in perfect condition, and that it stays that way."

Holly held up a little spray bottle. "I sincerely advise you to put this product in your Lady Lily Wear arsenal. It's absolute genius."

Elizabeth dropped her head onto the table in exasperation. *Is this woman going to show me how to run a business? Or sell me more stuff?*

Holly cradled the mug between smooth manicured hands. "But most important of all is *you*, and the way you present *yourself*. You, that's right, you are the face of this company. When your customers think about Lady Lily Wear, whose face is it that will pop into their minds? Yours. So, it's critical that you look current. If fashion isn't your thing, I suggest you get a subscription to *Vogue* and see what people are wearing. Don't worry about the expense. It's a business write off. Now, as a Lady Lily Wear stylist, you have access to the most *au courant* styles. Of course. But accessorizing can get tricky for some of you gals, so do your homework. Also, put yourself in the hands of a gifted hairstylist and have your hair cut in a style that actually flatters your face."

Holly put down the mug and drew a circle with her fingers. "For example, if you have a big round face, you do not want to cut your hair in a chin-length bob. Trust me. You will look like a pumpkin in a wig!"

She picked up the mug again, which Elizabeth doubted contained anything but air. She looked at the clock. *Stop wasting my time, Holly. Are you going to tell me how to run this business, or not?*

"Now, as far as makeup goes, again, put yourself in the hands of someone who knows what he or she is doing. If you're over forty, please, please, please do not line your lower eye lid. It drags your entire face down and makes you look a hundred years old. Maybe, if you're old enough – because we're signing up lots of you college ladies into this business – woot woot! – you'll remember some of those photos of Princess Diana taken just before her tragic car accident. If you Google them, you'll notice that she not only had liner on her lower lid, but her hair had been cut short in the back and longer at the top of her head. Highly unflattering! The person who did that to her – well, that person should not have had that job. Poor Diana was only thirty-six and looked five years away from assisted living. Do not let anyone do this to you, Ladies. If you need a recommendation for a good stylist and/or makeup artist, Facebook is your friend. Every town has a moms' page. No doubt yours does too, and it can be a brilliant source of info you can use in your Lady Lily Wear business."

She has no intention of telling me how to run this business.

"Okay, now that we have the fundamentals out of the way, I want you to pull out your order sheets. You can place orders online, or you can fax them or call them into us using the toll -free number you see at the top." Holly held up the order sheet. "Do you see it there? In big numbers next to the Lady Lily Wear logo?"

She's giving lessons on how to fill out an order form.

Elizabeth snapped the laptop closed and poured the remaining tea in the sink.

A group of parents waited outside the classroom window, waving at their children and distracting them from what appeared to be the task of gluing fuzzy balls of colorful fabric to construction paper. One of the younger teachers glared at them through the window. The more experienced one corralled the children back into their seats.

"All right, Boys and Girls, line up single file the way you practiced with Miss Natalie, so I can return you to your parents," she told them.

Elizabeth recognized her ankle-length skirt as a Lady Lily Wear *Delphine*. She had Small, Medium, and Large *Delphine*s chilling in a corner of Bailey's room. This woman, Miss Donna, wore a small. She carried herself with a glamour one did not usually associate with a veteran nursery school teacher.

Bailey stepped to the front of the line. Miss Donna checked the tag on the little girl's dress.

"Bailey Candew," she announced.

Elizabeth made her way through the crowd of eager parents. "She's mine."

"Photo ID, please."

"Are you serious?"

"It's not that I don't recognize you, but it's a new policy we've put in place after that kidnapping last summer."

"It turned out to be a parent, right?"

"As usual." Miss Donna shrugged. "So, we have to check."

"It's a weird world we're living in," Elizabeth said. "I like your skirt, by the way."

"Thank you. I wore it to Greece over the summer. It travels well."

"So I've heard."

Bailey reached for her mother's hand.

"What do you say to Miss Donna?"

"Thank you, Miss Donna!"

Elizabeth moved off. She had a fleeting idea to introduce the idea of a Lady Lily Wear business to Miss Donna, although if she'd already been to a trunk show, the opportunity had probably been presented and rejected. Elizabeth dismissed that line of thinking as defeatist and decided to bring up the subject the next time she saw her.

She strapped Bailey into her car seat. Her phone lit up with a familiar number she couldn't place.

"Mrs. Candew, it's Irene Solom at the Five-Six School."

"Is everything okay?"

"We'd like you to come in and meet with the principal."

"Sure. What is this about?"

"Trevor's behavior needs to be addressed."

"He's a straight-A student."

"He's doing fine academically. However, his behavior has become an issue."

"In the second week of school? What kind of issue?"

"His behavior towards some of the girls has been inappropriate."

Elizabeth sucked in her breath. Those nights he spent at Russell's! Had Russell left his magazines around?

"Inappropriate how?"

"Can you come in tomorrow? We'd like to discuss this with you in person."

"Yes." Elizabeth watched the reunion of happy parents and children from the windshield, her own excitement about asking Bailey about her first day drained away. "Will ten o'clock work?"

"Yes, Mrs. Candew. We'll see you then."

FIFTEEN

E lizabeth put Bailey in for a nap before she tried Toni Badden again. The call from Trevor's school rattled her. This time she wouldn't be so easygoing.

The call went to voicemail.

"Hi, Toni," she said. "This is Elizabeth Candew. This is the third time I'm calling. Do you check your messages? Because my understanding was that you are a successful businessperson who could teach me how to be a successful businessperson, or at least that is the impression you gave me when you and my recently murdered sponsor, Louisa Davenport, suckered me into this deal. I am stuck with a roomful of clothes I can't return. The so-called training videos online are useless. I'm guessing Lady Lily Wear is concerned about the way they want their brand presented, so get back to me, or I'll unload my inventory for pennies on the dollar on every tag sale page on Facebook. I'm a single mother, for Pete's sake. Throw me a bone."

Elizabeth clicked off. She went out to get the mail. She flipped through the pile over the sink, chewing her thumbnail. The electric bill arrived in a yellow envelope, signaling bad news. If she didn't pay within ten days, the power would be shut off.

She threw herself on the couch and sobbed.

ELIZABETH FELT SMALL warm fingers on her forehead.

"Mommy wake up. Mommy wake up."

Elizabeth opened her eyes. What was she doing on the couch? The sun slanted across the living room floor. She jolted upright.

"What time is it?"

The child had her thumb in her mouth and a raw spot on her chin from drooling.

"You have to stop sucking that thing." Elizabeth checked her phone. She should be at the bus stop by now. Bailey's hair stood upright in the humidity. So did her own, probably. She jammed the little feet into shoes.

"We have to run," she said.

Elizabeth didn't have time to let the kid examine every rock and leaf on the walk to the bus stop. She scooped her up and ran out the kitchen door. Bailey pulled at Elizabeth's hair.

"I wanna walk. I wanna walk." She clamped Elizabeth's hips between her shoes.

Elizabeth gritted her teeth. "If you want to watch *Frozen* again, knock it off."

Bailey buried her head in her mother's shoulder. They arrived at the stop just as the bus pulled up. Trevor got off last, hoodie up, head down.

"Aren't you warm in that thing?" Elizabeth asked him. "How'd it go today?"

"All right."

"Did anything special happen?"

"No."

"Anything I should know?"

"Nope."

"We're having spaghetti tonight."

"Big whoop."

"Excuse me? What happened to saying thank you? You love spaghetti."

"The problem with you, Mom, is that you make the same thing over and over. Spaghetti is totally played."

"I make it because you said you like it."

"Well, I don't."

"I'm sorry. That's what we're having."

"I'll make cereal."

"Suit yourself." She'd freeze his portion and serve it when he was in a better mood.

Bailey yelped "Ow, Mommy, you're hurting me!"

"I'm sorry, Baby, I didn't realize I was holding you so tight."

Get a grip, Elizabeth. Or less of one.

She set Bailey on the sidewalk. "We can take our time now. Pick out some rocks to take home if you want."

Bailey reached over and picked up a stick. "Bang bang. You a dead man, Trevor!"

Elizabeth held out her hand. "Hand it over. We don't go around pretending to shoot people. Where did you learn such a thing?"

"At school, probably," Trevor said.

Elizabeth crouched down to Bailey's level. "We don't pretend to shoot people, do you hear me? It's bad to shoot people."

"Then why does Daddy have a gun?" Trevor demanded.

Bailey's eyes widened. "Daddy has a gun?"

"Not your daddy. You don't have a daddy."

"Trevor!" Elizabeth shot him a silencing look. What did he know? Who told him?

"Trevor, what?"

"Don't you say another word. Do you hear me?"

"Why not? You're always telling me to tell the truth."

Bailey's legs stiffened. "I do so have a daddy. I do so have a daddy!"

"No, you don't. Tell her, Mom."

Russell must have told him. Or Mary Pat. Or maybe they both did.

"Trevor, I'm warning you. Be quiet."

Or you'll do what? Send him to his room? Take away his devices? You want him to be able to get you if he needs you, don't you? So, what are you going to do about it?

"I'm disappointed in you. More than I can even put into words."

There. That's telling him!

"Yeah," he said. "Maybe I'm disappointed in *you*."

Elizabeth thought her bones would shatter.

"Mommy," Bailey whispered. "Do I have a daddy?"

"Yes," she said, despite the fact the man didn't know the child existed. "Everyone has a daddy."

"Well, my daddy is taking me to Disney for Christmas." Trevor patted Bailey on the head. "And you can't come."

The child started bawling, through her thumb. "I want to see Elsa. I want to see Elsa! Mommy, I want to see Elsa!"

Elizabeth glared at her son with a hatred that would bring her to her knees later. In that moment, she regretted giving birth to him, but the ferocity of her loathing didn't approach what she felt about herself. She alone brought this upon her family. She bore responsibility for all of it.

TREVOR HAD LEFT HIS dinner cereal bowl in the sink, ignoring his mother's instruction to put it in the dishwasher. Twenty-two minutes before he had to catch the school bus, it remained there.

"No breakfast until you put that bowl away," Elizabeth warned him.

"Good. Then I won't eat."

"You have to eat breakfast, Trevor."

"You can't make me."

"I can't make you, but if you don't eat something, you'll have trouble concentrating at school."

"That's your problem."

"Trevor, it's *your* problem."

"That's what you think."

Before marriage, child, adultery, child, and divorce, a yoga instructor identified Elizabeth as a "shallow breather." Breathe through your abdomen. Inhale for a count of four, hold for a count of sixteen, exhale for a count of eight.

She followed this advice tying her daughter's sneakers. *Inhale. Hold. Exhale.* Maybe she should strike fear into Trevor by telling him about the call from school, but she thought the better of it. Why issue threats until after she spoke to the principal?

Except for an isolated incident in kindergarten when Trevor refused to stop rolling on the floor at rug time, teachers spoke highly of him. He got top marks and won monthly citizenship awards. Despite her mistakes, Elizabeth did her best to ensure that she could look back from her death bed and say, "I've raised a good man."

She and Bailey trailed behind Trevor on the walk to the bus stop. He ran a half block ahead. He refused discussion about the math test he had coming up and the pinhole camera he planned to make for the science fair. He made it clear he didn't want to be near his mother, or be seen with her.

She pictured his reaction if they happened to cross paths during her appointment with the principal. Maybe she would pretend she didn't know him. See how he liked it. She smiled at the idea, knowing she'd never go through with it. What was it about seeing one's own children in a different context that made a parent's heart leap? The same kid who caused you to scream like a lunatic over a lost button at breakfast could fill you with unfathomable joy later that day when he sang "Rudolph the Red Nosed Reindeer" out of tune in a cafeteria that smelled of sour milk.

The bus arrived before Elizabeth and Bailey got to the stop. Elizabeth watched Trevor mount the stairs and plop into a seat next to a girl he did not greet. The STOP signs retracted, and the bus emitted its familiar hiss. Elizabeth's lungs filled with leaden sadness. She reached for Bailey's hand and watched the bus until it was out of sight.

BAILEY WANTED TO WEAR her Elsa dress. Elizabeth put her in the Elsa dress. Bailey wanted the Elsa barrettes and shoes, so Elizabeth put them on, too. Mary Pat had purchased these things after finding out Bailey belonged to someone other than her brother. Elizabeth's distaste for princess-y things was well known to Russell's family, who told her to get over herself. Elizabeth suspected Mary Pat bought the items precisely because she objected to them.

She arrived at Trevor's school at the end of a school-wide assembly; crowds of students darted from all angles. Fourth and fifth grade girls spotted Bailey and squealed.

"How cute she is!" shouted one in a Katie Perry t-shirt.

"I love your dress," said her friend. "Where can I get one like that?"

Bailey arched her back shyly.

A boy rushing past almost knocked her over. "Sorry about that, Junior," he said.

Elizabeth scooped her up, loving the attention. "Say hi, Bailey. Say hi!"

Bailey popped her thumb into her mouth and dug her head into Elizabeth's underarm. Elizabeth smiled, waved goodbye to the girls, and headed for the principal's office.

She sat on a blonde wood chair with a square brown cushion perusing the dog-eared selection of periodicals. She'd rather read the book she'd uploaded to the Kindle app on her phone but feared the principal would see her staring at her phone and take her for a disinterested social media addict. She had to make a good impression. She'd painstakingly avoided the harried mom look by blow drying her hair and putting on lipstick.

She heard the click of the latch on the beige door adjacent to the secretary's desk.

"Mrs. Dispo." A woman in her late sixties approached. She had a hair style that approximated a mushroom cap and did not shake hands. "Good to meet you."

"And you, Mrs. Caffee. My name is Candew now. Trevor's father and I are divorced."

"Oh, I'm sorry." Mrs. Caffee glanced at the paper she held.

"Thank you," Elizabeth answered. "It was for the best."

The principal shifted her weight, and it dawned on Elizabeth she wasn't sorry about the divorce, but that she'd called Elizabeth the wrong name.

"It must be hard to keep up when you have so many students to think about," she said. She'd bet this woman had her son mixed up with somebody else. She made a mental note to bring up Trevor's citizenship awards from second and third grade.

"Seven hundred," Mrs. Caffee said, "but we do our best. And what is this little girl's name?"

Bailey responded by staring intently at the speckled linoleum floor.

"This is Bailey. We're working on her manners."

"It's better when they don't trust everyone," the woman answered matter-of-factly "Why don't we go into my office?"

Elizabeth followed her into another beige room and lowered herself and Bailey onto a padded chair. What was it about a principal's office that could rattle a grown woman? She focused on the framed photographs in a bookcase, especially the one of a bride and groom. Mrs. Caffee stood to the side in it, looking like she'd gone for the full spa treatment. Elizabeth squinted, wondering what happened to Mr. Caffee? Maybe Mrs. Caffee's life was harder than her own. She made a silent vow to be kind and compassionate.

"Now, Mrs. Dispo." Mrs. Caffee looked at her paper. "Candew. You probably remember that you and Trevor had to sign our rules of conduct."

"I do remember. He and I discussed them."

"Right." Mrs. Caffee bent over, revealing a line of gray roots. She removed a copy of the student handbook from her desk drawer. "At this school, we take bullying extremely seriously. A first offense is reported to the parent. A second offense is reported to the police."

A wave of relief washed over Elizabeth. This meeting wasn't about Trevor's behavior. It was about Hughey's. *I can't wait to see Mary Pat's face.*

"Trevor mentioned there'd been a problem. I'm so glad you called me in to discuss it.

"I'm glad you see it that way because this behavior cannot continue."

"I heard bits and pieces of it. I think Trevor was embarrassed."

"Well, that's a good sign. You'd be surprised how many kids have no idea how their behavior affects others, or even care."

"I'm not sure I understand."

"I get the feeling that you're a concerned parent who doesn't put up with that kind of language."

Elizabeth swallowed. "What language?"

"Trevor has been using a certain word. On more than one occasion, he's called a girl a slut."

"That word isn't in our vocabulary." *Not mine, anyway. I can't vouch for his father.*

"According to his teacher, he's using it. He picked it up somewhere."

"Okay." Elizabeth rubbed Bailey's head in a self-soothing gesture. "Are you sure?"

"Is everything okay at home, Mrs. Candew?"

"Elizabeth. Please call me Elizabeth. Maybe the divorce has been harder on Trevor than I thought."

"Have you considered counseling? I can put out feelers for recommendations if you like."

"I'll sit him down first thing. If what you say is accurate, the first step is for him to apologize to those girls. Unless he already has. Do you know?"

Mrs. Caffee looked at her paper. "It doesn't say."

"Well, let's find out." *I mean, before you label the kid and ruin him for life.* "Is there anything else I should know about?"

"My understanding is that Trevor is a good student. His teachers say he is respectful, so no. There's nothing else."

Elizabeth stood up. The florescent light drilled a throbbing hole behind her eyes. "Well," she said. "Thank you then."

Elizabeth reminded herself to stand up straight. *Be businesslike. Show her you're no pushover and get the hell out of here.*

"Think about the counseling, will you?" Mrs. Caffee stood up and clasped her hands over a chartreuse belt that clashed with her orange shirt dress. Spittle appeared in the corners of her mouth when she smiled. Elizabeth didn't like her one bit.

"Let me get Trevor's side of the story first," she said.

SIXTEEN

Elizabeth tapped in Cathy's number. *Please do not be on a plane. Please do not be in a meeting.* Elizabeth missed the days when Cathy would show up on her parents' doorstep with her hair in braids. She missed the days when she gave Cathy advice – those days when Elizabeth had a pile of boys at her feet –and Cathy sought instruction on how to attract some of her own. How had Cathy wound up with the devoted, fun husband and Elizabeth with substandard Russell?

Cathy picked up immediately. Remembering Tom Stoddard's sage advice, she asked about Cathy's interests, not her own.

"Have you decided about Asia?"

"I was going to call you. Patrick is totally onboard. He says we'd be crazy to pass up the opportunity."

"Interesting how he said 'we.'"

"Which reminds me why I married him. He says that this experience is only going to benefit him and the kids."

"What about his mother?"

"The treatment is working. She said she wouldn't forgive us if we didn't go."

"That's it, then," Elizabeth said. "I can't imagine being without you. Give me a second to process this."

Cathy remained silent for bit. Finally, she said, "At least we have Skype."

"You know when you get down to it, with our schedules we get to see each other, what? Maybe three times a year."

Cathy paused. "Yeah, and you live five blocks away. I'll bet I see you more over Skype."

"Yeah, and maybe one day I'll visit you in Asia."

"You'd better."

"Need to make some money first."

"How's that going? The new enterprise? I've been trying to follow the Davenport murder, but there's no news as far as I can tell."

"Not as far as I can, either, but who knows what the police aren't telling us." Red's glinting eyes flashed into Elizabeth's mind. "As far as the business goes, it's not going anywhere. But, hey, you warned me. My upline isn't even taking my calls."

"Well, if it would help, you could host a party at our place."

"It's not a party, remember?" Elizabeth chuckled darkly. "It's a trunk show."

"Trunk show, right. Well, do one here."

"You'll be in the middle of a move."

"I'm entitled to one last hurrah."

"I don't know that an MLM party qualifies as a hurrah."

"I want to do this. Look at it as an excuse to drink wine."

As if Elizabeth needed one. She didn't want to accept Cathy's offer. Pride stood in the way. She dearly hoped to achieve some sort of success on her own, without anybody's help. Because what had she ever accomplished? Marriage? *Game over.* Children? Well, who could predict how they'd turn out? She did her best to raise humans who would be an asset to society, but if they fell in with a bad crowd, they could end up a liability. If Russell had his way, Trevor would grow up to be another entitled misogynist.

Right now, Elizabeth needed money. She said yes.

"Hey, look," Cathy said reassuringly. "You got burned. At least you tried. Let's see if we can make back some of your investment.

How's Wednesday? By midweek every woman in Stonesbury's itching for an excuse to drink wine."

"I'm glad I'm not alone." Elizabeth felt a shift in her anxiety. Now, instead of worrying how to pay her credit card bill, she dreaded standing in front of Cathy's well-heeled friends begging them to buy clothes they didn't want. "Seven o'clock?"

"It's on the calendar."

"I gotta tell you about Louisa's wake. She belonged to that church in that strip mall next to Angelina's Pizza."

"Oh, yeah. Someone gave me a flyer about it outside Stop & Shop."

"The pastor showed up in Bermuda shorts."

Cathy laughed. "Every girl's crazy about a sharp-dressed man."

"I had a conversation with a couple of the congregants. They didn't have a kind word for anyone."

"You know what Gandhi said about Christians."

"No. What?"

"He liked Christ but wasn't crazy about Christians."

"He wouldn't have liked this bunch. I didn't like the pastor. The guy's your typical garden variety misogynist. Complete bore. Anyway, I got the feeling Louisa may have pushed Lady Lily Wear too far at church, but a faction from the special needs community turned out. She was a hero to them. Apparently, she did a lot of good work for learning disabled kids."

"Does she have a kid with a learning disability?"

"Yeah. Nice little girl."

"I wonder if Louisa would have been so generous if her kid were a straight-A student."

"Few of us get involved with causes that don't affect us, so she gets a pass there." Elizabeth would write a list of people Louisa had royally pissed off as soon as she got off the phone. "Oh, I almost forgot. Guess who's the detective investigating the case."

"I don't know any detectives."

"You know this one."

"Give me a hint."

"His name came up the night we went to the movies."

"Red Garcia? Red Garcia is a detective?"

"Yeah, and he's still not fat and bald."

"Yeah, but he dumped you for Mary Pat, so it doesn't matter. He's a loser in my book."

"He's a hot loser. Don't worry, though. I won't let him suck me in with that charm and low-key manliness of his."

"Has he been in touch about the case?"

"A couple of times. I think anyone she convinced to join Lady Lily Wear is a suspect."

"So, your paths will cross again."

"I suppose. I need this stuff like a hole in the head. In other news, Trevor's principal claims he's been calling girls sluts on the playground. Furthermore, he's been made aware that his sister is not his father's daughter"

"Who the hell told him?"

"As big a jerk as Russell is, I don't think he would do it. My money's on Mary Pat."

"There's something wrong with that woman."

"I think her meanness is rubbing off on Trevor. After he told Bailey she doesn't have a father, he rubbed it in her face Russell's taking him to Disney and not her."

"Wow," Cathy said. "I'm surprised at him. That's pretty cruel."

"I can't blame him for being angry. I didn't say Bailey belonged to Russell, but I certainly gave Trevor that impression. It's a betrayal."

"What were you supposed to say? That you lost your mind when you found Russell's porn stash? He promised he wasn't into it and never would be. He knew what you'd been through with your father."

"I may have overreacted."

"Porn ruins lives. People act like it's innocuous. It's not."

"I probably shouldn't have retaliated by banging a stranger and getting pregnant."

"You didn't intend to get pregnant. Your mistake was telling Russell the truth about it."

"We've been through this, Cathy. I couldn't *not* tell him." Elizabeth visualized Russell watching Bailey take her first steps with the excitement he'd had in his eyes when Trevor took his. "That would have been cruel."

"We all have our secrets, Elizabeth. That's all I'm saying."

"You don't have any."

"Well, Russell sure did." Cathy paused. "Didn't he?"

"He did, but now my children are suffering because of my actions."

"Will you mention to him that Trevor told Bailey?"

"I have to." Elizabeth filled the tea kettle and put it on the burner. "I also have to address this business of Trevor calling people sluts."

"You don't even let him say 'shut up.' Where'd he learn a word like that?"

"I'm guessing his father."

"Russell's an idiot, but he wouldn't use that word in front of a kid. My money's on his sister."

"I'm guessing that Trev overheard her bitching about me."

Elizabeth opened the refrigerator. How had she forgotten to buy lemon? She couldn't drink tea without lemon. She shut off the stove.

"Have you considered family therapy?" Cathy asked quietly.

"The principal suggested it. I'm not sure I like her, however. She didn't seem to know Trevor or be overly interested in getting to."

"In other words, she doesn't know she's dealing with a good kid."

"Her desk and bookshelves were loaded with photos of her grandchildren. I get the feeling she's ready to retire."

With tea no longer an option, Elizabeth stood over the coffee maker. *Yes or no?* She didn't want another sleepless night. *No.*

The doorbell rang.

"Hold on," Elizabeth said. "I have somebody at the door. Let me stealthily check to ensure it's not a team of religious zealots."

Elizabeth whispered into the phone. "It's Red Garcia."

"What's he wearing?"

"A button-down shirt, bursting at the seams around his biceps."

"Is he trying to kill you?" Cathy gasped. "Be careful. He may be trying to butter you up for information."

"I wouldn't put it past him."

Elizabeth checked herself in the mirror above the sideboard and flicked an errant flake of mascara from under her eye. Good thing she hadn't skipped the blow dry.

"I'll let you go. Promise you'll report back," Cathy said.

"Definitely. I'll be over a half hour early Wednesday to set up my wares."

Elizabeth ended the call. She sucked in her breath and opened the door.

SEVENTEEN

Detective Garcia looked crisp in his button-down shirt. An absent tie served as the only indication he felt the heat.

"Would you like to sit down, Detective?"

Red laughed. "I like it when you call me Detective, Elizabeth."

Okay, he was definitely flirting with her, not that Elizabeth didn't appreciate it. Since she'd been relegated to the Land of the Ma'ams, it had been a long time since anyone did. However, Red Garcia had broken her heart in high school.

She gestured for him to sit on a living room chair with the view of Bailey's Pack 'n Play and the pile of Trevor's soccer equipment. She never could count on Trevor to put his things away, and she'd been so tired after the wake she hadn't forced the issue. Anyway, it didn't take a detective to tell housekeeping wasn't among Elizabeth's favorite activities.

"Coffee?"

"I'd love one. Thanks, Lizza."

"Nobody calls me that," she said.

"I hope you don't mind if I do." He shrugged. "It suits you. Nobody listens to this music either, in case you haven't noticed."

Elizabeth turned down slightly Jefferson Airplane's "Wooden Ships," which emanated from a speaker perched precariously on a pile of mail. "If I ask you a question, will you give me an honest answer?

"Depends on the question."

"I thought you might say that." Elizabeth left to make the coffee. From the kitchen she said, "If I'm a suspect, I'd like to know."

"You always did have excellent taste in music."

Between Russell's penchant for non-stop cable news and auto-tune Top 40, that taste had nearly been drummed out of her. One of the benefits of divorce was that you got to listen to music you want-ed as loud as you wanted.

"You're changing the subject," Elizabeth said.

"We still have a lot in common, is all I'm saying. But since you brought it up, where were you at the time of Louisa's murder?"

Elizabeth finished setting up the coffee and returned to the living room. "I don't know. Have you established a time?"

"Where were you before you arrived at the crime scene?"

"At home, but my alibi is a preschooler."

"Don't worry about it. Even if you were a suspect, you're not a suspect. You couldn't kill anybody, Lizza. I know you better than that."

"You *used* to know me."

Elizabeth detected a shadow of pain behind the remarkable eyes.

"People don't change that much," he said quietly. "You learn that in my line of work."

"I'll keep that in mind," Elizabeth said. When he'd flown off to Paris for the exchange program in which she was also enrolled but could no longer afford due to her parents' sudden divorce, he'd given her the impression they'd still be a couple when he got back. They'd exchanged no less than three letters a week for seven of the eight weeks he was away, and then his letters stopped. He returned to Stonesbury the boyfriend of another girl from the group. *Mary Pat.*

"I'm trying to get insight into Louisa Davenport, what kind of person she was. I thought you might be able to help me fill in the blanks."

"I don't know anything we didn't learn at the wake. She had a lot of ambition. She liked to garden. When I came to visit, she had her gloves on."

"You're sure about that?"

"I'm pretty sure." Did he think she was some kind of idiot? "When she greeted me, she was wearing gardening gloves."

He smiled and took the mug Elizabeth offered. "That's interesting. One of the first people we interviewed was her gardener."

"She told me she did her own gardening. Tried to come off all modest about it, too."

Red blew into his coffee. "Yeah, well. She lied."

"Is the gardener a suspect?"

"His alibi checked out. He was pretty broken up about her death. Said she provided a steady stream of cold beers in the heat. She paid on time. Not everybody does."

"Wow. She put on some show for me, then. It sounds pathological."

"She might have been."

"At some point, she must've lied to the wrong person. She had a kind streak though, which makes it hard to hate her, and I really want to hate her. I wish life could be black and white."

"That makes two of us." Red held Elizabeth's eyes for a moment too long. She wouldn't lie to herself. She still had feelings for him, but self-preservation dictated she ignore them.

"You signed up to join her business," he said.

"I'm embarrassed to admit it. It turned out to be a scam."

"If it makes you feel better," Red said. "I have a cousin who got wrapped up in a phone card scheme. The people who bring you in are Rembrandts of persuasion. Only the people at the top of those pyramids make any money."

Elizabeth chuckled darkly. "Don't call it a pyramid."

"They all say that, don't they?"

"Yep. It was stupid of me to wait to do the research after I signed. Do you remember my friend, Cathy?"

Red paused before he answered, not, Elizabeth guessed, because he didn't remember her. But because he had to know that Cathy, as Elizabeth's friend, remembered him and didn't like him.

"How is Cathy?"

"She's very well. She warned me about this business, but I ignored her."

"Why?"

"Because I wanted to believe."

"That's how they get you. Every single time." Red cradled the hot mug between his hands. Still no wedding ring. Had there been anyone after Mary Pat? Or had she broken his heart beyond repair?

"So how much did Louisa take you for?"

"Three thousand."

"Ouch."

"I'm going to get back that money if it kills me," Elizabeth said. "Or get what I can, even if I have to put my inventory on a bunch of tag sale sites and sell it at cost."

"That could work."

"A couple of other women signed up for the business the night I did. I wonder how they're doing."

"We've talked to them. About the same as you."

Elizabeth winced.

"Are they suspects?"

He deflected the question. "They've been helpful. They're angry, but that won't surprise anybody."

"It's a pattern then."

"Right. Louisa dropped the hook, and somebody named Toni Badden up in New Hampshire reeled them in."

"Oh, Toni Badden reeled me in all right. Then she filleted me and served me for breakfast."

"If it makes you feel any better, other people made even bigger investments."

"I thought I got in at Top Tier."

"Well, apparently you can get in at Top Tier as many times as you can be convinced. There's a family Louisa signed up for twenty-five grand."

"That's a lot of clothing."

"Definitely. Another family opened a Lady Lily Wear boutique in their house. They built a room for it, outfitted it with racks, mannequins, the works."

"How'd that work out?"

"They did okay at first, and then the neighborhood became saturated with Lady Lily Wear reps and revenue fell off. Louisa had convinced them to put the freight on a credit card, so they're under a lot of debt."

"And I thought I had it bad. It sounds like they have a motive."

"And an alibi."

"All of them? The whole family."

"Yeah, all five of them were on a plane to New Mexico for a wedding at the time of the murder. They hate her, though. The wife said she hopes Louisa rots in hell."

"Yikes. But the people in the Special Needs community would have her canonized."

"Her records indicate she didn't sign a single person from the advocacy group she founded, nor did she sign any of the parents who joined."

"It would be easier if people could be all bad or all good. That black and white thing again," she said.

"Human nature is endlessly fascinating." Red drained his coffee mug. "That's why I love my job."

Elizabeth poured him another and sat down across from him, noticing for the first time the wear in the arms of the chair in which he sat.

Through lowered eyelids, she stealthily watched Red sip his coffee. Perspiration bloomed above his black brow, the only evidence the lack of air conditioning affected him. In this situation Russell would be tearing off his shirt and moaning, "It's hot as Hades in here!" During their marriage, Elizabeth had observed that, despite all his macho contrivances, he couldn't stand the smallest discomfort. In her mind, this constituted a major weakness. What good would Russell be in an emergency? What if the power went out for days? She'd find him balled up in a beer cooler.

Red broke the silence. "How old are your kids?"

"Trevor is nine. Bailey will be three."

"That's an age gap."

"Yes." She wished he'd turn down the amperage behind those glowy green eyes of his. Why did he have to look at her like that?

It occurred to her she should put out some decent-looking bread or cookies, but trips to the bakery were another casualty of the divorce.

"My brother and I were thirteen months apart." He shifted uncomfortably. "Well. You remember."

"How is Brian?" she asked.

"He relocated to San Francisco with Laurel and their three kids. Do you remember Laurel?"

"Of course." How could Elizabeth forget Laurel? "We saw *Braveheart* with her and Brian before you left for France."

The week before.

Red brushed imaginary lint from his breast pocket.

"That was a fun night." Red looked into Elizabeth's eyes and blinked.

"So, you," she said, avoiding a trip down memory lane. "Do you have any children?"

"My daughter lives with her mother in California."

"So, I don't have to tell you about divorce."

"We were never married. We went to college together. She wanted to be an actress, and I'd pick her up after auditions. You know what ghosting means, right?"

Yeah, I know. You did it to me. "In other words, you stopped taking her calls."

"She stopped taking mine. She had a part-time job in a supermarket. I used to pick her up. One day, she didn't come out. The manager told me she stopped going in. I go to her house, and her father tells me he has a gun, and if I don't do the right thing, he'll use it."

"She was pregnant?"

"I tell him I'll marry her. I don't think twice about it. Her father shouts up for her to come down. She doesn't, so he goes up to get her."

"Don't tell me. She ghosted him, too."

"By the time we find the note she's halfway to California."

"Did she know anyone in California?"

"Yeah, a pen pal. From some Friends Across America project from fourth grade where the school hooked her up with a kid across the country. This was before the Internet. They sent letters back and forth for years. For all I know, she planned to take off all along."

"Did her father ever bring her back?"

"At that point, she was nineteen and of age." Red shook his head. "I'll bet he was sorry he bought the stamps for those letters."

"Do you get to see your daughter?"

"Once, twice a year, tops. She considers her stepfather her real father."

Elizabeth thought she had it bad. Russell might be playing games with child support, but at least he didn't take off with their kid.

"Didn't you have any recourse?"

"I could have taken Cindy to court, but her career took off. She married a director and had access to better lawyers. I was still working my way through college. I didn't want to put the kid through it."

"Would I know Cindy?"

"You might. Cynthia Morgan-Wells? She made the cover of *Vanity Fair* at the beginning of her career. She peaked around 2007. Now she does commercials and plays somebody's mother-in-law on HBO."

"Oh, I know Cynthia Morgan-Wells." Elizabeth pictured a pretty blonde she used to confuse with Reese Witherspoon. Had Cynthia Morgan-Wells been relegated to mother-in-law roles at the tender age of 42? Clearly, she needed better friends in the business than a director husband. She needed Reese Witherspoon.

"It must be tough turning on the TV and seeing your ex-girlfriend," Elizabeth said.

"It's not manly of me to admit it," Red said, running his fingers along the brim of an imaginary cowboy hat. "But I've had therapy."

"Did it help?"

"Absolutely. Now when Cindy shows up in my living room as the decoration in a luxury car commercial, I'm actually happy for her. And Lacy – that's my daughter – and I have been emailing back and forth. She wants to get to know me."

"Oh, that's great news." Elizabeth teared up, seeing the wet in Red's eyes. "I don't know if I could be happy for my ex. Usually, I want to choke him."

Red knuckled the corner of his eye. "If I didn't forgive Cindy, I'd be angry all the time. I didn't want to spend my life like that. You'd be amazed at what you can do when you set your mind to it. Especially if you want to be happy, you have to forgive."

"I'll try to keep that in mind," Elizabeth said. She turned the music back up.

EIGHTEEN

The phone buzzed with a text from Trevor: *Aunt MP is taking me home.*

Elizabeth wasn't in the mood for a showdown, but she'd be damned if she let Mary Pat roll over her.

Not today. I'll see you at the bus stop.

Dots danced on her screen and stopped, indicating Trevor edited his initial response. Finally:

I promised Hughey I would go to his house.

Elizabeth didn't equivocate: *No.*

Trevor didn't either: *I WANT TO GO TO HUGHEY'S!!!!!!!!!!!!!!*

This made no sense. Why would he want to spend time with Hughey after he sold him out to a bunch of bullies? Was she raising some kind of patsy?

AND YOU CAN'T STOP ME. AUNT MP IS PICKING ME UP

In her mind's eye, she saw Trevor stamping his foot. It would get him nowhere.

Take the bus. I am warning you. I will see you at the bus stop.

I AM GOING TO MP'S! SEE YOU LATER!!!!!!!!!!!!!!

Well, at least the kid remembered to use an apostrophe. Elizabeth texted Mary Pat.

Trevor cannot go home with you today. He has an appointment. Please make sure he gets on the bus.

It was not exactly a lie. Trevor did have an appointment, with his mother.

Mary Pat would take her time texting back, even if she saw the message. She thrived on power games. Well, if Elizabeth didn't hear from the witch in a half hour, she'd drive up to school and pick up Trevor herself. In fact, why hadn't she thought of that before? That's exactly what she'd do.

BY ONE-THIRTY, MARY Pat hadn't texted back. Elizabeth called the school secretary and asked her to keep Trevor off the bus. She packed Bailey into the van and waited for him in the pick-up circle in the front of the building. In her rearview, Elizabeth saw Mary Pat pull up two vehicles behind her.

She unstrapped Bailey and walked over to Mary Pat's car.

"Did you get my text?"

"You texted me?"

"Yes."

"What about?" Mary Pat smiled innocently. Elizabeth knew a game when she saw one.

"I'm picking up Trevor today. He has an appointment."

"What kind of appointment?"

"None of your business." ·

"He doesn't have any appointment. I'd put money on it." Mary Pat pulled up her sun glasses far enough to look into Elizabeth's eyes. "Everyone knows you're a cheater, so that makes you a liar too. Hughey was really looking forward to Trevor coming over today."

"I'm sorry, but Hughey is going to be disappointed."

"You might want to think twice before you drive a wedge between the boys, Elizabeth. It's not like Trevor has a lot of friends to fall back on."

"Are you kidding? It was Trevor who defended Hughey, who didn't have any friends. Not the other way around. And Hughey thanked him by throwing him to the wolves."

"You keep telling yourself that. The fact is, your son has a behavior problem. Nobody likes him. We're doing him a favor by giving him a chance to learn how to socialize in a controlled environment."

Elizabeth felt her own eyes shoot out of her head. She didn't believe in violence, had never laid a hand on her children, but right now she ached to pop Mary Pat's artificially inflated lips with her fist.

She turned on her heel. She leaned against her minivan to capture Trevor as soon as he exited the building, preempting an attempt to get into his aunt's vehicle.

"Oh, come on, Mom!" he said when he spotted her.

"In the van, my man. Let's go."

He stamped his foot. "It's not fair."

Elizabeth bent over so that they were at eye level. She spoke softly and clearly. "You want to know what *is* fair? Going right to your room as soon as we get home and spending the night there. How would you like that?"

"I want to go to Dad's."

"Not a possibility. Get in the van."

Trevor relented and got in.

Elizabeth pulled out of the circle. "Please take your feet off the seats."

"My feet aren't on the seats."

"I feel your shoes on my back, Trevor."

Trevor gave the seat a good shove, startling Elizabeth so that she accidentally accelerated.

"Are you trying to get us killed? What is the matter with you?"

"What's the matter with *you*?"

Elizabeth had no experience in trying to control a child who suddenly misbehaved, especially one who had formerly been easygoing from birth. What happened to that child? It seemed Trevor had been replaced by an evil twin.

She pulled into their driveway.

"This house is a dump," Trevor said, swinging his backpack on his way out of the car.

"Excuse me?"

"This driveway. Aunt Mary Pat says it needs blacktop."

"Oh, did she?" Once again, Elizabeth would like to remind Mary Pat that her brother ignored Elizabeth's pleas to improve the house when he lived in it.

"She asked me if I were embarrassed to bring friends here."

Elizabeth felt her blood pressure spike. She wondered how many 42-year-old women died of strokes.

"What did you tell her?"

"I said, why do you think I like to play over at your house?"

"Ah. Well, get into *your* house. We are going to have a talk."

"I can't wait. You're so interesting, Mom."

Inside, Trevor ripped open his backpack. "Here," he said, pulling out a large white envelope with big black letters. "The teacher said you have to look at this. She said it would be good if you bought something."

Elizabeth opened the envelope and found a catalog for a Lady Lily Wear fundraiser one of the other mothers was doing for the PTA. She threw it on the pile on the kitchen table.

"What's this about you calling the girls on the playground names?"

"I didn't call them names."

"Really? Because the principal called me up to school to look me in the eye and tell me you'd used an unacceptable word on the playground."

"What was the word?"

"I think you know, Trevor. It's not a word you heard in this house."

"It's not a bad word, Mom."

"Do you know what it means?"

"It means a girl that does bad things."

"A *girl* who does bad things, Trevor? A *girl*?" The women in the porn magazines Elizabeth discovered under Russell's side of the bed qualified as sluts. Russell, who paid for the magazines, did not. The women who worked in the brothels masquerading as massage parlors on Dickson Avenue qualified as sluts. The men who kept them in business did not. How was Elizabeth to explain misogyny to a nine-year-old?

"I don't know where you heard that word," she said, "but leave it there. And I'll tell you something. I hope I don't find out who taught you that word because I'll have lost all respect for them."

"I don't think they care."

"Then where did you hear it, Trevor? And this nonsense about Bailey not having a father. Why would you say such a mean thing to your little sister?"

Trevor shrugged. "All I know is what I heard Daddy and Aunt Mary Pat talking about. Daddy said – " Trevor deepened his voice – "that kid isn't mine," and Aunt Mary Pat said –he brought his voice up an octave – "Yeah, because her mom's a slut.'"

"Is that right?"

"And Daddy said, 'I wish I'd known what I was getting into when I married her.'"

"How did that make you feel?"

"It didn't make me feel anything."

The clock on the microwave said it was too early for a glass of wine. Elizabeth popped on a 1978 Grateful Dead show on YouTube, still holding a theory that nothing could ever go too wrong while listening to the Dead.

"Listen, Trevor." She tossed the remote on the couch. "You're my baby, and I love you. Nothing is going to change that. I'm sorry you overheard your father and aunt saying those things, but you can't take it out on other children."

"Those girls think they're so cool."

"Were they mean to you, Honey?"

"Look, can I just do my homework? I have a math test tomorrow."

"Sure, but you're going to have to apologize to those girls. Maybe then, they won't get their parents involved. We're going to have a talk with the principal about all this."

"I don't want to apologize."

"I know you don't, but you're going to. And this business about you going to Disney with your father. I'm glad he's taking you, but you cannot rub it in your sister's face. Do you have any idea how cruel that is? How would you like it if the situation were reversed, and she were going and you weren't? Would you like to ride all the way to the airport to watch her get on a plane and leave you behind?"

"I guess not." Trevor put his head on the table. He needed a haircut. He'd just had a haircut! Elizabeth would have to fit another appointment into their schedule: Principal. Haircut. She herself was about a year overdue for a mammogram.

With one foot he peeled his sneaker off the other. "Can I do my homework now?"

"Yes. Do your homework. And, Trevor."

"What?"

"I love you."

TREVOR FINISHED HIS homework and did not argue when his mother asked him to get into his pajamas and brush his teeth. On the contrary, he went up to bed almost gratefully. Elizabeth had peace of mind knowing he wanted to do well on his math test. Hughey, as far as she could tell, cared only about fitting in with other kids. He didn't excel at anything. Elizabeth thanked God that Trevor was her kid, and not Hughey. There was nothing remarkable about him.

She waited until the line of light under Trevor's bedroom door went out. She put Bailey to bed. Then she dialed Russell.

"Two things," she said by way of hello. "The support check has yet to arrive, and your son overheard the conversation between you and your sister in which you called me a slut and let out that you're not Bailey's father."

"Two things," Russell said. "The check is in the mail, and I am not responsible for the fact that I am not your daughter's father. Three things, actually. You are a slut."

"I get it. You're angry, but can you try being discreet? I know I did the wrong thing, but show some respect for your son and his feelings."

"You'd have shown respect for his feelings by not hopping into the sack with another dude."

"Are we going to do this again? I can't change the past any more than you can change the fact that you had a big fat porn stash after you promised you weren't into that kind of thing."

"All men are into that kind of thing. Grow the hell up, Elizabeth. It's reality."

"That's not what you told me."

Russell, who could go from zero to sixty in a second, roared into the phone. "I told you what you wanted to hear!"

Elizabeth wouldn't waste valuable energy by raising her voice. "You're a real prince, Russell. Did anyone ever tell you that?"

"As a matter of fact, I'm seeing someone who's actually reasonable. She actually likes my porn habit and uses it to her advantage."

"Spare me the visual." Elizabeth's stomach turned. "Oh, and that sister of yours is out of control. Rein her in."

"That's Mary Pat. Love her or leave her."

"Hughey ganged up on Trevor at school with a bunch of bullies. Did she tell you about that?"

"I'm sure it was just kid stuff. Trevor and Hughey are best friends."

"Let me fill you in. A bunch of boys ganged up on Trevor at the bus stop. These are the same boys Trevor stood up to when they went after Hughey. So now they're on Trevor, and your weasel nephew not only didn't stand up to them, he joined them in bullying your son. That's the story, Russell."

"You're reading too much into things. As usual. Kids fight. That's what they do."

Elizabeth heard laughter in the background. Feminine laughter, and not Mary Pat's.

"Oh, yeah, Baby," Russell said.

Elizabeth stomach did another back flip. The guy had the audacity to fool around during a discussion about the welfare of his child!

"Clearly, you're busy, Russell," she said calmly, "but your nephew is a weasel. If you want the story, ask the kid whose support check you use for a hockey puck."

Elizabeth stared at Russell's name on her phone and grimaced. Then she hung up.

NINETEEN

Cathy offered to pay for the food and wine for the trunk show, as was the custom for hostesses who stood to gain free product, but Elizabeth already felt like a charity case. First off, Cathy was doing her a favor. Second, she didn't need free clothing. Elizabeth would provide the refreshments, even if she had to add the cost to her mounting debt. She was going to sell off her inventory, right? The proceeds would put a dent in her credit card balance! And what was another hundred bucks for chips and wine when you already owed five grand? All would be right with the world. It would.

Elizabeth dropped Bailey off at school and hit the supermarket. She bundled four bags containing assorted chips, cheeses, and crackers, in addition to three hummus and two guacamole varieties, into the van and headed to the liquor store. How much wine did she need? Better to have too much than too little, and God forbid Elizabeth should look cheap in front of Cathy's well-heeled friends, schlepping in with her usual $10.99 jumbo bottles. Smaller bottles would make a better impression. Elizabeth debated buying French or Italian. No point in being stupid, though; she'd stick with Californian and chalk it up to patriotism.

She spotted a cheerful arrangement in the florist window, of orange gerbera and purple alstromeria, the woman inside told her. It would feel good to thank Cathy with flowers. Besides, Elizabeth wanted to make a good impression on the guests, who, she guessed,

did not live in ranch houses with crumbing driveways. To be successful, she must look successful. She vaguely remembered Louisa saying
something about being able to write off business expenses. Elizabeth
decided the flowers qualified and put another $73.73 on her credit
card.

She stepped out of the florist's bone-chilling air conditioning
back into the blanketing September humidity, buzzing with anxiety.
The haze of moisture on the horizon further disoriented her. A sudden dread knocked her for a wallop. She didn't like selling, she didn't
like standing up in front of a room full of strangers, and she didn't
like making small talk. What had she gotten herself into?

A white Nissan Altima crept along, impeding her slow progress
across the broiling parking lot. She juggled the bouquet and a shopping bag straining under the weight of five rattling bottles of wine.
Under her breath, she muttered an expletive.

The driver's side window went down, and Red Garcia flashed the
result of magnificent orthodontia, his sunglasses lending a movie-
star quality. By comparison, Elizabeth felt like a bag of laundry in her
flip flops and sweat-soaked capri pants.

"Well, hello there," he said, with a look in his eye that hit her like
lightning.

"Heh – hello, Red," she stammered.

"What brings you out this lovely morning?"

She wanted to be coy and say something you'd see in a movie,
like, "*Why, if I didn't know better, I'd think you were following me,
Detective.*" She wouldn't dare, though; she was an abysmal flirt. She
learned her lesson in high school when she tried waving and smiling
at Stephen Grossman and smacked into a beam.

"Party snacks and flowers," she said. "My friend is hosting a show
for me tonight. Fingers crossed I'll unload my inventory."

Red held up crossed fingers.

She blew damp bangs off her face. "Any leads on Louisa?"

"Let's just say things are coming along."

"Don't tease me."

"Loose lips sink ships. Has anything come to you that might be helpful to the investigation?"

"You're suddenly very formal." She couldn't decide if he liked her, or if he was using her. Buttering up insecure suburban mothers could be a tactic from the detective playbook. "I hope you're looking at the pastor. That guy creeps me out."

"Any particular reason? Other than the fact that he's a terminal blowhard?"

"Yeah, he uses the Bible to oppress women."

"That's pretty much all organized religion. It's nothing new."

"It doesn't make it okay."

"The pastor has the markings of a narcissist, but that doesn't make him a killer," he said.

"It doesn't make him not a killer."

"Touché."

"I guess you meet a lot of narcissists in your line of work," she said.

"I've arrested a few, and I've dated a couple."

Elizabeth hoped he meant Mary Pat. She adjusted the packages in her arms. "Well, I'd better get going."

"Listen," Red said. "Where'd you leave your car? Let me drive you over." Before she could object, he hopped out of the Altima and relieved her of flowers and wine bottles.

"The Great Gates of Kiev" by Emerson, Lake and Palmer came from the sound system. Elizabeth buckled up and smiled, remembering Red's affinity for progressive rock, a genre that had its heyday around the time they emerged from their mothers' wombs. Back in high school, she'd secretly learned to play both parts of "Karn Evil 9 First Impression," and some of Red's other ELP favorites on the piano for a birthday surprise. Due to the sudden traumas of their breakup and her father's affair, he never got to hear them.

Red smirked playfully. "I don't think you need the belt. We're only going across the lot."

"I'm obeying the law, Detective."

He looked her in the eyes. "Still such a Girl Scout. I do have a few more questions, actually. I could meet you after your show tonight."

"I'd better not," Elizabeth said, although she did want to see him. "It's a school night." *And I can barely afford to pay the babysitter.*

She directed Red to her van. She turned scarlet as he loaded in the wine and flowers, praying he didn't notice the snack wrappers and the odor of sour milk. All these years later, she still cared what he thought.

THE LADY LILY WEAR package Elizabeth purchased included clothes and accessories but no shelves on which to display them. She could hardly be pulling garments out of cellophane wrap and cardboard boxes; that would impress nobody. *It's not what you do, it's how you do it,* somebody once said. Audrey Hepburn? David Bowie? Madonna? She couldn't remember.

She trolled YouTube for presentation ideas before heading back out to the store for tissue paper and silk ribbon. Luckily, she already owned clear storage boxes in the basement that housed Christmas decorations she could evict. She scrubbed them until they shone, gently swaddled each item of clothing in tissue paper, and laid it into a box like a baby in a manger.

In front of the full-length mirror in her bedroom, she rehearsed her intro:

"Hello, I'm Elizabeth Candew, your Lady Lily rep."
Lady Lily Wear Stylist!

"Hello, I'm Elizabeth Candew, your Lady Lily Wear Stylist. I'm so excited to be here." (Gesture to hostess.) "I want to thank my friend, Cathy Allret—" (Smile. *No, not like that! You look like a stoned walrus.*) "—for inviting me here today."

Elizabeth felt ridiculous. Cathy's friends wouldn't be typical Lady Lily Wear customers. They had careers. They traveled. They could pay for college. Every single woman who showed up at this event would be doing Cathy a favor. It would be the definition of a pity party. Elizabeth would be the object.

"Hi, I'm Elizabeth Candew. You know why you're here. Drink up and buy something. If you hate it, give it to Good Will."

Just wing it. Give 'em enough wine, and they'll be too drunk to care.

She fed the children and gave instructions to the sitter to make sure they were asleep when she got back. This business of coming home to kettle corn all over the floor and having to bribe sugared-up children into bed at midnight would not be happening.

"All right," Chelsea replied, stealing a glance at her constantly lighting up phone. Clearly, she thought she was doing Elizabeth a favor, but she could be counted on to keep the children safe, if not put to bed on time. Most of the other kids in the neighborhood spent too much time preparing for scholarships on ball fields to find time for income-producing opportunities. Elizabeth resigned herself to slim pickings: Fifteen-dollars-an-hour Chelsea or Free Nancy. Elizabeth already felt like a charity case, so Chelsea got the job.

She drove to Cathy's. She wanted to park the van around the corner, in the hope that the guests wouldn't make out it was hers, but she had too much to carry.

Cathy opened one of her three garage doors.

"Pull up in here," she called. "I'll help you carry in the merch."

"Thanks," Elizabeth said, pulling the crappy van up beside Cathy's silver Mercedes. "I've got a ton of it."

"Yeah, but the stuff resists wrinkling, right? Let's push the travel angle."

Elizabeth never went anywhere, so she wouldn't know. "That's what they told me, but they told me lots of things."

Cathy rested a box on her hip and held open the door leading to the basement stairs for Elizabeth. Upstairs, the kitchen was lit up with candles. It glowed like a church.

"Are you planning to say Mass, Cathy?"

"Ha ha. I'm trying to set a mood. We gotta get these people to buy." She set the box on the gleaming granite island and inhaled dramatically. "Serenity is key."

George Michael's "Father Figure" wafted in from the speakers in the family room.

"Nice choice," Elizabeth said.

"I thought about Morrissey, but he might be too depressing."

"Endearingly depressing, but I take your point." Elizabeth peered into the living room and admired the antique furniture Cathy had paid to have refinished in white and turquoise. The effect complemented the historic nature of the house without feeling stuffy. "The house looks beautiful, as always."

Everything gleamed, from the panes on the fingerprint-free white cabinets to the glasses they held. Having a lovely home was easier when you had help.

"I'm nervous," Elizabeth confessed.

"Don't be. These women have a lot of money, but some of them have been where you are. One of them developed a jewelry line that sells in Macy's."

"Have I heard of it?"

"Eva and Evie?"

"Mary Pat wears six of their bracelets on one arm."

"Yeah, that's the genius of it. Stackable jewelry. Why sell one bracelet when you can get people to buy six?"

"My line of easy-care women's wear seems downright cheesy by comparison."

"Don't worry." Cathy poured two glasses of Cabernet. "I didn't invite anybody who's going to look down on you."

Elizabeth took the glass gratefully. "That reminds me. I left some things in the car."

She went out and brought in the snacks, wine, and flowers.

Elizabeth could count on Cathy not to say, "Oh, you shouldn't have," which would only underscore the fact that Elizabeth hovered above the poverty line.

Cathy arranged the flowers in a vase and set them next to a cheese tray. "Has there been any progress in the murder case?"

"No, but I ran into Red coming out of the supermarket."

"Do you ever wonder if he regrets breaking up with you?"

"I wouldn't mind if he did," Elizabeth admitted. "I'd like to mash his heart like a potato."

"You don't have it in you."

Elizabeth sighed. "I know."

"Just be careful not to let him suck you in with his charm. He dumped you for Mary Pat. Keep that in mind."

"Don't worry. Relationships are more trouble than they're worth. I'm not getting into a mess like that again."

"You've had some bad experiences." Cathy sighed into her wine glass. "First, your dad. Then Red. Then Russell. Am I leaving anyone out?"

"Russell was the nail in the coffin of my love life."

"I hope not. I keep hoping you'll meet someone worthwhile. Or worthy. That's the word I'm looking for. *Worthy*."

"Can you keep a secret?"

"You know I can."

"I never told you this, but when I first started dating Russell, I had an uneasy feeling about him. My mother used to tell me, 'Don't make snap judgements. Don't jump to conclusions,' so I ignored it. And anyway, Russell *looked* good on paper: Growing dental practice, came from a seemingly solid and decent family. His younger sister was the most popular girl at school who stole my boyfriend, for Pete's sake. It sounds crazy, but marrying Russell – being accepted by him – seemed like some sort of vindication. Marrying into that family seemed like a ticket to every good thing that ever eluded me." Elizabeth shrugged. "So, I dismissed the uneasy feeling. You do that enough, and you stop trusting yourself."

"I can see how that could happen." Cathy gently rubbed one of the purple petals between her fingers. "But you can learn to trust yourself. It's like building a muscle."

"You think so?"

"I know so. You can do it. Make it a goal."

TWENTY

The doorbell rang, fifteen minutes early. Cathy ran to answer it. Elizabeth brought her wine into the dining room and hastily set up a clothing display. The bell rang again. And again. Clearly, these women couldn't wait to get out of their houses. Elizabeth watched them trail in, laden with bottles of wine. Who brought wine to parties where you were expected to buy things? Either they turn out to be big spenders, or the wine signified the extent of their contribution.

"Tanya, Frances, Charla, and Gloria, come in and meet Elizabeth." Cathy led her guests back into the kitchen, her sleeves billowing like trumpets. "We've been friends since first grade."

"You have friends from first grade?" asked Tanya. "I'm lucky if I remember anyone from grammar school."

"I could never forget Elizabeth." Cathy handed out glasses. "And neither will you."

Elizabeth reddened under the praise, and also the pressure.

"We have something to celebrate tonight," Charla said, holding up a bottle of prosecco.

"Tanya founded an online language program," Cathy said. "It's officially a seven-figure business."

Tanya took a glass, bracelets jingling. She had big brown eyes accented by elaborate false lashes. The fluorescent orange on her fingers and toes picked up a shade in the pattern of her sundress. "Beats the hell out of teaching."

"Really? Teaching seems so straightforward," Elizabeth said. "Is running a business really easier?"

"Infinitely. No parents emailing me on a Sunday asking why Johnny failed the semester when he didn't turn in half his classwork." She ticked off additional points on her brightly colored fingers. "No administrators eyeballing my lesson plans. No senior citizens angling to have me laid off because they're kids are out of the system, and they don't want to pay school taxes. I've divested myself of all bullies."

"I'm glad. That sounds like hell."

"It was. The career advice I give to girls considering careers in traditional education is *don't*. I had colleagues who nearly drowned in the toxic soup and took early retirement. The ones who hung in for full benefits drank or ended up on meds. I got the hell out. My husband thought I was crazy trying to teach Spanish online, but it paid off."

"Seven figures. Holy mackerel, though," Charla said. "I hope you don't mind me harping on the money, Tanya."

"Not in the least. My mother told us that nice people don't talk about money. Well, if you don't talk about it, how do you make it? How do you show other people what's possible?"

"Did your husband support you eventually?" Elizabeth wanted to know. "Or did he just think you were crazy?"

"He accused me of wasting time and money. Then the business took off, and he got mad because I was more successful than him. Now we're divorced." Tanya took a gulp of Chardonnay. "If you're not helping, get out of the way."

Cathy rested her hand on the gleaming shoulder of a long-legged woman in white jeans. Her shiny blonde hair fell to the bottom of a navy halter top.

"Frances is the owner of Eva and Evie downtown."

"I follow your Instagram," Elizabeth said weakly. "Your products are beautiful. Cathy says you're in Macy's."

"We just cracked Nordstrom, too." Frances said it matter-of-factly. She didn't come off a braggart.

"So, how do all of you know each other?" Elizabeth asked.

"We're in a networking group Gloria started," Tanya said, raising her glass towards a fifty-ish woman applying brie to a multigrain cracker. "An old boys' network for women, she calls it."

"You're welcome to join." Gloria had a smattering of freckles on a bumpy nose and the beginnings of gray framing her face. "We like women with an entrepreneurial spirit. What did you do before you started the clothing business, Elizabeth?"

"Stay-at-home mother. Nothing interesting, I'm afraid."

Cathy rolled her eyes. "Before that, Elizabeth. You're out of practice selling yourself."

"I worked in marketing for Bullseye Entertainment. Do you know it?"

"Everybody knows it," Gloria said.

"Elizabeth didn't work in marketing," Cathy said. "She ran the department. Then she married a jerk, had a kid, and gave up her job."

Elizabeth sighed. "The jerk is now an ex who plays games with the child support check."

"Been there, done that. Show us what you're selling," Frances said.

"Make sure you show them how the fabric resists wrinkling," Cathy told her. "Frances, this blouse and skirt will get you off a plane looking as crisp as the moment you left the house."

"I need travel gear, but I'm not into florals," Gloria said. "Does that skirt come in navy?"

"I don't have any navy," Elizabeth said, fearing she'd lost a sale. "Just a lot of prints."

"I'm sure I'll find something I like." Frances dug through Elizabeth's inventory. It occurred to Elizabeth that these women would buy something to help her cause if it killed them.

"Cathy set up a fitting room next to the bathroom," she said weakly. "Try on anything you like."

"No need," Tanya said, flashing her credit card, and holding a green floral skirt Elizabeth guessed would end up in a pile destined for Goodwill.

"Do you have a blouse to go with it? In a small?" Tanya asked.

Elizabeth combed through her inventory and brought out a white button-down with a collar that now struck her as smug and overly pointy. "Would you like to try it on? They run kind of big."

"That won't be necessary," Tanya said, and Elizabeth made her first sale.

After fifteen minutes, Cathy had sold seven hundred dollars' worth of Small and Medium clothing none of these women would ever wear. The Larges didn't sell, though. She'd still have to figure out a way to unload them. She packed the remaining inventory, while the other women huddled around Cathy's kitchen island drinking and laughing.

George Michael kept on singing; Cathy owned every CD the man recorded. "Freedom" came over the speakers. From the dining room, Elizabeth saw Tanya dancing with her wine glass.

"I'm Linda Evangelista," Charla shouted, referencing the video starring the biggest supermodels of the 1990s.

"I get to be Christy!" Gloria said.

Elizabeth looked on, mortified. There was not enough wine in the world to induce her to participate in this scene.

"I'm Naomi!" Cathy declared, surprising her. Elizabeth would think Cathy would sooner imitate Mia Hamm, but she threw back her shoulders. "That means I am the boss!"

"I'm Cindy." Tanya declared. "Get me a bathtub!"

"Stay out of my bathtub," Cathy shouted back.

"Elizabeth, get in here," Gloria called. "We need you to be the Russian one!"

"I don't know who you mean," Elizabeth called back, knowing damn well who she meant.

"Pretend then!" Charla demanded.

Elizabeth crossed the floor listlessly. "Can't we play Scrabble or something?"

"No!" Tanya shouted. "And show us some attitude!"

"Attitude is everything." Gloria stuck a sunflower between her teeth.

"I need a drink." Elizabeth flushed with embarrassment. "I need a lot of drinks, actually."

Blessedly, the song ended. For the second time, George sang "Father Figure."

Tanya sat back on her stool and poured drinks all around. "This song used to make me think unholy things."

"Too bad for you he was gay," Gloria said.

"Too bad for all of us." Frances shook her head. "Man, this song gets me every time."

"This is a song about a stalker." Cathy reached into a bowl and grabbed a fistful of chocolate covered almonds. "What is the matter with you people?"

The other women fairly flopped back onto their stools. Gloria eyed Elizabeth, her eyes massive with wine. "So, how did you do?"

"How did I what?"

"In sales?"

"Well. Really well. Thanks to all of you."

"Can I give you some advice?"

Elizabeth had a strong feeling she didn't have a choice.

"I strongly advise you not to make this your career," Gloria said. "Your next step is to try to sign up one of us to join your business, right?"

"Yes, it's supposed to be. There's a script."

"You didn't seem like you were using any script, honey," Gloria said.

"I didn't want to use it," Elizabeth said. "It didn't feel natural."

"It didn't feel natural because it's not natural. You don't strike me as much of a phony."

"I'm not feeling the passion from you, Elizabeth," Frances agreed. "No offense."

Tanya cut in. "What she means is, is that if you wanna be successful at something, you gotta be feeling it."

"Yeah, so, this isn't the business for you," Frances said. "If you're halfway decent at sales, you need to sell bigger ticket items, like real estate, like Gloria. Or you have to sell something you have a passion for, like me with jewelry or Tanya with language. Trying to find people to throw parties and join your downline is like rolling a boulder up a mountain. You're better off doing something geared to your talents."

Cathy opened another bottle of wine. "Frances is right."

Gloria held out her glass for a refill. "I was exactly where you are five years ago, embroiled in some MLM company I got talked into joining, going to dumb meetings in hotels, trying to convince myself I could make a good living."

"What kind of products?" Elizabeth asked.

"Happy Honey. You hear of it?"

"I'm guessing artisanal honey." Elizabeth rolled her eyes when she said *artisanal.*

"More like artisanal marital aids."

"Are you serious? Artisanal?"

"Not about the artisanal. Yes, about the marital aids. I made it to Regional Manager and hit the wall. There are only so many people on the PTA who want to buy dildos. The real money is in the down-line, but how many people do you know who want to be known as the Sex Toy Lady at church?"

"You did, apparently."

"I told myself it would be a lark. Women would come to my parties and drink. It would be revolutionary talking about sex in a way that's been taboo for females. My feminist mission," Gloria raised her carefully-tended eyebrows, as if about to reveal a secret. "But I ended up with a bunch of drunks looking for a therapist. You'd be absolutely shocked how many women are victims of sex abuse."

"That sounds rough."

"Totally. Also, I got kind of tired of making jokes about edible underwear. When I left the business, I ate my inventory for dessert over the course of several months. The blueberry was fabulous."

Cathy bent across the island tipsily. "Gloria is currently an extremely successful real estate agent."

"I'm not going to lie," Gloria said. "I am."

"She sold my last house in two days," Tanya said.

"And helped me find my new one," Frances added.

Gloria met Elizabeth's eyes. "Are you coachable?"

"I think so."

"Elizabeth is highly coachable," Cathy said.

"Here's my advice. Unload your stock for cost. Take a real estate course. Cathy and I have a proposal for you. Tell her, Cathy."

"Gloria is going to list my house. She'll show you the ropes and split the commission with you. Sound like something you'd be interested in?"

Elizabeth swallowed. "Yes, but split the commission? Are you sure, Gloria?"

"This is what gets me high," Gloria said. "Selling houses and help-ing other women succeed. That's why I started the old boys' network. We all need a hobby."

"Tell her how much money you made last year." Cathy asked.

"Seven hundred thousand dollars."

Elizabeth swallowed. "When can I start?"

TWENTY-ONE

Nancy had been AWOL since the murder. Elizabeth hadn't laid eyes on her since her trunk show. Trevor made it plain that Nancy gave him the creeps, but Elizabeth chalked that up to Trevor not wanting a babysitter. So, what if Nancy was stuck in the early 1970s and kept a lunchbox with rusty tin corners on her mantlepiece? And performed spells to get rid of inconsiderate poodle walkers? It occurred to Elizabeth that Trevor might have sensed about Nancy something she hadn't.

She picked up the phone.

"I've been out of town," Nancy said in answer to Elizabeth's question. "My brother in Des Moines lost his wife, and he needs help getting adjusted. Man couldn't fry an egg."

"Oh, I'm sorry. Had your sister-in-law been sick?"

"Massive heart attack."

"Oh, that's awful, Nancy. That's why I didn't see you at Louisa's wake."

"Talk about awful. I've seen her husband at church, and he looks just shattered."

"Your brother must be shattered."

"Eh, he'll bounce back. Knowing him, he has another lady on deck."

Elizabeth winced. "About Louisa. Do you have any theories?"

"About who did it? A beautiful, classy lady like that couldn't have enemies."

"Some people at the wake indicated she did. They claimed Louisa got people to invest in Lady Lily Wear and left them holding the bag."

"What does that even mean? Holding the bag?"

"She took their money and made promises she didn't keep. She didn't help them build their businesses."

"That wasn't my experience."

"Did she try to bring you into the business?"

"Of course," Nancy said. "She tried to bring in everyone. What's the harm? I have a spine and said no. Why all the questions, Elizabeth?"

"Because I did join her business."

She heard Nancy inhale on the other end. "And now she's not here to help you."

"She talked me into making a bigger investment than I could afford, but that's my fault. She didn't put a gun to my head."

"She was so pretty and put together she inspired people. She seemed to know things the rest of us didn't."

"She had confidence," Elizabeth agreed. "Did you know of her involvement with kids with special needs?"

"I heard good things about that."

"Anyway, so I'm holding a bag. That's why all the questions. I invested a lot of money. I'm trying to make sense of it all."

"I'm so sorry I dragged you into this."

"You didn't. You've been a wonderful friend to me and the kids."

"Can you get your money back?"

"No, the company is stonewalling me. Louisa's upline isn't returning my calls."

"That's despicable." Nancy paused. "Let me get my book. I'll bet I can find a spell to remedy *that* situation."

"No, really. Don't. I'm selling my inventory and getting out. I wondered if you'd like some of it at cost."

"Oh, I'm sure I'd love to, but I can pay full price."

"Cost is good. I insist, Nancy."

"I could use a couple of skirts. Do you know my brother had the nerve to say I looked dated? Do you think that's true? If you have any of those gauzy scarves in the jewel tones, I'll take a couple of those too."

Elizabeth had at least twenty. "I'll bring them over."

"Louisa did my colors, and I'm a Winter. I'll take anything navy, red, scarlet, emerald."

Elizabeth pictured Nancy sitting at her Formica kitchen table in one of the fruit-themed blouses she favored. The jewel tones would mark a departure.

"Definitely, Nancy. I'll bet you'd look great in all kinds of solid colors."

"Pastels wash me out, so you can keep those. Listen, about Louisa. Do the police have any leads?"

"They're looking at the usual suspects, I'm sure." What if Nancy's trip to Des Moines turned out to be fiction? What if she didn't have a dead sister-in-law? What if she'd repeatedly stabbed Louisa in her kitchen before hopping a plane to a Partridge Family fan club convention?

"My understanding is," Elizabeth said, "the spouse is always a suspect, and the detectives must be looking at any Lady Lily Wear reps Louisa screwed over."

"Well, if anybody asks about you, I'll assure them they're running down the wrong road."

"Thank you, Nancy."

"Did they question you?"

"Yes. I told them everything I knew. I told them I'd called Toni – that's the upline I mentioned – and she hadn't called me back. It might help them establish some sort of pattern."

"I can't believe she didn't call you back." Nancy huffed into the phone. "That's not very professional."

"She didn't call me back twice."

A light went on in Elizabeth's head. Maybe Toni didn't call back because she couldn't.

ELIZABETH TYPED "TONI Badden, dead, New Hampshire" in the search engine. *Bingo!* She got multiple hits, the first from the *Nashua Record*:

> A Nashua woman was found dead in her driveway Sunday morning after suffering multiple gunshot wounds. Police report that John Santini, 38, discovered the body of his neighbor, Antonia B. Badden, 52, mother of three, while jogging. Police ask that parties with any information pertaining to this matter contact the department.

TWENTY-TWO

Elizabeth called Red Garcia to tell him about Toni Badden.

"I appreciate the information," he said. "We heard."

Elizabeth poured water over her teabag, feeling betrayed. "When? You didn't mention it," she said with more annoyance than she'd intended.

"Look, this is a murder investigation. We kept it under the rug to see if anything else crawled out."

"Give it to me straight, Red." *Unlike the time you left for France as my boyfriend and returned to the States as Mary Pat's.* "Am I a suspect? Don't play with me."

"Everybody's a suspect, Elizabeth. Do I think you did it? No, I do not. You don't have it in you."

"People change, Red. I might have it in me."

"You haven't changed," he said quietly. "You haven't changed at all."

Elizabeth cleared her throat. "Isn't it strange that the killer used a gun on Toni and a knife on Louisa?"

"It might be, if the killer turns out to be the same person."

"I hope it is the same person. Otherwise we've got two killers on the loose." Elizabeth winced at her use of the word *we've* as soon as it left her mouth.

"We might."

"I don't think so. I don't think you do either. But it's weird he used two different weapons."

"Maybe."

"I'm thinking the killer knew Louisa well, and Toni not so well. He had access to the inside of Louisa's house but not Toni's. Or maybe he had access to both but wanted it to look like the work of two killers."

"I've already said more than I should," Red said. "You've heard about loose lips."

"Look, I'm not some bored housewife angling for gossip. I mean to find out who killed these people. I'm invested, you know what I'm saying? It's not just about the money."

"Are you considering a job in law enforcement?"

"Don't patronize me."

"I'm sorry. It was a joke."

"That joke isn't funny anymore." Elizabeth wound the teabag around her spoon. "Tell me something, Red. Do you think I have good instincts?"

"About this case?"

"About anything."

"Yeah, I'd say you have good instincts."

"Thanks. Good to know." Elizabeth disconnected.

THE TEA TASTED BITTER. Elizabeth checked the expiration date on the box, which indicated it should still be okay. Maybe the murder investigation put the bad taste in her mouth. It didn't thrill her one bit that Red had left her out of the loop on Toni Badden. In her frustration, she'd forgotten to mention Nancy's excuse for being out of town the time of Louisa's wake.

Elizabeth jotted some ideas on the back of the envelope containing her overdue electricity bill.

SUSPECTS
Pastor
Tom Davenport
Nancy
Me

Elizabeth wanted the pastor to be the killer. She longed for it. She hoped it wouldn't be the widower, Dave Davenport. His little girl would need an advocate. She didn't want Nancy to be guilty, either. Did her story check out? Elizabeth typed "Spinner death notice Des Moines" into a search engine, feeling like a skunk. She came up with zero results.

Nancy lied.

Elizabeth let that sink in for a minute. Nancy, who had been so kind to her and her children, could be a killer!

She rubbed her face in her hands. *No, I don't believe it.*

And for all she knew Red had been playing with Elizabeth when he said he didn't believe she – Elizabeth—had it in her to kill somebody. Maybe he wanted her to let her guard down.

She sipped the bitter tea, her mind spiraling. What if she, Elizabeth, was indeed a suspect in Louisa's murder? And Toni's? She couldn't afford to pay her divorce lawyer, let alone a defense attorney! And what if she went to prison? Russell would get full custody of Trevor, damning the kid to life as a misogynist, flogged by the miserable prognostications of Mary Pat. And Bailey! She'd end up in foster care, bouncing around from family to family. She'd end up on drugs living on a bench!

Elizabeth poured the tea into the sink. She had motive to kill both Louisa and Toni, probably more motive than anyone. And Red knew it. So did Michaels, that windbag of a partner of his. But if Elizabeth had motive, so did all the others Louisa and Toni suckered. Red said he'd tracked them down, but what if he missed somebody?

So far, he didn't seem to have any strong leads. Not that he let on, anyway.

Elizabeth picked up the phone.

"It's me again," she said. "The other guests who came to the trunk show at Nancy's house. Did you talk to them?"

"I told you we did," Red answered. "Alibis checked out."

"Okay, well, it kills me to say this, but you might want to look at Nancy. She claimed to have been in Des Moines at the time of the murder, but her alibi didn't check out."

"Okay, Detective." Red chuckled.

"It's not funny. I've told you that." *What didn't he get?*

"You're right. I am sorry." He went quiet for a second. "I'm not making fun of you. I just – "

"Look, *I* just want to help you. The least you could do is wait to laugh your head off until after we hang up. This is really bothering me about Nancy. I don't want to believe she could have done it. I don't believe she could have, but I have to be sure."

"I'll look into Nancy. Again, I'm sorry. I mean it, Elizabeth."

"Okay. I'm still rooting for the pastor."

"Listen, if it makes you feel any better, he gave us an alibi which did not check out."

Elizabeth emitted a small squeal of happiness. "You know, Red, I could be enlisted to take a closer look at him."

He laughed again, good naturedly. "I don't think so. And I've said way too much."

"No, listen to me. I can go in and attend services. My friend, Nancy, belongs to his fake church. I won't raise any suspicions."

"I appreciate the offer, Elizabeth, but we're on top of it."

"A lot of women at that wake carried on like that creep was the Second Coming."

"And that ties into Louisa's murder, how exactly?"

"I don't know, but I'd like to take a look."

"It's not a good idea."

"It's a great idea. Is there a law against it?"

Red paused. "You're free to join any church you want."

Elizabeth debated whether she should ask again if she were a suspect. She had already lost enough sleep over bills and Trevor's problems at school.

"I don't mean to be a pest, but are you telling me the truth that I'm not a suspect?"

"Oh, come on, Elizabeth."

"But I have more of a motive than anybody."

"You have a motive, yes. But you didn't arrive at Louisa's residence until after the murder."

"Maybe I had been there earlier, though. Maybe I went back there to make myself look innocent, like I was on my way to meet Louisa for our appointment."

"You couldn't have done that."

"And why not?" A gleeful revelation dawned upon her. "Right, of course. There were security cameras. If I'd been there earlier, you'd know it."

"The security cameras were non-operational."

"Are you serious? You're saying someone tampered with them?"

"Uh, no actually. It turns out the high-end builder installed the cheapest system on the market. Those cameras hadn't been working for months."

"Wow."

"Yeah, wow."

"So, how are you so sure I didn't murder Louisa?"

"The security guard."

Elizabeth carried the phone into her bedroom and changed her shoes. "But he wasn't there when I arrived at the development."

"Elizabeth, he wasn't there because he had been called away on an emergency. He was there *until* the emergency. If you'd driven over there to kill Louisa, he'd have seen you."

Elizabeth fell back onto her bed, her eyes spilling tears of relief. "Right. Of course."

"Do you feel better now?"

"I feel stupid and paranoid. Of course the guard would have seen me."

"You're under a lot of stress."

"I'd better get it together." Elizabeth wiped her face with the back of her hand. "But the pastor, then. If he'd gone to see Louisa, the guard would have seen him."

"All I'm saying is that he didn't see *you*. I have to get back to work."

"Oh, come on, Red!"

"Come on nothing." He said it playfully. Was he flirting with her?

Elizabeth's stomach flipped in response, a bad sign.

"All right then, Detective," she said with all the coolness she could manage. "Thank you for your time."

A LIGHTBULB WENT OFF in Elizabeth's brain. She drove over to Louisa's development. If none of the staff reported the non-functioning the cameras, they probably slacked off elsewhere. Elizabeth circled the perimeter of the so-called exclusive community, past the hissing of unseen sprinklers and the row of tall hedges lining a fence meant to keep outsiders out.

The minivan crept along, towards the back of one of the club-houses and continued past the tennis court. She spotted what she hoped to find: a break in the fence and a hole in the hedge, both large enough to accommodate a fat pastor without causing damage to his madras shorts.

She pulled away, hit with the sorry realization that if the pastor could breech the development, so could Nancy. So could *Elizabeth*. Did Red know about the hole in the fence? Probably, but now she did, too.

TWENTY-THREE

Nancy came to the door in the Lady Lily Wear jumpsuit she wore to her trunk show, music loud enough to inflict acoustic trauma. Elizabeth had her hands full with a box of scarves. She couldn't cover her ears.

"Partridge Family?"

Nancy frowned, a number eleven etched between her eyes. "The Monkees."

Elizabeth shrugged. "Also before my time."

"You don't know what you're missing. All these golden oldies are on the classic sitcom station. It's good wholesome entertainment for the whole family. You and Trevvie can bond over it."

Had Nancy used the expression *good wholesome entertainment*? "It wouldn't hurt for Trevor and me to bond over something. I might give it a try."

"He is a musician, after all."

"Yes, he is." Elizabeth's stomach dropped, remembering she was late paying the piano teacher. She plopped the box on Nancy's kitchen table. "Ready to go shopping?"

"Let me put on some coffee." Nancy ran the pot under the tap and sang along to the music. Elizabeth had planned a quick in-and-out visit. Clearly, she had been optimistic.

"Cheer up, Sleepy Jean!" Nancy pirouetted over to the coffee maker. "Life was so much simpler in the sixties and seventies."

"Yeah, if you're into a war nobody wanted, assassinations, and the Manson murders."

"So, you know some things."

"Only because I studied fifth grade history."

"Well, your curriculum fell short if it didn't cover the Monkees and the Partridges. Charles Manson? Who wants to remember that jerk?"

Elizabeth pulled a mirror from the box of clothes and held an emerald scarf against Nancy's face. "Jewel tones really do flatter you."

"I'll take that one. What else you got?"

"This fuchsia?"

"Bright is good. Let me see." Nancy took in her reflection and nodded. "I'll take it. What else?"

"Skirts? Blouses? Jumpsuits?"

Nancy bought six large skirts without trying them on. Elizabeth knew a favor when she saw one. *Again!*

"You could put the rest on Craigslist," Nancy suggested.

"Or just give them away," Elizabeth answered, sensing an opportunity to get into Nancy's church. "Does anybody in your congregation need clothing? Is there an outreach program?"

"We don't have an outreach program. As yet." Nancy's back stiffened. "Um, we're a new church. I'm sure that's on the pastor's list of projects. Hey, if you join, it's something you could spearhead. What do you think?"

Elizabeth folded the rejected garments back into the box. "I can't promise, but I'd be willing to attend a service to get a feel for the place."

Nancy bounced on her toes. "How's this Sunday? Pastor has a prophet coming up from Texas."

"A prophet? Like Daniel?" This Elizabeth had to see.

"The last time he came, he prophesied the Lord had big plans for me."

"Does he prophesy over everybody, or is it kind of a lottery system?"

"He tries to get everybody. He stays for hours."

Hours? Good thing Russell had Trevor this weekend. Bailey could serve as the excuse to exit the second the scene became tiresome. "What time should I be there?"

"If we go together, I can introduce you around. Except, would you mind driving? I don't have a car seat for the wee one."

"What time, then?"

"Service starts at ten, but we need to be there by nine if we want parking."

"We have to get there an hour early?" Elizabeth didn't mean to grimace.

"It'll be worth it," Nancy reassured her. "Trust me."

TWENTY-FOUR

A classmate's mother invited Bailey over for a playdate at the last minute, which freed Elizabeth to scope out the church without distraction. It also canceled her excuse to pull out of there early.

Nancy's place of worship squatted between a bank and a nail salon in a newly built strip mall. The strip mall replaced the Hewitt Family Farm, established 1710. Once upon a time, Elizabeth and Russell took Trevor there every year to pick pumpkins and pose for Christmas cards. After the farm sold, Elizabeth and hundreds of others petitioned the town to buy it and designate it as open space. That didn't happen.

Nancy's church didn't look like a church to Elizabeth, who grew up attending a house of worship with stained glass and a pipe organ. But, since she'd largely avoided it over the past two decades, she didn't have the right to an opinion.

She pulled the minivan into the last open spot, in front of Angelina's Pizza on the far end of the lot. The blacktop glistened under the hot September sun.

"As long as we're out of here by noon, you won't get towed," Nancy said, adjusting a violet Lady Lily Wear scarf around the strawberry turtleneck. She'd set it off with a pair of dangly strawberry earrings.

"We'll be out by then," Elizabeth said. "It's not even nine."

"Oh, but the pastor is such a wonderful preacher you won't want to leave. He's like a drug." Nancy wore an expression Elizabeth doubted was inspired by anything holy.

"What happens at noon that we have to be out of here?"

"The pizza place opens, and the owner doesn't want our flock taking up all the parking spots. She had words with the pastor," she huffed. "Some woman from *Queens*."

Elizabeth, whose mother grew up in Queens, chose not to react to the insinuation. Right now, she was more interested in the pastor's response to a woman who dared speak up to him.

"How'd he take that?"

"He said she's a devil on high heels, and I don't disagree. You should have heard the profanities coming out of that mouth."

Elizabeth's mother had forbidden profanity. Calling someone *stupid* got you sent to your room. "Sounds unpleasant," she said.

"That's an understatement, but Pastor held his own." Nancy looked into Elizabeth's eyes meaningfully. "He has God on his side. It served her right a week later when some punk came along and shot a hole through her window."

"Shot? As in a gunshot?"

"Yep. Some of the congregants stayed away from church for a number of weeks, fearing we could be next. You never know with these mass shootings going around. But everything's back to status quo."

"And what about the pizza lady? Was her business affected?"

"I hear it's mostly deliveries these days. The sit-down diners have dropped off, but hey, that's what you get when you mess with the Lord, right?"

"She didn't mess with the Lord, Nancy. She messed with the pastor."

Nancy shrugged. Apparently, she hadn't considered the possibility the pastor shot out the pizza lady's window. Elizabeth yearned to sneak off and alert Red to this morsel, but she'd better see what else she could find out inside this so-called church.

Anyway, Red could wait.

A SHARP ODOR EMANATED from an indoor-outdoor carpet the color of a mini golf course. Congregants milled around a table covered with donut boxes and a coffee urn.

Elizabeth noted that somewhere between the car and the church entrance, Nancy had reapplied her frosted pink lipstick. "Get yourself some coffee," she said. "It's not great, but it's free."

Nancy bolted across the small room and lost her footing alongside a drum kit, smashing into a cymbal. She mounted a small step to greet Pastor Jim, who ostentatiously thumbed through a Bible from behind the podium. Nancy giggled into his ear. The pastor responded by hugging Nancy at arms' length with a smile that didn't quite meet his eyes.

A sixty-something woman in a familiar top with a boatneck slipped up next to Elizabeth at the coffee urn. "Would you mind passing the sugar packets?"

"Sure," Elizabeth said. "Pretty blouse. Lady Lily Wear, right?"

The woman rolled her dartlike eyes. "I should've bought Powerball tickets with all the money I poured into that scam. Now I'm stuck with a bunch of clothes nobody wants."

"Oh, you got caught up in it, too," This woman couldn't be a recruit of Louisa, who would have steered her away from this particular blouse. It made her neck look like a stump.

"And now," she said, stirring a lump of powdered creamer into her coffee, "My husband's forbidden me to buy another piece of clothing until 2036, so I'm stuck with the ones that fit. The rest went to my daughter-in-law. Did you get suckered too?"

"That's one way to describe it," Elizabeth said. "What went wrong with your business?"

"I couldn't give the stuff away. Couldn't get a woman to sign up to host a," she put her fingers in air quotes, "*trunk show* if my life depended on it. Every other woman in this church is a Lady Lily Wear Stylist and has the same problem. I'll bet you do too."

"I managed one show," Elizabeth said. "A friend hosted it for me out of pity."

"And did you sign anyone up?" The woman sipped her coffee. "Of course not. Are you one of Louisa's, too?"

"As a matter of fact." Elizabeth held out her hand and introduced herself.

"I knew I hadn't seen you before. I'm Penny Jissop." The woman chuckled darkly. "Nobody in this church shakes hands. It's all hug hug hug and a ton of gossip. Watch your back."

Over Penny's shoulder, Elizabeth spotted the sisters she met at the wake. She prayed they wouldn't spot her. "It's my first time here. I'm a friend of Nancy Spinner."

"The Nancy with the short curly hair?" Penny raised an eyebrow.

"Yes, she's a good friend," Elizabeth said, watching her neighbor take a stack of pamphlets from the pastor and press them on congregants. "I got the Lady Lily Wear bug at a show she hosted."

Penny's tiny eyes tracked Nancy's movements around the room. "She makes a good cheesecake."

"I've never had it." Elizabeth thought back to the pigs in blankets Nancy served. "Maybe our businesses would have a chance if poor Louisa were still alive."

"Oh, baloney. She set us up." Penny sipped her coffee, but kept her eyes trained on Nancy. "Look, I'm sorry she got what she got. She didn't deserve it. I mean, if anybody did, she did, but nobody does, so she didn't. If you know what I mean."

"I think I know what you're getting at." *Although it doesn't especially strike me as Christian.*

Dave Davenport walked through the door holding Quincy's hand.

"What's he doing here? He never comes," Penny said. "But I feel sorry for him. And those kids. Say what you want about Louisa, but she took good care of her kids."

"I didn't know them well."

"This kid has some sort of retardation."

Elizabeth debated the wisdom of advising this woman that the word *retardation* didn't fly anymore. Anyway, she needed information. "I met the older daughter."

"Oh, that hot shot. Her mother was always bragging how she goes to a private university in Rhode Island."

"Brown?"

"Maybe."

"I hope my son gets into a school like that."

"Good luck paying for it. Do you know those private schools can cost upwards of seventy grand a year?"

"Yes."

"I mean, I can understand why you'd spend that kind of money on a son, but a daughter is another story."

"I don't know what you mean." Elizabeth had heard enough. She wanted to get away from this person.

"God's plan is for us to be wives and mothers," Penny said, oblivious to Elizabeth's eyes dancing feverishly over her shoulder. You don't need a fancy degree for that."

A screech came out of the sound system, startling the congregation. A quiet came over the room.

"Are you trying to scare the hell out of us, Joel?" the pastor barked from the back.

A balding guy in his early thirties scrambled to adjust a microphone. "Sorry, Pastor."

"Sheesh, Joel-y Boy. You should've warned us we'd need a second pair of underwear."

The poor guy ran back behind a music stand, fiddling with the reed in his clarinet and blushing wildly. Elizabeth's desire for Pastor Jim to be Louisa's murderer bloomed with an ungodly fervor.

"Although the pastor's wife didn't seem to get that memo," Penny was saying.

"I'm sorry." Elizabeth had lost the thread altogether. "You said something about the pastor's wife?"

Penny waved her arm dramatically in the direction of a pretty brown-haired woman in a sapphire Lady Lily Wear *Contessa* dress that drew attention to her dainty ankles. The older couple in matching polo shirts shook her hand listlessly and shuffled off. The pastor's wife greeted the next group who came along, but they nodded perfunctorily before elbowing their way to seats nearest the podium. Elizabeth guessed her age at 35, which made her a good fifteen years younger than Pastor Jim.

"She's a university professor." Penny made a point of dragging out every syllable in *university* to further emphasize her disdain of women in higher education.

Elizabeth had a mental picture of pastors' wives who wore dirndl skirts and cardigans. "She's very attractive."

Penny rolled her eyes. "She teaches math."

"At the university level?" Elizabeth let out a low whistle. "I barely squeaked through three-term algebra."

"Math isn't getting anybody into heaven, and she needs to button her lip. Last weekend, she asked us to pray for pastors' wives because they have a – let me see if I remember the exact quote – *particularly* difficult path to walk. She's always feeling sorry for herself."

Elizabeth watched the pastor's wife, who appeared distracted but trying her best to be friendly. "Does she have a name?"

"Rosalita. She married Pastor right out of college, apparently. Letting her become a doctor," Penny made air quotes around *doctor*, "was his first mistake."

ELIZABETH HAD A HUNCH Rosalita's work paid more than her husband's, but if she mentioned it, Penny's head would pop off. How an attractive, accomplished woman like Rosalita ended up with the likes of Pastor Jim Dunfore qualified as the Eighth Wonder of the World. Right now, he had his meaty paw clamped on the shoulder of a teenage boy. The boy's mother stared into his eyes with a terrifying adoration.

"Pastor met Rosalita," Penny lowered her voice to a whisper. "At a Grateful Dead concert."

"The pastor is a Dead Head?" Maybe Elizabeth had misjudged him. Now she had something to start a conversation with him about. She herself had never seen The Dead perform live. Jerry Garcia died the week after she bought tickets to her first show.

Penny sucked her teeth. "The pastor is no such thing as a Dead Head. He infiltrated rock concerts to minister to the fallen."

Elizabeth tried to picture a younger pastor, a predator who seduced young women between scripture readings and hits of acid.

"He's a wonderful man." Penny beamed.

"He's something," Elizabeth said. "That's for sure."

TWENTY-FIVE

The pastor opened the service by reading Matthew 16:26. After he finished, the congregation trailed up to the podium and dropped little papers into a metal bowl.

"I'm guessing those are prayer requests." Elizabeth said.

"I've been so busy yakking I forgot to write mine." Penny looked regretfully into her empty cup. "Shoot."

"God in heaven, despise not our petitions but answer them according to your promises," the pastor intoned. He tapped his thigh three times, as if calling a dog. Rosalita Dunfore approached the podium and set the bowl's contents afire with a candle.

The congregation whooped its approval. The drummer smashed his symbol. Joel-y Boy blew dolefully into his clarinet while a lavishly tattooed young man rhythmically slapped the face of an acoustic guitar and shouted PRAISE! GOD! Somebody grabbed Elizabeth's hand and pulled her into the circle of worshipers, who joined in exclaiming PRAISE! GOD! Black smoke ascended menacingly to the white foam ceiling.

Jim held up a hand, commanding silence. Nancy broke out of the circle, inched closer to him, and beamed.

"Come, Prophet, come!" intoned Pastor Jim. "Spread your good news, Paul."

The prophet darted to the podium, high-fiving congregants along the way. He hopped onto the stage wearing Air Jordans like the ones Trevor begged Elizabeth to buy, and which Russell ultimately did. She disliked the prophet immediately.

"I'll start off with some generalities before I address you individually." Paul stuck his hands in the pockets of his Levis. The hems swam about the tops of his sneakers. "Your senator here in Stonesbury – what's his name? Anderson? – will face an assassination attempt or be assassinated."

"One up for God," shouted one of the congregants. "That guy's a baby killer!"

The prophet's bald head gleamed under the recessed lighting. "That actress – that bold one who God humbled when she tripped in her high heels at the award ceremony." He snapped his fingers.

A petite teenage girl in torn jeans shouted, "Lorna Siciliano!"

Snickers ensued. Elizabeth noticed they came mostly from women.

"Right, Lorna Sic—*Sic*—oh, you know what I mean," the prophet agreed. "Miss Lorna will continue to make movies that offend our Lord to her very grave peril."

"This guy's like the *National Enquirer* of prophets," Elizabeth cracked.

A male congregant threw her a hot glare over his coffee cup, but she didn't care. She would include him in the clever report she mentally formulated to give Red.

Paul loped to another side of the room and rested his palm on a forehead. "Now, as for you, young man, the devil has you by the tail. You are enslaved by pornography. You must break this stronghold or be condemned."

Elizabeth stood on her toes to see the reaction of the recipient. She couldn't. But she saw his mother, the woman who'd beheld Pastor Jim with adoration at the beginning of the service, begin to cry.

"My son does not use pornography," she said, sounding as though she'd been strangled.

The prophet cleared his throat. "I know it hurts a mother's heart to learn her son has given into the temptations of the flesh, but men are weak and women treacherous. Pray for your son, Mom, that he be delivered."

The boy and his mother shuffled, round-shouldered, to the back of the room. Other women trailed fingers along the mother's arm consolingly as she passed.

The prophet turned to a girl barely out of her teens, her lovely figure hidden under a beige skirt that reached her ankles. "I know you're worried about the clock ticking, as ladies are wont to do, Dear, but you will marry and please God with many children."

The trim tall man at her side wore a crew cut and khakis. He clamped his arms around her shoulders, and she beamed.

The prophet shook his head. "Not this guy, though. He isn't the one. The man you marry will be older and well-established in his profession. He will be a godly man."

"Yeah, a bald fraud named Paul," Elizabeth muttered.

"Jackson *is* a godly man!" the girl protested. "You don't know anything!"

The prophet shrugged and moved along. The young woman fled the building. Jackson ran out after her.

Paul approached Elizabeth.

"Let me ask you, Sister, are you a believer?"

"You're the prophet," Elizabeth answered. "You tell me."

If she'd embarrassed him, he didn't show it. He merely turned and trotted back to the podium. Pastor Jim seized him by the shoulder.

"Okey dokey, Family, let's give Prophet Pauly a Texas-sized round of applause. Let's dig into our pockets and show him how much we appreciate him making the long trip from the Lonestar State." Jim closed his eyes for emphasis. "Remember when you bless the prophet with your good, the Lord will amply bless you with his."

Elizabeth tossed a dollar into the basket and checked the time on her phone. She had to get out of there before the pizza place opened in twenty-five minutes, or she'd get towed. She waved to get Nancy's attention, but Nancy remained at the pastor's elbow, glassy-eyed.

Elizabeth spotted Rosalita pouring a cup of coffee. She accidentally knocked it over, spilling it all over the plastic tablecloth and the floor. Elizabeth seized the opportunity, balling up a bunch of napkins to help clean the mess.

"Oh, thank you. You don't have to." Rosalita threw her hands to her head. "Sometimes I'm so clumsy."

Rosalita was even prettier up close, with an almost perfect oval face and gray eyes. No wonder Pastor Jim had tried to "save" her.

Elizabeth tossed the wet napkins into the bin. "I'm Elizabeth Candew. I'm new."

"Welcome to our little church." Rosalita's eyes darted towards her husband. She smoothed her hands on her skirt, nervously, Elizabeth thought. "Hats off. I caught that shot you took at the prophet. I take it you don't think much of our prophet."

"I don't, but my neighbor, Nancy over there, convinced me to check him out."

"Nancy Spinner?" Rosalita pressed her lips together tightly. "How do you know Nancy?"

"She helped me out when I was going through my divorce."

"She's a helper all right." Rosalita glanced back to watch Nancy hand out a pile of pamphlets which said, *I'M GOING TO BE SAVED, AND IT FEELS SO GOOD!* "Nancy just loves to help."

"That's a good thing, right? At my church – well, I haven't been inside the place in ages – they struggled getting volunteers."

"What church is that?"

"St. Stephens."

"You're a Catholic."

"I mean, yeah. I had my children baptized, but we're busy with activities. We don't go to Mass."

"I used to be a Catholic," Rosalita said wistfully. She glanced at her husband, who appeared to be giving advice to the mother of the son of the prophesied porn addiction.

"Sometimes I miss it, too," Elizabeth said, hoping to build rapport. "I liked the rhythm of the Mass, the smell of incense. The hymns are in my blood, you know what I mean?"

"Oh, yeah. 'Joyful, Joyful, We Adore You.'" Rosalita smiled. "'How Great Thou Art.' Sometimes I find myself singing them in the shower. Quietly, of course."

Elizabeth took a beat. Should she say it? "Catholicism may be a male-dominated institution, but at least nobody isn't hitting you over the head with Ephesians 5 every ten minutes."

Rosalita sighed appreciatively. "Where would these guys be without Ephesians 5? My husband founded this church on Ephesians 5. I'm glad I met you. I may be the pastor's wife, but I feel a little out of step. It's nice to have someone normal to talk to."

Elizabeth laughed. "I don't know if I qualify as normal. My ex certainly doesn't think so."

Rosalita laughed, too. "Well, if you're abnormal, you're my kind of abnormal. I have to warn you, though, if you're looking for a no-judgment zone, this church is the wrong place. These people gossip like it's their job, my husband included."

"I had a feeling." At least the priest who baptized Bailey hadn't judged Elizabeth for the circumstances surrounding the child's conception. It also occurred to her she'd need a new friend now that Cathy was moving. Maybe Rosalita would fit the bill.

"Is it true you met your husband at a Dead show?"

"Yes." The pastor's wife smiled into her coffee. "I love the Dead."

"I have some shows on CD. I could burn a couple for you."

"Seriously? Thank you!" Rosalita lowered her voice to a whisper. "I'll upload them to my phone and listen to them in the car. Jim won't have it at home."

"Jim sounds like a lot of work."

Rosalita didn't seem offended. Elizabeth figured she had nothing to lose.

"Can I meet you for a drink one of these days?"

"Not allowed, either, but yes. Weeknights are better. Name the place."

Elizabeth would need someone to watch the kids, but she'd figure it out. "How's Murphy's on Tuesday? Six o'clock?"

TWENTY-SIX

The air held a golden quality. Elizabeth headed towards the preschool, grateful for the smell of fallen leaves. Bailey emerged from the classroom with a sheet of paper and the letters *Aa* she'd practiced writing in its wide spaces. For a not-quite-three-year-old, she made a good start. The glittery paper star pinned to her sweater had *SUPER WRITER* written on it.

"You're a very bright person," Elizabeth told her.

"Thank you. I want to go on the swing, Mommy."

Elizabeth checked the time on her phone. "What's the magic word?"

"Please."

Elizabeth strapped Bailey into a swing and pushed. Her phone rang. She'd promised herself not to be a parent who spent more time on a device than making eye contact with her child, but when she saw the caller's name she couldn't resist. She could hate herself later.

She let it ring some more. No point in looking eager.

"So, I went to that church," she said when she answered.

"Of course you did." Red sighed, but she got a feeling he didn't wholly disapprove.

"It's a weird place," she said. "They eat donuts during the service."

"Real donuts or supermarket donuts?"

"I can't say. I stuck with coffee. One thing I do know: They all hate the pastor's wife."

"Most pastors are charismatic. Women love them. They always hate the wife."

"Yeah, well, I find him repellant."

"We've established that."

"My neighbor Nancy was all over him."

"You think there's anything going on there?"

"Not on his end. She hugged him, but his body language made it clear he's not into it. I did talk to his wife, though."

"Good going," he said. Elizabeth pictured Red rubbing his hands together.

"Story in a nutshell: Her name is Rosalita. She married the wrong guy when she was too young to know better. Met him at a Dead show."

"Too young or too high?"

"Too young, definitely. We didn't get far enough to discuss drug use. Her husband posed as a Deadhead on the pretense of saving people, but I'm guessing he limited the ministry to attractive women in her age group."

"The pastor's a Deadhead?"

"The wife is. The pastor is not. She's no longer allowed to listen to them."

"Not *allowed*?"

"I don't get it either. She's a professor. She has to be making more money than he does at that fake church. What does she need him for?"

"Humans are highly complicated, Elizabeth. Cops will tell you stories about trying to break up a domestic situation, and the wife ends up breaking an officer's jaw to protect the guy who just broke hers."

"Are you serious?"

"Dead serious."

"I don't think that's the case with Rosalita. However, she seems too smart to be with him, yet she is. I'm fascinated."

"Hey, just because she teaches at the college level doesn't mean she doesn't have issues."

"I guess. Meanwhile, I wonder if that fathead pastor ever did like the Dead," Elizabeth said. "I hope not, though, because I like the Dead, and I don't want to have anything in common with that guy. Oh, and listen to this. Somebody shot up the pizza place a couple of doors down from the church."

"Right, Angelina's. So far, we have no suspect, but the shooter used a BB gun."

"You already knew?

"Yeah, sorry. We don't think there's a connection."

"Rats," Elizabeth said.

Bailey squealed. "Higher, Mommy!"

Elizabeth pushed harder with her free hand, causing the swing to zig zag. To push properly she needed both hands.

"Listen, I'm at the playground with my little one. Can I call you later?"

"Why don't we meet and discuss things eye-to-eye?" Red cleared his throat. "Can you meet for a drink?"

"To discuss the case?"

She hoped he'd say yes, even though she wanted him to mean no. Her vow never to fall in love again was fraying to a thread.

"Sure," he said. "To discuss the case."

"Okay, then." As long as they were discussing the case, how could she refuse? Now Elizabeth would need a babysitter for two nights. Expenses were adding up fast. Unless she asked Nancy, whose alibi hadn't checked out.

"How's tomorrow?"

"Tomorrow's Tuesday. Believe it or not, I'm meeting the pastor's wife for a drink."

"You're a slick one," he said. "How's Wednesday then?"

"Perfect," she answered. "I mean, it should be fine."

Maybe she would ask Nancy to babysit. Sure, she was a low-key witch who coveted another woman's husband, but she couldn't kill anybody. Could she?

TREVOR DID HIS HOMEWORK, ate the tuna fish casserole Elizabeth made for dinner without complaint, and headed upstairs. Lately he didn't say much, which bothered her. The little boy who used to seek her guidance on every subject could solve his own problems. That was a good thing, right? It wouldn't be normal for a fourth grader to cling to her leg like a kindergartner. Elizabeth should be grateful he'd ceased teasing his sister about her lack of an involved father. She should enjoy the peace and quiet.

She gave in to Bailey's insistence to watch *Frozen* and unloaded the dishwasher. Ten minutes into the movie, the child fell asleep with her thumb in her mouth. Elizabeth would address the matter of the thumb soon. Not tonight, though. To let it persist would elicit further criticism from Mary Pat. It would also endanger the proper development of Bailey's teeth. Elizabeth didn't have dental insurance.

She laid Bailey in her crib and went downstairs. Tonight might be the night to open the extra bottle of wine Cathy returned to her after the trunk show. It would kill the low-key anxiety percolating in her stomach. She uncorked the wine and set about pinpointing the anxiety's source. She still hadn't negotiated an oil contract for the coming heating season. If Russell's check arrived after the fifteenth, she'd incur another late fee on the mortgage. She had agreed to meet Red. In a bar.

Bingo.

What did she know about this guy, except that she was still attracted to him? For all she knew, a wife lurked in the shadows. He'd given her a sob story about an ex-girlfriend who fled across the country with his child, but that didn't mean he didn't marry someone else. Anyway, the story could have been made up to play on Elizabeth's sympathies. People did stuff like that to get what they wanted.

Maybe all Red wanted from her was forgiveness. Maybe he didn't like being swallowed up by guilt for dumping her for Mary Pat, especially now that he lived in Stonesbury again. He risked bumping into Elizabeth like a sore tooth every time he left the house.

She poured a glass of wine. And another. Two glasses of wine didn't qualify as drinking alone, did it? For that, she'd have to drink a whole bottle. She debated having one more glass, but that would mess with her blood-sugar, and she'd be ravenous the next day. She corked the wine. She took the Agatha Christie off her night table, but she'd been away from it so long she lost the thread. Elizabeth turned off the light, her mind racing.

She fell asleep. She must have. She bolted upright, soaked in perspiration: What if she did fall in love again?

She'd be damned if she gave any man that power over her.

TWENTY-SEVEN

Chelsea showed up ten minutes late in a sweatshirt and shorts, carrying her phone and an SAT prep book. Elizabeth had a feeling she'd get the kids to bed early so she wouldn't have to deal with them.

"Hey, Chelsea," Trevor said with the eagerness of a boy who doesn't know to play it cool. It pricked Elizabeth in the heart to see her son had a crush on this thoroughly undeserving girl.

"Are you by any chance a Jonas Brothers fan? Because I know how to play 'Sucker.'"

"I guess that means you're going to play it for me." Chelsea slumped into a living room chair, her slender tanned legs dangling halfway across the floor.

"Yes, I am!" Trevor scraped the bench from beneath the piano.

Elizabeth watched her son's fingers move effortlessly across the keys, the innocence in his voice splintering her in the ribs like a stab wound. Chelsea jiggled her sandal and scrolled at something on her phone.

"I'm out of here. Bedtime's at nine-thirty, Chelsea," Elizabeth said. Ordinarily, she'd insist the kids had to be in bed by nine, but if her hunch was right about Chelsea getting rid of them early, she'd try to buy them an extra half hour.

202

ELIZABETH GOT TO MURPHY'S via Uber, figuring the fare would cost less than a DUI. Also, Mary Pat's criticism, combined with Trevor's bullying girls at school, hadn't induced anybody to perceive her as a good mother; being labeled a drunk driver would make things worse.

She took a seat at the bar and waited. The bartender set out a bowl of pretzels, which she would not eat. She wouldn't. Carbs inevitably caused facial swelling, tight waistbands, and self-disgust. She studied the clock over the pyramid of gleaming liquor bottles. After fifteen minutes, she ordered a glass of Cabernet.

Rosalita came running in, finally, looking less put together than she had at church.

"I am so sorry," she said, blowing hair out of her eyes and settling onto a stool. "First, a staff meeting. Then Jim called saying that Isaac needed to be run up to the ER."

"Is that your son?"

"Yes, the oldest. Got hit with a hockey puck. Has a goose egg on his forehead, but he should be fine."

"No concussion."

"No, thank God." A second bartender flew over and held eye contact with Rosalita a smidge too long. Elizabeth could tell she had an effect on men. Maybe that's why women didn't like her at church. If Rosalita noticed the bartender's attention, she didn't show it. She smiled at him and pulled a recipe out of her purse.

"My favorite martini," she told him. "I came up with it myself."

He smiled back at her, fetchingly. "I'll do my very best with it then."

She removed her wallet, and Elizabeth, who did not smoke, was heartened to spot gum and a pack of cigarettes in Pastor Jim's wife's purse. "Tall, Dark Handsome Stranger" by Heart, came over the jukebox.

"That's a Lady Lily Wear skirt, isn't it?"

Rosalita fingered its hem. "You heard about Louisa Davenport, the woman who was murdered? She sold it to me."

"Louisa was my upline."

"You poor thing! What rotten luck. I spent a few hundred dollars with her, but I didn't get caught up in the business." Rosalita thanked the bartender, who carefully placed the martini on a napkin. "Jim insisted I buy it, which amused me. He usually watches my spending like a hawk."

Elizabeth liked Jim less by the second, especially since Rosalita made the money. Where did he get off telling her how to spend it?

"These are for you," she said, handing over the Dead CDs she'd burned. "I've labeled them. The one from Red Rocks is my favorite."

"Oh, thank you!" Rosalita didn't glance at the song titles Elizabeth had painstakingly noted on the cases but chucked the CDs into her tote bag. "I hate listening to the radio on my way to work. It's all bad news or some loudmouth yelling at you to buy a donut and a new car."

"I don't bother with the radio. It's Dead all the way. Either that, or the *Frozen* soundtrack. There is a monumental version of 'Morning Dew' in that collection. Once you hear it, you will never be the same."

"'Morning Dew?'" Rosalita looked at Elizabeth blankly.

"The song. You know. By the Grateful Dead."

"Oh, God, of course. Right." Rosalita covered her ears with her hands. "I'm so frazzled I thought you said *Mountain Dew*. You know, like the soft drink?"

"Of course you're frazzled. Your kid got hit with a hockey puck. Are you just back from the ER?"

The bartender brought Rosalita's martini. She took a sip, a long one. "Yep, and it has been a day. It's no party balancing work and motherhood, let me tell you."

"I'm sure Jim helps out," Elizabeth said, not sure of any such thing.

"He doesn't, actually. Anything to do with the kids is on me. Pediatrician's appointments, parent/teacher's conferences, helping with homework, and on and on."

"And on. I get it." *What's the point of a husband if you're working yourself to nub like a single mother?* "That can't be easy."

"It's not. Four kids in five years, a full-time job, and zero help with cooking, cleaning, or shopping."

"Who watches the kids while you're at work?"

Rosalita rolled her eyes. "His mother. She lives with us, rent free. Thinks her God-given role on the planet is to clothe her son's wife in womanly holiness. I teach three days a week and do my best to stay clear of her the rest. I'm sorry. You didn't come out to hear me complain."

"You're entitled to a sounding board." Elizabeth's own marriage and divorce had left her so frustrated she felt compelled to help another woman in a similar situation. "I have a sister-in-law who's a holy terror, so I know where you're coming from. It's hell."

Rosalita's eyes widened. "So, you understand!" She reached for Elizabeth's hand and squeezed it. She threw up her arms and wrapped her hands around her neck. "I feel like I'm being choked to death."

"How'd you manage to get out to meet me in a bar?"

"I told them it's back-to-school night. Jim doesn't pay attention to that stuff." Rosalita gulped her martini. "I've become a liar. I never used to lie."

"Why don't you leave him? You're attractive, educated, and self-supporting. What's stopping you?"

Elizabeth signaled for another round. Rosalita smiled gratefully.

"The truth?" she said. "I'm afraid I'll lose my kids. I'll be depicted as an unfit mother by Jim and She Who Spawned Him. The whole congregation will gang up on me."

"Yeah, but you can't just throw out a charge like that. You have to provide evidence."

Rosalita's eyes darted around the bar. "I'm not going to take that chance."

"Listen," Elizabeth said. "If you ever need anybody to talk to, I have two good ears. I was in a bad marriage myself."

"I may take you up on it." Rosalita put her second drink to her lips and downed it in three gulps. For a pastor's wife, she could really put it away. "Why'd you get divorced? If you don't mind me asking."

"My husband had a porn problem."

Rosalita signaled the bartender for another drink. "Our church is lousy with porn fiends. Did you hear the prophet's take on it?"

Elizabeth dropped her voice an octave to imitate Paul. "Men are weak and women treacherous."

"I'm surprised Jim hasn't put that one on a plaque."

"It must be great to be a guy. Everything's the woman's fault. Guy cheats, it's the other woman's fault. Or the wife's, because she's fallen down on some responsibility or another. Guy's getting off on porn, it's those slutty ladies on the website's fault."

Rosalita clapped her hands. "Hear, hear."

"And we're supposed to accept our husbands' infantile obsessions. His sex drive reigns supreme. One time my husband spent so much time in the bathroom, I thought he'd died. I didn't know what he was doing in there," Elizabeth paused for emphasis. "Until I found out what he was doing in there."

"What did you do then?"

"He says I overreacted. Everybody does it, *blah, blah, blah*, you're a prude, Liz. I should've known he was up to something when he started spanking me in bed. I was so naïve."

Elizabeth said too much. *Eek.* How would she walk that one back?

"Spanking is a thing." The pastor's wife said this without judgement, which encouraged Elizabeth to continue.

"Actually, my husband served me papers. I cheated on him after I found out about the porn habit."

Rosalita's eyes widened. "You cheated on *him*?"

"At the time, I felt justified because I consider porn adultery. I wanted to even the playing field. I'm not proud of it."

"That takes nerve," Rosalita said, not without admiration. "I could never cheat on Jim. Not that I haven't thought about it. There's this guy at work."

"Another professor?"

Rosalita reached into her purse and ran her fingers along the cigarette pack. "I'm pretty sure it's mutual, but it'll never happen. Again, can't lose the *kids*."

"Do you need to go out?"

"Yeah. When I drink, I smoke. Do you mind?"

Elizabeth drained her glass and followed Rosalita out of the bar. Rosalita cupped her hands to keep the wind off the match.

"My daughter is the product of a one-night stand," Elizabeth said. "I'm not proud of it."

Rosalita exhaled a long line of smoke. "Holy moly."

"Yeah, I kind of lost my mind. I love that little girl, though."

"Sure you do. You have a photo?"

"Do I have a photo?" Elizabeth whipped out her phone and scrolled to a new favorite. "This is Bailey on her first day of school."

"She really is into *Frozen*."

"Yeah. Can I see a pic of your kids?"

Rosalita brought up a shot of her wedged between Jim and the children. Jim stood with his legs spread apart and his chest puffed out, his wife barely in the frame. The children wore eerily meek expressions, except for the second boy.

"Nice looking family," Elizabeth lied. Only the second boy qualified as good looking, but she couldn't take her eyes off him. If she saw him on the street, she'd never peg him for a pastor's kid. "And the girls are wearing Lady Lily Wear skirts."

"Jim picked out our clothes. You're not going to find his ladies wearing jeans as long as he's head of the family."

"What does that make you?"

Rosalita blew a trail of smoke rings and watched them fade into the distance. "I make the money, but Jim is militant when it comes to gender roles. He pulls quotes out of the Bible and twists them to support his argument. He is sovereign in our household."

"I don't think Jesus said anything about gender roles."

"Forget Jesus. Jim sticks with Paul."

"There's all sorts of scholarship about Paul's message being lost in translation. Even if it wasn't, Paul isn't God. Jesus is. Who cares what Paul thinks?"

Rosalita stamped out her cigarette. Elizabeth had a vision of her as a teenager passing a joint.

They headed back into the bar.

"Jesus is a means to an end for Jim," Rosalita said, getting back on her stool. "Jim craves power. He likes to be in control. A lot of men in the congregation have the same need. The bottom line is, I'm in a quasi-abusive marriage. I blame myself because I let him get away with it. I let him get bigger and bigger. I figured if he was happy, we'd all be happy. I ended up making myself really small."

"Define quasi-abusive."

"Well, he's never hit me. Not with a closed fist."

Elizabeth needed another drink. She signaled the first bartender, who brought another round and winked at her. Or maybe he had something in his eye. She couldn't remember the last time a man had looked at her with any kind of enthusiasm, unless you counted Red. And she didn't.

"Just to be clear," she said. "You're telling me your husband hits you."

"Jim believes it's his role as head of the family to discipline his wife and children. That includes corporal punishment."

Elizabeth's stomach turned. She really did have to help this woman. "Your husband spanks you?"

"On occasion."

"Where are your children during these spanking sessions?"

In the bar's low light, Elizabeth watched the color rise in Rosalita's face.

"He thinks they gotta watch." She swung the martini under her chin, spilling half of it on her lap. She pulled a face. "Guess that means we're gonna need another round."

Elizabeth looked at the clock. "I have some time."

Rosalita reached for a napkin. "So, my sons get a lesson on how to lead their families one day, and my daughters learn how they are to obey their husbands."

"And your mother-in-law. Where's she?"

"Oh, she's there too, looking all smug and satisfied." Rosalita took a large swallow of what remained of her drink. "I'd like to slap her."

"You know none of this is okay, right? What would happen if your students found out their professor's husband spanked her for being disobedient?"

"Believe it or not, I use my maiden name at work. I never got around to changing my Social Security card. Anyway, I don't need anybody knowing I'm married to the guy who runs the church in the strip-mall. MYOB, you know?"

"I'm surprised Jim lets you use your maiden name."

"As long as they pay me, right?"

"Can I ask you a question?" Elizabeth breathed into the bottom of her lungs. "Why do you think Jim wanted you to wear Louisa Davenport's clothes? He complained at the wake that she didn't know her place as a woman."

"He wanted her."

Rosalita leaned towards Elizabeth with the languidness of a comfortable drunk. "He saw her as some sort of a conquest."

"How did Louisa take that?"

"Oh, she loved the attention. It didn't hurt her bank account, that's for sure. I don't think she was having an affair with my husband, if that's what you're asking. She was way out of his league."

"Yeah, but you're out of his league too."

"Once upon a time, the attention of an older man seemed romantic. It pissed off my parents royally." Rosalita giggled. She slipped off her stool and punched selections on the jukebox. Elizabeth looked into the bowl of pretzels, which gleamed invitingly in the low light.

Rosalita came back to the bar. "I think Jim got off on taunting me. Told me I was jealous because Louisa was prettier."

"She wasn't prettier. She was pretty, sure, but different. Not that it matters."

"Jim also told me a man needs variety."

"Is that in the Ten Commandments?"

The Dead's "Shakedown Street" came from the jukebox. A guy who'd been slumped over the bar slapped on a cowboy hat and started dancing.

Rosalita eyed Elizabeth glassily. "I wished to God Louisa and Jim were having an affair. To get him off my back. Now she's dead."

"What do you think happened to Louisa?" Elizabeth's fingers found their way into the pretzel bowl. She would eat just one.

"She crossed the wrong person. Sweet talked them into her business and left them high and dry. I warned people, but no! Who the hell listens to the pastor's wife? Louisa was a predator, and my husband knew it. I told him to rein her in. He said I was jealous."

"Right. Because you're so ugly." Did Rosalita have reason to kill Louisa? No, Elizabeth believed she'd welcome the distraction of another woman. She reached for another pretzel, which, it turned out, paired excellently with the wine.

"Rosalita raised her glass. "Far be it from me to tell my almighty husband I told him so."

The new friend was sufficiently drunk. Elizabeth moved in for the kill. "You probably have a couple of suspects. In Louisa's murder, I mean."

"That's the thing. I got a list as long as my arm. That lady screwed over so many people it could be anybody. I've fantasized about it being Jim, though. If he went to prison, I'd throw his mother out on the street so hard she'd bounce."

"Do you think it could have been Jim?" Elizabeth crossed her fingers in her lap.

"I don't know. On one hand, I'm freaked out thinking I could be sharing a bed with a man who stabbed someone to death. On the other, I kind of hope so!"

Rosalita clamped her hand to her mouth. "Please don't repeat that. Please don't."

"I won't say a word." Elizabeth dug into the pretzels. "What about Dave Davenport? You think he had it in him?"

"I only met him once or twice. He seems kind of quiet to kill anybody."

"You know what they say about the quiet ones." Elizabeth drained her final glass of the evening. The pastor's wife was too drunk to drive. "I'm getting an Uber. Leave your car here, and I'll drop you off."

Rosalita turned her ankle sliding off the stool. "Okay," she said. "But that means I gotta come up with another story."

TWENTY-EIGHT

Trevor took his seat on the bus. Elizabeth watched it disappear around the corner. Her head felt like it would splinter into a thousand pieces. She drove towards Bailey's school with the intention of heading back to bed after she dropped her off. First, though, she needed reinforcement dose of ibuprofen. The first one hadn't put a dent in her misery.

The minute she got home, she flung off her leggings and got back into her pajamas. She had two blessed hours before she had to be back in the van. She crawled between the sheets and closed her throbbing eyes. The phone rang.

"Is this Trevor's mom?" a woman asked.

"Yes, this is Elizabeth."

"This is Andrea Atler. Your son is in my son Joseph's class."

Oh, Lord. What did Trevor do now? Elizabeth had no time for a big long conversation and recriminations.

"How can I help you?" she asked cautiously.

"That's what I'm calling about. You signed up to be a helper, and I need a helper."

So. Trevor wasn't in trouble. What a relief. "Tell me what I can do."

"I have good news. You originally signed up to chaperone the Steam Engine and Steamboat field trip, but, as you know, you didn't get picked. However, two of the three moms who did backed out last minute, so you're our lady."

Elizabeth surmised she'd been passed over the first time because of Trevor's behavior with the girls. She felt like a sloppy second. "I'd be delighted. When do you need me?"

"The buses leave at 9:30."

"Today?"

"Yes, today. Did you remember to send Trevor in with a snack in addition to a bagged lunch?"

Elizabeth didn't like the woman's tone. Anyway, she had sent Trevor in with lunch, as usual; it cost much less than the school's hot meal plan. She dropped the ball on the snack.

"Oh, yes," she stammered. "I'll be right there."

Elizabeth pulled on her jeans, which strangled her waist. An image of the pretzels she'd consumed at the bar flashed in her mind. *Damn!* She left the button open and threw on a long shirt to hide it. In the bathroom mirror, her face looked big as the moon.

It hadn't occurred to her to say no to Andrea Atler. Despite the clanging hangover, Elizabeth couldn't pass up an opportunity to observe Trevor among his peers. But now she'd need someone to pick Bailey up from school. Whom could she get to do it? Chelsea would be at school, Cathy would be at work, and she'd be damned if she asked Mary Pat. That left Nancy. *Who didn't kill anybody!* Elizabeth punched in the number and reached for another ibuprofen. Nancy picked up the phone and said she'd be delighted to get Bailey. Elizabeth thanked her profusely. *She didn't kill anybody!* With no time for a shower, she rubbed deodorant under her arms with all her might and made a run for the door.

ELIZABETH SAW TREVOR, from his seat on the field trip bus, spot her from the window. The look on his face betrayed his discomfort at seeing her there. She noticed the empty seat beside him and resisted the impulse to take it.

"Hey," she said, passing him. "I'm subbing for another chaperone."

"Cool." He returned his gaze out the window.

Elizabeth continued her way to a seat in the back. As she sat down, she spotted Rosalita sitting across the aisle from her next to a hollow-cheeked woman she guessed to be Andrea Atler.

"Hi, there," she said gaily.

The one who might be Andrea pinched her lips together in an approximate smile, but Rosalita refused eye contact altogether and pulled her pocketbook tightly into her lap. She looked worse than Elizabeth felt, with skippy black liner around her bloodshot eyes. Her complexion looked ruddy, as though she'd been slapped.

"Hello," she muttered finally.

"How did it not come up that our kids are in the same class? We should set up a playdate, or something like a playdate." Elizabeth said brightly, hoping Trevor didn't overhear. "They're much too old for playdates."

Rosalita didn't look at her. "We'll have to see. We have a lot coming up."

The smile on Elizabeth's face froze. *Was it something I said?* Last night, she and Rosalita had a gay old time together. Now the other woman gave her the cold shoulder. Elizabeth became acutely aware of a pain blooming over her eyebrow.

Well, she could take a hint. She wouldn't force herself on anybody. She popped in her earbuds and pulled up a Dead show on her phone, but her child sitting all by himself a few rows ahead distracted her from enjoying it. Where were Trevor's friends? Where was Hughey?

Elizabeth yearned to throw her arms around her little boy, but that would mark him for additional bullying. She kept her distance.

She got off the bus and spotted Hughey descending the steps from a second school bus. The sky blackened. Elizabeth joined the line of students, teachers, and parents waiting to board a historic steam train. She watched Trevor climb onto it and take another seat by himself at a window. Nobody joined him. Hughey tumbled into the row behind him with another boy.

AFTER LEAVING THE TRAIN, Elizabeth and the pastor's wife corralled their charges to board a steamboat named the *Becky Thatcher*. Elizabeth changed her mind about playing it cool and took another shot at engaging Rosalita.

"I loved *Tom Sawyer*," she told her, meaning the movie and not the book, which she hadn't read due to the learning disability.

"Is that so?"

"Which one is yours?" Elizabeth stammered.

"Which one what?"

"Sorry. I meant which kid."

"Oh." Rosalita let a long silence hang in the air. Finally, she said, "Noah is the one in the Spider-Man shirt."

Elizabeth spotted a prematurely adolescent boy surrounded by smaller boys, whose body language indicated they wanted to impress him. "He's even better looking than his picture."

"We think so," Rosalita said.

Elizabeth figured she had nothing to lose. "Did I do something to offend you?"

"Starting with putting me in an Uber?"

She should be thanking me. "You were in no shape to drive."

"I was fine to drive. Picture for a minute how it went when my husband noticed the car gone this morning. Now he's tracking my phone, and I can't talk to you."

Elizabeth caught Noah's eye in the distance. He probably didn't know of her involvement in the missing car, but he gave her an icy glare.

Her voice came out like a squeak. "Did your husband hit you?" she asked Rosalita.

"What do you think?"

The pastor's wife turned her back.

Elizabeth caught her breath. "Hey, you three," she called to a group of girls whacking each other with celebrity-themed backpacks. "Come over here with me."

She guided her group up the ramp and onto the boat, watching Trevor. He took a seat in the front row, directly beneath the tour guide. She scouted around for Hughey and saw his funnel-shaped head rise along the ramp behind his chaperone. He took a seat behind Trevor, whom he ignored, and leaned too far towards another boy to get his attention. *The kid's a follower.*

Noah and another boy took seats next to Trevor. *Good.* So maybe Elizabeth and Rosalita wouldn't be friends, but that didn't mean Noah and Trevor wouldn't. Elizabeth prayed her son's days as a pariah were over. She took a seat several rows back, which provided good views of both her son and the Connecticut River.

A young bearded guy copiously tattooed with dolphins, whales, and sea turtles introduced himself as Sharkey the Tour Guide. After noting that the Connecticut River may or may not have been discovered by Adrian Block, he identified eagles, egrets, and swans along the grey landscape and pointed out a house that belonged to the inventor of the Chia Pet. From the distance, Elizabeth watched a feminine figure walk a dog along the property. She imagined how lovely it would be to wake up in a room with a view of the longest and widest river in New England. If the Chia Pet held a clue to its inventor's personality, Elizabeth guessed he threw excellent parties.

The sound of her son's voice snapped her out of her reverie.

"I *didn't* do it! I swear I didn't do it!" Trevor shouted. He flung himself out of his seat in an appeal to the tour guide. "I promise I didn't do it."

Sharkey chuckled. "Happens to the best of us, Junior."

"I didn't do it, though. I didn't!"

"He did so do it," Noah got up on his chair holding his nose. "Dispo farted!"

"Sit down, Buddy," the guide warned him. "Or you'll be swimming with the fishes."

Elizabeth stood to get a better view. She saw Hughey elbow Joseph with the rat-like face.

Noah clambered back into his seat, clamping his nostrils. "Dispo farted!"

"Dispo farted!" Joseph echoed.

"Dispo *stinks*!" Hughey screamed, catching Joseph in the ribs.

"I do not. I did not!" Trevor protested. Elizabeth spotted his tears of indignation from three rows back.

She scanned the boat for Andrea and Rosalita. Would they correct their children's behavior, or would they let it go? She spotted Andrea at the snack counter handing a coffee to Rosalita. Clearly, they wouldn't intervene, but should she? It was her job to protect her child. Elizabeth could slap those boys so hard she'd leave marks, but she didn't go for violence. She wouldn't hit anybody. But shouldn't she step in, though? Or, should she allow her son to fight his own battles? A line existed between being a good mother and a woman who smothered her children. Right now, Elizabeth couldn't find it.

Her function on this trip was to chaperone. *Chaperones intervene!* Elizabeth made her way back into the aisle, gingerly avoiding stepping on fourth grade feet.

"What's going on here?" she demanded.

Noah covered his nose with both hands and announced, "Dispo farted."

Elizabeth gave him her best death stare. "Even if he did, you don't have to embarrass him. It could just have easily been you."

The kid had a look in his eye that took her breath away. "*I*," he said languidly, "do not fart."

"It wasn't me, Mom!" Trevor shouted.

"It was him." Noah ran his eyes over Elizabeth, as though she were his to accept or dismiss. "You're Dispo's mom?"

Her entire body reacted, a line of perspiration blooming on her brow. She found herself questioning her authority in the situation. *Get a grip!* "Yes, I'm his mother. And that's *your* mother over there."

"I'm so scared," he said. "Like *she* can do anything."

Elizabeth saw Rosalita and Andrea chatting in the distance.

"Let's break it up boys!" Sharkey clapped his hands, startling Elizabeth. "Ma'am? We gotta get this show on the road."

She went back to her seat. After the group left the boat and lined up in the drizzle to re-board the train, she tapped Rosalita on the shoulder.

"It's a shame you let your husband treat you like a child, but how do you think it's going to work out when you let your son disrespect you?"

"First off, MYOB. And second, stop overreacting," Rosalita said. "As you're clearly prone to doing."

"Excuse me?"

"You're the one who banged a stranger because your husband likes porn. As normal men do."

Elizabeth felt punched in the stomach. She looked around to see if anybody overheard, but they were buried in their phones. "I told you that in confidence. "I thought we were going to be friends."

"We're not."

"I guess our sons aren't either."

Rosalita stole a look at her nail polish. "I got a feeling Noah's not going to perceive that as much of a loss."

"As a dutiful pastor's wife," Elizabeth put *dutiful* in air quotes, "you might want to teach your kid to treat others as he'd like to be treated. He may be a grammar school hot shot now, but life has a way of catching up with people."

"Are you threatening my son?" Rosalita asked.

"Don't flatter yourself." Elizabeth walked away.

TWENTY-NINE

The rain came down. Elizabeth splashed through puddles of scary depths all the way home. She questioned her judgment. First, because she'd trusted Rosalita, a perfect stranger, with her secret. Second, because she hadn't handled the (alleged) digestive event on the steamboat with grace or efficacy. Not only that, she'd let herself be bullied by the nine-year-old who bullied her son.

And then there was Hughey. Elizabeth hated him. She despised the little runt. *He's a child, though!* Well, Hitler was a child once, too.

She fretted that Mary Pat and Russell could be right about her being a bad mother, the extra-marital baby Exhibit A. And, if Trevor was indeed guilty of the episode on the boat, was Elizabeth partly responsible? She'd fed him orange juice on top of bacon and scrambled eggs for breakfast, a volatile combination. So, probably.

THE RAIN STOPPED AS Elizabeth pulled into Nancy's driveway. Her phone rang. Red's name came up. In the excitement, she'd forgotten she'd agreed to meet him. She checked herself out in the mirror on her visor. She looked like hell. She scrambled for an excuse to cancel.

But she didn't want to cancel. If she squeezed in a nap and blow dry, she could make herself look presentable. Maybe. She hoped. Elizabeth wanted to see Red more than she wanted to admit.

"Hey, there. Any leads?" she answered casually.

Nancy stood at the window bouncing Bailey, who appeared to have just woken up.

"Can I pick you up at 6:30?"

Elizabeth needed another half hour to facilitate the nap. Also, she didn't want to look eager. "How's seven?"

"Sure. You want to try Harry's?"

Harry's made stellar habanero martinis, but its overhead lighting made patrons look like Gollum from *Lord of the Rings*. Elizabeth required a more forgiving environment, especially after the booze fest from the night before. "Would you mind Murphy's? It's cozier."

Cozier? She regretted the word as soon as it came out of her mouth.

"Murphy's it is. See you at seven."

Elizabeth disconnected. She hopped out of the van to retrieve Bailey, who busied herself smearing Nancy's window with her fingers.

"There's no point in taking her now," Nancy said. "Why don't I keep her? Have a quiet cup of tea before you have to get Trevor at the bus. We're having fun, aren't we, Bailey?"

Bailey pointed at the television. "We're watching *Frozen*."

"You're already taking the kids later, Nancy. I can't put you out."

"It's no work at all. Bailey and I are great friends, aren't we, Bailey?"

"Friends," the child repeated. She slid her head into Nancy's chest, settling the question. Well, at least that went well. *I really hope my kid hasn't fallen for a killer.*

Elizabeth went home and put on the kettle.

THIRTY

If Red showed up and honked the horn instead of ringing the doorbell, Elizabeth would banish all romantic notions about him. Her mother had taught her not to consider any man too lazy to walk up the steps to meet her at her front door. "What's he going to be too lazy to do for you later?" she asked, but her admonishment didn't guarantee a happy relationship. Russell always came to the door.

Elizabeth checked herself out sideways in the mirror; her stomach hadn't recovered from the pretzel binge of the night before. She untucked her blouse. *Better.*

She opened the door. Red stood on the step, disconcertingly trim and youthful in chinos and a blindingly white button-down shirt. Elizabeth wondered if he pressed his clothes, or if he sent them out to be laundered. She pictured him standing at an ironing board, muscles pulsing at the effort. She pushed the image out of her mind.

"You look great," he said.

Elizabeth told herself he probably didn't mean it. The guy was a detective. He wanted information.

"You look pretty good yourself. I'm eager to get your read on Nancy when I pick the kids up later. Like I said, the story she gave me for why she skipped town didn't add up."

"Skipped town?"

"Don't make fun of me."

222

"I wasn't making fun of you." He looked genuinely hurt. *Wow, he's good.* "You're just so cute."

Elizabeth still didn't know whether to believe him. Anyway, what right did he have to say such things?

"We didn't come up with a death notice for a Skinner in Des Moines, either," he said.

Elizabeth's stomach did a flip, having left her kids in the care of the woman whose alibi didn't check out. She consoled herself that if something went wrong, Trevor knew to call her immediately. She turned up the ringer on her phone as high as it could go. Red could have her back from the bar to Nancy's in ten minutes, less if he used a siren.

She led him down her grass-cracked steps towards his Altima; she liked that he didn't need to drive a flashy car. It suggested confidence. She caught a whiff of woodsy cologne as he opened the passenger door for her. She slid in without turning her ankle or accidentally flashing her underwear. Things were off to an excellent start.

"AH, YOU'RE BACK," SAID the bartender, the one who'd winked at Elizabeth the night before.

"Can't stay away," she answered casually. "Seltzer and lime, please."

"You'd have a sore head from last night, sure."

Then, between the height and accent, Elizabeth deemed him somewhat attractive. Now the poor fellow paled next to Red, whose eyes and teeth gleamed in the low light of the bar.

"You're sure I can't get you anything stronger?" Red asked her.

"She had more than a few last night," the bartender remarked. He set a bowl of pretzels in front of her. "Here's your dinner, Love."

Elizabeth squinted. "I thought being discreet was in your job description."

"I'm a barman, not a priest." He slid a coaster over to Red. "What are you having, Sir?"

"Whatever's on tap. Surprise me."

"You're sure I can't get you a glass of wine?" Red asked Elizabeth again.

"I am sure." *Was he trying to get her drunk?* Well, she'd be damned. She wasn't about to have her judgement clouded again, not for this guy.

Roger Daltrey's voice came shrieking from the jukebox. Red thanked the bartender for the beer.

"About the pastor's wife," he said to Elizabeth. "What did you think?"

Guy doesn't waste time getting down to brass tacks. How much did she want to tell him? Everything, if it would help her find out who killed Louisa.

"Last night, she came on like my best friend. I saw her today, and she iced me. Completely. She said the pastor won't let her talk to me. He doesn't allow her to drink, but she drinks a lot. She smokes too."

"So, she came home tanked, and her husband blamed you?"

"She told him she was going to a parent/teacher conference. He found out she lied when she came home wasted in an Uber. I'm guessing my name came up, and now he considers me a bad influence."

"And this woman is how old?"

"I'm guessing thirty-five."

"Young for him."

"Way young. She has a PhD, if you can believe it. She said he spanks her."

Red put down his glass. "For fun or discipline?"

"Discipline. In front of the children."

"Man." Red let out a low whistle. "It's one of those churches."

"What churches?"

"A spanky church. Google it. There's an entire faction of whack jobs who distort the Bible to justify spanking their wives."

"If he were my husband, I'd knock his teeth out."

"I hope so," Red said. "But Rosalita. How much you wanna bet she gets off on it?"

"I don't think so. She seemed pretty over it last night."

"But today?"

"Back in her box." Elizabeth shook her head.

"Domestic situations are not straightforward. I hate to say it, but she might get off on it."

Despite Rosalita's betrayal, Elizabeth felt compelled to defend her. "Let's not blame a woman for being abused by her husband. She said she can't leave because he'd smear her and take the kids. I believe her."

"You could be right," he said. "A lot of victims diminish themselves to keep the peace. It's a coping mechanism."

"I am right." *Thank you very much.* Elizabeth stabbed the lime in her seltzer with the stirrer. "By the time my father left, my mother was the size of a pebble."

Red shifted uncomfortably. "I'm sorry."

Simple Minds came over the jukebox: *Don't You Forget About Me.* Elizabeth changed the subject. "Rosalita thought Jim had a thing for Louisa."

"Do you think she'd kill her over it?"

"She didn't seem to care that much. Is she a suspect?"

"We have a number of suspects."

Red looked into her eyes so deeply her stomach warbled. Elizabeth could still lose her head over him, no alcohol required. She chewed on the stirrer.

"Who are the other suspects?" she asked.

"I'm not at liberty to say."

"Do detectives really say that? 'I'm not at liberty to say?'"

"I can't say." Red ordered another beer and a bacon cheeseburger.

"Ha ha." Elizabeth's waistband dug into her stomach. No burger for her. "It bothered me how easily Rosalita blew me off today. It was a little psycho."

"Psycho enough to kill?"

"After the one-eighty she did on me this morning, I guess anything's possible. But psycho enough to blow me off after I burned two Dead shows for her."

"You still burn CDs?"

"Doesn't everybody?"

"I'm not sure. I don't think so."

"She didn't even offer to give them back." Elizabeth stared at the banged-up lime in her empty glass. "So rude."

U2 took over for Simple Minds. If Elizabeth were drinking, she'd be pirouetting in the aisle like a fool.

"What does your gut tell you?"

Elizabeth closed her eyes and got a picture of Rosalita's cold expression earlier in the day. "She could be."

"I'll take that under consideration." Red excused himself to go to the men's room. He brushed her arm. Her entire body tingled unsettlingly in response.

"I have an early day tomorrow," she said when he got back.

"Two beers is my limit, anyway."

"Really?"

"No, but I'm driving."

"Oh. Right." Elizabeth searched his face for signs of disappointment. She didn't find any. He was a detective, though, and hiding feelings was part of his job, although he probably didn't have any feelings for her, which simplified things because she didn't have any feelings for him.

She didn't.

A STEADY RAIN CAME down as Elizabeth and Red left the bar. The streets shone under the lamplight. An old woman with creases in her face emerged from the doorway next to the bar with a sack of umbrellas.

"'Brella, five dollars," she said.

"Thanks, but we're just going to the lot," Elizabeth told her.

Red handed the woman a five. He accepted an umbrella and held it over himself and Elizabeth.

"I've got you covered," he said.

They got to the car just as the sky opened. Rain pounded the windshield. Red steered back on to the street in front of the bar. Even with the windows closed, Elizabeth heard the commotion outside. She saw two guys in hoodies yanking umbrellas from the vendor's sack.

"Give me a minute." Red stopped the car and got out.

Elizabeth rolled down the window.

"Those don't belong to you," she heard him tell the perpetrators.

"Yeah, and what are you going to do about it?" the one with untied laces taunted. The kid had the blue-white skin of an unloved ghoul.

"I'm telling you to give them back."

"Like he said," shouted his small round companion. "What are you going to do about it?" He had a face that emerged from his tightly drawn hood like an un-popped pimple.

"You don't want to find out," Red said wearily.

"What are you? A cop?"

"As a matter of fact." Red reached for his badge, but the ghoul scrambled and threw a right hook, which Red deftly caught. He threw the kid on his back. The small round one tore off, the wet hems of his pants flapping under the street lights.

"Hey, Man," the ghoul said from the wet sidewalk. "What the?"

"Let me see your wallet," Red said. The kid complied, and he flipped it open. "Twenty-three years old. Let me guess. Still living with your parents."

"Listen, Man, I was teasing. I wasn't going to steal anything."

"Yeah, you were. Admit it, or I'll call your mother."

"No. No. Don't do that, Man. I'll pay the lady."

"Get up." Red tossed the wallet into one of the potted evergreens flanking the brick entrance to the bar. "Pay the woman for two umbrellas and throw in an extra five for her trouble."

"That's fifteen bucks, Man. I got student loans."

"Yeah, I'll bet you do. If I have to take you to the station, it'll ruin my night. You don't want that to happen."

The kid retrieved his wallet from the plant. He thumbed out some bills and handed them to the umbrella vendor. "Can I go?"

"Go."

The kid took off. Red handed back the umbrellas. An incandescent look came upon the old woman's face. Suddenly, she looked beautiful.

Red got back in the car, shirtsleeves soaked to the arms.

"That was impressive," Elizabeth told him.

"I hate bullies."

"So do I." Elizabeth rolled up her window, silencing the sound of cars splashing along the street. Before she knew it, she was confiding in Red about what happened to Trevor on the field trip. "They ganged up on him. I didn't know if I should get involved or not. I didn't know what to do."

She watched the old woman return to her place in the doorway. Red pulled out of the spot. All he had to do was say something stupid like, *boys will be boys* or, *it's not like someone stole his umbrellas*, and the spell would be broken.

Do me a favor. Break the spell.

"You know," he said. "Maybe I could be of some help here."

NANCY GREETED ELIZABETH and Red in jeans and a t-shirt that bore the logo of a popular brand of soup. Elizabeth didn't wear clothes with logos. Her mother said she'd be damned if she'd given birth to a billboard.

Nancy held up a pot of tea. "The kids are asleep in front of the TV. Can I get you to stay?"

Elizabeth wanted Red's read on her neighbor. "What do you think?" she asked him.

"I love a good cup of tea," he said.

Nancy clapped her hands together excitedly. She set the pot on the stove and turned up the volume on an LP Elizabeth couldn't identify.

"*Cherish*, right?" Red remarked.

"Don't tell me. The Partridge Family," Elizabeth said.

"David Cassidy, actually," Red answered. "His solo album."

Elizabeth rubbed her temples. "How would you even know that?"

"Seventies music trivia: Did you know that David Cassidy and Carl Palmer were friends?"

Nancy gave Red a blank stare.

"Carl Palmer, the drummer from Emerson, Lake and Palmer," Elizabeth said. "I guess that means you're not the only one stuck in the Seventies, Nancy."

Red elbowed her. "Says the Dead Head."

"Well, I don't know anything about Emerson, Palmer, and Whoozie-Whats-It, but I'm glad somebody here knows who David Cassidy was." Nancy looked wistful. "The year I turned ten, he did a concert at the New Haven Arena, but my parents wouldn't take me."

"Parents," Red said. "Can't live with them."

"Can't live without them!" Nancy laughed so hard she snorted. When she recovered, she announced she'd bought tickets for a *Star Trek* convention in New York City.

Red responded by recounting his all-time favorite *Star Trek* episode, in which a transporter malfunction split Jim into two separate people. Elizabeth had to admire the ease with which he could find common ground with strangers.

Nancy poured the tea. Casually, he asked, "So you and Elizabeth met at church?"

She tucked a small curl behind her ear and smiled. "No, not at church. We met during her divorce."

"She was a big help," Elizabeth said.

Nancy set out a plate of 'Nilla Wafers. Did Elizabeth want a 'Nilla Wafer? It had been decades since she'd had one. A memory came to mind about her late grandfather.

Pay attention!

"I heard Louisa Davenport was a member at your church." Red nibbled on a wafer innocently. "That was a shame, wasn't it?"

Nancy passed a pitcher of milk. "Louisa was a lovely lady. And those children. I'm so sorry for them, especially that little one." The curl sprung from behind her ear. She tucked it again and smiled. "I'm sure the father will do his best, but Louisa." She met Red's eyes and blinked. "Louisa was special."

"Do you have any idea who could have killed her?" Red asked.

"I can't think of anyone. She didn't have enemies, as far as I know."

Nancy held his gaze for a second too long. *Is she flirting? Or is she messing with him?*

"Well, we don't have to talk about that." Red smiled, smooth as syrup. "Elizabeth mentioned you lost your sister-in-law. I'm very sorry."

"I'm sorry, too," Elizabeth said. "I meant to send a card, Nancy, but I didn't know your sister-in-law's name. Sometimes Google isn't much help."

"Oh, you were probably searching for a Spinner. My brother's wife never took his name. Big old feminist." Nancy rolled her eyes.

"Oh, that explains it," Elizabeth said.

"Her name was Samantha Nelson." Nancy winked. "I'll bet you'll find it now."

THEY FINISHED THEIR tea. Elizabeth carried Bailey back across the street under the light drizzle. Red and Trevor trailed her, deep in conversation.

At the door, Red gave Trevor a high-five. "Hope to see you again, Man."

The overly delighted look on her son's face stabbed Elizabeth in the heart. "Take your sister," she said. "Teeth time. I'll be there in a sec."

He went in without protest. Red handed Elizabeth the umbrella. "Take this as a free gift," he said.

She laughed, even though her insides churned with a bunch of different feelings: an unwise and growing attraction to Red, fear about her son's situation at school, sadness about said situation, anger over Rosalita's betrayal, and determination. She would find out who killed Louisa if it killed her.

"Do you think she did it?" she asked.

"Nancy? I guess we'll see."

"I hope not." Elizabeth said. "I'm still rooting for that pastor."

"No kidding." Red cleared his throat. "Listen, about Trevor."

"We'll figure it out." She looked up into his eyes. His dark hair had a blue gleam running across it from the lamplight. "I still don't know if I should swoop in, or let him fight his own battles."

"I could teach him to defend himself. I could show him a couple of kung fu movements. If he likes it, he could take lessons."

Elizabeth didn't have money for lessons. "Between piano and soccer, he barely has time to do his homework. But thank you. I mean it."

"Sure," he said. "Is Russell around much?"

"Not for the day-to-day stuff. He is taking Trevor to Disney, though."

"Maybe it would help the kid to have another male influence. I don't mean to muscle in."

She reached for the door handle. "I have to think about it."

"You're his mother." Red made a little rolling motion with his hand, indicating a bow. "I defer to you."

Elizabeth's eyes wettened. She hoped he didn't notice.

SHE PUT THE CHILDREN to bed and made another cup of tea. She opened her laptop. She entered "Samantha Nelson Des Moines" into the search engine. Instantly, a link to a death notice came up for a woman by that name who'd been survived by a husband, Edmund Spinner. Nancy Spinner's name appeared among the other survivors. Samantha's funeral coincided with Louisa's. Nancy had indeed been in Iowa at the time of the murder. Elizabeth sighed with the special relief that comes with learning the woman to whom she'd entrusted her children is not a killer.

She knew there was something else she wanted to look up. Right: *Spanky churches*. She put it into the search engine and came up empty. However, the search term *Churches where men spank their wives* returned 3,800,000 results.

THIRTY-ONE

A leaf dangled from the maple outside the kitchen window. Elizabeth watched it shimmer in the morning sun, and fall. She felt happier than she had in months, having kept her promise not to drink. Her head felt clear and good, her stomach free of the insatiable hunger that inevitably followed a night of alcohol abuse. Best of all, she remembered every detail of the outing with Red. She felt blissfully free of anxiety. She had not said the wrong thing.

In the time it took Trevor to get dressed, Elizabeth read *Green Eggs and Ham* and *The Lorax* to Bailey. After both children were at school, she sorted through her remaining clothing inventory. Before she wasted time taking photos and writing product descriptions, she searched eBay for Lady Lily Wear and found it flooded with offers. Nobody wanted the stuff. Elizabeth had no choice but to donate hers to a thrift shop on Main that helped domestic abuse survivors. At least that way, somebody would benefit from her stupidity.

The phone rang with an unfamiliar number. Something told Elizabeth to pick it up.

"Hey, it's Gloria." Elizabeth didn't recognize the voice right away. It sounded bigger on the phone. "Remember me? We met at Cathy's."

"Yes, of course I remember you. Thanks for calling."

"Listen, I signed a new listing in Westport, and I thought you could come along when I get the house ready for market. The homeowner's prickly, and I thought it would give you an idea of the challenges of the business before you decide to get involved."

Elizabeth fingered the pile of unsaleable clothing. "When were you thinking?"

"This weekend. The sooner I get this house staged, the better."

"Would Saturday work?" Russell would have Trevor for the weekend, and Elizabeth would rather not ask Nancy to watch Bailey on a Sunday. Heaven forbid the kid got dragged to that weirdo church.

"I'll get you at nine o'clock."

"I'll be ready. I appreciate you thinking of me, Gloria."

"At this rate, I'm so busy I need another me. Cathy says you have the skills and personality to be an asset to my office."

Mary Pat's remarks came to mind as Elizabeth looked out the window onto her torn-up driveway. She dreaded Gloria pulling her car up on it. "I have to warn you. My house isn't going to make the cover of *Architectural Digest*."

"Honey, you just got a divorce. If you pursue this business and put the work in, you can renovate with the money you make."

This sounded pie-in-the-sky to Elizabeth, who'd heard similar speeches from Louisa about the benefits of joining what turned out to be a scam. "I'm nervous about real estate. I hear it's feast or famine."

"If you do the right thing with your money during the feast, you'll be fine during the famine," Gloria said. "I won't sugar-coat it. It's a cyclical business, but real estate always comes back. Nobody's making more land."

A LOW HUM SIGNALED the arrival of the mail truck. Elizabeth put on her lipstick and waited until the postal worker turned the block before going to the box, which contained a coupon magazine, the cable bill (*time to stop paying for cable?*), and an envelope from Russell, which contained a check. She tossed the mail on the microwave and called her ex-husband.

"Are you dying?" she asked.

"Why?" he asked cheerfully. "Do you know something I don't?"

"The check you sent is for three months."

"That's what I owe you, right?"

"Yes, but – "

"But what? What's the problem now, Elizabeth?"

"You haven't paid me consistently since the divorce, and now you send me a check for three months? Is it going to bounce?"

He chuckled. "It's not going to bounce, Dear."

Elizabeth squinted at the phone, as if it would give her a read on him. "You'd better not be playing me, Russell."

"Sweetheart. Take a breath. You know it would really behoove you to learn to trust more. You need to look at the issues that are holding you back, Elizabeth."

Yeah, okay Porno Boy. "Well, I'm glad you decided to do the right thing."

She opened her mouth to say thank you, but why should she thank a condescending yo-yo for meeting a court-ordered obligation?

"See you around," she said and hung up.

ELIZABETH PHOTOGRAPHED the check. As she attempted to deposit it to her online bank account, a call from the school secretary interrupted.

"Can you hold for Mrs. Caffee?"

"Yes," Elizabeth answered, anxiety blooming in her solar plexus. *What now?*

Mrs. Caffee got on the line, her voice more irritatingly nasal than it sounded in person. "I'm afraid Trevor's been at it again, Mrs. Dispo," she said.

Afraid? You don't sound remotely afraid to me.

"He's been at what, Mrs. Caffee?"

"Your son has been involved in an altercation."

"What kind of altercation?"

"Physical, this time. I'm afraid things are escalating."

Afraid, again.

"The other boy's parents want to meet with you and Mr. Dispo to discuss the situation."

"Well, I'll let you be in touch with Mr. Dispo because he and I are divorced."

"Oh, right. You mentioned that."

"When would you like to have this meeting?"

"The sooner, the better. I understand that people have work obligations during the day, so I can make myself available this evening." She said it as though she was doing Elizabeth a big favor. "How's six-thirty?"

THE SCHOOL BUS HISSED to a stop. Trevor trundled down the steps, jacket slung over his shoulder. Elizabeth spotted the bruise on his forearm.

"What happened to you?"

"I got beat at dodgeball."

Dodgeball? Did schools really still allow this form of sadism dressed up as a gym game? "I hated dodgeball. In fifth grade, some kid made me a target. I had a black eye for a week."

"I didn't get beat at dodgeball. I got beat *at* dodgeball." Trevor's shoelaces flopped menacingly as he walked. Elizabeth's desire to hear the story overrode the impulse to tell him to tie them.

"Okay, so you were beaten at dodgeball. Please elaborate."

His ears reddened. "Remember that kid who said I farted on the boat?"

"There were several."

"Noah. Do you know which one that is?" The wind sent up a raft of fallen leaves, but it didn't induce him to put on his jacket, nor did it stop Bailey from squatting every few feet to study rocks.

Elizabeth shivered. "Yes."

"Uh huh. When I got the ball, I decided to take him out."

"So, what's the problem? It's dodgeball. The point of the game is to take out your opponent."

"Yeah, so I did, but he didn't like it, and his friends didn't like it. So, we get to the locker room, and he takes me like this." Trevor twisted up the collar of his t-shirt. "And he slams me against the locker like this. And I tell him to put me down, but he starts laughing, and his goon friends start laughing, and of course Hughey – that giant loser – starts laughing."

"Okay, and then what happened?"

Trevor stopped walking. He held out his hands. "Well, Dad told me I needed to protect myself better. He gave me these things to put on my hands in case I needed to punch anybody out."

"What things?"

"Um, some metal things."

"What kind of metal things?"

"Knuckle things."

Cold air swirled around Elizabeth. She became aware of a stinging sensation on her face. "Are you telling me that your father gave you brass knuckles, Trevor."

"He didn't say anything about brass."

"May I see these knuckle things?"

Trevor's backpack slipped off his shoulder as he exhaled. "The principal took them."

"Of course she did. We have a meeting tonight."

"Okay."

"Trevor, did you hurt Noah?"

"He has a bruise. I didn't break anything. Anyway, I have a bruise too."

Excellent point.

Elizabeth couldn't punish the kid for defending himself, especially when she'd witnessed how the so-called Christian boy and the other boys mistreated him. But she couldn't let him go around whacking people with brass knuckles, either.

She did the only thing that made sense. She fell to her knees and hugged the poor fellow. A lock of hair curtained his sad, uncertain eyes.

"As God as my witness, Trevor," she told him. "I will defend you to the ends of this earth."

THIRTY-TWO

Confidence is key. Not only would Elizabeth have to face Mrs. Caffee, Rosalita, and the fake pastor, but she'd have to facilitate the impression that she and Russell, despite their divorce, qualified as decent parents. After searching the Internet for self-confidence tips, she followed the instructions from a TED Talk by standing in front of a mirror, widening her stance, and shooting her arms over her head. The speaker claimed this would stimulate a flow of emboldening chemicals in her body.

It worked. The fizziness in Elizabeth's stomach subsided a bit. If she had time, she'd hit a restroom before the meeting and do it again. She put on a shirtdress and a low heel and examined her face. The pores could be smaller, but the eyes looked fresh, delightfully free of bags and shadows. Skipping alcohol had all sorts of benefits, it turned out. She prayed to God that Rosalita would appear at the meeting with a whopping hangover. She said another prayer asking to be forgiven for such a thought.

"This is getting old," Trevor said, as she packed the children's supplies to go to Nancy's.

"Yeah? You think the principal's office is my idea of fun?" Elizabeth answered. "Give me a break."

THE RESTROOM SMELLED of pine cleaner and brought back unpleasant memories. *Elizabeth is a polite little girl who wants to be liked. Elizabeth's reading is way below grade level.*

She blew her nose and practiced the TED Talk move, the fabric under her arms damp against her skin. The clock on the tile wall in the empty hall put her at ten minutes early. She waited under a blinking fluorescent light on the bench outside Mrs. Caffee's darkened office.

The principal and the Christians turned the corner at the bottom of the corridor at six-thirty-three. In the distance, Elizabeth watched Jim stride alongside Mrs. Caffee in his usual shorts. As they got closer, she worked out the saying on his t-shirt: *I COME TO SAVE!* Rosalita fluttered behind in a Lady Lily Wear skirt and flat shoes.

"Oh, he's a wonderful student," Elizabeth heard the principal say. "Mrs. Altricher nominated him for Citizen of the Month."

"Noah made Citizen of the Month six times last year," the pastor said. "You follow the JIJO principle, and everything falls into place."

"The JIJO principle?" the principal asked.

"You heard of GIGO? Garbage in, garbage out?"

"Of course,"

"JIJO is the opposite. Jesus in, Jesus out."

Elizabeth detected a slight broadening in the distance between Mrs. Caffee and Pastor Jim. "Well, if it's not broke," she said. "Don't fix it."

Elizabeth stood up to be noticed, smoothing the front of her dress. She shook Mrs. Caffee's hand, which felt cold and powdered. Rosalita's felt creamed, warm and slippery. Pastor Jim clamped Elizabeth's fingers so hard she yelped.

"We're just waiting for your husband, Mrs. Dispo," Mrs. Caffee said.

"Ex-husband. My name is Candew," Elizabeth reminded her.

"Right." Mrs. Caffee unlocked her office door. She turned on the lights. "We'll give him a few minutes."

"We understand you must be under a ton of stress," Pastor Jim told Elizabeth. "Being a single mom isn't easy. It's hard on the children when a male role model isn't present."

Elizabeth stared at him.

"Right," Mrs. Caffee said again, making a show of flipping through some papers on her desk. "We'll catch Mr. Dispo up when he arrives."

"I'd like to start," Elizabeth told the principal. *Sit up straight. Confidence is key.* "Rosalita, Jim. Your son is bullying my son. He knocked Trevor up against the lockers in gym class."

The pastor shook his head. "Far be it from me to call a child a liar, but you've been misinformed. Your son came to school with brass knuckles. He was looking for trouble."

"My son was put in the position of having to defend himself. Are you aware that your son bullied him on the field trip? I saw it with my own two eyes. So did your wife."

Rosalita folded her hands in her lap.

"Rosalita," Elizabeth pleaded. "Tell them what you saw. Put yourself in my place. How would you feel if a bunch of kids ganged up on Noah?"

"I didn't see anything of the sort."

Mrs. Caffee rested her hands on her datebook. "This isn't getting us anywhere. Mrs. Dispo – Candew – your son came to school carrying weapons, which is an offense that warrants expulsion. It's clear there are problems in your home, and I'm not unsympathetic to that reality. Now, the Dunfores and I have discussed the matter, and they have very generously agreed that we can drop this whole thing as long as Trevor gets help."

"Therapy," Rosalita whispered.

Pastor Jim rested his palm on his stomach. "*Christian* therapy, which I would be happy to provide."

"Thanks," Elizabeth said, eying the door that still presented no sign of Russell, the cause of this drama. "I wouldn't want to put you out. I'll find somebody."

"I can make a recommendation," Mrs. Caffee said. "If you'd prefer to go with a non-religious source." To Jim, she said, "I'm afraid we can't force a parent to pursue Christian therapy."

"That's too bad, the government getting in our faces again." Jim held up a finger. "If I agree to let her kid stay, what stops him from showing up next time with a gun?"

"Your concerns are understandable, Pastor. I will look into the possibility of having a police officer on site for the foreseeable future – or at least until a qualified counselor can assure us we're out of the woods on this."

A police officer? To monitor my *child?* Elizabeth rubbed a damp eyebrow. *Stay calm. Do not say a word.*

The pastor scratched the inside of his wrist, revealing a small tattoo of a skull. "But if my boy feels unsafe, I reserve the right to have this kid Trevor suspended or expelled. Is that right?"

"Absolutely," Mrs. Caffee said. "It is my job to keep every student in this school safe, and I take that responsibility seriously."

"Okay, then," Jim said.

His wife didn't offer her opinion, and he didn't ask.

BACK IN THE MINIVAN, Elizabeth called Russell.

"Yes?" he answered mildly.

"Where were you?"

"Where was I when?"

"The meeting."

"We had a meeting?"

"Yes, we had a meeting. Stop playing games." Elizabeth was driving too fast. She blew a stop sign. "Give me a sec. Let me pull over before I get somebody killed."

"Look, Elizabeth, I'm in the middle of something."

She stopped the car in front of a Cape decorated with orange Halloween lights. The life-sized Frankenstein on the lawn raised and lowered its arms.

"The meeting with the principal, Russell."

"Nobody told me about any meeting with the principal, Babe."

"I'm not your babe, Russell. We had a meeting about the brass knuckles you sent our son to school with. The principal said she's getting the police involved."

"The police? Oh, come on. These people are ridiculous."

"I'm not going to argue with you. Are you telling me you didn't know about the meeting?"

"Let me check my recent calls. Nope, nothing from the school."

"That insufferable woman dropped the ball."

"What insufferable woman?"

"The *principal*! I've told her a million times we're divorced, and that *she* would have to contact you about this meeting."

"Well, she didn't."

"Clearly, Russell!"

"Listen, take a breath," he said. "Calm down."

"Do not tell me to calm down." The man had the attention span of a squirrel. She'd better get to the point. "You sent our kid to school with lethal weapons, and I'm the jackass who had to sit there and be lectured to by some woman who does not know or care about our son. And be judged by the smug and sanctimonious so-called Christians whose son he used them on."

"Smug *and* sanctimonious so-called Christians?"

"It's a long story."

"Give me the Cliff Notes."

"The so-called Christian Trevor hit with the brass knuckles is one of the bullies. He's bullied him mercilessly."

"Good. That's why I gave them to him."

Elizabeth exhaled loudly. "I want you to know this is the first conversation I've had in my entire life about brass knuckles. That's how low I've sunk."

"Okay, so, was that everything? What's the upshot?"

The upshot is you're lucky I don't drive over there and hit you with a pair of brass knuckles. "The principal said she won't expel Trevor as long as he gets therapy. So, prepare to blow the dust off your wallet."

"Insurance will cover it."

"Not the co-pay, it won't. Is that all you have to say about this? She's getting a cop to patrol the school to keep Trevor in line."

Russell didn't say anything. Elizabeth pictured him rubbing his hair over his forehead, the way he did when he got frustrated. "You want me to straighten these people out?"

"No, I don't want you to straighten these people out. And do not give our son any more ideas about defending himself."

He hardened his tone. "Look, my kid is not going through life as a target. Newsflash, Babe, the world is full of bullies. Until Trevor learns to handle them, he's screwed."

"I don't need *you* to tell me the world is full of bullies," Elizabeth said, thinking of Russell's sister. "But sending a nine-year-old with brass knuckles never got anybody into Mensa. Now, as far as therapy goes, I'm thinking we should all be involved."

"Yeah, that'll be the day I sit around whining about the July 4th my father dropped my sloppy joe. That's your department, Elizabeth."

"Okay, then." Tonight, she decided, warranted a bottle of wine. If she hurried, she could get to the package store before it closed. "Thank you for your time, Russell."

ELIZABETH SLID THROUGH the store entrance just under the wire. She headed directly to the section that held her favorite vintage in the jumbo bottle that went for $8.99 and picked two off the shelf. She headed back to Nancy's to pick up the kids, where she begged off the offer of tea and tried not to let Nancy's disappointment get to her. She worried her neighbor might be feeling used. Elizabeth worried she was indeed using her.

Nancy had already changed Bailey into her pajamas, so all Elizabeth had to do when she got her home was rock her and sing, "Do You Want to a Build a Snowman?" Bailey fell asleep in her arms. Elizabeth knocked on Trevor's door, kissed him goodnight, and poured a giant glass of wine.

Gulping it, along with the calcium and multivitamin tablets she steadfastly took to avoid thin bones and premature death, she thought about the day's events. *Could Caffee be right? Is Trevor traumatized from the divorce?* Her own parents' divorce shattered her. She'd been practicing the song for months; Mr. Saunders claimed she sounded better than Carole King, his all-time favorite singer. Elizabeth took the stage and sat at the piano. She looked out expectantly into the first row and spotted the empty seat next to her mother. Who didn't look proud or excited but limp and defeated with red wet lumps stuck on her face where her eyes should be. From then on Elizabeth locked the two experiences together in her mind, her father's betrayal and what would have been her own triumph on stage.

Elizabeth finished the first glass of wine, her insides balled up with crisscrossing wires. She took the empty glass over to Trevor's piano and ran her fingers along the keys, soundlessly.

THIRTY-THREE

After several more nights of wine, Elizabeth woke up with yet another firmament of pointy pains covering her head, like stars. She downed three cups of coffee.

"But I don't want to go to the doctor." Trevor stood up from his half-eaten egg and threw his calculator in his backpack. "I hate the doctor."

"Don't start." Elizabeth handed him a slip of paper and led him out of the house. "Give that to your teacher. You're leaving early today."

"Big deal."

Bailey held them up, squatting to examine rocks and leaves. They were running late, and Elizabeth scooped her up. Bailey flailed in protest and stuck her thumb in her mouth.

"You're getting too old for that," Elizabeth told her. *Says the 42-year-old who still thinks alcohol is the answer to her problems.*

She sprinted to catch up with Trevor. Her phone buzzed in her pocket. Who had the nerve to be calling at this hour?

Red.

"Running to bus stop," she said breathlessly.

"I won't keep you. Can I take Trevor this afternoon? Thought I'd show him some of the moves we talked about."

"He's got a doctor's appointment." How much did Elizabeth want him to know? "He brought brass knuckles to school to fight off bullies, and now he has to go to therapy."

"Where'd he get brass knuckles?"

"Russell."

"Russell's a bonehead."

Elizabeth liked this answer. Until now, Red had kept his opinion of her ex-husband a mystery. What would he think of Russell's porn habit? If she were to believe late-night comedians, probably nothing. According to them, all men had porn habits.

"Can I call you back?"

"Can you meet for coffee?"

Elizabeth sucked in her breath. What did he want, really? She didn't want to harbor feelings for him. He was casting a spell. She conjured the antidote: a vision of him logging on to Porn Hub.

"Okay. What's up?"

"I have news about the case. Meet you at the Common Bond?"

The school bus came into view beyond the stop sign. Trevor vaulted over a pile of leaves to catch it. *News about the case!*

"I'll meet you after I drop Bailey at school."

TO KEEP THE SUN FROM boring into her tender skull, Elizabeth chose a table next to the window with the half-lowered canvas shade. Red brought over the coffees.

"Remember I said Pastor Jim's alibi didn't check out?"

Elizabeth rubbed her hands together greedily. "So, he *is* our suspect?"

Unfortunately, no." Red sat down and handed Elizabeth a napkin. "And now we can rule Nancy out, too."

"I found her sister-in-law's death notice online."

Red shook his head. "Of course you did, but there's something else."

Elizabeth sipped her coffee, the caffeine blurring the edges of the pain in her skull. "What are you saying?"

"You'll never believe it."

"Nancy was in Des Moines at the time of Louisa's wake, but she was in town at the time of the murder."

"You just said she didn't do it."

"Jim's alibi didn't check out, but he was also around at the time of the murder."

"Are you telling me Jim was with Nancy at the time of the murder?"

"Bingo."

"Let me guess. They were working on a pamphlet."

Red shook his head slowly. He tore open a sugar packet, a surprise. She didn't remember him having a sweet tooth.

"They're not having an affair, Red, if that's what you're saying. She has a thing for him, but he does not reciprocate."

"I'm not saying he's in love with her, but they are having an affair." In the sliver of light coming through the space between the shade and window, his eyes shimmered like sifting gemstones. She suspected he was trying to kill her.

Porn habit. Porn habit. Porn habit.

"Are you for real? Jimbo is sleeping with Nancy?"

"That is correct."

"Ew. That's a picture I'll never scrub out of my mind. But why? I mean, if he doesn't care for her? I hate to say it, but she's not what anyone would call conventionally attractive. His wife is pretty. Louisa was pretty. Nancy is more of an acquired taste."

"It's about power. The guy has a harem. Nancy's not the only one he's messing with."

"But he's repellent." Elizabeth's stomach turned as she imagined the fake man of God's hairy calves. "How did you come by this intelligence?"

"We questioned him."

"He's such a jerk. I wonder who else he's fooling around with."

"Let's just say that church is rife with willing participants." Red rolled his eyes. "The Pastor Syndrome."

"If you say so." Elizabeth covered her eyes. The vision of Jim and Nancy clanged around in her head, worsening the hangover. "It's horrifying."

"Your teen-idol obsessed babysitter isn't so innocent, after all. Although I wouldn't have put Jim Dunfore and David Cassidy in the same league."

"I admit I was surprised when I caught her flirting with you."

"What are you talking about?" Red glanced over the rim of his cup.

"At her house. I saw the way she looked at you."

"Can we change the subject, please?"

"Sure," Elizabeth said. "She's into witchcraft, you know."

"I didn't."

"You'd better hope she doesn't cast a spell on you. Who knows? Maybe she cast one on Pastor Jim."

"She didn't. Trust me." Red cleared his throat. "Listen, about Trevor. He should know how to defend himself. I can teach him without hurting anyone. Also, that police officer at school can work to our advantage."

Work to our *advantage?*

"How do you mean?"

"I talk to the officer, get him to keep an eye on things and report back to me. He may be able to vindicate the kid."

"That would be great, but –"

"But what?"

"It's above and beyond. I appreciate your kindness, but none of this is in your job description."

Red chewed his stirrer. He dropped it on his napkin and pulled back the shade for a quick look out the window. "I went into police work because I like being of service. I get off on putting bad guys away and protecting good ones. I'm not doing anybody any favors."

"If you insist, then thank you." Elizabeth eyed the other tables to make sure nobody overheard. "Russell hasn't been much help."

"Let me take Trevor to the gym after you get back from the therapist. Again, I'll show him some moves. If he's interested, I'll sign him up for lessons. My treat."

"I can't accept that, Red."

"I'm not doing it for you. I'm doing it for the kid. You just said his father hasn't been much help."

Elizabeth sighed. "He hasn't."

Red leaned in. "Russell has always been very limited. Not just him, though. That whole family." He said this through the side of his mouth.

"What do you mean?" she asked.

"They're always trying to impress somebody. And those dopey billboards. They're so full of themselves," he said. "It was never my scene."

THIRTY-FOUR

It turned out Gloria drove a Mercedes, not the Audi Elizabeth envisioned. The rain cleared, and she drove onto the glistening leaves on Elizabeth's driveway with the top rolled down.

"Can you believe this Indian summer?" Elizabeth said, bouncing into the front seat. "Thanks for doing this."

"Hey, it's my pleasure. Somebody helped me get started. Now I'm helping you." Gloria backed out. "Ever hear of the good ol' boys' network?"

"Sure."

"We're the good ol' girls' network. I firmly believe that if every woman set her mind to helping another woman, we would rule the world."

"I hope I can help someone else one day," Elizabeth said.

"You will." Gloria headed down Rocky Hill, towards the entrance to the parkway. "I'll persuade you to join the business, and you'll take it from there. Remember, you're getting half the commission on the sale of Cathy's house."

Elizabeth squirmed. "I'm pretty sure I shouldn't."

"Knock it off. Cash the check and take me out to dinner. We'll call it even.

Elizabeth's mind swirled with the names of restaurants she wanted to try. "If you insist."

"I'll pick out someplace really expensive. That'll assuage your guilt."

"I'm overdue for expensive." Elizabeth removed a loose thread from the pair of black pants she wore everywhere from baby showers to soccer practice.

Gloria pointed out a billboard along the parkway. It showed Mary Pat and Tom giving the thumbs up in front of a lavishly land-scaped McMansion with a *SOLD* sign on it.

"Is that individual really your sister-in-law?"

"Ex-sister-in-law. She and her husband are very successful."

Gloria headed for the exit. "Money-wise, maybe. They don't have a great reputation in the industry."

"Really?" This was news to Elizabeth.

"Yeah, really." Gloria snorted. "Wouldn't it be outstanding if you could beat them at their own game?"

GLORIA INTRODUCED ELIZABETH to the homeowner, a saltine of a woman in a housecoat named Eleanor Fitch. Pulling a fat cat into her lap, Miss Fitch sat down in a faded armchair. With the flick of a finger, she signaled her guests to take seats on a couch covered with a brown and orange patchwork quilt.

"I have some demands," she said.

Something – dust or a cat hair? – caught in Elizabeth's throat. She emitted numerous coughs into her elbow, quietly as possible. The woman raised her voice.

"Nobody," she said, "steps on this property unless I am here to supervise."

Gloria turned up her palms. "I understand your concern, Miss Fitch, but quicker sales result when buyers can walk around freely and imagine themselves in the space."

"The space. Is that what we're calling it now? We used to call it a house. In this case, *my* house. Nobody allowed, am I making myself clear?"

Elizabeth became aware of a talcum powder smell, which she deduced to be the cause of the throat tickle. Everything about the small, boxlike house dated back to 1958, when it was built. The neighborhood had once been solidly middle-class but recently became a haven for professionals attracted to good schools and easy access to Manhattan. No doubt, the buyer would tear down Miss Fitch's house and replace it with a palace featuring a chandelier that lit up the entire street from a second-floor window.

"Rule number two," Miss Fitch announced, stroking the cat. "I get twenty-four hours' notice before buyers show up. I have to prepare Edward for visitors."

"Is Edward your son?" Gloria asked.

"Yes." Miss Fitch kissed the cat's head. "Aren't you, Muffin?"

"Oh, the cat is Edward."

"He's an excellent judge of character. So far, he approves of you two, and he'll be the one to decide who gets to buy this house."

Elizabeth had heard crazier things before, but having the cat's approval gave her a measure of confidence.

"What if Edward doesn't like any buyers?" she asked Gloria when they got back to the car.

"Did you see the boxes lined up in the hallway? She's already packing. Notice she didn't haggle about commission. She's paying full price," Gloria noted. "Trust me, she wants out. It's the cheap ones who make you work the hardest. Miss Fitch's bark is worse than her bite."

"I guess you learn a lot about human nature in a job like this." Jim and Rosalita Dunfore came to Elizabeth's mind.

"You sure do."

Gloria recited a litany of horrible things homeowners could do to an agent, including withdrawing their house from the market after accepting a bid. She told her about the worst buyer she'd handled, a woman who'd made ten offers on different properties and changed her mind at the last minute every time.

"I was so naïve," Gloria said. "We won't let anyone do that to you. Buyer breaks a deal, and it's *hasta luego!*"

She went on to recount a couple of nightmares about radon leakage and buried oil tanks, but none of this deterred Elizabeth. As she and Gloria flew back up the parkway, a fantasy took shape in her mind: She would qualify for her license in record time. Then she would set about beating her former sister-in-law's sales records. She would wipe the floor with Mary Pat. It would become her life's work.

THIRTY-FIVE

Red called to check on Trevor, as he did almost every day. Things had frozen up on Louisa's case.

"We want to believe there's a link between Toni and Louisa's murders, but the methods are throwing us off."

"Louisa was stabbed. That's personal, right?"

"Yeah, consistent with a husband or a lover," Red said. "But Badden was shot to death. Not so personal, or not *as* personal."

"Could the murders be unrelated? I keep thinking about that church. This cranky goat named Jackie mentioned somebody else Louisa screwed out of money. Ombianelli, I think her name was."

"We talked to that one, too. She's clear."

"Jackie said Louisa had affairs," she said. "I wanted the pastor to be guilty with such a passion it clouded my thinking. What if she had an affair with someone else?"

"You've given me an idea," Red said. "EZ Pass had Badden in Connecticut several times in recent weeks."

Red seemed to be opening up more about the case. It made Elizabeth feel important. She found herself wanting to live up to his trust.

"Right, okay. Can you let me in on your theory?"

"Let me check it out first." Red paused. "I know it's last minute, but I'd like to take Trevor to the Mets game tonight. If it's okay with you."

"You want to take a fourth grader to Flushing, New York on a school night?"

"I think he could use a friend, you know?"

Elizabeth did know. Her heart quickened, unsettlingly. "I'll ask him when he gets off the bus. I'm sure he'll be up for it. He had a great time with you at the gym."

"Good, I'll sign him up for lessons. What nights don't conflict with the therapist and soccer practice?"

"After a bit of back and forth, we've decided on Tuesdays for therapy. He could use a diversion afterwards."

"Tuesday it is, then. And, Elizabeth?"

"Yes."

"I'll look forward to seeing you tonight, too."

WALKING HOME FROM THE bus stop, Elizabeth told Trevor Red invited him to a baseball game. The sadness that had filled the boy's eyes for weeks evaporated. He jumped and grabbed at a branch on a tree.

Elizabeth let him run ahead. She didn't rush Bailey when she stooped to examine a rock. She didn't want Trevor to see her face.

Bailey looked up from the sidewalk. "Why you crying, Mommy?"

TREVOR FINISHED HIS homework in record time. Red rang the bell.

"Remember to say please and thank you," Elizabeth told him.

She opened the door. She should have put on lipstick. No, she should not have.

"Thank you so much for this, Red."

"Any excuse to see the Mets." Red winked at Trevor. "You ready, Champ?"

Trevor smiled shyly and stepped out from behind his mother. Elizabeth watched him jump into the back seat of the Altima with a wrenching mix of joy and fear in her stomach. The kid needed a good role model, and Red fit the bill. But the cost of gas, tolls, parking fees, and tickets might obligate her somehow. It didn't help that her resolve not to fall in love with this guy was dissipating by the second. *Get over yourself, Elizabeth. Who said he even wants to be with you? Maybe he's just a good person doing something good for a friendless kid.*

Her phone buzzed. Mary Pat.

Damn! Elizabeth forgot soccer practice. If she ignored the call, Mary Pat would report the absence to Russell, and things would escalate.

"What's up, Mary Pat?"

"I'm at practice, and I don't see my nephew."

"He went to a Mets game."

"My brother didn't say anything about a Mets game."

"He didn't go with your brother."

"Okay, so does he know about this then? Because I don't see him letting his son go to New York on a school night."

"With everything that's happened lately, I thought it was important to let him go."

"With all what that's going on lately?" Mary Pat paused. Elizabeth imagined her screwing up her mouth in that indignant way of hers. Elizabeth wouldn't be baited into breaking the silence. She counted silently. *One, two, three.*

"So, your answer is to let him blow off practice?" Mary Pat said finally. "What are you teaching him? That it's just fine to let the team down for a baseball game. Mike is furious. You're lucky if he doesn't kick Trevor off the team."

"I'll call Mike."

"How would you like it if Mike blew off practice because he got tickets to a Mets game? This guy volunteers his time for the benefit of our kids. The least you can do is get Trevor to live up to his end of the deal."

"I said I'd call him, Mary Pat."

"Oh, and if Trevor didn't go to the game with Russell, who did he go with?"

"He went with a friend of mine."

"Does my brother know this person?"

Elizabeth stomach tightened. "Yes."

"Does he have permission to cross state lines with him?"

"He had my permission."

"Yeah, but he didn't have my brother's permission. For all we know, this so-called friend of yours is a pedo on wheels."

"He's not a pedo."

"And you know that for a fact?"

Elizabeth sighed. "I'm pretty sure, Mary Pat. Yeah."

"Pretty sure? I'm pretty sure I'm going to nominate you for Mother of the Year."

Mary Pat clicked off. Elizabeth stared at her phone in disbelief. She searched her memory; she hadn't agreed to a clause about Trevor not crossing state lines. Had she? No, she had not. But she knew how her sister-in-law relished a good drama. No doubt she'd already dialed Russell to give him a full report.

Her phone rang again. Gloria, this time.

"Cathy wants us to come over and sign the contract."

"Oh, that's great. But you don't need my signature, do you?"

"No, but I want you there to see how I determine a price on a property. Did you sign up for your real estate course yet?"

"Classes start Wednesday at the community center."

"Excellent. Any chance you can make it to Cathy's tonight? The sooner we get this show on the road, the better."

"I don't have a sitter. Is it okay if I bring Bailey?"

"Ordinarily I wouldn't recommend it, but it's Cathy. Meet you at 6:30."

Elizabeth left a voicemail for Mike apologizing for Trevor's absence at practice. She fed Bailey, took another shower, and slipped into a navy shirtdress and her mother's pearls. She would look and act like a professional. She would live up to the faith Cathy and Gloria showed in her.

THIRTY-SIX

Elizabeth wanted a glass of wine. She deserved a glass of wine. Entire sections of her brain lit up imagining its plummy taste on her tongue as she put Bailey to bed. Downstairs, she reached for the bottle in the cupboard and had a revelation: She fretted constantly about the cost of piano lessons, pre-school tuition, and soccer equipment, yet she always had money for wine. She did the math. Even the cheap stuff added up. She considered the ramifications of pouring one glass, which would inevitably lead to four:

You don't want to be a wreck when Red drops Trevor off, do you? Do you need a headache in the morning? Do you want to spend the day replaying what you said, and if it was the wrong thing? Will you enjoy feeling like you're starving to death tomorrow no matter how much food you eat?

She replaced the bottle in the cupboard. She made a cup of green tea. If she managed to cut her alcohol consumption, she'd have money to pay babysitters while she attended classes, met buyers, and attended open houses. The goal was to rely less on Nancy. The revelation she'd been sleeping with that disgusting pastor made Elizabeth downright queasy.

What else had she learned?

Red reported that Toni Badden drove to Connecticut four times before the murders, but why? Louisa's business seemed to be a well-oiled machine. Why would Toni drive all the way from New Hampshire to supervise? Louisa had a reputation for disappearing on recruits. Maybe Toni wanted to set her straight and ended up stabbing her to death out of frustration. And then, maybe Dave Davenport drove to New Hampshire to avenge his wife's death.

Sounds farfetched, but anything is possible with these people.

The front door squealed open, followed by the sound of sneakers.

"We won the playoffs, Mom! We won!" Trevor bounded into the kitchen wearing a Mets cap.

"Nice head gear," she said.

"Red bought it for me."

Red appeared behind Trevor. Elizabeth mouthed *thank you.*

"Is it playoff season already?" she asked. "And, you're telling me the Mets won? That in itself is amazing."

"Hey, hey, what are you? Some kind of Yankees' fan?" Red leaned against the archway that divided the kitchen and living room. "When it comes to the Mets, ya gotta believe!"

"What I can't believe is that you took Trevor to a playoff game. That is beyond generous, Red." Mentally, Elizabeth tried to calculate the cost of tickets, which could be thousands of dollars. But Red was a cop. Maybe somebody did him a favor.

Trevor bounced on his toes. "Picture this, Mom: It's five-to-two Cubs in the bottom of the ninth, and then Pete Alonso comes along and *whoosh*! Grand slam, Baby!"

"It sounds like quite a game."

"And then," Trevor said, waving a team yearbook Red must have supplied. "Dom Smith comes along and *whoosh*! hits another homer, and it's goodnight Cubbies!"

"Trevor is good luck, it turns out," Red said. "If it's all right with you, Elizabeth, I'll take him to a couple of games next season."

Next season? Next season didn't begin for six months. Did Red plan to be around that long? Elizabeth broke into a sweat.

"I'm glad everybody had a good time, but it's a school night. Light's out in ten minutes, Trev," she said.

He stiffened his legs. "Oh, come on, Mom!"

"Listen to your mother, Trev."

Trevor bumped Red's fist and waved the yearbook. "Thanks again, Man."

"Thanks again, Man?" Elizabeth muttered. "Really?"

"Hey, we bonded." Red moved closer.

"Clearly."

"He wants to quit soccer, Elizabeth," Red said, after Trevor's bedroom door clicked closed.

"He never mentioned it."

"He doesn't want to disappoint anybody. He's under the impression he needs soccer to get into college."

"That's silly."

"But that's what he thinks. Quitting soccer will free up time for kung fu."

"And what if he loses interest in that?"

"I don't think he will. He's learning how to stand up for himself while being respectful. He needs that. He's already a pretty disciplined kid, and kung fu will only help him in that regard."

"How many kids are in a class, usually?"

"It depends. I think he'll make friends."

Trevor didn't have any friends. Elizabeth was sold. "Okay, then. I'll see what he wants to do."

"Good." Red smiled. Lines shot like stars from the remarkable eyes. Elizabeth thought about asking him to stay for a cup of tea.

"I'd better go," he said. "I have an early morning."

"Sure. Right. Me too."

"Tell Trevor I'll see him Tuesday."

"I will."

Elizabeth luxuriated in the imagined sensation of her lips against Red's. She snapped out of it. She turned to the empty sink, where she could pretend to wash non-existent dirty silverware.

"I'll let myself out," he said. "Goodnight, Elizabeth."

Shutting out the sound of her heart hammering in her chest, she listened for the squeal of the door closing behind him.

ELIZABETH STARED AT the ceiling, stewing. She'd wanted to kiss Red with a breathtaking intensity. She still did.

She bolted upright and thrashed back onto the mattress. *What is wrong with you?* It was bad enough she'd fallen for the guy again, but now she was taking favors from him. She owed him. She owed Cathy, Gloria, and Nancy, too.

Elizabeth Candew, Connecticut's biggest charity case!

Well, no more. *She* would be the one to sell Cathy's house. *She* would be the one to solve Louisa and Toni's murders. *She* would earn her keep.

THIRTY-SEVEN

After a shower and coffee, Elizabeth brought up the MLS specs for Cathy's house on her laptop. The headline, *CHARMING HISTORIC COLONIAL CLOSE TO TRAIN AND SHOPPING* didn't inspire her. She came up with this:

RESIDE IN REVOLUTIONARY SPLENDOR

Gloria might be a crack real estate agent, but she didn't know Cathy's house as well as Elizabeth did, nor did she share her affection for it. Her photos couldn't show it to its best advantage. After Elizabeth dropped Bailey at school, she drove to Cathy's and angled her camera lens under the Palladian window so that it sparkled like a jewel of many colors in the sun. She imagined Mary Pat would criticize the photo as stupid, but Elizabeth had a hunch that buyers for such a house valued historic detail over stainless steel appliances. She took several other shots to include the formal garden that made her forget she lived in the twenty-first century.

She rushed back home to design a flyer. At pick-up time, she got permission to tack it to the parent board at the pre-school. She drove downtown to the beautifully restored lavender Victorian that housed Goody Smith's Ice Cream Shoppe. She bought herself and Bailey each a scoop of Rocky Road and asked permission to hang the flyer in the shop's window. Elizabeth figured at least one of their customers might interested in buying a house like Cathy's. She would be the one to sell it. She would.

264

SHE MET TREVOR AT THE bus stop.

He dropped his backpack on the kitchen floor. "I want to quit soccer."

"Red mentioned that. I wish you'd said something sooner. Pick up that bag and do your homework."

"No kidding, Ma."

"Don't call me *Ma*. It's *Mother*, *Mommy*, or *Mom*. Don't make me say it again."

"Yeah, like I'm going to call you *Mother*, Mom."

The kid exasperated her. She remembered what Red said about kung fu teaching respect and discipline and picked up the phone. "You were right. Trevor wants to quit soccer."

"I'll pick him up Tuesday."

"After therapy."

"Right." Red sighed. "After therapy."

TREVOR CLEARED THE table after dinner without complaint. Elizabeth sent him to take his shower. She put Bailey in her pajamas and read three books to her before guiltily setting her in front of the TV and queuing up *Frozen* for the umpteenth time. She opened her laptop and typed *how to find out if someone owns a gun* in the browser. It turned out gun ownership isn't public information. She didn't want to ask Red's help in finding out if Dave Davenport had one. She wanted to solve this murder on her own.

Also, she worried about her insistent attraction to Red. She found an index card and wrote *France. Mary Pat* on it in bold type with a black marker. She taped it to the mirror in her bathroom, where she would see it twice a day when she brushed her teeth. Red could be a real jerk. She would be wise to keep that in mind.

THIRTY-EIGHT

On Tuesday, Red picked Trevor up from the therapist's office and took him to kung fu. When he dropped him off later, he came inside instead of staying outside on the step as Elizabeth hoped. He looked too happy to see her; his posture emanated hopefulness. Or maybe it didn't. Elizabeth could be imagining things. It wouldn't be the first time.

"Hey there, Red," she said, resenting the obligation to turn down the volume of a favorite Dead show on YouTube. "How'd your lesson go, Trevor?"

The boy whirled around the kitchen and pulled some moves.

"He's off to good start. We stopped for cheeseburgers. I hope you don't mind."

"The ketchup in the corner of his mouth was my first clue," Elizabeth said.

Red's ears reddened. He ran his knuckle across his lip. "There's ketchup on my face?"

Elizabeth laughed, charmed by the unexpected vulnerability. "No, Trevor has ketchup on *his* face."

"So, anyway," Red said. "Well, we had a good time."

"Okay."

Jerry Garcia warbled, "They Love Each Other." Elizabeth's face burned in horror. She wanted to turn it off, but she couldn't move her feet.

"Yeah, so, I'd better be going." Red angled one of his feet awkwardly towards the door.

"It is a school night." Elizabeth raised her voice in an effort to prevent Red from hearing the lyrics coming from the television. "Hey, do you know if Dave Davenport has a gun?" she blurted.

So much for solving the murder on my own.

"Why do you ask?"

Elizabeth turned to Trevor. "It's pajama time."

"Yeah, yeah." He fist-bumped Red. "Thanks, Man."

Elizabeth watched her son walk down the short hallway and close the door to his room. She might as well let Red in on her theory. "What if Toni got sick of fielding complaints about Louisa's business practices, tried to reason with her, and ended up stabbing her. And then Davenport drove up to New Hampshire to shoot Toni?"

"That's good thinking, but it didn't happen."

Elizabeth's shoulders collapsed. "Oh, come *on!*"

"If it makes you feel any better, Michaels had the same idea, and he's been a detective for twenty-five years. Davenport's alibi is rock solid. And not only does he not own a firearm, he writes letters and makes donations to support all kinds of gun legislation."

"I really want to solve this case." Elizabeth shook her head. "I have to."

"Are you trying to put me out of a job?" Red stepped closer. Elizabeth felt the heat from his skin. He looked her straight in the eye. Involuntarily, Elizabeth exposed her throat. That he'd kiss her was a foregone conclusion. Even though she shouldn't, she'd kiss him back.

Instead, he said, "You have good instincts. Trust yourself."

He had his hand on the door knob when she stopped him.

"Red?"

"Yup?"

"What happened in France?"

"I made a mistake."

"Yeah," she said. "You did."

"If it makes you feel any better, she's not half the person you are."

It did make Elizabeth feel better, but she said, "It doesn't. Don't compare me and Mary Pat."

"She's your sister-in-law. That was a stupid thing to say."

Elizabeth shrugged. "We're not friends."

The door emitted its familiar squeal as she opened it. Red walked out onto the brick steps. A wind swept into the house, carrying the scent of dried leaves.

"I just want you to know that I know I made a mistake," he said. "The biggest mistake of my life. If I could make it up to you, I would. I'm so sorry, Elizabeth. I've been sorry for years."

"I never really got over it." She couldn't believe she said it out loud.

"I'm sorry," he said again. He looked into the distance. "For what it's worth, I would never hurt you again."

Even though she had a lot to say, the ability to manage a coherent sentence failed her.

He shrugged. He slipped his hands in his pockets and headed for his car.

ELIZABETH LAY AWAKE wondering what might have been had Red not dumped her. She wouldn't have a son, nor a daughter. *He* wouldn't have a daughter he barely knew living across the country. Despite the pain of the breakup, things had worked out for the best.

I just want you to know that I know I made a mistake. The biggest mistake of my life.

But maybe he hadn't made a mistake. Maybe everything unfolded in perfect order: Elizabeth had given birth to the children God intended, and now the time had come to find happiness with the man she once lost. In the morning, she took the index card off the bathroom mirror.

THIRTY-NINE

A week later, Gloria still hadn't been in touch. Elizabeth hadn't heard from Red, either, although Trevor reported receiving a text from him. Elizabeth kept herself busy fiddling away on her laptop, dreaming up social media ads to sell Cathy's house. Gloria already knew her way around social media, but marketing had once been Elizabeth's superpower. She had a hunch it still was.

The phone vibrated on the table.

Red.

She heard her mother's voice. *Let it ring. Don't let him think you're eager.*

Oh, but she was.

"Hello," she said casually.

"Hello." Red cleared his throat. "Um, I wondered if you'd like to come with Trevor and me to kung fu this afternoon. In case you wondered what they're teaching him, I mean."

"I guess I should probably know. Should we meet you there?"

"Or, I can pick you guys up. We could get a pizza after."

"I love pizza."

"I remember."

Elizabeth thought back to Matese Pizza where they used to go in high school. One day Red went to use the garlic shaker, but some joker had loosened its top, and he wound up with a mountain of yellow powder burying his Sicilian slices. He didn't get angry about it.

He went back to the counter and politely asked for replacements. His unflappability was one of the things that made Elizabeth fall in love with him. If it had happened to her, she would have been furious.

"I'll see you after school then." She disconnected and stared at the screen on her laptop. What had she been working on again? For a good minute, she had no idea.

ELIZABETH SET A BUDGET of thirty dollars – the approximate equivalent of three bottles of wine she wouldn't buy – on two social media platforms, placed her ads, and said a *Hail Mary*. She caught sight of herself in the decorative mirror above the dishwasher. Her hair looked dry and lifeless. She spooned some mayonnaise into a small bowl. In the bathroom she spread it through her hair and covered her head with a plastic bag for a half-hour conditioning treatment. She'd be damned if she looked like a scarecrow when Red picked her up to go to kung fu.

THE PHONE BUZZED. ELIZABETH adjusted the plastic bag to uncover her ear.

"It's Gloria," said the caller. "We've got six people who want to get into Cathy's place before the open house this weekend."

"Is that normal?"

"In this market where there's a ton of inventory, not really. One of the buyers said she saw something on a bulletin board. Was that you?"

"My daughter's preschool. Is that okay?"

"Yeah, it's okay. I got one buyer from your bulletin board, and three others from social media. It's funny. I placed those ads days ago and *crickets*. Now all of a sudden, we're getting bites."

Elizabeth smiled into her greasy phone.

"Can you be around Friday? So far, everyone's who's called can make it then. Some of them are bound to be no shows, but we'll still be in good shape."

"As long as I'm back in time to get the kids," Elizabeth said. "If we sell the house Friday, do we cancel the open house this weekend?" She hoped so; the weather looked excellent for pumpkin picking.

"We do the open house, regardless. The goal is to make sure everyone is prequalified for a mortgage, get as many offers as possible, and take the best one."

"Which invites a bidding war."

"Yep, and thrills the homeowner to no end."

"Which means good word of mouth for you, Gloria."

"That's the name of the game, Elizabeth. And you can be sure it also means good word of mouth for you, too."

ELIZABETH TOOK A SHOWER. Between the mayo treatment and a new brand of shampoo and conditioner, she knew she'd hit the jackpot as soon as she removed the towel from her head. The bent and droopy locks she's suffered lately had been replaced by buoyant and shiny curls. This day kept getting better.

She swabbed her phone with alcohol to dissolve the mayonnaise and noticed the missed call from Trevor's school.

Please, God. No bad news.

Usually, she'd skip the voice message and return the call immediately. This time, listened to brace herself. The police officer assigned to the school wanted to speak to her. He didn't say why.

A wave of anxiety rushed over her. *What now?* At the rate things were going with Trevor at school, she'd end up putting any commission she made with Gloria towards a down payment on a house in a district where nobody knew her family. She called back.

A nightmarishly long succession of rings ensued. Finally, the school secretary picked up. "Oh, hi, Mrs. Dispo," she said. "Officer Kenneth needs to speak with you. I'm going to put you on a quick hold."

Elizabeth waited. *Deep breaths.*

An older, gravelly male voice came on the line. "Is this Ms. Candew, Trevor Dispo's mom?"

"Yes, it is, and thank you for getting my name right."

"Oh, I should be able to get that much straight, I hope. My name is Kenneth O'Neil. I'm the officer assigned to be at school in – uh—the matter with your son, Trevor."

"Okay, yes?"

"We have good news," he said. Elizabeth pictured him speaking into the phone with his hand on his stomach. "Or bad news. Depends on how we look at it."

"I'm hoping we can look at it as good news."

"Your son was involved in another bullying incident."

"Okay."

"Thing is, I witnessed it, and I can say unequivocally that your son was the victim and not the aggressor."

"Well, that's good news." Elizabeth looked at the ceiling and mouthed, *Thank God.* "What happened?"

She heard the shuffle of paper. "This kid Noah Dunfore is the ringleader. He and his buddies jumped your boy in the school yard. Red Garcia filled me in on the situation, so rather than strut around the playground making myself obvious, I observed things from the cafeteria window, so these boys would act naturally, if you know what I mean."

"Yes, thank you. Good thinking."

"This leaves you with three choices. You can press charges, or *not* press charges but issue a warning that you will press charges should these boys interfere with your son ever again. Or you can just let the whole thing go."

"Let's go with the warning. I want these boys to leave my child alone, but I don't want to ruin anybody's life."

"Fair enough, and more than generous under the circumstances Detective Garcia relayed to me."

"Well, thank you, Officer. Your help means more to us than you know."

"You have a good day, Ms. Candew,"

"Oh, this is the single best day I've had in years, Officer. Thank you again."

RED DROVE UP AT FOUR on the dot. Elizabeth remembered they'd have to take her messy minivan to kung fu because it contained Bailey's car seat.

"I hope you don't mind if I drive," she said, removing a coffee cup from the holder. The van's interior was littered with flattened juice boxes.

"Not at all." Red strapped in Bailey.

Trevor flew down the front steps behind them in his uniform, his face shining with excitement. "Yah!" he shouted.

"Remember your seat belt," Red told him.

Elizabeth started the engine. "You're pretty good at this. You sure you don't have kids?"

Except he did have a kid, clear across the country. "I'm so sorry. I forgot."

"It's fine." He put his hand on her arm. "Really."

Elizabeth turned the corner. A half mile away, Trevor announced he forgot his water.

"Can you be more careful?" Elizabeth blew her bangs out of her eyes. "You know I hate buying water in plastic bottles."

"I do too," Red said, "but we don't have a choice. There's a store near the school."

Elizabeth pulled into the lot. Red said he'd make the run. Trevor asked to go with him.

Bailey writhed and kicked her mother's seat, her shrieks drowning out "Terrapin Station."

"Knock it off." Elizabeth met the child's eyes in the rearview. "They'll be right back. Be a good girl, and you can watch *Frozen* after you practice your letters."

Red and Trevor hopped in the car. Red whispered, "Is it okay I got some pretzels for Bailey?"

"Sure. Thank you."

Red handed them back. Bailey batted her eyes at him.

"Anyway, that was weird," Trevor said.

"What was weird?" Elizabeth asked.

"It wasn't that weird," Red said.

"We ran into Aunt MP and Dad," Trevor said. "And Creepy Hughey and Tammi, Dad's girlfriend."

Elizabeth pulled out of the lot. "I hear she's nice, Dad's girlfriend."

"That's because I told you that." Trevor said. "Tammi, nice. MP, on the other hand, not so nice."

In the rearview, Elizabeth watched her son make airplane motions with his arm. "I wish MP would pack up and fly to Albuquerque."

Elizabeth laughed out loud.

"Albuquerque," Red said. "Where'd you get that one?"

"One of those songs Nancy listens to," Trevor said. "She sings in-to a hairbrush."

"And how's Aunt Mary Pat doing?" Elizabeth slid her eyes side-ways for Red's reaction, but her peripheral vision didn't go that far.

"Grim. As usual," Trevor said.

Red said nothing.

"Right, well, let's not be late." Elizabeth pulled the car around in-to the adjacent lot. She and Bailey followed Red and Trevor into the building.

EVERYONE ATE TWO SICILIAN slices, except for Bailey, who left a paper plate of half-eaten mozzarella sticks in a puddle of mari-nara. Elizabeth walked back to the van with a warm glow in her stomach, her hand dangling close to Red's. A sense of relaxation came over her, as if she'd drunk two glasses of wine with dinner. But she hadn't.

On her doorstep, Red handed Bailey to Elizabeth.

"I'd ask you in for tea," she said. "But I'm showing Cathy's house. Big day tomorrow."

Red gazed at her with an intensity that made her skin burn. "Would you be up for dinner sometime? Just us?"

"Sure." She'd find the money for a babysitter.

He cupped her elbow. "Well, then, I'll be in touch."

From the door, she watched him until he got into his car and drove away.

FORTY

Elizabeth pulled into Cathy's driveway, her stomach dropping when she saw the FOR SALE sign next to the mailbox. *This is really happening.* Her best friend was moving across the planet.

Already at the front door, Gloria fiddled with the lock box. Two cars pulled up behind Elizabeth. A young couple made teamwork of removing a baby in a carrier from the SUV. A fair-skinned woman with silver hair and red lipstick got out of the shiny Mercedes behind it. Her husband followed her up the walk, coat flapping in the wind.

Elizabeth snapped off "Wharf Rat" and gathered the navy and silver folders that contained the specs on the property.

She climbed the steps towards the pumpkin display Cathy had arranged on the porch. Gloria introduced herself and Elizabeth to the buyers. She ran her hand along the historic marker on the white clapboard. "Isn't this a lovely home?"

"It looks like something out of a history book," the young mother gushed.

"Let's take a look inside," the silver-haired woman said, twisting her mouth. Elizabeth suspected she wouldn't be easy to impress.

Gloria led everyone into the large foyer. The buyers craned their necks to take in the ceiling. Gloria winked at Elizabeth.

The silver-haired woman's husband complained about the size of the master bedroom, but in the end, both couples made offers.

A third couple came along and outbid them. Mentally, Elizabeth worked out her share of the commission.

"Those older two, the Maguires," Gloria said, when she called Elizabeth later, "showed me a screenshot of an ad I didn't place."

"I placed it. I hope you don't mind," Elizabeth said.

"The young couple said they saw it, too, and it *captivated* them. You're off to a good start in this business."

"Thank you. So, what now? We hold the offers until after the open house?"

"No. By law, we have to report all offers to the homeowner as they come in, but I'd still like to do the open house and see if we can do better."

"See you then."

Elizabeth clicked off. She started a text to Chelsea, but her phone rang again.

"Forget the open house," Gloria told her. "Cathy wants us to wrap it up. That means you sold the house."

"We sold the house, you mean."

"No, you sold it," Gloria said. "Get yourself a glass of champagne."

ELIZABETH WOULD CELEBRATE without champagne. Why would she ever dull this buzz of exhilaration with alcohol? She'd take the kids out to dinner and let them pick out the restaurant! She'd send Patrick the check she owed him for piano lessons!

She picked up Bailey and called the office at Trevor's school to make arrangements to get him, rather than have him take the bus. Officer Kenneth intercepted her when she arrived. He was thinner and balder than Elizabeth imagined.

"I didn't see it coming," he said. "I'm sorry about the trouble, Ms. Candew."

"What trouble? What did I miss?"

"I've been a police officer thirty-five years. Used to be we called a kid's parents, and the kid had to face the music. Nobody accused us of making up stories."

Elizabeth spotted Mary Pat and the Dunfores huddling in the office with Mrs. Caffee. "You're scaring me."

Officer Kenneth scratched his eyebrow hard. "The parents of the boys involved in the incident with your son are contesting my report."

"That's ridiculous."

"That's what I said."

"What did Mrs. Caffee say?"

Officer Kenneth hooked his thumb towards her office. "Let's find out."

THE OTHER PARENTS BROKE from the huddle. They blinked at Elizabeth. Mrs. Caffee seated herself on a radiator next to a bookcase that contained few books but many wedding pictures, presumably of offspring.

"What now?" Elizabeth said.

"Oh, nothing." Mary Pat's nostrils flared. "We were just discussing how you managed to pin Trevor's behavior on our children."

"And how we can vindicate them," said Andrea Atler. "I know my son, and he would never do any of the things this officer said."

"None of our sons would," Pastor Jim agreed, reaching down to scratch a hairy shin.

"I didn't make it up," Officer Kenneth said.

"You don't know my son," Joseph's mother said. "I do."

Elizabeth rolled her eyes. "Oh, so this man's a liar?"

Pastor Jim jammed his fists into the pockets of the shorts he wore even on a windy October afternoon. "We believe you've had undue influence on Officer Kenneth, Mrs. Dispo."

"What are you suggesting, Pastor?" Elizabeth let go of Bailey's hand. She made air quotes around *Pastor*. "I just met him, for crying out loud."

"Okay, but you're sleeping with another member of the police force," Mary Pat declared.

"I'm not sleeping with anybody. As if it's any of your – any of *any*body's business! And even if I were, what has that got to do with Officer Kenneth, who's just minding his business trying to do his job?"

"All right, maybe you're not sleeping with Red Garcia, but I know for a fact you're seeing him." Mary Pat looked over at Mrs. Caffee. "That's the detective I told you about."

"Mary Pat, you're wrong. I'm not seeing him." *Not officially.*

"I'm right, Elizabeth."

"Does your brother know about this meeting?"

"He's at work," Mary Pat told the others. "Trevor's dad is a dentist. He has patients."

"Dr. Dispo, the dentist?" Rosalita piped up. "Jim, he did the emergency filling for Isaiah when Dr. Sonas was on vacation."

"Dr. Dispo is your ex?" Jim asked. "I was thinking about Dr. Dispo when I spotted that billboard of his on Route 8 the other day."

Elizabeth sighed. "By any chance, is it a picture of him leaning against a tooth?"

"A tooth*brush*. I'm surprised you haven't spotted it. It's hard to miss. I'd stick with Dispo, but we've been with Dr. Sonas for too many years."

"Maybe Dispo wouldn't see you if he knew how you treated his son," Elizabeth said wearily.

Mary Pat's eyes blackened. "Your son has become a menace due to your behavior, Elizabeth. He's traumatized. It's not my fault he's bearing the brunt of a divorce caused by your wanton actions."

Under the institutional light, Mary Pat looked brittle, her lipstick stark against the broken capillaries in her skin. The word *unhinged* came to mind. Elizabeth glared into her eyes and every eye in the room, one by one. Jim puffed up his chest. Rosalita studied the loafers peeking from under her Lady Lily Wear skirt. Mrs. Caffee checked her watch.

"The truth will come out," Elizabeth said.

A smug smile crept across Mary Pat's face. Elizabeth wanted to slap her.

"You're right, Sweetie. The truth will come out." Mary Pat smiled harder. "You wait."

FORTY-ONE

Elizabeth lost the desire to celebrate. She didn't feel like going home and cooking, either. She drove over to Henry Hobbins Burger Emporium and asked for a table.

Trevor examined the menu excitedly. She hadn't the heart to tell him he'd been blamed again.

"What's the occasion, Mom?"

"I sold Cathy's house. Things are going to be a little easier financially from now on."

"Fin-*an*-shully," Bailey repeated, picking up a purple crayon. "Fin-*an*-shully."

Cold air blew on Elizabeth from an overhead vent. She shivered.

She couldn't talk Bailey out of mac and cheese, even though they had a ton of it at home. Trevor ordered a cheeseburger with a hockey-oriented name. *A themeburger*. Elizabeth wanted iced tea and South-western chicken salad, but the cold air put her off. She settled for hot tea and fish and chips. She zipped up her jacket and tried to block out the autotuned song coming from the sound system.

She wanted Red's insight. He hadn't been in touch about dinner. Despite her reluctance to look eager, she decided to initiate contact.

"I know the rule is no phones at the table, but I have to text Red," she told her children.

Trevor reached into the middle of the table and broke off a piece of bread. "Go for it, Mom."

I need your opinion, she typed.

Elizabeth turned on the ringer and said a silent prayer Red would text back quickly. She wrapped her hands around the mug of tea, grateful for the small warmth. Her children seemed impervious to air conditioning in the middle of October. She retrieved Bailey's jacket from under the table and laid it across her lap.

The phone pinged.

Meet me for dinner? Red texted.

Let me see if I can get a babysitter.

The meals arrived. Trevor squeezed out a mountain of ketchup next to a cheeseburger the size of a small planet.

Elizabeth texted Chelsea, who agreed to babysit. Elizabeth asked the server to wrap the fish and chips. If all went according to plan, she'd be home in an hour, giving her plenty of time to freshen up before she went out with Red for another meal.

RED RESERVED A BOOTH tucked into a corner at Mariani's. A waiter came along and popped open a bottle of champagne to celebrate Elizabeth's sale. Their glasses fizzed happily in the candlelight.

"To you," Red said.

"To me," Elizabeth agreed, touching her glass to his. "Although it was almost too easy. What if I can't do it again?"

"You will." He had on an impeccably pressed turquoise button-down that brought out his eyes. "I believe in you, Lizza."

Elizabeth dipped bread into a plate of olive oil. "Poor Officer Ken. The way those people treated him."

"Ken's a big boy. He can handle himself. Those people are idiots. I'd talk to that principal myself, but I don't think it would help."

"It wouldn't. She's stubborn, and I get the feeling she's ready to retire." If Red confronted Mrs. Caffee, it would give weight to Mary Pat's accusation of an affair. "You've been so helpful as it is."

"It's been my pleasure." Red's remarkable eyes shined in the candlelight. "The pleasure is all mine."

Elizabeth would kiss him tonight. She knew it in her bones. *Just put those awful people out of your mind!* She sipped her champagne slowly. She didn't want to lose her head. She would know exactly what she was doing when she kissed him tonight. She would remember everything clearly in the morning.

ON THE WAY OUT TO THE car, Red took Elizabeth's hand. Her palm in his felt right and familiar. When they got inside the car, he put the key in the ignition, but he didn't start the engine.

"I'm sorry about what I did to you, Elizabeth."

"You've already apologized. I believe you."

"No, let me finish. When Cindy split for California, I thought I had it coming. I've been having this conversation with you in my head for years. Like a loop, you know? I was such a jerk. I don't know what I was thinking."

Elizabeth ran her thumb against his cheekbone, the way she did when they were kids. In that moment sitting under the parking lot lights it seemed like none of it ever happened. "Water under the bridge," she said.

"Nobody could ever compare to you. None of them."

Elizabeth thought Red would kiss her, but he started the car.

At her house, he walked her to the door and watched her unlock it. "Can I see you tomorrow?"

Elizabeth stepped into the house. She hadn't gotten around to replacing the screen door with the storm panel yet. She leaned her forehead against the screen.

"Sure," she said.

"Forget the babysitter. Let me come over and make dinner for you and the kids."

"I would love that. We all would." She smiled. How easily she could see them becoming a family.

"I can drop off the food when I pick up Trevor for kung fu."

"Sounds like a plan."

Elizabeth closed the door and tossed her keys on the counter. Mentally, she went through her closets and put together an outfit. Twenty-four hours from now, the kids would be safely tucked in their beds again. She would kiss Red then. Oh, yes, she would.

FORTY-TWO

The oven needed cleaning. Heaven forbid Red should see it full of burnt American cheese, meat drippings, and crumbs. Elizabeth sprayed the heck out of the thing with a toxic foam. Then, while it ate up the grime like a piranha, she headed out for Cabernet. Now that she'd cut down on drinking, three bottles should be enough to cover her and Red for dinner. She counted on him to drink wine, but she tossed in a six pack of that lame beer he liked just in case.

Back at home, she learned the oven cleaner had fewer teeth than advertised. She dug up a pair of rubber gloves and set about scrubbing the oven. After her shower, she drove to a salon for which she'd received a coupon in the mail and paid for a manicure. She wanted to look her best tonight.

ELIZABETH HAD AN IDEA to surprise Red. She'd surprise Trevor, too. Once her nails were fully dry, she sat at the piano. Could she still play it? She found some ELP footage on YouTube and hummed along to the opening to Part I of "Karn Evil 9: First Impression." Her fingers failed at first, but muscle memory kicked in. Her hands followed the notes taking shape on the screen in her mind. And why wouldn't they? Years ago, she'd practiced this piece to the point where she played it in her dreams.

Elizabeth forgot the time. Too late to walk up to meet Trevor, she strapped Bailey into the van and arrived at the stop as the bus turned the corner.

Trevor dived into the seat beside his sister. He caught his mother's eye in the rearview.

"What are you so happy about?" he asked.

"I'm just glad to see my boy," Elizabeth said. "Anything wrong with that?"

THROUGH THE WINDOW, she watched Red pull up. Elizabeth liked that he never made her wait, a blessed contrast to Russell, who once admitted he liked keeping her on her toes. Red walked towards the house in a button-down shirt and chinos, seemingly impervious to the dip in temperature. The expression on his face made her uneasy.

"There you are," she said cheerily.

"Can I talk to you out here for a minute?"

Elizabeth had no desire to stand in the wind without a jacket, but maybe he had news about the case. "Sure."

"I need you to clear something up for me."

"Sure," she said again. "What is it?"

"I've heard a rumor Bailey isn't Russell's kid."

"Wait. What?"

"I'm asking. Is it true?"

"Russell is not her father, no. Why do you bring it up?"

"Mary Pat contacted me about Officer Kenneth. When she didn't get her way, she threatened to report me for conflict of interest. Then she told me the thing about Bailey."

Elizabeth felt her temperature spike. "The thing about Bailey? Are you assigning some sort of stigma?" *Are you labeling my child a bastard?*

"Why didn't you tell me? Why did I have to find out from –." he spit out the name, "*Mary Pat?*"

"Find out what? What has any of this got to do with you?"

"I don't know. It seems like a subject that should have come up."

"Really, Red?" Elizabeth wrapped herself up in her arms against the wind. "That doesn't strike you as a tiny bit presumptuous? When exactly in this fledgling relationship, or whatever this is, would you have had me bring it up?"

He looped his thumbs over his pockets and stared straight over her shoulder. "It's strange you didn't mention it. That's all I'm saying."

"We can talk about it after dinner. I'll tell you the whole story. Once the kids are in bed."

"Yeah, about dinner. I think we should cool it for a while."

"So, no dinner?" Elizabeth stood motionless, the wind sticking her hair to her lipstick. She felt as though he'd slapped her. "What do I tell Trevor? Are you not taking him to kung fu?"

"Oh, come on. This is between you and me. I'm not going to take it out on a kid."

"Right."

"Tell him I'll be in the car. Don't worry about dinner. We'll get pizza or something."

"That's really generous of you." Elizabeth was done being polite. "I guess I'll make myself a piece of toast."

She went into the house and let the door fall shut behind her.

FORTY-THREE

Without having to be reminded, Bailey used a fork. She ate her mac and cheese while her mother sat staring into space. Elizabeth couldn't eat. She had no room in her stomach for anything except a leaden stunned sadness. Her lungs swelled with grief.

Your child deserves your attention! Snap out of it! She looked at her daughter, shocked to see the child had a napkin in her lap. And when was the last time Elizabeth had to tell her to take her thumb out of her mouth? The girl's hair had grown, falling to her collarbone in gentle curls. Her eyes were no longer blue but a serene gray. Elizabeth didn't have a baby anymore.

After dessert, she offered to put on *Frozen* for the four thousandth and seventy-sixth time, but Bailey asked to watch *The Partridge Family* instead.

"Since when do we watch *The Partridge Family*?"

"I saw it at Nancy's house. They sing very good songs."

"Do they really?"

"Yes. I'm going to be Laurie."

"I don't know who that is."

"Nancy likes being Laurie, so she makes me be Tracy. But she's not here, so now I get to be Laurie."

Elizabeth didn't know whether to be charmed or freaked out. She searched for the show on her TV and put on an episode. Assured it was wholesome as Nancy promised, she logged on to her real estate course. She still felt kicked in the stomach, but she'd be damned if she wasted time balled up on the couch spouting tears about Red Garcia. She had an exam coming up. She would make something of herself. She would set a good example for her children.

TREVOR BOUNDED INTO the house after his lesson.

"Check me out, Ma." He showed off some moves.

"I'm very proud of you, Trev, but what did I say about calling me *Ma*?"

"Check me out, Mom," he said.

"I'm checking." Elizabeth took the last sip of her tea and closed the laptop. She'd been immersed in her lesson, but now the sadness came back.

"I'm impressed, Trevor. In case I haven't told you lately, I'm proud of you," she said.

FORTY-FOUR

To squeeze in extra steps for exercise, Elizabeth pulled into the spot farthest from the supermarket entrance. As soon as she cashed a couple of commission checks, she'd join a gym. Right now, she headed for the baking aisle. She needed organic cake mix for the cupcakes she promised Bailey she'd make for her birthday celebration at school, which coincided with Halloween. The house embarrassed Elizabeth, so she planned what Bailey called "the real birthday party" at the cineplex, inviting three school friends and their mothers for pizza and a movie.

At the checkout, Elizabeth perused the magazines for sale. The photograph of clam chowder on *Living in New England*'s cover caught her attention. She wouldn't mind learning to make a good clam chowder, instead of resorting to a canned version packed with sodium as she usually did. She took the magazine from the rack and thumbed through it. A headline struck her: *Multilevel Marketing: Good Business or Financial Disaster?* She skimmed the article, which claimed that 99.7% of people who became involved in an MLM lost their money. She tossed the magazine in the cart.

AFTER ELIZABETH FROSTED the cupcakes and put them in the refrigerator, she made a cup of tea and returned to the article in *Living in New England*. It detailed the hardships that befell partici-

291

pants in several MLMs, two of whom lived in the next town. A full-page photograph showed a well-dressed middle-aged couple seated in a restaurant booth. Both the woman and the man had rings under their eyes.

Elizabeth read, "...Shelly and Mike Allen of Seabright, Connecticut saved for two-and-a-half decades to provide for their children's education.

'We met a seemingly wonderful woman in a support group for special needs parents,' Shelly, whose children include a son with Down Syndrome, reported. 'She convinced us to join a clothing business. She said we could make more than enough money to ensure Billy's care after we die. It was too good to pass up.'"

'We fell for it hook, line and sinker,' Mike, who owns a successful Irish pub and restaurant in Seabright's bustling center, admits. 'I'm a businessman. If anybody should have known better, it was me. I sank my kids' college money into this scheme. I let my family down.' He wiped away a tear as he recalled how his older son, Michael, was forced to leave Brown University in his senior year after he couldn't make his tuition payment."

Elizabeth re-read the article: Special needs support group. Brown University. *Hey, doesn't Stephanie Davenport go to Brown?* "She's very determined," Louisa had said of her daughter. "She's a force of nature."

Elizabeth had an idea. She checked Instagram and combed the profiles of five different Stephanie Davenports until she found the right one. Elizabeth scrolled through Correct Stephanie's feed and discovered numerous photos of a lanky guy with tufted hair named Mike: *Mike on skis, Mike on the soccer field, Mike with his arm around a surfboard, Mike on a Ferris Wheel with his arm around Stephanie.* A look at his profile revealed his name: *MikeyAllen777.*

Elizabeth stared at her phone in disbelief. Could Stephanie have killed her own mother? If so, she almost felt sorry for Louisa, who was so desperate to secure her children's futures she'd schemed and defrauded innocent people. She also felt a strange sorrow for Stephanie, who, if she did indeed commit the murder(s), had blown all her dreams to smithereens. The girl might very well waste her life in prison. Elizabeth put her face in her hands. *Why couldn't the killer be that damn pastor?*

Her heart pounded anticipating Red's reaction to her discovery, but surely he had already looked at Stephanie. *Surely he had.* Elizabeth could hardly call him after what happened the night before, though. She didn't want him thinking she meant to apologize or talk things over. Red could take a hike.

She considered calling his obnoxious partner to reveal her findings, but no. If her detective work checked out, that clown seemed the type who'd take credit for it. Elizabeth would bask in that glory herself, thank you very much.

She dialed Red.

"By any chance," she said by way of hello. "Did you look into Stephanie Davenport for the murders?"

"She's a family member, Elizabeth. Yeah, we looked at her," he said brusquely. "Her alibi checked out."

"Okay, so you know her fiancé's parents signed up with Louisa and lost his college fund?"

Red didn't say anything.

"Did you know that, Red?"

"Of course I know it. Look, my partner talked to her and the fiancé. They were out of town together the days of the murders. They were on a Ferris wheel outside of Hartford the day of Louisa's murder."

"And the day of Toni's?"

"At a park, also in Hartford."

"Did Michaels find anyone to corroborate?"

"He's a detective, Elizabeth. I think he knows how to do his job."

"So, that's a yes."

He hesitated. "Yes."

"Yeah, because I'm wondering if he used her Instagram feed to corroborate. You see, I'm looking through it now, and it backs up what you're telling me."

"So, what's the problem then?"

"Instagram doesn't prove anything. Just because they posted a photo doesn't mean it was taken that day. Did Michaels look into that? I mean, I'm no legal expert, but if you got a warrant to look at their phones, couldn't you find out when the photos were taken, as opposed to when they posted them?"

"Michaels is an excellent detective. I'm sure he explored that possibility." Red cleared his throat. "Let me talk to him."

He hung up.

FORTY-FIVE

Bailey wasn't having it.

"Knock it off." Elizabeth told her. She had a flashback to a fight she'd had thirty-five years ago with her own mother when she'd forced her to wear a coat over a Halloween costume. "Put it on. It's cold out there."

Bailey clamped her arms across her chest. Her legs stiffened into exclamation marks.

"Fine, then. No trick or treating this afternoon."

The child narrowed her eyes. Lately everything came down to a fight.

"I can call off the *real* birthday party at the movie theater. Don't push me."

Bailey stood stock still. Elizabeth wiggled her arms into the coat over the Elsa costume. She lifted her and carried her out to the minivan.

She left the girl and her birthday cupcakes at school with Miss Alice, a woman in late middle age dressed as Little Bo Peep. On her way back to the van, she got a text from Cathy suggesting an impromptu farewell breakfast at the Walton Street Café. She stopped at the light on Church Street and sang along to "Box of Rain." Amber leaves drifted among thin headstones in the pre-Revolution cemetery.

AT THE CAFÉ ENTRANCE, Elizabeth made her way past a family of stuffed scarecrows seated on a bale of hay. She spotted her best friend at a booth near the window.

Cathy looked up from her coffee. Her eyes matched the pale blue of her windbreaker.

"Did you run this morning?" Elizabeth asked.

"Yoga."

Elizabeth slumped into the seat opposite her. "You had time for yoga class the day before a move across the planet?"

"A person has to take care of herself, Elizabeth."

"You're annoying."

Cathy shrugged. A waitress flew over to take their order in an ankle-length black fringed dress, turned on her stiletto heel, and rushed off.

"Morticia Adams or Elvira Mistress of the Dark?" Cathy asked.

"I'm thinking Morticia." Elizabeth squinted. "The hair, though. Maybe Elvira."

Cathy finished her coffee. "My money's on Elvira."

They discussed the logistics of Cathy's move to Asia. A series of tunes came over the sound system, including "Witchy Woman," "Evil Woman," "Devil Woman," and "Devil in a Blue Dress."

"I'm sensing a theme," Elizabeth said.

Cathy rolled her eyes. "Some men will never forgive us for giving birth to them. Oh, listen. It's the 'Monster Mash.' Didn't we play Spin the Bottle to 'Monster Mash' at Randi Kellogg's party?"

"Yeah. Randi insisted on a glass bottle. It spun better than plastic."

"Spun too well if you ask me. I aimed for Mickey Nelson and ended up kissing Bart Farder with that film of saliva all over his lips." Cathy wiped her mouth with the back of her hand. "I can still feel it."

"Yuck. I remember that. I heard Randi became some sort of nuclear physicist."

"Oh, good. So now she can blow up the world."

The waitress brought the food.

"I love your costume," Elizabeth told her. "Morticia or Elvira?"

The girl's face sunk with disappointment. Looking at her now, she couldn't have been more than twenty.

"I'm Kiley Jenner," she said.

"Oh, we were just teasing. We knew you were Kiley the minute we saw you." Cathy thanked her for the scrambled eggs and bacon – no potatoes or toast – and picked up her fork.

"Nice save," Elizabeth said. "What time is your flight tomorrow?"

"We have to be at JFK by 10AM."

"Well, that's civilized at least."

Cathy squeezed ketchup on her eggs. "I'm counting on you to keep selling houses so you and the kids can visit us."

"Pray for me."

"You're going to be fine. Give yourself some credit."

"I think I will be. I can see my way forward at least."

"How's Red Garcia? Is he still on the scene?"

The less Elizabeth said about Red, the better. If she talked about him, she'd start thinking about him. She didn't want to think about him.

"He's become a good friend to Trevor."

"Well, that's something. Any breaks in the murder case?"

"So far nothing's checked out."

"Does Red have any ideas?"

"Not that he talks about with me. Anyway, forget the case." Elizabeth swallowed hard. She'd been determined not to cry about Red. So far she hadn't, but it was hard not to when his name came up.

She blinked back tears. "I am going to miss you so much, Cathy."

"I'll miss *you*. I was thinking about it, though. How often do we get to see each other as it is? You live five minutes away, and I'm lucky if I see you six times a year."

"When did we all get so busy?" Elizabeth dabbed at her eyes with her napkin. She cut into her omelet, which oozed with a variety of cheeses. "You know, if I meet my sales goals, maybe I could fix my front walk *and* bring the family to Asia. Maybe we could even visit next Christmas, if you still want us."

"Of course I want you. I also have faith in you." Cathy removed a small datebook from her purse. "I'm putting it on my calendar."

A grenade of anxiety exploded inside Elizabeth. She gave her friend a wet smile.

FORTY-SIX

Once upon a time in college, Elizabeth worked as a campaign volunteer, making cold calls to procure votes for then-Congresswoman Nettie Monaco. She didn't like cold calling then, and she didn't like it now. In those days, a third of the people on the other end hung up on her, a third cursed her out, and the remainder either listened politely or seized the opportunity to discuss their ailments. Twenty-three years later, Elizabeth could recite a conversation about bleeding hemorrhoids verbatim.

She learned that not much had changed after Gloria emailed numbers for one hundred homeowners for her to cold call, the goal being to get appointments that would lead to listings for houses they could sell. Elizabeth plowed through the names and logged her results. By two o'clock, she'd left dozens of voice messages. Some of the people who answered the phone impugned her for ruining naps of both seniors and toddlers. One man revealed details of acid reflux and creaky knees. In the end, Elizabeth managed to secure only one appointment, with a woman named Millie whose current contract with a "crap" realtor would expire in a week. Elizabeth smelled a possible nightmare client, but she booked her anyway. She notified Gloria to meet up at Millie's house Saturday morning.

She poured a third cup of tea. The phone rang: Stonesbury Elementary School.

Please be good news.

"Elizabeth Candew," she answered without thinking – instead of *hello* – the way she'd done before marriage and kids took over.

"I'm sorry," said the caller. "I thought I had the Dispo residence."

"Trevor Dispo is my son," she said. "I take it you're calling from Mrs. Caffee's office."

"Mrs. Caffee needs to speak with you. Can you hold?"

Elizabeth looked at her nails. "Sure."

"Trevor has been involved in another incident, Mrs. Dispo," the principal said.

"Okay. Do you have any details? Can I speak with Officer Kenneth?"

"Officer Kenneth isn't available. Your son assaulted another student."

"Assaulted how?"

"He kicked one of the other boys. We're going to need another meeting. Can you come in this afternoon?"

"Trevor has music lessons and therapy, and then we're going trick-or-treating."

"Do you think rewarding Trevor with trick-or-treating is a good idea considering his behavior?"

"Are you telling me how to raise my child, Mrs. Caffee?" Elizabeth felt her temperature spike. "Because I'm not at all convinced Trevor is the problem. Officer Kenneth vindicated him. You have a bullying problem at your school, and you know it."

"Look, Mrs. Dispo. We're debating whether to take your son's case to the board. If you want a say in the matter, you'll come in this afternoon."

"Let's make it after therapy."

The rattling of bracelets came over the line. "Can you do 5:30?"

Therapy ran until 5:30. "I can do 5:45. How long is this going to take?"

"As long as it *takes*, Mrs. Dispo, but it's Halloween for the other families, too. Their children want to go trick-or-treating as much as yours do."

As if I give a damn what their children want to do! Smoke came out of Elizabeth's ears. "I'll see you then, Mrs. Caffee. Mark my words, I will get to the bottom of this."

She disconnected and went to the cupboard where she kept the wine. A glass – just one – would ease the tightening spots in her temples; two would dissolve them altogether. *Until the inevitable headache takes over.* She closed the cupboard. The piano called to Elizabeth. She sat down. When she was small, music made everything better. When she stopped playing after making the irrational link between her success and her parents' divorce, she'd only hurt herself.

She played "The Great Gates of Kiev," *her* favorite by Emerson, Lake and Palmer. In high school, she dreamed of singing it for an audience. Red, the proud boyfriend, would be seated in the front row. She imagined his reaction, the expression on his face. She would wow him.

Now, she fantasized about *showing* him. She wanted him to see what she was capable of, and what he'd foolishly thrown away. She wanted to show Mrs. Caffee and the pastor and his stupid wife, too. She wanted to show Russell and Mary Pat and Hughey. She would show them all.

Above all, Elizabeth would show herself.

TREVOR DROPPED THE pen and cradled his wrist.

"Finish your homework," Elizabeth told him. "We're on a tight schedule."

"Finish your homework," Bailey mimicked. She sat at the kitchen table in her costume and ticked off the reviews of Elizabeth's cupcakes on her fingers.

"Taylor, Tyler, and Cameron liked them. Ryan said they tasted like poo."

"Did Ryan eat his cupcake?" Elizabeth asked.

Bailey carefully held up her fingers. "He ate two cupcakes."

"Do you think they tasted like poo then, Bailey?"

She shook her head. "I told him, you are *rude*, Ryan."

"Ryan is extremely rude, Bailey. Hey, Trev," Elizabeth said. "Tell me what happened at school today."

"I don't want to talk about it."

"Come on. Before Christian gets here for your piano lesson. I can't help you if you don't talk to me."

Trevor plunked his head onto his math book. "Joey and Noah jumped me and stole my lunch money. They said it's open season since nobody believes me or Officer Kenneth."

" Mrs. Caffee said you kicked somebody. Is that true?"

"Yeah, Joey. Noah had me on the floor with his foot on my wrist, and Joey had his hands in my pockets. I tried to get free, and my sneaker somehow ended up between his legs."

"Poor Joey." *Maybe now the little cretin won't be able to reproduce.*

Did Elizabeth say that out loud? She didn't think so, but she was so angry she couldn't think straight. She ordinarily abhorred violence, but right now it would feel good – *so good!* – to punch Mrs. Caffee and those parents one by one in the face.

She needed time to think. She shut herself in the bathroom and fluffed her hair in the mirror. They'd get through this. She didn't know how, but they would. She closed the bathroom door behind her and put one foot in front of the other.

DETERMINED TO SPARE Bailey the drama at the principal's office, Elizabeth called Nancy to ask her to babysit. She didn't pick up. *Strange. Nancy always picks up.*

Elizabeth went out and pretended to look for mail she'd already collected. Up the street, she saw Nancy on her lawn fiddling with an inflatable ghost. Elizabeth called to her, but she didn't answer. She must not have heard. She went back into her house.

After his piano lesson, Trevor followed his mother to the van.

"Wait here," she told him.

She took Bailey's hand and headed to Nancy's house. She hated asking a favor last-minute, but she knew Nancy would enjoy showing off the little one in her Elsa costume to trick-or-treaters.

She rang the bell. From the other side of Nancy's door, Elizabeth heard the volume lower on some hit from yesteryear. Elizabeth squinted to see through the door's small window and spotted the back of Nancy's head. Nancy stood stock still in the little hallway beside the kitchen.

She's avoiding me.

"How much you wanna bet that meatball pastor turned her against us?" Elizabeth said out loud.

"I don't know what that means." Bailey said.

They headed back to the van.

FORTY-SEVEN

At the therapist's office, a diffuser behind the empty reception desk emanated lavender. Elizabeth inhaled it as though her life depended on it. In the mad rush to get there on time, she forgot her real estate books. While she waited for Trevor to come out from his session, she thumbed through parenting magazines, filled with the usual conflicting advice, and a *Vogue* from the previous spring. She slid the magazines back in the rack and scrolled through social media notifications on her phone. Bailey fell asleep in a chair in her costume and coat.

A recent update from the Stonesbury Moms and Dads page got Elizabeth's attention, especially since it included a photo of her house with its crumbling front walk.

> *Once again, this loser is a danger to our kid's at Stonesbury Elementary. He did something disgusting (!) on the field trip to Essex, and now he has caused another incident in the lunchroom. It is time he is expelled from our school system! We do not pay taxes to have to worry about our kid's being hurt by a bully like Trevor Dispo. Apparently, he comes from a troubled family, and I feel bad for him, but this is NOT OUR PROBLEM. My husband and myself are going up to the school first thing tomorrow to demand this kid get sent home FOR GOOD! Who is with us?*

A thread of responses ensued.

Look at the trash can on that wreck of a driveway. You'd think they'd know to hide their garbage until garbage day like the rest of civilized society. My wife and I will definitely be at the school tonight.

The following comment incited a torrent of responses, including screeds about racism and pedophile priests.

This is why we send our kids to Catholic schools. It eliminates the possibility of having to deal with this element.

Another:

Is it true this is Dr. Dispo's kid? My family has been going to Dr. Dispo since we moved here to Stonesbury. We recommend him highly. If this is his kid, I feel terrible for him. His ex-wife must be some piece of work. Obviously, he needs to have full custody. I hope he takes action and gets this boy the help he needs!!!!!!!!!!

Elizabeth rubbed her temples. Trevor returned to the waiting room, followed by his therapist, Gina, a thin young woman with kind eyes and an open face.

"Trevor and I had a good talk today," she said.

"Really, Trevor? Is that true?"

"I guess so." He smiled and tucked his head. Elizabeth suspected a crush.

"Well, I'm glad."

"Is it all right if I talk to your mother privately for a sec, Trev?"

"Okay." Trevor dropped into the chair Elizabeth abandoned, next to his sleeping sister.

"I see a lot of kids in here," Gina said, behind a closed door in her office. "As you can imagine."

Elizabeth braced herself.

"You need to know that Trevor is a really good kid. Everything he says indicates he strives to do the right thing."

"I'm not kidding myself then?"

Gina shook her head. "It's obvious to me the problem at school isn't Trevor's fault. They're making a good kid a scapegoat. I've seen this kind of thing before. From what Trevor tells me, you're doing the best anyone can in an unacceptable situation. You're doing everything right."

Elizabeth's eyes stung with tears, but she didn't have time for a good cry, which if she thought about it, was long overdue. Until then, Gina's words would serve as a shield when she faced those dreadful parents in Mrs. Caffee's office.

THEY SPRINTED ACROSS the dark parking lot and leapt back into the van, rain thrumming on the windshield.

"We're not going to get to go trick-or-treating, are we?" Trevor asked.

She squinted at him in the rearview. "Not unless this rain stops."

Who cares?" came the response from the back seat. "They'd slam the door in my face anyway."

Elizabeth sighed. "You're probably right."

She hoped it kept raining. She didn't feel like ringing doorbells and smiling at people.

"I'm sleepy," Bailey said.

"What do you have to be sleepy about?" Trevor asked. "You were snoring your head off in Gina's office."

"I was not."

"Were to."

"Listen," Elizabeth interrupted. "We can stop for a pizza if we can't go trick-or-treating. I'll even let you have soda."

Bailey kicked up her legs happily and sang a song she made up about soda. *Caffeine-free soda.* Elizabeth turned the van onto Totem Lane, headlights streaking across the glassy blacktop, and snapped on a Dead show. "The Wheel" came on and nobody protested. *Another good sign.*

A gang of parents and children shining flashlights crossed her path, undeterred by the weather. Elizabeth rolled past and proceeded north on Wexford Road. She pulled into the school's parking lot with the enthusiasm of an inmate headed for the electric chair.

"That's weird. What's a school bus doing there?" Trevor said.

"Maybe a team's back from a meet?"

"That's high school, Mom."

"Maybe a class is back from a field trip."

"On Halloween? Anyway, where's the kids? It's weird."

"A school bus in a school parking lot is not that weird, Trev."

The rain picked up. Elizabeth steered the van through a running sheet of water into the spot nearest the bus and the school's back entrance. She stepped out into the storm and rammed open the sliding door to the van. She unbuckled Bailey, who wailed about getting wet at the top of her lungs.

"Come on," Elizabeth demanded, rivulets of water pouring down her neck. "Let's make a run for it."

Trevor pulled at the glistening door to the school, but it would not budge. Elizabeth pressed her face to the window. Except for a faint light at the back of the cafeteria, every light had been extinguished.

"How much you want to bet they canceled and called your father instead of me?" Elizabeth said. "These people are pathetic."

"I'm freezing." Trevor's soaking bangs stuck to his forehead.

"Back to the van," Elizabeth told him. "Run!"

She strapped Bailey in and climbed behind the steering wheel, dripping rain. She cranked up the defogger.

"You still want pizza?" she asked the children.

"I just wanna go home," Trevor said.

"Is that okay with you, Bail? We'll order in, and you can still have your soda?"

"Go home," Bailey agreed, kicking the seat.

"We can put on our pajamas. I'll make hot chocolate. I'll make popcorn, too, if you want."

"Yes, please," Trevor said quietly.

FORTY-EIGHT

The minivan splashed through abandoned streets. All trick-or-treaters had vanished. Elizabeth turned off Wexford and stayed on Lane Street for three miles. The heat in the van warmed her bones sufficiently when something – a shadow, a deer? – crossed her path.

She slammed her foot on the brake. The van shrieked to a stop.

"Mom," Trevor shouted. "You scared me!"

Bailey wailed.

Elizabeth rolled down her window. Three small figures in black hoodies huddled on the corner.

"Well, they look familiar," Elizabeth said.

Trevor squeaked open his window. "What are they doing all the way over here?"

"On this side of town," Elizabeth agreed. "They're in fourth grade, for Pete's sake."

She pulled up beside the boys.

"Mom, don't."

"Hughey, Joey, and Noah, do your parents know you're out here?"

She could see Hughey had been crying and felt an unexpected pang of sorrow.

"Can you take us home, Aunt Elizabeth?" he pleaded.

She didn't have seats for all of them, let alone seatbelts. By law, a child under twelve had to ride in the back. If she got pulled over, she'd end up in court with a big fat ticket. Her photograph would be splashed all over Facebook.

I can't just leave them here though, can I?

"Get in the front, next to me, Hughey. Buckle up. Your friends can squeeze in the back. Trev, one of them is gonna have to sit on your lap."

Trevor groaned. "They're soaking wet, Mom!"

"We all are."

The shivering boys filled the van, dragging heavy wet pillowcases.

"Sorry, Junior," Noah said, knocking Bailey's feet.

"My name is not Junior," she replied.

Hughey wiped his nose on his sleeve. "We thought we knew the way home, but then it got dark."

"Does your mother know you're out here?"

"No."

Elizabeth checked the other two in the rearview. "I take it yours don't, either."

Joey shook his head, but Noah said, "Mine probably don't even know I'm gone."

Elizabeth let the van idle. She pulled out her phone and brought up the Stonesbury Moms and Dads page. It was lit up with speculation about the three missing boys.

"If I were the cops, I'd be talking to that bully Trevor Dispo right now."

Elizabeth called the police station and left a message for Officer Kenneth. She put the car in Drive. Her phone rang, and she slid it back into Park.

"The driver told us the boys jumped off the bus at the wrong stop," Office Ken told her. "We've had three calls this afternoon from residents reporting a group of boys egging houses."

"Can you hold for a sec, Officer?" Elizabeth eyed the boy next to her. "What's in the pillow case, Hughey?"

"Nothing."

Elizabeth seized the wet sack from the floor mat. It contained wet chocolate bars, a can of shaving cream, and a gloppy mess of broken eggs.

"I think we've solved your case," she told Officer Kenneth. "Give me your address, Joey."

Joey gave it.

"Officer, can you meet me at 16 Wayfair Circle in ten minutes?"

"I just finished dinner," he said. "You got it."

"Hughey and Noah, call your parents and tell them to meet us at Joey's," Elizabeth said. "You're going to tell them the truth about everything. About the field trip, about every single instance where you made Trevor the scapegoat for your malfeasance."

"Mom," Trevor said. "We don't even know what *malfeasance* means."

"You're smart boys," she said, putting the car back into Drive. "You'll figure it out."

FORTY-NINE

Elizabeth shielded Bailey from the downpour and followed the boys up the broken walk to Joey's house. Andrea stood under the light of the small awning, her slight frame wrapped in a long beige sweater.

"Who gave you permission to drive my son?" she demanded.

"You want me to put him back where I found him? Don't push me, Lady."

Bailey's wet shoes sideswiped Joey's mother as Elizabeth marched into the house, which harbored the terse odor of mothballs, uninvited. Officer Kenneth stood beside a worn couch with his hands in the pockets of his windbreaker. Headlights from two vehicles streaked into the driveway.

"There's your mother, Hughey," Elizabeth said. Between his lumpy preadolescent body and triangular head, she really did feel sorry for him. He was way out of his league with charismatic Noah and even Joey, the Rat.

Elizabeth stole a look at Noah. Already, he'd made himself at home in one of Joey's mother's faded armchairs. "I guess that'll be your parents, too," she told him.

Mary Pat burst into the living room, loaded for bear in a blue M&M costume. Jim appeared behind her in his shorts. Rosalita wore an ankle-length Lady Lily Wear skirt with a wet hem.

"What the hell is going on here, Hughey?" Mary Pat demanded.

Jim put up his hand to silence her. "Let's all calm down, Ladies. We're gonna let the boys tell us what happened."

Officer Ken looked at him sideways.

Joey spoke up. "It was Noah's idea."

Hughey studied the puddle forming around his sneakers.

Jim folded his arms. "What was Noah's idea?"

"He said we're too old for trick-or-treating, and we should go egging instead."

"Trick-or-treating?" Jim addressed the boy staring holes in the wall from the armchair. "Halloween's of the devil, Champ. You know that. Since when do the Dunfores celebrate Halloween?"

"Your son didn't go trick-or-treating," Elizabeth said levelly. "He went on a vandalism spree."

Andrea placed her hands on her Joey's shoulders. "I knew somebody put you up to it."

Elizabeth noticed the cracks in the dining room ceiling. "Tell them what you told me in the car," she directed Hughey.

The boy shifted his weight. "Trevor didn't fart on the boat. He didn't kick Joey for no reason."

"Make it crystal clear, Hughey. You're saying you three bullied Trevor. Is that correct?"

Noah clasped his hands behind his head. "That's what he's saying."

"So, you back Officer Kenneth's account?" Elizabeth asked.

"Yep," Noah said.

Mary Pat wobbled forth in oversized red foam shoes, which matched her red foam gloves. "I don't believe a word this kid is saying."

"You have a problem, which will not be resolved until you get around to doing something about it," Officer Kenneth told her. "Ms. Candew has three choices here. She can press charges on Trevor's behalf. Or, she can issue a warning stipulating that she will press charges the next time your boys so much as blink at him."

Jim interrupted. "That sounds like two choices to me."

"I wasn't finished."

Joey's mother raked her fingernails through her hair. "So, what's our third choice?"

"It's not your choice. It's Ms. Candew's choice, and that's to let the whole thing go. Which, obviously, I don't recommend."

"We can settle this among ourselves, Elizabeth," Mary Pat said hopefully. "Let it go. There's no reason to press charges."

"Let me ask you a question." Elizabeth took three steps towards her former sister-in-law. "Did you go out trick-or-treating tonight, Mary Pat?"

"By myself? Stop being ridiculous. I'm a grown woman."

"But you're dressed up like a piece of candy."

"A lot of moms wear a costume when they take their kid out on Halloween."

"Yeah, but your kid didn't come home on Halloween, did he? In fact, he went AWOL on a bus driver while you're standing around pointing your big fat foam finger. Any sane person can see you have a problem, and I don't trust you to handle it."

From beneath the oily blue makeup, Mary Pat's mole gleamed. "Are you questioning my parenting skills, Elizabeth? Don't *you* talk to *me* about parenting skills."

"Think before you speak, Mary Pat. Do not try me."

Mary Pat opened her mouth to say something. She closed it.

Elizabeth met her former sister-in-law nose-to-nose, noticing the suffocating pores. "Right this minute, the Stonesbury Moms and Dads page is lighting up with lies about my family. If I agree not to press charges, I expect every parent in this room to get on that page and set the record straight. Is that clear?"

"It's still Trevor's word against the other boys," Rosalita said, ever so quietly. "And he doesn't have a good track record."

"Damn straight," Jim said.

"Yeah, Mrs. Dunfore, you might want to give that some thought," Officer Kenneth said. "I got a call from a resident who has your sons egging his property on a security camera. His wife is in a book club with my wife. If you do the right thing, I might be able to get *him* not to press charges. We might even get him not to post the video on social media."

Elizabeth doubted such a resident existed, but a look of defeat came over Mary Pat. Her head seemed to shrink into the costume, giving her the look of a hypothermic turtle. "If he presses charges, Hughey will be lucky to get into community college."

"Not that there's anything wrong with community college," Officer Kenneth said.

"Maybe in your family," Mary Pat gasped.

Officer Ken shook his head.

"Let me apologize for my former sister-in-law," Elizabeth said. "There's something seriously wrong with her. Mary Pat, are you crazy? Apologize to this man before he frog marches your kid into the police station."

"Yeah, do that," Jim said. "So, we can all go home and put this business behind us."

Mary Pat stuck out her chin, the hard lump in her throat plainly visible.

"If you want me to say I'm sorry, I'm sorry."

"That's not much of an apology," the policeman said, blowing his nose. "But I promised my wife tonight we'd catch up on *Grantchester*, instead of me getting stuck at the station doing paperwork. I guess it'll have to do."

A FEW DAYS LATER, ELIZABETH buttered an onion bagel. She opened the *Stonesbury Herald*, which included screenshots of the accusations about Trevor on the Moms and Dads social media page, along with his subsequent vindication. The article featured an additional photo of Elizabeth, the children, and the house, which managed to make them all look respectable. The half-hour she'd spent with the reporter yielded a single quote: "Bullying is an epidemic that crosses all class and age lines. It's up to all of us to stop it."

FIFTY

G loria called to say she'd be late for their meeting with the homeowner Elizabeth recruited, which meant Elizabeth would have to tread water and hope she made the right impression until her mentor arrived.

She rang the bell and waited. A newspaper sat on the top step. Shouldn't she pick it up and hand it to the woman when she opened the door? Elizabeth hopped from foot to foot nervously. *Stand still. Try to at least* look *like a professional.*

The homeowner, Millie, came to the door in the type of house-coat Elizabeth's grandmother used to wear. Elizabeth's grandmother had been dead for decades.

"Are you Elizabeth or Gloria?" Millie asked, stepping back to allow her guest to enter.

"Elizabeth." She recognized the smell of canned spaghetti from her childhood. She smelled something else, too. "Orchids," she said aloud.

"My son sent them. Aren't they something?" Millie pointed to the crystal vase standing on the type of wood TV console Elizabeth had seen in old magazines. Nancy would love it.

"What happened to Gloria?"

"She should be here any minute."

"Well, Elizabeth, let me tell you. I got suckered." She gestured for her to sit at a kitchen table covered with notepads she'd stapled together of uneven scraps of paper. "I figured if those two had the money for a billboard on the interstate, they had to know what they were doing."

Wait. Were Mary Pat and Tom the crap realtors? The sheer size of Mary Pat's kitchen attested to the fact she and Tom made sales which led to sizeable commissions. Why hadn't they been able to sell this house?

"Don't be so hard on yourself. That billboard would lead me to think the same thing," Elizabeth said. She prayed Gloria would hurry up and ring the bell.

"It just goes to show, appearances can be deceiving," Millie said. "If I got a dime every time I forgot, I'd be living on a yacht on the French Riviera with Cary Grant."

She flopped into the chair opposite and creased the padded plastic tablecloth with her thumbnail. "I'm supposed to move into Gladden Suites at the end of the month," she said, referring to the assisted living facility that just went in on the Post Road. "If I can't sell my house, I won't be able to swing the rent. It costs a pretty penny to live in one of those places. Even so, they've got a waiting list. They'll give my place away."

"We'll do our very best for you, I promise." Elizabeth didn't know what else to say. "Gloria should be here any minute."

The house needed a major update, but it had what Gloria called "good bones." Its location on a quiet cul-de-sac with a partial view of the lake should have attracted a buyer the minute Mary Pat and Tom listed it. Elizabeth's stomach cartwheeled. What if it turned out the house had a problem that rendered it unsaleable? Maybe it had a leaky oil tank in the basement. Or, worse, a leaky oil tank underground in the back yard! She and Gloria wouldn't be able to sell it, either. *So long, Fat Commission Check!*

"I won't get fooled again," Millie said, pushing a plate of chocolate chip cookies across the tablecloth. "If I give you the listing, you get until Thanksgiving. If you don't sell by then, I'll cut my losses and take it off the market until spring. Provided I live that long."

Elizabeth accepted a cookie, but her mouth was so dry with anxiety, she nearly choked trying to swallow it. "We'll do our very best," she said after she managed.

Gloria arrived, finally. Millie gave her and Elizabeth, now damp under the arms, a tour of the house. The oil tank had been replaced within the last five years, she said. Gloria deemed the alcove in the master bedroom "charming." She suggested a price.

Millie's eyes looked like weary raisins. "The billboard people said I'd get more than that."

Gloria handed over a binder filled with testimonials from former clients. "Look, you don't know me or my colleague from a hole in the wall, but I have helped people in similar positions. Forget Thanksgiving. Give us one weekend, and if we don't sell this house at better than asking price, give it to our competition."

"You're telling me you can sell this house in a weekend when it's been dying on the vine for six months?"

"Make it available to us this Saturday. We promise to do our best."

"You'll do your best. That's what the billboard people said." Millie pointed at Elizabeth with her thumb. "That's what your colleague here says. I won't say I trust her, but there's something about her that makes me willing to take a chance. What the heck? What's the worst that could happen in a weekend?"

Millie signed the contract. Elizabeth followed Gloria out of the house, winds of triumph howling through her shaking bones.

Getting into her van, Elizabeth asked Gloria, "You really think we can sell it?"

"Absolutely. The previous realtors are infamous for listing dated houses at inflated prices. They use them to let buyers think that's the only type of property they can get at their budget. Then they show them something grander for fifty thousand dollars more, and guess what?"

"The buyer finds the money, and the realtor banks a bigger commission."

"Bingo."

"You're saying they never intended to sell it?"

"Yes. You'll learn not everyone in this business is in possession of a soul. Luckily for you, I can let you know who they are before you make the mistake of trying to split a sale with them." Gloria opened the door to her car. "I'll text you details for the open house Saturday."

Elizabeth's hand flew to her mouth. "I just remembered. My daughter's birthday party is at four o'clock."

"I usually run open houses from noon to three. Any chance you can cover for an hour?"

"Absolutely. The party's at a movie theater, so besides baking cupcakes and filling goodie bags, I don't have a lot to do to prepare."

"Perfect." Gloria said. "Let's sell a house then."

AFTER THE MOVIE, BAILEY'S guests filed into the small room the theater staff decorated with crepe paper streamers to play games. A girl named Keisha won Pin-the-Tail on the Donkey. Bailey handed over the prize, a 12-inch Elsa doll she had picked out herself. The children ate their cake. Elizabeth's phone buzzed. She excused herself from the other parents milling around the edges of the room to take the call.

"Three offers," Gloria said.

"You're kidding."

"Each for more than asking price."

"Which means a bidding war."

"Exactly. Listen, Elizabeth, this could be a niche for you. Elderly people looking to downsize. You'd be good at it. Think about it, will you?"

"I will do that, definitely. And thanks, Gloria. Really."

Elizabeth disconnected. If all went according to plan, she'd have another commission check to put in the bank. She resisted giving herself a high-five, lest she freak out the other parents.

FIFTY-ONE

Russell started texting, making financial demands. Elizabeth knew that, as a realtor, Mary Pat kept abreast of recent house sales in the area. She also knew that Trevor was proud of Elizabeth for facilitating two of them. He'd probably mentioned it to his father and aunt, which would account for the list of clothing and toiletries Russell expected Elizabeth to provide for Trevor's Disney trip at Christmas.

Elizabeth texted back.

YOUR VACATION. YOUR RESPONSIBILITY

She knew he'd retaliate. He'd be late with the child support check, but that would be on him. Both Russell and Elizabeth would die eventually. If Russell wanted his son to remember him as a giant yo-yo, it was fine with her.

She studied for her real estate exam. She drank tea and played the piano. Every time her mind took a wrong turn in Red's direction, Elizabeth set it back on course. Despite all efforts to distract herself, she felt an underlying layer of sadness she couldn't shake. It sat at the bottom of her stomach like wet cement.

He would come that afternoon to pick up Trevor for kung fu. Elizabeth didn't know what to do if he came to the door. Part of her wanted to determine if their breakup had caused him any suffering, but looking into those eyes would throw her into a tailspin that could set her back for weeks.

Let him wait for Trevor in the car.

Elizabeth got up from the piano. She should probably do something with her hair just in case. Lipstick wouldn't hurt. She put on the pale pink angora sweater she'd treated herself to after Millie accepted the best offer on her house. She came out of the bathroom pressing in a pearl earring.

Trevor looked up from his homework. "Wow, Mom. You look pretty."

Bailey put down her chocolate milk. "Mommy's wearing a different color lipstick!"

"I have a lot of lipsticks," Elizabeth told her. "I've been known to change it up from time to time."

"No." Bailey shook her head. "Not so much."

FIFTY-TWO

To calm herself, Elizabeth turned up the Dead, "Morning Dew" this time. The doorbell rang. She sucked in her breath.

Trevor slammed his book closed. "Gotta fly!"

Why should the effort Elizabeth put into her appearance to go to waste? She looked good. Red should be made aware of it. He should be forced to behold her. Then again, she wasn't going to race her son to the door to make that happen. Maybe the satisfaction of knowing that today she didn't look like somebody's worn out mother would be enough.

Trevor came back into the house. Red followed, square-shouldered and freshly shaven, his skin tight and slightly gleaming. Elizabeth caught a whiff of woodsy aftershave. Why did he have to make it so hard for her?

"Trevor," Red said. "I need to talk to your mom for a minute. I'll meet you out in the car."

Trevor went out, and Elizabeth's heart leapt. She swallowed.

"You were right," he said.

"I was?"

"About the case. Turns out the Instagram stuff she posted was taken last spring."

"So, she did it then?"

"Yep. And shot Toni Badden."

Elizabeth felt wobbly. She took hold of a chair. As much as she'd wanted to solve the case, she really didn't want the killer to be a young woman with her life ahead of her. She figured she already knew the story, but she'd let Red tell it.

"Yeah, Louisa and Toni bankrupted her future in-laws." Red shrugged. "The fiancé had to drop out of Brown. They planned to marry in the university chapel after graduation."

"She still could have married him. What did it matter if he dropped out?"

"She wanted to marry a man who went to Brown," he said, confirming Louisa's fear that Steph hadn't necessarily gotten engaged to the *right* boy but one who met Steph's primary specification.

"Well, good luck with that now. How many boys from Brown are lining up to marry a woman who killed her mother?"

A charmed smile crept across Red's face. "I can't think of any."

"I actually feel sorry for her. What a value system."

"You may be interested to know that her father didn't take the news as a complete shock."

"Oh, that poor man. He's a victim in all this, too," Elizabeth said. "The little girl is the one I really feel for, though. Her mother's dead. Her sister's going to prison. Why couldn't Pastor Jim be the killer?"

"You gotta let it go, Elizabeth." Red shook his head. "I have a feeling karma will catch up with that clown. Anyway, Trevor and I are going to be late."

He turned to go. Elizabeth followed him out onto the crumbling front steps.

"Listen," he said.

"Yes?"

"I was way out of line. I had no right to expect you to tell me about Bailey."

"Yeah." The words stuck in her throat. "You were."

"I was a jerk. I'm sorry. Can you find it in your heart to forgive me again?"

"I've already forgiven you, Red."

His eyes gleamed turquoise in the golden November sun. "Seriously? Really? I promise to make it up to you."

"There's no point in holding a grudge." Elizabeth felt chilly and wrapped herself up in her own arms. "I wish you every good thing. I hope you'll wish the same for me."

"Wait, what? I'd like us to start over. That's what I'm asking. Forget everything."

Elizabeth turned back towards the door. She saw Bailey bent over with a crayon at the table. "Forgiveness is one thing. Forgetting is another, Red. I'm not setting myself up for you ever again."

"Lizza, listen to me. Let me make dinner like I promised. We can put the kids to bed, have a couple of glasses of wine, look into each other's eyes." He balled his hands in his pockets and smiled. "You know how it goes."

"You make a lot of promises," she said.

"It's not like that."

"Okay."

His shoulders lost their relentless squareness. "Maybe you'll change your mind."

"Sure."

"Maybe you will change your mind," he said again. He turned to go.

He walked back down the broken path, and Elizabeth did change her mind. She opened her mouth to say she wanted dinner. She couldn't wait for dinner! They'd laugh. They'd drink a boatload of wine. She'd get sleepy and rest her head on his chest in front of the TV. She could already smell the soap in his shirt.

Again, the ability to form a coherent sentence failed her.

If Elizabeth kept letting this guy bounce her around, she'd never be able to trust herself. She had to be able to trust herself. She had to set a good example for her children.

She let him go.

FIFTY-THREE

Via webcam, Cathy's cheekbones looked sharper than Elizabeth remembered.

"Have you lost weight?" she asked.

"The food's different here," Cathy said. "So, yeah."

"Don't you like it?"

"I like it a lot. It's lighter than I'm used to. Not a lot of pork roast." Cathy held up a coffee mug decorated with a sketch of Stonington Green. "I'm going to miss Christmas in Connecticut."

Elizabeth felt a pang of sadness. "I'm going to miss *you* at Christmas."

"How's work going?"

"Gloria and I made two more sales. If all goes well, I'll have my license early in the new year."

"All will go well, Elizabeth."

"It will." She nodded. "I've decided."

"I hope you're enjoying all the money you're making," Cathy said.

"Oh, I am. We even sprang for a live tree this year." Elizabeth angled her laptop to provide a view. "We cut it down ourselves and took pictures for our card and everything. The best thing is, I got rid of that dusty fake thing hogging up the basement."

"Anything else?"

"Yeah, a washer and drier that don't do the Macarena."

"Although that could've been festive at this time of year."

"And I got estimates for the front walk," Elizabeth said. "Which we'll take care of in the spring."

"Are you saving anything for retirement?"

"Why, yes, Cathy." Elizabeth laughed. "Believe it or not, I am making regular contributions to a Roth IRA."

"I'm impressed." Cathy nodded approvingly. "And what about future business? How does that look?"

"Things are quiet at Christmas, but I've got three listings lined up for January. Do you remember that client I told you about?"

"The one Mary Pat screwed over?"

"Yeah, Millie. She belongs to every church and senior organization under the sun. She calls me – wait for it—her *savior*, which has led to loads of referrals. She is also actively badmouthing Mary Pat all over the universe."

"Good," Cathy said. "She had it coming."

"Also, I got a side job playing the organ at St. Gabriel's."

"You're going to church?"

"Not exactly. I play the organ *in* a church. If I didn't play, I probably wouldn't go. That could change, though. Maybe someday I would go just to go. It's possible. You never know. It can't hurt to have a spiritual life."

"You're full of surprises, Elizabeth."

"Yeah, well, buckle up because here's another. I've been looking at airfares. If you still want us, we'll spend next Christmas with you in Beijing. Trevor's obsessed with Asia ever since he started kung fu."

"Of course, I still want you!" Cathy shrieked. "The year can't pass fast enough."

"It will, though. Before you know it, I'll be waking the kids up to go to the airport, and I'll be on my way."

"I'd say you're already on your way, especially after everything you've achieved these past few months."

"So much has happened, I haven't really had time to think about it," Elizabeth said. "But you're right. I am absolutely on my way."

THE END

ACKNOWLEDGEMENTS

This book would not have been written without the help, guidance, and support of many people.

Thanks to The Two Marks at BXP Team, Craig Martelle, Mark Dawson, and the Writing Gals for making the seemingly insurmountable surmountable. I will forever be grateful to Ronnie Ryan, Catherine Robotis, Bernadette Starzee, and Valerie Lauria for wading through early drafts of this book and making valuable suggestions. Susan Cristini and her eagle vision came as last-minute gifts and made for a better story.

Thanks to the EFT/Tapping community, particularly Andrea Lewis and Heather DeRome, for helping me to get out of my own way. Love and gratitude go to my husband and daughters for their unwavering belief in me.

Special thanks to my late father, who, many years ago, read over his fifteen-year-old's submission to *Circus* Magazine's Write a Review Contest for an Emerson, Lake and Palmer show. When he finished, he remarked, "You can write."

His encouragement meant everything.

THANK YOU FOR BEING A READER

If you enjoyed *Stitch by Stitch*, please sign up for my mailing list, and I'll make you the following promise:

I will not clutter your inbox with unnecessary nonsense.

I will, however, drop you a line to let you know when my next book is due to come out and offer you the first chapter free of charge, if you'd like it. I welcome messages from readers.

Join me at marie-theresehernon.com.

YOU CAN MAKE A DIFFERENCE

Honest reviews help bring books to the attention of new readers. If you enjoyed this one, I would be eternally grateful if you would drop a line on the platform where you purchased it. Thank you.

About the Author

A native New Yorker, Marie-Thérèse Hernon moved to Connecticut in 2003. Besides writing, she loves books, travel, and music. She is very good at her Spanish lessons, but her attempts at conversation still require much improvement.

Read more at www.marie-theresehernon.com.

Made in the USA
Middletown, DE
01 April 2021

36708490R00203